THE MERCHANT'S YIELD

THE LEEWARD ISLAND SERIES - BOOK 2

LORRI DUDLEY

WILD HEARt
BOOKS

Cover design by: Carpe Librum Book Design

ISBN-13: 978-1-942265-17-7

For my parents,
Your love and encouragement bless me.

"We are hard-pressed on every side, but not crushed; perplexed, but not in despair; persecuted, but not abandoned; struck down, but not destroyed."

2 Corinthians 4:8-9

CHAPTER 1

London, England
May 1814

I should keep his secret, but it is bursting within me. My brother mentioned in confidence he shall request a dance if your mother is not in attendance.
~ *From Miss Priscilla Middleton written to Miss Charlotte Etheridge*

"Of course, the islander would come."

Charlotte Amelia Etheridge stiffened at Mama's acidic tone. She followed her mother's gaze to the entrance of the Middleton's modest ballroom where guests arrived in hordes of navy and formal black jackets bobbing amid a sea of colorful gowns. They filled the ballroom with boisterous chatter and a bouquet of expensive perfumes and colognes.

Mama flicked her fan in sharp increments. "Even dressed in English finery, he appears barbaric and uncivilized."

Lottie focused on the landing where Nathanial Robert Winthrop bowed to Lord Gibbons and his wife. His large frame and broad shoulders dwarfed Lord Gibbons's, making the average-height man appear slight in stature. Winthrop's hand tossed back the coattail of his fitted charcoal jacket and tucked into his right pant pocket. He exuded a relaxed, casual self-assurance that uniquely contrasted with the pretentious lords and ladies of the Quality surrounding him. Their grandiose displays sought approval, a favor they would be hard-pressed to receive from her mother, for Lady Etheredge's acerbic tongue could elevate or cut down a person with a single remark.

Winthrop nodded at something Gibbons said, and his teeth gleamed the same bright white as his cravat and shirt front.

Mama nodded in the direction of the gentlemen. "I will make certain Lord Gibbons reserves a dance for you. His mother owes me a favor."

A favor. The jab struck its soft target, but Lottie had numbed to most of her mother's verbal attacks.

"There she is now." Mama stepped away to speak with Lady Gibbons.

Lottie plucked at the sides of her skirt and searched for Priscilla, her closest friend. The large mirrors reflected shimmering light from the overhead multi-tiered chandeliers and exposed her abandoned position. A retreat to the retiring rooms to freshen up might be in order.

Captain Anthony Middleton eyed her.

Lottie paused mid-step.

He weaved through the cluster of people to her side.

This was it. Her pulse leapt. How long had she fancied Pricilla's handsome elder brother and dreamed of this moment?

"If it isn't Little Lottie Ethridge." The deep rich tone of Anthony's voice sent a wave of tingles up her arm.

Lottie fought to subdue a grin she knew would cross the lines of decorum.

The boyishness in his face had disappeared, and he exuded

virile sophistication in his navy captain's jacket and highly polished boots. "It has been an age."

She longed to say something witty like how she practiced in front of the mirror while he'd been at sea, but all that came to mind was, "Indeed."

"Green is a lovely color for your complexion." His gaze swept over her like a soft caress. "It also happens to be my favorite color."

Of which she was keenly aware. That, and the fact he despised snakes, took four lumps of sugar in his tea, and sang a little off key. Such knowledge was a boon of being close friends with his sister.

"Would you like to—" He glanced away and shifted his feet. "Would you care to—"

"Captain Middleton" Mama drew alongside the two of them. "Your mother is looking for you. I believe she said it was urgent."

Anthony craned his neck toward the entrance. "Perhaps another time." He stole one last glance at Lottie, bowed, and excused himself.

A whimper sounded deep in Lottie's throat as she watched him go. The opportunity had been within her grasp.

"You don't want to dance with the likes of Middleton." Mama frowned at his retreating form.

She gaped at her mother. "Whyever not?"

"He lacks a spine."

"For mercy's sake." Lottie gritted her teeth. "He commands a ship."

"I'm saving you from future heartbreak." Tiny lines framed Mama's pursed lips. "I have it on the best authority that Middleton dips too deep. I will not abide having a spineless, drunken wastrel as a son-in-law."

"You find fault in everyone." Lottie's fingers curled into tight balls. "Besides, it would have only been a dance." One she'd hoped turned into courting, and soon after, marriage, but Mama didn't need to know that at the moment.

"You shouldn't be overexerting yourself." Mama fluttered her fan. "The last thing you need is to have another spell."

She hadn't had a fever in over four years. What would it take to prove she was well enough to be like everyone else? If only she could have been able to make her own choice about the dance with Anthony. But once again, her mother had chosen for her. She sucked in a deep breath through her nose to curtail the roiling boil churning inside her.

"You'll find Lord Gibbons has exquisite dance form."

She didn't want to dance with someone instructed to oblige her. She wanted to dance with Anthony.

Mama glanced at Lottie's coiffure and sighed. "I wish you had used powder."

Lottie resisted the urge to put a hand to her hair. "Mama, no one has powdered their hair in a decade."

Her mother's mouth pursed into a thin line. "I'm well aware of the fashion trends, but the powder tones down your color, making your hair a much-preferred strawberry blonde. I daresay blonde is more fashionable than this"—she circled a finger in the direction of Lottie's head—"vibrant red."

Lottie waited for Mama's next line. She could repeat it verbatim.

"Red hair is for opera singers and ballet dancers. Proof of the tainting of our pure bloodline."

Lottie's periphery darkened as the rush of blood filled her ears, blocking out the lively background conversations. She fought to regain a measure of control. Her red hair was a constant reminder she was a disappointment. Not only was she born a girl and not a male heir, but her hair was red. Not a dark Auburn or strawberry blonde, but carrot red. Her mother blamed her father often with a mouthful of venom about the Etheridge line being tainted. Of course, Mama implied that had she known the family's indiscretions, she never would have infected her pure blood with his. It was rumored Lottie's great-grandmother on her father's side had indulged in a fling with an Irishman. In mother's opinion, Lottie's red hair was proof that her grandfather was baseborn.

An ember of hope ignited. If her ancestors had risked for love, then maybe—just maybe—she might have some of their blood running through her veins.

"He thinks he's one of us." Mama crossed her arm and raised a haughty brow. "As if he can buy his way into the Quality."

"Who?" Lottie shook her head to clear her negative thoughts and pivoted to find Nathaniel Winthrop scanning the crowd with a hint of resigned amusement. For a stranger, he owned the room with his subtle manner, as if he didn't care a wit about the pomp and circumstance of the *ton* or its social rankings.

Priscilla said his father had grown wealthy through the sugar trade. Winthrop contributed to his father's legacy by becoming a savvy merchant, trading in sugar and other goods. Clearly he was his own man, and she could picture him standing proudly at the helm of his ship, sailing the vast sea with wind ruffling his hair.

Lottie's eyes drifted closed. What would it be like to hold such freedom? An imaginary breeze pressed against her skin and whipped her undone tresses behind her. Her palms turned out to cup the air.

"Lady Reinhart's daughter danced with him at the Mayfair ball."

Lottie's eyes sprung open, and she dropped her hands to her sides.

"She complained about feeling hardened callouses under his gloves." Mother shivered and a look of utmost disgust deepened the creases around her lips. "You must give him a wide berth tonight."

Lottie withered under the constant weight of her mother's

commands. Her lips had parted to offer the expected *yes, mama,* when the islander's gaze met hers from across the room. Their eyes held, and she saw the confidence in their depth, the defiance, as if he were proud of being an islander and not one of them. Deep down within her being, buried under layers of insecurities, a spark of rebellion ignited.

Mama issued her a sideways glance and lowered her voice. "Straighten up, dear. Etheridges do not slouch. You are the daughter of a viscount. Hold yourself with poise in accordance with your station. Hunching isn't going to make you appear less gangly..."

She would never raise herself high enough for her mother's standards, so why should she bother? It was her life, and past time she lived it. Lottie lifted her chin and pulled back her shoulders, but not because of Mama. She ignored her mother's droning and drifted in Mr. Winthrop's direction as if a magnetic force drew her.

"Charlotte Amelia Etheridge?" her mother called.

Lottie weaved through the crowd toward the entrance of the reception hall, her eyes never leaving her target.

He slanted a brow as if to say, *have we met?*

Lord Gibbons touched Mr. Winthrop's shoulder and gestured to Lady Reinhart as if offering an introduction.

The spell was broken.

Lottie froze. What had come over her? Curious stares of other guests bored into her skin, leaving her feeling naked. She pretended to wave to an imaginary acquaintance and hastened to the retiring rooms.

After freshening up, she faced herself in the looking glass. "This can't continue any longer. You are not a puppet. You have your own mind." Her pale blue eyes darkened. "If you want to dance, then you should dance. You're not going to collapse dead on the dance floor as Mama believes." She inhaled a deep breath and, with a curt nod to herself, returned to the ballroom.

Lottie's brother, Gerald, and Anthony, her would-be dance partner, stood on her right with a crowd of their friends. She sidestepped a particularly tall guest and slid next to her brother. "Pardon my intrusion." She dipped into a polite curtsy. "Gerald, I was hoping you would be a dear and allow me some reprieve from..." Her gaze flicked in their mother's direction.

Gerald groaned, and she could practically read his thoughts. If she was here, Mama was bound to follow shortly. "I was about to meet some chaps in the card room."

"Hmm." She leaned closer to Gerald and whispered. "I'd hate to have to retire early due to an oncoming headache, which would leave you to escort Mama home."

Her brother's Adam's apple bobbed. "Let me introduce you to my friends." He nodded to Anthony. "Of course, you know Middleton."

She smiled at Anthony, and he briefly returned it before he flashed a nervous glance in her mother's direction.

Lottie turned toward the other man and stiffened. Her stomach dove for cover. The guest she'd rudely stepped around had been the islander.

Gerald continued. "Lottie, may I introduce you to Nathaniel Robert Winthrop, of the Leeward Island Winthrops. You know, St. Christopher's Island, in the Caribbean."

She winced, for his reference made her appear dimwitted. "I'm conversant with St. Christopher, or St. Kitts, as its natives refer to it."

Winthrop bowed his head.

"Winthrop," Gerald gestured in her direction, but his eyes panned the crowd, "this is Lady Charlotte, my sister. We fondly refer to her as... as... Lottie."

Gerald craned his neck to peer between Anthony's and Winthrop's shoulders. She followed his line of sight to where Mama left her dowager friends and searched the room.

7

Lottie grasped Mr. Winthrop's sleeve, using his body to shield her from view.

The man's brows snapped into a *V*.

"I-I believe, we've already met." She forced her gaze to meet Mr. Winthrop's assessing one.

"I didn't know you and Winthrop were acquainted." Gerald turned to the Kittitian.

Curiosity and a flash of wonder glinted in the depths of Mr. Winthrop's eyes. He arched a quizzical brow.

"Indeed, I'm sure you remember." She wracked her brain for a plausible explanation.

Mama spotted Gerald and headed toward them.

"Gerald introduced us at the Leicester dinner party. You requested a dance at our next meeting and"—she pleaded with her eyes—"here we are."

Her heart thundered as he studied her for a long moment.

Gerald cleared his throat. "I don't recall attending the Leicester's... Ah." He slapped Anthony in the gut. "Was that the night you brought out that bottle of port? If my mother found out..." His voice faded into the background, for she couldn't tear herself from Winthrop's intense gaze.

"Er—what do you say we finish this conversation in the card room?" The pitch in Gerald's voice raised, and he dashed away. Anthony followed, nodding to guests as he went.

"Pleasure to meet you for the second time." Winthrop bowed slightly.

He moved to pursue Anthony, but she clutched his arm, using his tall frame for cover.

Steely blue eyes locked on her and displayed exactly what he thought of her—a desperate, featherbrained, nitwit who must be nicked in the nob.

"I'm dreadfully sorry. This is very forward of me and completely out of character, but I would love to dance."

She leaned left to see past his large form, only to find Gerald pointing Mama in her direction. Lottie ducked back behind Mr. Winthrop.

He crossed his arms and glared at her with a sharpness that should have chilled her to her core, but her desperation for refuge overshadowed her embarrassment.

The islander's jaw clenched. His nostrils flared. She bit her lower lip and implored him with her eyes.

Her anxiety must have struck a chord somewhere deep down in that statuesque physic, for he nodded and held out his hand.

She released a breath and placed her clammy fingers in his. Thank heaven for the satin gloves that hid her perspiration.

His grip was strong and warm as he pulled her onto the dance floor. The orchestra struck up another song, however, this one had a fast cadence. She hesitated. Did islanders dance? "Do you know the quadrille?"

One side of his mouth drew into a crooked smile. "A bit late to be asking now."

He jerked her into his arms and began to propel her around the ballroom. For a foreigner, he was an expert dancer. He commanded the floor with power, moving with panther-like grace in the waves of rhythm. She held an awareness of Winthrop's every move as if she were an extension of him. The thrill of being whisked around in the brace of such strong hands set her pulse racing. Funny, but Melinda Reinhart had been correct. She could actually feel the roughness of his calloused skin through the thin material of his gloves. Mama would be justified.

Within the safekeeping of his strong arms, Lottie dared to peer into the crowd. Mama's pinched expression and lethal gaze foretold of a future tongue-lashing, not merely for avoiding her mother, but for dancing with someone Mama found beneath her. Not yet ready to surrender, she flashed what she hoped was a coquettish smile at Winthrop.

Perhaps, she'd try her hand at flirting.

~

*N*athan beheld the titian-haired beauty in his arms. Bright copper curls laced with tiny inset pearls crowned a face with skin as smooth as the cream from the coconuts back home.

She moved as one with him, adjusting to the slightest pressure of his hand. For the first time in a long while, he forgot about sugar, trade agreements, and the *Amory's* missing crew, and merely enjoyed dancing with a beautiful woman in his arms.

It was her unguarded openness that drew him. The few women on St. Kitts and at sea were hardened for good reason. To dance with a lady so unaffected was refreshing.

She smiled at him, and he bit back his laughter. Miss Etheridge was an innocent, of that he had little doubt, and she had no idea of her allure. He didn't dare allow his gaze to wander down the white expanse above her gown's neckline. Instead, he refocused on the most expressive pair of blue eyes he'd ever seen.

Those bewitching eyes had caused him to relent, despite the fact he should be focused on business with Middleton to obtain British naval escorts for his ships. The merchant company he'd built through his own grit, hard-earned labor, and sugar profits had come under attack of privateers. Now the safety of his crews was his primary concern.

Yet, with one flash of those blue eyes, he'd lost his focus. She had held his gaze, pleading for him to accept her challenge. In that long moment when she hadn't dared to move, and he hadn't dared to answer, he'd sensed her desperation, and it drew out his protective instincts.

He pivoted them into a turn, and she craned her neck once again toward the crowd.

His jaw tensed. "I'll not be used as a pawn to inspire jealousy in a suitor."

"It's not like that."

He maneuvered her around an overzealous couple lacking rhythm. "Really? For I'm completely certain we didn't meet at the Leicester dinner party." He'd attended, but arrived late and sat at the end of the table next to the Leicester's governess. When the meal was over, he joined the men for cigars and solidified a merchant deal with Lord Leicester himself. That had been a fruitful, yet unadventurous, evening. He would have remembered being introduced to Miss Etheridge, if not for her eyes, then for her red hair.

"It's a complicated story." Her gaze continued to rove about the room until it settled on one place.

"Try me. Or, this dance is over."

Her eyes widened. "But the song hasn't ended."

"It has for me." He stilled.

"Wait." Her fingers dug into his sleeve. "I can explain." Her gaze returned to its previous position.

He followed the direction of her eyes to a dower woman scrutinizing them with flared nostrils and a hostile glare. He felt Miss Etheridge stiffen.

"Mama and I are at odds."

Those revealing blue eyes gauged his reaction. "I see." He forced a deadpan expression. "So, you danced with a lowly islander to upset her."

Her lashes lowered. "I'm sorry."

To her credit, she was an honest chit.

The last note of the music sounded, and everyone clapped, but Miss Etheridge wouldn't release his arm. She shifted direction, like a frightened rabbit, uncertain where to hide.

"Shall we take a turn about the room"—he tucked her hand

into his arm—"so we may finish our discussion?"

The tension in her fingers relaxed. "A lovely suggestion."

He turned away from her mother and circled the perimeter of the room. "So your plan is to retaliate?"

"How can I get you to understand?" She sighed. "I walked around with an oversized volume of the History of Scotland on my head for three months to keep myself from growing too tall for Mama's tastes. She reprimanded my embroidery stitches saying they were too large for her liking. I pricked my fingers trying to please her until the handkerchief stained red with my blood. I have powdered my hair, for she despises its color."

He paused in his stride, and she turned to look at him.

"It's time I show her that I am my own person." A servant passed, and she plucked a glass of champagne off his tray. "I can make my own decisions."

"And you believe you'll show her by being irresponsible?" He'd once had similar conversations with his younger sister. The familiar pang of sorrow constricted his chest.

"Precisely. No… Well, maybe."

A low chuckle resonated from his throat. "Spirits heighten your emotions and addle your wits." He removed the glass of champagne from her gloved fingers. "Unless you want tomorrow filled with regrets, I suggest refraining." He passed it off to a servant.

Her eyes followed the glass weaving its way through the crowd back to the kitchens. She rounded on him and narrowed her eyes. "I don't need another person to lecture me."

She gasped and drew a hand to her lips as if stunned by her own words. A becoming rose color spread across her nose and cheeks. He half-guided, half-pushed her behind a potted hibiscus to keep curious eyes from wandering in their direction.

"You haven't lived with her." Miss Etheridge stepped toward him so close her chin tilted up to continue to meet his gaze. "I'm a grown woman, of a marriageable age. Lord willing, I will be running a household soon enough, yet she treats me like a china doll."

Her fingers dug into the sleeve of his jacket. Tomorrow he'd probably find bruises."I'm made of stronger stuff." Her chest heaved against the lace of her gown,

Was Miss Etheridge desperate for an ally? He placed his hand over hers to relax her grip. "I can tell."

A breathy laugh burst from her lips.

He leaned in close enough for any passersby not to overhear. "Be who you are." The heady scent of her hair filled his nostrils. Lilac. "You need not be a puppet, nor go to the opposite extreme to prove otherwise. You are beautiful the way you are."

She drew back. Confusion shrouded her eyes, changing them to the color of an impending storm. Her lips parted in a silent gasp. The temptation to bewilder her further by pressing a kiss on those rosy lips straightened his spine. He was here on business. No time for complications.

He stepped back but continued to hold her gaze. "Pain is unavoidable, but misery is optional."

An array of emotions chased each other across her face—hope, fear, denial, anger. He wished his meaning would absorb into her heart. They hadn't known each other long, but he felt a connection with her, a shared desire to be respected. He admired her passion and vulnerability. Their paths may never cross again, but he wished her well.

He searched the room for Anthony Middleton, but to no avail. The man was probably still relieving his pockets of some coin with Gerald Etheridge in the card room. "Would you like me to return you to your..." Lady Etheridge plowed through the crowd from the far side of the room, her gaze intent on reaching her daughter. "...mother?"

"Heavens, no!" The shrill sound of her voice resonated her panic.

He nodded to a set of doors on their right. "Why don't you

convalesce in the retiring room for a spell?"

"Brilliant." She shouted a bit too loud. "I mean... it would be good to freshen up a bit. It was—er—pleasant meeting you, Mr. Winthrop." She bobbed a rapid curtsy and escaped to her place of refuge.

He sighed. It seemed his big-brother instincts hadn't faded over time. Then again, neither had his sorrow.

No more distractions. He'd allowed himself one dance with Miss Charlotte Etheridge. Now back to business. There were too many people counting on him.

He spun on his heel to seek out Capitan Middleton for a meeting, but came face to face with Lady Etheridge instead.

"Who do you think you are?" Her scathing tone afforded no false impressions about how she felt about him. "How dare you dance with my daughter? You haven't been introduced. You haven't gone through the proper channels. Do you have no qualms for etiquette?" She didn't wait for his reply. "Of course not. You're a foreigner who believes money can buy you ranking and the esteem of your peers."

Though he stood a head taller than Lady Etheridge, she still endeavored to peer down her nose at him with the amount of disdain only the true British could muster.

And she wasn't finished. "It is good breeding that gains you respect and admittance to mingle with the aristocracy who are, quite frankly, above your station. It would serve you well to remember that."

"Yet, here we speak, Lady Etheridge, a lowly Kittitian and a highborn, privileged aristocrat."

"What flippant speech from someone here to do business within my sphere of influence."

Nathan's stomach dropped anchor.

Her lips pressed into a white slash, and her eyes narrowed into slits. "Keep away from my daughter. Am I clear?"

His jaw clenched, and he bit out through tight lips, "Quite."

CHAPTER 2

I'm tempted to add him to my list of potential suitors, but his calloused hands left little doubt of his status.

~ *From Miss Melinda Reinhart to her mother, Lady Reinhart*

*L*ottie fanned her face and paced in front of the large looking glass in the ladies' waiting room. How dare Mr. Winthrop speak to her so, and in such a know-it-all tone? He didn't understand the extent of her troubles.

The intensity of his gaze had sent a shiver of anticipation through her body, and she could still feel its aftereffects. She closed her eyes against the echo of his words—*you are beautiful the way you are*. She wanted him to be right, but then she'd have to give credit to the other thing he'd said. *You need not be a puppet nor go to the opposite extreme to prove otherwise.* What did he care if she went to the opposite extreme? Wasn't it right for the pendulum to swing back the other way?

For once in her life, she wanted to act courageously.

Pain is unavoidable, but misery is optional. She wanted to press her hands over her ears to block out his words, but they nagged at her like a constant dripping. Her mother made her miserable.

Feeling that way wasn't Lottie's choice. Or was it? What if, for one night, she rebelled? What if she ignored her mother's demands and enjoyed herself? What if she numbed herself with a sip or two of the brandy Pricilla had found in Anthony's study?

Yet, she knew God's commands. "Honor thy mother and father," and, "Be not drunk with wine." How could she honor her mother and still be her own person—the one God created her to become? She rubbed her hands over her face. She needed to get away, far away from her mother. Maybe she could beg for a visit to her aunt in Lincolnshire. Some time alone in the country might be a grand idea.

With one last check to ensure her coiffure remained in place, she strode back into the ballroom. Her mother accosted her before she'd even taken two steps.

"Charlotte Amelia Etheridge!"

Lottie winced. It was the second time that evening her mother had used her full name—not a good sign.

"How dare you disobey me and dance with that—that—foreigner?" Two angry red circles marred her mother's cheeks.

Another bad sign. Lottie braced herself for an affront. *Inhale... exhale...*

"You disgrace yourself and your family when you associate with the likes of Mr. Winthrop. A person is known by their associations. You are playing a dangerous game. Mark me, if you cavort with the working class you will wind up smelling of shop. My job is to protect your virtue. How can I do so when you directly defy my orders? I'm having our coach brought around. Say your good-byes, because I'm sending you home. Tomorrow you'll pack your things. I want you back in the country, where I can tame this unruly streak of yours."

"Actually..." Lottie's voice wavered. "I wanted to speak to you about visiting Aunt Genevieve in Lincolnshire."

"Absolutely not. I will not have you traipsing over the countryside cultivating this impertinence. You will stay under my watchful eye at all times until I'm reassured you've resumed your biddable disposition."

A tremble ran up her arms, and Lottie realized her hands were shaking. She clutched the folds of her gown until the tiny nubs of her chewed fingernails dug into the material. "It was one harmless dance." The dead calmness of her voice seemed strange to her ears.

Her mother snapped her fan open with a resounding crack. "That is still to be determined."

"If you loved me, you'd allow me a semblance of independence." The cutting words poured from Lottie's mouth. "Instead, you treat me like an insolent child."

"It is my love for you that forces me to keep guard over you. I spent hours of sleepless nights by your side when you were a sickly child. I'll not stand by now and let you to ruin your life."

Memories of peeking through curtains to watch the rest of the world from her sickroom flashed through her mind. She'd spent most of her childhood ill, bedridden, and sequestered away in the dark as her mother doted on her until her fevers passed. Back then, she'd appreciated her mother's company, but she'd also felt like a prisoner. Thankfully, she grew out of her sickly state. However, the freedom to which she'd aspired still seemed unattainable.

"Say your good-byes. It may be a while before you see your friends again." And with that, Mama stalked off leaving Lottie in her wake.

The brandy suddenly became more appealing. Lottie drifted to Priscilla Middleton's side to bid her friend farewell and wish her a lovely season—without her.

"Oh, there you are, Lottie." Priscilla's face lit up, then quickly fell. Her eyes darted over Lottie's shoulder. "Where's your mother?"

"She's having our carriage brought around."

Priscilla's eyes filled with sympathy. "Does that mean you're leaving?"

"I'm afraid so."

She clutched Lottie's arm and pulled her away from their peers. "Is it because you danced with Mr. Winthrop? How was it?" She flushed, and even though she lowered her pale blond lashes, they couldn't hide the unmistakable curiosity in her eyes. "I mean, he's handsome in a rugged sort of way. Don't you think? His shoulders make those of his English counterparts seem lacking." Her head nearly touched Lottie's as she whispered. "I'm afraid if your mother has her way, which she will, you'll be under lock and key until he returns to the Leeward Islands."

"I daresay, it is her intention."

Priscilla frowned. "She wouldn't. Would she?"

Lottie nodded. "We pack tomorrow to retire to the country. We'll be cutting the season short."

Priscilla's face melted into a somber expression. "Oh, Lottie, and just when Anthony had begun to show you favor."

Lottie's simmering anger blazed anew over the reminder of how her mother had chased away her only prospect. The mantle clock, illuminated by the groupings of candles on either side, read five minutes until midnight. The men would soon begin to disseminate to the billiards room to smoke cigars.

Her eyes grazed over the exit to the hallway. Anthony's study door lay a few paces down the hall. Tonight, she was older than the girl who turned her nose down at the taste of his liquor. And maybe—at least for this night—she was braver. She pictured the look of horror that would appear on her mother's face when she smelled spirits on her daughter's breath. If Lottie was going to be punished, she might as well have a valid reason. She'd toast to her fleeting night of freedom and show her mother and Winthrop who was really in control. Indulging in spirits would be her decision to make.

She turned to Priscilla. "Does your brother still have the decanter of brandy in his study?" Priscilla's parents were the opposite of Lottie's mother. They barely paid her any heed, which was one of the reasons Lottie appreciated her friendship. Priscilla lived the life she wanted.

Priscilla's pale eyes illuminated. "Indeed."

Mother still had to say her good-byes. How long would that take? Lottie rolled her lips to hide her smile. *Long enough.* "I thought it might be a last hurrah before my relegation to Mama's austere surveillance."

Priscilla grabbed Lottie's upper arms. "Lottie, you're brilliant." Her eyes scanned the ballroom. "I shall have Anthony join us."

Priscilla walked to the hallway, but hesitated at the entrance. "Oh fig, there's Lord Dalton. He's coming to claim the dance I promised him." She gestured to the door of Anthony's study. "You remember where he keeps it?"

She nodded.

"Go ahead and pour the glasses. I'll join you shortly." She squeezed her arm and smiled.

"But—"

"Miss Priscilla." Lord Dalton cut Lottie off. "I believe this dance is mine." He bowed and pulled Priscilla away, but she held back, peering at Lottie. "I won't be long." She turned and melted into the jovial throng of guests.

Lottie slipped into the hallway. The heavy oak door to Anthony's study beckoned her. Her palms perspired. She quickly pulled her gloves off, wiped her hands on the sides of her gown, and pushed the door open. No candles were lit within. She slid into the room and closed the door behind her. The latch clicked into place, and she stood in the peaceful solitude of the darkness. The only sound was the murmur of the guests on the other side of the wall. The aroma of aging books and the smoked-cherry scent of Anthony Middleton's favorite cigars lingered in the air.

With her hands stretched wide in front of her, Lottie shuffled her way across the oak floorboards until the tips of her slipper met with the leg of Priscilla's favorite reading chair. She hesitated, and her fingernail found its way to her mouth. She nibbled on the small snag that had been catching on the inside of her glove. Her nails were already ruined anyway. Besides, that was the last thing she had to worry about. Mama would be too livid to notice she'd resumed her nail-biting habit. She pictured her mother's face. Her lips would pinch, her nostrils would flare, and then her voice would shriek.

Lottie sighed and felt around for the candlestick and matches that usually rested on the nearby side table. A wall clock chimed, and she jolted, releasing a startled gasp. It was midnight, and although her hands shook, the match lit with one strike. She held it to the wick until it caught, then waved out the matchstick and placed it in the metal tray. The cheery glow assuaged her frazzled nerves.

She spied the decanter of brandy and up-righted two glasses. The decanter stopper fought her, but finally relented with a pop. She lifted the crystal bottle and took a whiff. The potent vanilla-sweet smell of fermented wine burned her nostrils. She coughed and poured two glasses. The amber liquid sparkled in the candlelight.

After replacing the stopper, her hand hovered over a glass.

Her nerves gave out. She would wait until Priscilla joined her.

Lottie picked up the candlestick and moved to the bookshelf. The light was dim, so she held the candle higher to read the embossed titles on the bindings of the books. *The Pirate's Treasure.* A sappy title for one of Pricilla's romantic novels. The pads of her fingers ran down the leather cover. From Priscilla's retellings, Lottie knew it would feature a helpless heroine who needed repeated saving, but she pulled it out anyway. Her mother would never allow her to read such drivel.

Balancing the book in one hand and the candle in the other, she flipped open the cover with her thumb and skimmed the first page. The flow of words transported her mind from the night's events and opened a door into someone else's world, someone else's life.

She leaned against the side of the high wingback chair and flipped the page, starting chapter two. The back door to the office swung open. Lottie jumped and dropped the candle, snuffing out its light. She bent down and felt for it on the floor, to no avail.

A dark figure appeared, illuminated by the backlight of the doorway. She knew by the height and breadth of the shadow's outline it was Mr. Winthrop. He didn't look her way but reached back into the parlor from which he'd come and brought forth a lit candle from off the fireplace mantle.

She ought to say something, clear her throat and give away her position. Instead, she swallowed her voice and remained crouched behind the wingback chair. The light reflecting off brandy glasses winked at her.

What was she doing? Her reputation would be compromised if she were found alone in a dark room with a man.

She still didn't move. What would Priscilla think when she entered? Her breathing quickened into silent, shallow pants.

The dark figure set the candle on the desk. He lifted one of the glasses she'd poured to his nose and said to no one in particular. "Middleton's already prepared a toast to our deal. It's as good as done." He placed the glass back on the desk, and it clinked against the other glass. A smile donned his face. "With Middleton's backing, our cargo route will be safe from privateers." His voice grew with enthusiasm. "Winthrop Sugar and Shipping." He raised a hand and rubbed his chin as if decided upon a name. "No. Katherine Winthrop Shipping." He glanced at the ceiling and smiled.

He shifted to the other side of the desk within feet of where she crouched. Her breath caught. He pulled out a leather chair and sat. Her legs cried out in pain from their half-crouched position as he settled into the seat. He propped his elbow on the arm of the chair and rested his chin on his fist.

"By Jove," he said in more of a sigh to himself. "I knew I should have stayed by Middleton's side. He'll converse with every soul in the place on his way here."

He slung his other arm over the back of the chair, and his fingers dangled so close to her face that she could smell the salt on his skin, the oaky scent of his cologne, and...what was that other scent? Smoke?

He must have smelled it too because he sniffed and straightened in the chair.

Lottie turned to where the smoke was stronger and spied a reddish glow at the hem of her gown.

The candle.

Her gown!

Fire!

CHAPTER 3

Scandal!
~ Headline of the "Morning Post" gossip column

*L*ottie screamed and leapt from her hiding place.

Two steel bands grabbed her arms and threw her into the wingback chair. Smoke burned her lungs and eyes, and she gasped for air. She pulled her legs in to get as far away from the fire as possible while Winthrop beat out the flames with his gloved hands.

"It's all right," he said in a strained voice. "The fire's out now."

She stared at him, too stunned to move.

He coughed into his charred gloves. "Are you hurt?"

Gray eyes held hers. His concern stole her voice and froze her to the spot.

"Will you be all right if I take a look?"

Lottie shook herself out of her stupor enough for the barest of nods.

With gentle hands, he pulled her foot down and turned it left and right to examine the skin around her ankle.

She peeked over her knees to find her slippers blackened with ash and her gown ruined beyond repair.

"You look none the worse for wear, but that was close, I must say."

"Winthrop, what in the devil is going on? I heard screaming."

Lottie cringed as Anthony Middleton charged into the room with Priscilla close on his heels. He skidded to a stop when he saw Mr. Winthrop bending over her. And not just leaning near...*folding down her skirts.* "God's thunder, man. Unhand her!" A pitcher of ale Anthony carried sloshed onto the floor as his face turned crimson.

At that moment, Lottie's mother burst through the hallway entrance, followed by a gaggle of dowagers. Her mother sucked in a loud gasp and paled two shades lighter than her cream-colored gown.

Winthrop pushed away from the reading chair and rose to face the crowd. Lottie hastened to stand also.

Anthony sniffed and glanced about the room. "Why does the room smell like smoke?"

"I dropped a candle," Lottie burst out. "It slipped. It caught my gown on fire and Mister—ah—Mister..." She knew his name, but at that moment, the word escaped her.

"Winthrop," he added.

"Yes, Mr. Winthrop put out the flames before I was harmed" —a shudder swept through her body at the realization of the true danger she'd averted—"or killed." She turned to him. "You saved my life. I'm indebted with gratitude."

He allowed her a wobbly smile before fixing wary eyes back to the ever-growing crowd.

Mama, instead of launching into an angry tirade, stood eerily still.

A warning bell in Lottie's head sounded, and her stomach dropped under the crushing weight of her impending doom. She followed her mother's gaze as it lanced Mr. Winthrop like a bayonet. Lottie sensed him tense beside her, but when she dared to flick her focus in his direction, he appeared cool and detached.

Lady Gibbons peered over Mama's shoulder. "Miss Etheridge, what, may I ask, were you doing in a room alone with a man in the first place?"

Lottie felt Mr. Winthrop's gaze boring into the side of her face, and her cheeks burned hotter than her skirt had only moments before. She glanced at the untouched glasses of brandy and then to Priscilla's stricken face. Lottie swallowed down the bile rising in her throat and stared at the floorboards. "I...came here to read."

"During a party?" Lady Gibbons's head drew back.

"I needed a few moments of reprieve. Ask Pricilla."

Priscilla nodded, but her guilty expression didn't help Lottie's case.

Anthony put the pitcher down and stepped toward Winthrop. "Why didn't you leave when you discovered the room was already occupied?"

Winthrop opened his mouth, but Lottie interrupted.

"I was reading when Mr. Winthrop entered. He startled me, and I dropped the candle. I'm certain Mr. Winthrop would have excused himself if he hadn't noticed my skirt on fire." It wasn't a lie. If he'd known she was in the room, certainly he would have left.

Anthony grabbed the brandy and tossed it back in one gulp before fingering the other.

A low, deadly growl sounded from Lady Etheridge. "We're ruined."

Lottie's head whipped around to stare at her mother, and her heart missed a beat.

Hushed whispers flowed through the crowd gathered in the hall.

A stillness fell over the room. The silence blared like a siren in Lottie's ears. Her arms stiffened, and fingers curled into the folds of her gown, clenching the material into hundreds of tiny wrinkles. No matter, her dress was already ruined.

Papa pushed his way through the crowd. "Honoria? What are you screaming about now?"

Lady Gibbons whispered into his ear.

Little by little, red seeped into Papa's face, darkening to purple as he turned rage-filled eyes on Winthrop. "You cur. You've ruined my daughter." His voice started out low and menacing, but rose in volume with each word. "By Jove, you shall marry her or meet me at dawn!"

All eyes shifted to Winthrop, awaiting his verbal consent.

"No."

Winthrop's single word set the room buzzing. Lottie reeled from the impact. She didn't expect Mr. Winthrop to want to marry her. She had no intension of marrying a stranger, yet his firm rejection—without even a second's hesitation—hurt deeply. Did she hold so little value?

Papa lunged at Winthrop, but Anthony grabbed his shoulders to restrain him.

This was outright insanity. How could her life and reputation be ruined in a moment? This was all a grave mistake. She stepped forward on wobbly legs toward her parents.

"Papa, it was an accident. Mr. Winthrop doesn't want to marry me and"—she forced the words past her lips—"I don't want to marry him. Nothing untoward happened, and there is no need to take this to such an extreme."

Anthony's face had grown as pale as a powdered wig. He kept a firm grip on Papa's shoulder.

She swallowed her embarrassment. Would Anthony believe her? Would he step in and save her from her plight? Or had her chance at capturing his affections been ruined along with her reputation?

Mama brushed past her and stood directly in front of Mr.

Winthrop. "You despicable rogue. You aren't fit to feed swine. You dare compromise my daughter and refuse to do the honorable thing? You've sullied her reputation beyond repair and will pay with your life."

A crease between Mr. Winthrop's brows deepened, and a small muscle twitched in his cheek. He no longer appeared cool or detached. "I have done nothing of the sort, Madame."

Mama's head snapped to Anthony, who downed the other glass. "You will second."

Anthony coughed on the brandy. "In a duel?"

Mama didn't answer, merely glared at him.

"But it's illegal."

Papa rounded on Winthrop. "You will do your God-fearing duty, Mr. Winthrop. If you have an ounce of honorable character in you, you *will* marry my daughter."

Lottie had never seen her father act so forceful. Mama had always been the demanding one.

"Our daughter will never marry the likes of him," Mama spat.

Papa thrust out his chest and glared at Mama. "Indeed he will and before the week is out." His voice boomed, and for the first time in her life, Lottie witnessed her mother shrink back. The rest of the crowd did likewise to avoid Papa's fury.

Lottie overheard her papa once say he'd wished he'd called out the odious man who ruined his sister. She'd asked about the aunt she'd never met, but Papa refused to speak of it. Would she share a similar fate as her forgotten aunt? Was this Papa's way to atone for not taking action on his sister's behalf?

The room grew eerily silent as they awaited Mr. Winthrop's response. His eyes blazed brighter than the earlier fire. Lottie's heart went out to him. It might be too late for her, but he should run—catch the next ship back to the Caribbean—because he'd eventually come to despise this life as much as she. At the same time, she wanted to drop to her knees and beg him to take her with him—away from all this—out from under the daily pressure to perform in a manner that pleased her mother and the ladies of the *ton*. Her breath came in quick pants, and she bit her bottom lip until it throbbed to the rapid tempo of her heartbeat.

He assessed her as if deciding what color jacket to wear to an evening of festivities.

Her mother snorted a *harrumph*, and Lottie flinched. Her eyes closed against the painful misery that would be her future. Because her mother caused such a fuss, rumors would fly. People would believe what they wanted to believe, which would be whatever cast her in an unfavorable light, because savory gossip was more enjoyable to spread than the truth. Her reputation would be tattered worse than the hem of her burnt gown, blackened and irreparable.

Priscilla would be banned from associating with her. If Lottie were lucky, her mother would send her to live with a distant relative. If she weren't, then she'd face her shame for the rest of her life under her mother's constant disapproving glare.

Her stomach churned, and her knees weakened. Lord help her, she was either going to cast up her accounts or faint dead on the spot.

Mr. Winthrop's strong hand steadied her elbow.

The heat of his touch seared her arm, and their gazes locked. His blue eyes flashed under a set of thick dark brows. She could feel his anger simmering under his façade of cool detachment.

Papa widened his stance and peered up at Mr. Winthrop. "You have ruined my daughter. What you wretched foreigners may consider a bit of sport is a grave manner here in England. You have overstepped. If you do not atone for your lecherous actions, I shall ensure the Winthrop name becomes an abomination. You shall not receive another farthing in trade with the mother country. Do not underestimate my reach."

"If your daughter survived the voyage, she could never

endure the hardships of the island." Winthrop crossed his arms. "You'd be condemning her to death."

"Thanks to your appalling actions," Mama said, "if she remains, she will be dead to us already."

Lottie gasped. Mother didn't mean that. Her coloring was high, and Mama sometimes said things she didn't mean during an outburst. She'd regret her words later. She wouldn't apologize, not in so many words, but she'd leave a cup of tea on Lottie's nightstand and have her favorite dishes made the following day.

Winthrop's lips moved as if he were about to growl, but instead, he unleashed his fiery gaze upon Lottie. "You heard the risks. Is this what you want?"

Was he asking her opinion? Did she actually have a say in the matter? Papa's gaze dared her to say no. Mama's gaze dared her to say yes.

Her entire body began to shake under the intense pressure not to explode, especially in front of the gathered guests licking their lips at the gossip they'd spread on the morrow. Her life was over. She would become a disgraced old maid tethered to her mother's side, for she'd never be able to marry.

Run! Her mind screamed. *Get away, as far from here as you can.*

"Yes," a faraway voice whispered. Heaven above, did that word come from her lips?

His mouth curled with a cynical twist. "Very well, then. We shall both be sacrificed on the marriage altar."

CHAPTER 4

The outcome of recent events should not affect our dealings.

~ From Nathaniel Winthrop, written to Captain Anthony Middleton

After three days of scrounging to get a special license and a clergyman, Nathan seethed in the back room of the small church in his finest suit. "What do you mean, you won't do the deal?"

The vicar's head rose. "Gentlemen, perhaps this could be discussed at a later date. Guests await in the sanctuary, prepared to see man and wife joined in holy matrimony."

"No." Nathan blocked Middleton's exit. "I need to hear his reasoning." Men's lives were on the line, but he couldn't let Middleton know how desperate he was without losing what small advantage he still held. "The deal is a sound business venture. Profitable on both sides. You know it, and I know it."

Anthony crossed his arms. "It is a good venture, but I refuse to do dealings with a libertine."

"You don't believe that. You've heard the retelling. It was an innocent mishap, for which Miss Etheridge and I are paying the penalties." When Middleton's countenance didn't soften, Nathan's fingers balled into fists. "You've done dealings with Littleton and Gillett, both notorious rogues with reputations blacker than...than"—he glanced around—"than the priest's garb."

Vicar Benson's eyebrows lifted.

"That is not the reason." Nathan stepped forward. "And no one is leaving this room until I get a straight answer."

"Then explain the two draughts of brandy. I saw the way you danced with her, your secret conversation behind the potted plant. You're a cur. You planned to get her in her cups and seduce her."

"I swear, before the presence of piety, those glasses had been poured before I arrived. I was under the impression *you* were prepared to drink to our deal. I don't partake of spirits. Coffee, tea, and"—Nathan glanced at the vicar—"the occasional watered ale or small beer, but that's because seawater would kill a chap."

"Priscilla." Middleton spit as he said his sister's name. "She and I will have a discussion later."

Nathan's breath caught. "Then you concede my encounter with Miss Etheridge was an unfortunate accident?"

Middleton hesitated and licked his lips as if to savor the deal being back on the table. "No."

Nathan's nose twitched.

Middleton crossed his arms. "You don't know the extent of what you've done to her." Middleton leaned in, and his eyes flared. "Lottie was a lady of stature. She's good-natured, with an unmatchable sense of duty, and tolerant beyond comprehension. Only God understands how she's been able to withstand Lady Etheridge's verbal slayings."

Nathan's fingers uncurled, and he grew still. "Lottie, is it?"

Middleton's eyes jumped between the vicar and Nathan.

"My sister and Miss Etheridge were the closest of friends. She was practically family."

Nathan locked eyes on Middleton. "You left out beautiful." He would pull the truth out of the man by any means possible. "Lottie is very becoming, with those big eyes, her mass of vibrant hair, her slender figure."

Middleton's face reddened, and he lunged at Nathan. "You'll not speak of her in that manner."

Nathan stilled him with a hand. "You believe yourself in love with her?"

Middleton paled as if the comment sucked the wind out of him, but he either would not, or could not, answer.

Nathan rubbed his face. "You can't do the deal because you can't stand the fact that I'm marrying her and you're not." His fingers dragged down the edge of his hairline and dropped back to his sides. "You've had all this time to make your intentions known, yet you stayed quiet." He peered into Middleton's eyes. "If I could trade places with you, I would."

Middleton's nostrils flared. Nathan's words only appeared to incite him further. "I hope someday you come to realize the gift with which you've been blessed."

He brushed past Nathan, thumping him hard on the shoulder with his own in the process. The door slammed shut behind him.

Nathan glanced at the priest. "That went well."

The somber man laced his fingers in front of him. "You fared slightly better than John the Baptist."

With a sigh, Nathan pulled out his pocket watch and glanced at the time. "I'm afraid it's the next undertaking where my head gets served on a silver platter."

～

*I*n the quiet of the room next door, Lottie stiffened in her best gown of pale lavender satin. Priscilla fiddled with Lottie's veil and pretended not to hear the conversation going on next door. How could she not hear them? Their voices penetrated the thin walls clear as day. Poor, dear Anthony. Lottie'd had no idea of his true feelings, but one thing she did know—he didn't have the fortitude to rescue her.

If I could trade places with you, I would.

Winthrop's rejection stung. She wanted to yell, "I don't want to marry you, either." Instead, she swallowed around the ever-increasing lump in her throat and held her tongue.

Priscilla smiled, but the lack of joy in her eyes proved it to be forced. "You look beautiful."

Lottie choked back tears that threatened to suffocate her. "I powdered my hair." She let out a chuckle, but it sounded hollow to her own ears. "I decided I'm no good at defying Mama. I made a horrific rebel, didn't I?"

"Joan of Arc would have hung her head in shame."

Her comment brought a smile to Lottie's lips, but tears blurred her eyes.

Priscilla took her hands. "It's going to be all right. I've heard the islands are beautiful. Palm trees, colorful flowers, turquoise water, and blue skies. Anthony says everything there is wild, but the cities are modern. He'll visit you whenever he travels for business, and one day, I will accompany him." She squeezed her fingers. "Think of it. You'll have the freedom you've always wanted."

Lottie nodded and wrapped her friend in a fierce hug. "I'm going to miss you. You're my dearest and only friend."

"You'll see. Without your mother to scare people off, you'll make oodles of friends in St. Kitts."

"I do hope so." She released Priscilla and wiped away her tears with gloved fingers. Priscilla was right. Everything would work out in the end. God had a plan for her life. She desperately needed to believe it.

Priscilla touched her arm. "Why did you hide instead of making your presence known that night?"

She twisted the index finger of her glove. "I don't know. Perhaps, I feared being discovered partaking of spirits. Perhaps, I'd been annoyed by his interruption and hoped he'd merely turn and leave." She lowered to a whisper. "Or perhaps, I was curious."

"Curious?"

Lottie closed her eyes and conjured up the memory of that night. "After we danced, he looked at me with such intensity, as if he found me interesting." Her eyes opened and met Priscilla's gaze. "He even complimented me." She bit her bottom lip.

A knock sounded to inform them the priest was ready. They both stared at the closed door.

A nervous giggle escaped Lottie's throat. "I guess my curiosity shall have its fill."

Priscilla nodded and swung the door wide.

Lottie smoothed any wrinkles from her gown and braced herself. All she had to do was get through the next hour and try not to think about the complete stranger—who didn't want her —to whom she was about to pledge her life.

She relied heavily on her father's arm to aid her down the aisle, for her legs were anchors trying to catch hold on a sandy bottom. The small church was packed tighter than a wealthy man's coin purse, which was easily attributed to the gossip surrounding their hasty wedding.

She could hear the whispers, feel the judgmental glances of relatives and acquaintances. She passed her mother, who was wearing the darkest gown possible without being in mourning blacks. For the past three days, Mama had wailed about the injustice of it all and tried to recant Papa's decision, stating they'd relocate to the northern mountains. But her father held firm as if he could right the wrong done to his sister through her. Never had Lottie seen her father so resolute—nor her mother capitulate.

Lottie barely heard the words the priest spoke, over the thumping death march of her heart. She assumed her place next to the groom and successfully avoided eye contact, but his presence loomed like a hangman's noose. The vicar's kind eyes did not match the life sentence he laid upon her, but she raised her chin and stood with enough regal dignity to do Mama proud.

However, when it came time to face her groom and say her vows, Lottie's resolve slipped.

If I could trade places, I would.

She'll never survive.

If she remains, she'll be dead to us already.

The vicar skimmed the crowd. "If any man do allege or holds just cause to impediment why these two persons should not be coupled in holy matrimony, declare it now or forever hold your peace."

Lottie peeked over her shoulder and held her breath. Mother shifted forward in her seat as if to protest, but Papa put a restraining hand on her arm. Lottie's gaze sailed to Anthony. Anthony's eyes met Lottie's for the briefest of moments before his head sagged, and he stared at his hands.

Her throat went dry. She angled to accept her fate, and the stained-glass window blurred into a kaleidoscope of colors. *God, please intervene. I'm sorry I ever prayed to be free from Mama. I don't want to be alone.*

"Let us proceed," said the vicar. "Please, take each other's hands."

Winthrop's strong grip engulfed her own and transferred a great deal of warmth. Her fingers felt colder than a jar fresh from the cellar. His steely eyes showed no emotion but boredom. He spoke out his vows in a succinct, businesslike manner, as if to get the deal done so he could focus on the next proceedings. He slid a ring on her fourth finger.

Instead of the simple silver band she expected, Lottie blinked at the sparkle of a large sapphire placed in a rose gold setting. Her lips parted in surprise. Where did he find such a ring, and why would he waste it on her? Did he see hope for them? Despite the trivial way he spoke of her, did he believe she may yet hold value? Or, was this another way for him to show off his profits? She met his cool eyes and witnessed a flash of apprehension, but the emotion disappeared.

The vicar cleared his throat, jolting Lottie. Everyone waited for her to say her vows.

"With…" She started in a strangled voice. "With this ring…" She paused to breathe. Had her maid pulled her stays too tight? "I thee wed."

Winthrop's eyes locked on hers with a *hurry up, we have a ship to catch* sort of look.

"With my body…" She murmured past the thick and cumbersome feel of her tongue. *Inhale…exhale.* "I thee worship." Her cheeks burned with embarrassment. How had he said these same vows with such ease? "And with all my worldly goods." *Inhale…exhale.* Where was the brave woman of less than a fortnight ago?

Winthrop leaned forward as if to coax the words from her mouth. His tilted brow distinctly communicated, *get on with it.*

"I thee endow." *Inhale…exhale.* "In the name of the Father, and of the Son, and of the Holy Spirit."

There. Done.

She sucked in a breath, blew it out past her lips, and issued the priest a curt nod.

Winthrop dropped her hands as if he'd tolerated enough of her touch, and stepped forward to the annals. He dipped the pen and signed in a slanted script, then passed the quill to her. Lottie dipped and signed what was now her maiden name. Her hand shook like an old woman's, and she stared at the wiggled lines. It would be the last time she signed Etheridge. She would forevermore be Charlotte Amelia Winthrop.

Inappropriate, bittersweet mirth welled up within her throat like bubbles of champagne. Marriage, she'd always known, would be her escape from her mother's tyrannical rule. She'd just never thought she'd take it to such an extreme. She'd married someone her mother despised. A foreigner. A stranger. And worse, a common merchant who worked for a living.

She should be celebrating her long-awaited freedom. However, the urge to squeeze her eyes shut and bawl like a child had never been so overwhelming. Oh, the irony.

A small snort leaked its way through her nose.

Winthrop's head jerked in her direction.

She rolled her lips tight and bit the insides for added suppression. What must Winthrop think of her? A bumbling nodcock who caught her skirt on fire and forced him into marriage, then dared to hold back a fit of giggles during their wedding ceremony.

What was the matter with her? Had she gone mad? Where were her manners? She dared not breathe in case more unladylike snorts attempted an escape. Her cheeks ached, and her face felt red and pained. The priest announced them man and wife, causing another snort to slip. Winthrop grabbed her wrist and yanked her down the aisle. He burst through the doors into the sunlit morning sky.

Lottie blinked against the bright sun until Winthrop's frame shadowed over her. His face a mask of fury. Her laughter dispelled faster than the pop of a soap bubble.

"Get hold of yourself. You will play the part of the cheerful bride and not dishonor your family or me with childish antics. Say your good-byes to your friends and family. My ship awaits us to depart for St. Kitts."

A blast of cold shock pelted Lottie in the face. "We leave today? But—"

"We leave immediately following the ceremony."

"But my things—"

"Are being loaded onto the *Katherine* as we speak."

"The reception—"

"To celebrate would be a mockery of God's marriage sacrament. You've brought this upon yourself, and now you will deal with the sober reality of it all."

Mama exited the church, followed by Papa and Gerald. Lottie jerked her spine into a straight line out of habit.

"There you are, Charlotte." Her mother drew up alongside her. "I've seen smoother weddings, but considering all, it was well done."

Other guests departed the church, and Mama acknowledged them. Lottie did her best, but the scene commencing around her seemed surreal, as if she were watching through someone else's eyes. "Thank you, Miss Chatham, you are too kind." A curtsy, a nod. "Yes, Lord Franklin, I shall endeavor to look up your second cousin when I arrive in St. Christopher." Another curtsy. "Thank you, Lady Sylvan, may I say you look lovely as well." Only when Priscilla approached, did Lottie snap out of the numbness.

"I shall miss our escapades, my friend." Priscilla's eyes welled with tears.

Lottie didn't care what the others around her thought. She hugged her dearest friend in a tight squeeze. "I shall miss you." She choked out. "Write often. Your letters will be a light in my dark days."

"You'll be too happy enjoying your newfound freedom to await my letters."

Priscilla pulled away with a weak smile, and Lottie returned hers with a wobbly one. Tears flowed freely down both of their cheeks. She wasn't sure how, but Lottie knew Winthrop was staring at her. His gaze burned like a matchstick flame too close to one's fingers, but she refused to let him ruin the moment.

Instead, her mother did. "Well, that's the last of the guests. Run along, Priscilla. Your brother is waiting in the carriage."

Lottie waved a final farewell as Priscilla stepped into the coach. Anthony had sneaked out without saying his congratulations or good-byes, and wouldn't make eye contact as Priscilla alighted into their family carriage. It was for the best.

Lady Etheridge turned to her new son-in-law with a raised chin. "Winthrop, we may have our differences, but you are now family and shall be treated as such."

Winthrop's gaze flicked to Lottie's with a sardonic arch to his brow. He knew her complaints about how Mama treated family.

"Thank you, Lady Ether—"

"I expect you to treat my daughter with the utmost of care."

"Of course—"

"We shall ride together in the Etheridge carriage to the reception at our—"

"Lady Winthrop and I have a ship to catch."

Mama's face paled. "The ship can wait. You're expected at the party."

"The ship is already a week off schedule due to the unplanned marriage. If we leave today, there's a chance we can make up time. If we wait until tomorrow and the weather doesn't hold, then we would be responsible for any perishables on board."

Mama's lips thinned until they almost disappeared. "The devil with the perishables—"

"Honoria," Papa interrupted. "The man shows prudent business sense. Say your good-byes, and let's see them on their way."

Mama's face morphed through a tumult of emotions before she exhaled and faced Lottie. She grasped Lottie's hand in hers, an uncharacteristic gesture. "If you lack for anything, I will be on the next boat. Charlotte, I …" She swallowed back what appeared to be tears. "I …" She blinked several times, but never finished that sentence. Instead, she said, "You look lovely." Mama straightened even taller, if that were possible, and turned to Winthrop.

Papa approached Lottie and leaned down to wrap her in an embrace. Even though he didn't like to be bothered with the raising of children, Lottie knew her papa loved her by his words of encouragement or the occasional measured hug. "God has a way of turning all things around for His good," he whispered into her hair.

Tears scratched at the backsides of her eyes, and a sob escaped through a shuddered breath. She'd loved when Papa used to visit her sickroom to offer Mama or the nurse a reprieve. He'd sit by her bed and read to her from the *Morning Gazette*. She'd dream of a life beyond her window. She just never imagined he wouldn't be part of it.

Papa nodded and stepped back to wait for his wife.

Gerald hung in the background, awkwardly shifting his weight and staring at the tips of his shoes. Lottie stepped up to her brother and planted a kiss on his cheek. "I shall miss you."

He grasped her elbows. "Not as much as I shall miss you." His gaze flicked their mother's way, and he reluctantly released Lottie. She'd always been the buffer between her parents, and now she was leaving.

Mama pointed her closed fan into Winthrop's chest. "I hope we have an understanding."

Winthrop didn't respond, but his scowl darkened.

Mama tapped her fan in Lottie's direction. "She is and will always be an Etheridge. It would do you well to remember that and—"

"Noted." His eyes slanted in Lottie's direction.

"I will visit as soon as I can." Having said her peace, Mama grasped Papa's arm. "Very well, then. The guests await, and someone needs to notify them of the lack of bride and groom."

"I see no reason for the celebration to cease on that account," Papa muttered as the footman opened the door to the coach.

Winthrop didn't move. He watched the pair alight before he turned to her and held out his arm. "Time to depart."

She forced the tense muscles of her hand to slide around the crook of his elbow and rest in between his forearm and bicep. He was no waif. His muscles strained against the material of his jacket. She spared him a sideways glance. His piercing blue eyes penetrated her soul, and an oddly primitive warning struck the cords of her heart. He was a stranger, yet he was her husband.

God help her.

CHAPTER 5

Increase rations for an additional passenger. I seem to have acquired a wife.

~ From Mr. Nathaniel Winthrop to Captain Jeremiah Fielding

athan inhaled the briny seaport air as the carriage drew closer to the wharf. The tightening band around his chest that had formed the night he met Miss Charlotte Etheridge finally lessened a notch. Soon he'd be aboard the *Katherine* and one step closer to home. Even though the island of St. Kitts was a British territory, England itself was a strange land to which he was not accustomed.

Miss Etheridge—*no*—Lady Winthrop, *his wife*, stared out the window at the passing buildings. He had to admit, she was a beauty, with fine cheekbones, ripe lips, and a delicate nose. Even if her hair wasn't the vibrant red he'd remembered from the Middleton party, and her cheeks no longer held a rosy flush from when they'd danced, she still held an incomparable freshness. In fact, her coloring had waned to a milky white. Such fair skin would blister in the strong Caribbean sun. He would have to ensure she remained covered at all times.

Nathan rubbed his temples with one hand. How did he end up in this predicament? The last thing he needed was to be leg-shackled, and to an English socialite to boot, especially since he'd invested a significant amount of funds into another shipping vessel. He needed to focus on keeping his father's legacy afloat, not jumping into marriage.

He hadn't conceded to the marriage out of the threat of a duel. He hadn't feared he'd be bested and end up with bullet in his gut. Nathan had grown up in the wildness of the islands. His father taught him to be a crack shot out of necessity, for one never knew if the French would return to claim the island or if wild Caribes would attack from the jungle.

He'd agreed to the union because, while chaos had broken out in Middleton's study, a sense of clarity unlike Nathan had ever known settled over his body. He no longer heard the rumbling voices around him, Lady Etheridge's wails, nor Lord Etheridge's threats. Instead, the clearest thought he'd ever heard said, *marry her.*

Charlotte's fright had almost been palpable. She'd needed rescue. Thoughts of his younger sister overwhelmed his good sense, and he was driven by the same need to protect Charlotte as he had desired to protect Katherine. He'd opened his mouth to accept his fate when Lady Etheridge attacked his honor. His pride raised its prickly hackles, for if there was one thing he believed in, it was honor. However, the Etheridge elders had no idea the dangers to which they would be subjecting their daughter. It had to be her decision. To his surprise, and to what appeared her own, she'd said yes.

A terrible mistake.

He tapped his thumb against his thigh. His anger ignited anew merely thinking about his dreadful mother-in-law. He'd been tricked into marriage so Charlotte could exact revenge upon her overbearing mother. Her little episode of delirium at the church only meant the unwanted consequences of her actions were coming to light.

Charlotte still stared out the window. She hadn't peeked in his direction the entire carriage ride. Most in her situation would probably be lamenting over their last glimpses of home, but the jittery look in Charlotte's eyes vacillated between apprehension and excitement. One hand still clutched her bouquet of white roses, while her thumb on her other hand fiddled with the wedding band he'd placed on her finger.

"Charlotte."

She startled at his voice and jerked around to face him.

"I've taken the liberty of using your given name since we are now married."

Her wide blue eyes peered at him, and she gave the barest of nods. "Of course."

"Nathaniel is my given name, but those closest to me call me Nathan."

She didn't respond. She didn't even blink. Silence grew between them.

"Did those roses come from your garden?"

She nodded.

Couldn't she see he was trying to extend an olive branch? He raised both brows to prod her further.

"Indeed." She cleared her throat. "They did. I-I care for them myself. Our gardener says I have a way with flowers."

Of course, she'd have a liking for roses. "Roses don't grow well on the island. The ground is too sandy. At least, I don't see them often."

"Oh." She plucked a growing bud from the arrangement and held the single rose out for to him to take. "For you."

He accepted it with a nod.

She curled her fingers back around the cluster of stems in a grip that seemed a bit too tight. "Since you don't see them much."

"How kind." Her offering surprised him. He studied the delicate petals—so pale, so fragile, not unlike his new bride. He inserted it into the buttonhole on his lapel. "Have you ever sailed before?"

"Once. To France." She picked a speck of lint from her pale lavender gown. The clip-clopping of the horses' hooves permeated the quiet.

"And did you like it?"

"Traveling or France?" she asked.

"Either."

A slow, demure smile spread across her face, like the early morning sun stretching its rays across the ocean's horizon. His breath hitched.

"I loved it. The sights, the adventure, the people, the food—all lovely."

"You went there for pleasure?"

"Mama purchased authentic furniture used by one of the King Louises, I forget which, but she was intent on supervising its shipment." Her eyes sparkled. "She berated the poor merchant for an entire day and completely left me to my own devices."

"How did you fare?"

"Quite well. I met two elderly French women, Desiree and Aurelie, with whom I still write, and they to me."

"I meant, how did you fair with the boat ride?"

She blushed, and the healthy glow resumed in her cheeks. Something stirred in his gut, but he ignored it. Youthful lust was the last thing he needed right now, even for his wife. The safety of his ships and crews was paramount.

"I didn't cast up my accounts, if that's what you're asking."

"Good," he mumbled, but his mind drifted to the *Amory* and her crew. Since he'd not brokered the deal with Middleton, there would be no returning of his men. They would remain enslaved or, as the British termed it, "impressed into service," until he could figure out another plan. How hard it would be to return to the ports and tell their wives and children that they would be without their husbands or fathers, most likely until the war with France ended—if at all.

The anger he'd fought hard to repress returned in a flash. He shifted in his seat and squeezed the seat cushion with his right hand. It did nothing to cool his temper.

"I need to understand one thing." He ran a hand down his face and scratched the skin on his neck. "Why didn't you make your presence known that night?"

She shrank back into the seat cushions as if she could make herself disappear.

There was nowhere to hide. "Was it your intention to trap me into marriage?" It wasn't unheard of for the peerage to marry for money, even if it meant settling for an untitled mister, whether he be a nabob from India, a new-money cit from America, or a sugar baron from the islands. If that were the case, Miss Marry-for-Money would be in for a shock.

Her eyes widened—feigned or otherwise. He didn't know her well enough yet to distinguish. He prodded her further. "Was this your plan to escape your mother?"

"No. I..." She shook her head so vehemently that a puff of white powder haloed her head.

She'd powdered her hair. That was why it wasn't as red as the other evening. "In the future, you'll find it will serve you well to be honest and forthright."

"As you wish." Her eyes darkened to the color of a turbulent ocean, but her complacent reply did nothing to denote the emotions swirling in their depths.

"And don't powder your hair."

The coach jerked to a stop, and he reached across to keep her from sliding onto the floorboards. She let out a yelp as her stomach collided with his hand and forearm.

"God's thunder." He rapped on the ceiling of the carriage.

∾

*L*ottie righted herself and pushed his hand away. Heat further burned her cheeks, and her stomach felt branded by his touch. His accusations also raised her alarm. He believed her to be a wicked monster who would risk public shame and humiliation to force him to the altar?

Mr. Winthrop—or rather, Nathan—drew aside the curtain to see out the window. A bustle of activity crowded the streets. "The wharf is less than a block away. We can walk from here."

He thumped again on the carriage roof with the heel of his hand, and within seconds, the footman sprung to open the door.

"We've hit a bit of a jam, sir," the footman said.

Nathan stepped out and assessed the situation. A deep crease formed between his brows at the bridge of his nose, and he reached back to assist her. His warmth penetrated even through her gloves. Her hand felt like ice in comparison.

The busy port hummed with people and the commands of the ships' captains coming in and out of the harbor. Gulls cried their mournful screech overhead, and the stench of fish permeated the air.

His chest lifted as he spied the *Katherine*. Crossing his arms, he assessed their surroundings with hard eyes. "Have the rest of her trunks brought down to the *Katherine* and her maid follow us."

"Right away, governor." The footman bowed.

He handed the footman some coin for his trouble before he took her hand. Lottie had no other choice but to be pulled along in his wake as he pressed through the crowd toward his ship. She struggled to keep up with his long stride, as did Franny, her new lady's maid. The poor petite girl fell hopelessly behind. Edith, her regular maid, had been too old to travel. Lottie missed the kindly woman's eyes. As the crowd thinned, she tugged her hand away, but stayed by his side. How dare he treat her so? How dare he condemn her for crimes she didn't commit?

The *Katherine* loomed over them, ready to steal her away from all things familiar.

Nathan stepped onto the gangway and turned to assist her up. He searched her face and his eyes narrowed. Lottie's heart clenched at his frosty glare. She fought to hold his gaze and placed her hand in his. His fingers wrapped around hers like a fetter. Would he treat her well? Should she entrust her life to this stranger? Was it too late to run? She tried to pull away, but his grip clamped down. The crease between his brows deepened into a slash. She'd been the recipient of such a look many times in her life. *Oh God, please help me.* Had she married a man whose temper would rival her mother's?

With a snort of disgust, he shrugged and released her hand as if to say, *so be it. Go back to your family if you like. All the better.*

Lottie hesitated. Should she turn around? Could she return to the safety of her family?

If she remains, she'll be dead to us already.

No. She must see this through and suffer the consequences for her misdeed. Lottie maneuvered up the incline ahead of him, grateful the plank only allowed for single file passage. The thin soles of her dancing slippers were not meant for the rough splintery boards below her feet. Her fingers slid along the rope railing. The swaying green water below sloshed against the side of the ship.

"Well, well, who have we here?" A deep voice startled her.

Her foot slipped, and she pitched toward the water below.

CHAPTER 6

Egad! I have pledged my life to a stranger.
~ *From Lady Charlotte Winthrop to Miss Priscilla Middleton*

*L*ottie's right foot touched only air, and her left slipper teetered on the edge of the gangplank. She flailed her arms, and a scream tore from her throat.

Nathan's hand clamped on her shoulder and yanked her back into balance.

"Watch your step." He grasped her hand. "We don't have the time to fish you out of the drink."

She barely got out a *thank you* before he turned and hauled her up to the rail of the ship. Her heart still pounded in her chest from her near swim. She stared at the snug fit of his muscular shoulders straining against the fine material of his jacket. Her husband had proved most capable. Her jaw tightened. But she didn't want to be grateful to such a maddening man.

"If I didn't see her with my own eyes, I never would have believed you'd done it—gone and got yerself leg-shackled."

"Capt'n Fielding," Nathan yelled back a greeting. "How's my ship? Itching to set sail?"

"Worse than an ivy rash. The wind is steady, and the men are bitin' to hoist those sails."

A big mitt of a hand, tattooed with a small bird in the webbing between his thumb and index finger, reached out and encased Lottie's elbow. Captain Fielding hefted her onto the deck. His face was tanned like tough leather, and his hair bleached white with the sun. All the captains she'd ever met had been naval captains like Anthony, and dressed in the standard uniform with gold fringe that matched the gold buttons on their navy-blue jackets. Captain Fielding wore loose pants and a fitted jacket with extra-long coattails. His stature was tall like Nathan's but thinner in build. He reached down to shake Nathan's hand and yanked him onboard.

"Good to see you, my friend."

Nathan's features softened into a boyish grin with even white teeth and shining eyes. Her breath caught at the transformation. *Thank heavens*, there must be an endearing side to her husband. She merely hadn't seen it yet.

"Friend," Captain Fielding scoffed. "A friend is invited to a man's wedding."

Nathan shook his head. "I'll explain when we join you for supper. Right now, I'd like to get Lady Winthrop settled."

The captain whistled. "Gone and gotten yerself a lady. Won't that put a thistle in—"

"Shouldn't you be preparing to sail?"

A look passed between the two before the captain's weathered face split into a broad smile displaying a set of full teeth. "The crew's got it all underway, and I'm still waiting fer an introduction to this pretty young thing."

Nathan's boyish grin reappeared. "Charlotte, please meet Captain Jeremiah Fielding, the best sea captain east of the Prime Meridian. Capt'n, this is Lady Charlotte Winthrop, my wife."

The name sounded strange to her ears, yet it was her name. Captain Fielding bowed low, and she followed with a curtsy.

"I hope you feel at home on the *Katherine*. If anything isn't to yer liking, then make sure you inform yer captain, whether it be yer husband or me." He pointed to a sailor in cut off pants and a red scarf looped around his neck. "Charlie here will show you to your quarters."

Her maid climbed aboard, carrying one of Lottie's bags. Poor Franny's chest heaved, most likely from the exertion of keeping such a fast pace.

Lottie waved her over and nodded to the young sailor. She turned to thank the captain, but he'd already stepped closer to Nathan. "I have news of the *Amory*."

Nathan's smile faded, and the furrowed brow returned.

"Five men were impressed into His Majesty's Royal Navy. Two were killed."

Nathan's stance grew rigid. "Who?"

"Skitter and Knuckles."

"Blast." Nathan turned and pounded his fist on the railing.

"Right this way, miss." Charlie gestured for her to follow him down a steep set of stairs. She hesitated, wanting to hear more about the men who died. Were they part of Winthrop's crew? Was the *Amory* one of his ships? Why would the British navy impress men who were engaged in activities crucial for the homeland's trade?

Below deck, darkness sank over them and boards creaked under her feet. The ship seemed clean and appeared in sound enough condition. The scent of lemon oil rubbed on wood partially covered the musty smell. But with it being a ship, must and mold would likely be a never-ending battle. Charlie walked with a wide stance as if to balance himself, even though the ship was docked. The long, lanky lad couldn't have been older than six and ten. She and Franny followed him down a narrow hall to an opening.

Charlie pointed to the right. "This here's the galley if you get hungry. Our cook serves a fine meal." He lowered his voice. "But eat well early on 'cause her meat becomes a bit tough out at sea." His brows wiggled. "Tiller once chewed the same piece of meat for three days."

"I heard that," called a woman's voice from within the galley. "Go on and git before I take you over my knee and beat the devil out of you."

Charlie darted around the next corner as the cook waved her spoon in his direction and laughed a raspy cackle. "If yer needing anything, ring the bell in yer room, and I'll send someone yer way."

Lottie bobbed a small curtsy and started after Charlie. Franny scurried to keep up.

"Here's yer cabin, milady." Charlie swung open a heavy wooden door and bowed a bit too low to be proper.

Lottie stepped into the opulent room containing a large, lush bed, complete with hand-turned posts, an ornately-carved headboard, silk pillows, and satin bedding. Sunlit-paned windows lined the back of the room, filling it with natural light. A small eating table was nailed into the floor on the right, a large writing desk to the left. Maps and charts were tacked up around the room, and a painting of two tall ships ensconced in battle hung in a gilded frame on the wall across from the bed. Lanterns hung on thick black chains suspended from the wooden ceiling. A large trunk rested at the foot of the bed, and she half expected the box to be filled to the brim with gold doubloons.

She turned to face Charlie. "But, this must be Captain Fielding's room."

"Ah, it is, but the generous captain has given up his room as a wedding gift fer you and Mr. Winthrop. He'll be bunking with his men fer this voyage."

Tonight was her wedding night.

She stared at the large bed she and Nathan would soon share. A cold sweat broke over Lottie's brow. This morning her mother had sat her down, but instead of explaining what happened between a husband and wife, she'd coached Lottie on how to feign a headache or pretend to be sick to avoid Winthrop touching her.

The thought of Winthrop alone with her on their wedding night washed Lottie anew in a fine cold sweat. Her fingers found their way to her mouth, and she bit her nails through the fabric of her gloves. At least Mama wasn't here to reprimand her.

"I'll leave you to freshen up," Charlie said. "If you need anything, give the cord there a good pull"—he pointed at a gold rope near the bed—"and cook will tend to you. You'll have to release the clapper first. Otherwise, it won't ring. And make sure to hook the clapper back up when yer done, or the bell will ring with every sway of the ship."

A scuffling sounded from the hall, and Charlie stepped aside as two stout men carried in her trunks. They anchored them against the wall with ropes and turned to take their leave. As they passed Charlie, each let out a chuckle and shook their heads. Charlie followed in their wake and said to their backs, "It could have happened to anybody. It's not my fault." She heard the guffaws of the crewman's laughter until she closed the heavy wooden door.

"Do you need anything, milady?" Franny clutched her hands in front of her.

"Not at the moment. Go ahead and find your accommodations. When you're settled in, you can return and help me dress for supper."

After her maid left, Lottie paced the perimeter of the room. The captain was an orderly man. Even his bookshelf was categorized in alphabetical order by title: *Common Sense* by Thomas Paigne, *The History of the Decline and Fall of the Roman Empire* by

Edward Gibbon, *The Holy Bible,* and *MacBeth* by Shakespeare. His library held a plethora of subjects.

Sitting on the bed seemed too intimate, so she pulled out the Bible and sat at the small desk. Her finger flipped open the pages, but the words blurred before her eyes.

Dear God, what have I done? This is all a big mistake. I'm not brave enough for this. I can't be married to a man who doesn't care a wit about me. One who has a foul temperament and believes the worst of me. I don't have the courage to start a new life in a strange land. Please don't do this to me. I'm not strong enough. I promise I will never rebel against my mother, or You, or anyone else ever again.

Hopeless tears plopped down onto the Bible's pages. She blotted at them with a handkerchief Priscilla had thoughtfully stuffed up her sleeve. She'd never touched a Bible before. In the past, her Papa had cracked open the family Bible and read to them, but recently he'd fallen out of the habit. She riffled through a few of the pages, reading a few lines here and there, hoping to find something to lift her spirits and gather her strength. Her finger traced the lines of Isaiah 61:1-3, and she read the words.

The Spirit of the Lord God is upon me...he hath sent me to bind up the brokenhearted, to proclaim liberty to the captives, and the opening of the prison to them that are bound...to give unto them beauty for ashes...that they might be called trees of righteousness, the planting of the Lord, that he might be glorified.

Bind up the brokenhearted? Free captives? Beauty for ashes? Trees of righteousness? What did any of those things mean? She slammed the book shut and put it back on the shelf. She needed to know how to survive on a rugged island—and how to be a dutiful wife to someone who despised her.

Shouts thundered above deck. Lottie moved to the window, and a tingle of dizziness swirled through her body down to her feet. The ship drifted with the current. People waved their scarves in farewell, and the end of the pier slid past her window.

She raised her hand as if she could reach out and grab hold of the last wooden piling to keep them moored, but her fingers met the cold glass of the window pane. A bleakness settled over her as she watched the pier grow smaller in the distance.

When England—the only home she'd ever known—faded out of sight, Lottie choked back a sob. Nathan's words filled her head. *Pain is unavoidable, but misery is a choice.* She covered her ears as if she could block out the thought. But he happened to be right. There were two choices afforded her. One, she could cry, fall into a pit of despair, and hope death would come early. Or two, she could see this as an adventure and the beginning of another chapter of her life.

Every miracle began with a problem. Did it not?

CHAPTER 7

The ship has set course, yet I feel adrift, uncertain
whether to celebrate freedom or despair at the loss of
everything known. Lord, help me to trust your plan.
~ Penned in Lottie's prayer journal

*N*athan leaned against a flour sack and watched
Captain Fielding smooth his beard. The ship's
cargo hold was the only private room in which he could speak
openly about his disastrous marriage. Fielding rested an elbow
on a crate filled with tea and scratched the bottom of his chin.
"You're telling me you were tricked into marriage by a stunning
beauty? How wretched."

Nathan pursed his lips at the captain's sarcastic undertone.
"The last thing I need is the added worry of a wife." People were
counting on him. He had a crew to protect and a staff of people
at home to provide for—so many who relied on him to put food
in their stomachs. "I need to be out with my ships, developing
merchant relations, increasing our profits, protecting my men
from privateers. Not at home catering to a woman who's never
done a lick of hard work in her life."

Fielding snorted. "Indeed. How dreadful to have to stay at home with a woman who keeps yer bed warm at night."

"I had hoped my new wife would have some spirit in her, but everything after the night we met has led me to believe Lady Winthrop is as timid as a mouse. She nearly fainted during our wedding. She'll probably fall into hysterics when she meets the rest of our crew. I can't see to her comfort, nor protect her from all the possible mishaps on a ship." Nathan ran a hand through the top of his hair. "Confound it. If she endures the voyage, she'll never survive the hardships of the island. My mother was the strongest woman I ever knew, and even she succumbed to the fever."

"You might be hasty in making yer judgments. Maybe she's more spirited than you think."

"She landed us in this unseemly mess by hiding from her mother. The pea goose was in such a dither she dropped a candle and caught her skirts on fire."

Captain Fielding chuckled and crossed his arms. "Didn't you say your mother-in-law was a hardened tyrant?"

He snorted. "She makes Napoleon seem like a puppy."

"Yer lady may have a gentler disposition, but the mother's blood still runs through her veins. I'd be willing to bet yer woman is stronger than you think."

"Stop calling her *my woman*. This is not a love match." He paced back and forth a few steps before rounding on the captain. "If what you say is true, then I have more reason to be concerned. I may have a devious trickster on my hands. I assumed it was all an unfortunate accident, but I still wonder."

"I'm certain it—"

"If the mother's same conniving blood flows through my wife's veins, then I should be sleeping with one eye open." He pointed a finger at Fielding's chest. "Her mother is a charlatan. Lady Etheridge knows the truth about my situation. Why else would she have had the gall to bribe me?"

Fielding drew back and blinked at him. "Bribe you?"

"If I don't consummate our marriage"—Nathan fought back a snarl—"she'll not only release Lottie's dowry, she'll double it." He crossed his arms. "I can only guess she plans to annul the marriage and keep her daughter hidden away as her own personal servant until the gossip dies down."

Fielding let out a low whistle. "That's a hefty sum. You could recoup all yer losses from the last failed voyage and then some." His brows rose. "Did you agree?"

"Of course not. I have my pride."

"Yer pride is worth the price of a brand-new schooner?" He tossed back his coattails and rested his fisted hands on his hips. "If she's like her mama, at least you know yer woman has a mind on her, albeit a shrewd one."

"Rightly so, but most unfortunate."

"The crew is not going to take well to your wife if they pick up on your ill feelings. They're loyal to you." Fielding's eyes shadowed. "To a fault."

"Let them believe what they will. If she survives, which the chances are barely even half, then I'll return home after a time to sire a brood of children. The rest of my time I can spend at sea. Once my boys are old enough, they can accompany me."

Captain Fielding shook his head. "You don't want a sailor's life. Besides, you're needed on the plantation."

"Marcus has the estate under control."

"Marcus works better with direction," he murmured under his breath.

Nathan braced for a lecture.

Fielding eyed him. "One way or another, yer going to have to come to terms with the woman yer bound by God to protect." The captain folded his arms. "Depositin' her among strangers and sailing off is not fulfilling yer vow."

"You've done it for thirteen years. I don't see any fault in your marriage."

"I'm a lucky man for having an understanding wife, but I regret every leaving."

"Charlotte desires freedom." He crossed his arms. "I'm merely letting her have it."

The captain blew air across his lips. "The way this all came about, the mother-in-law, yer shabby marriage. It makes me think that curse is real."

Nathan's jaw tightened. The curse grated his skin like a wool sweater. If only he could pretend it wasn't real. He'd worked too hard, and too many people counted on him, but how could he explain Skitter and Knuckles, and now the candle incident that forced him to the altar?

The boat creaked and groaned as it crested a wave.

Captain Fielding rubbed his chin. "Yer right. The island's superstitious nature has gotten into my head." He waved his hand in a circle, and the frill on his cuffs swayed. "But perhaps you need to give your marriage a chance. Help her adjust to the island. It could be a honeymoon of sorts. Enjoy yer time creating a brood of sons who'll take over the family business. Me and Little Cap' can handle the voyages."

Nathan strummed his fingers on his biceps. "It might be best for her to stay with your wife for a time."

"You want your wife to stay at the inn?"

A rush of nervous energy filled his chest. "Calico Manor isn't in condition to house a woman of her station, not since the hurricane. Besides, the events that led up to our wedding were wretched. This will give me an opportunity to court her properly. Julia's man, Paul, can see to their protection. Not to mention, Julia will be a good influence on her. She may help toughen up Charlotte."

"Aye." The captain crossed his arms. "But are you certain? Not living under the same roof can create another nest of problems, unless yer thinking of takin' Lady Etheridge's deal?"

"I'm not, but I'm willing to throw some coin your way for the hassle, and I'll pay for all her expenses."

"Even still, I think ya should stay with yer wife. Marriages can be difficult enough to navigate."

"All the more reason to come at it over time and with a calculated route."

～

*L*ottie pulled a more sensible dark blue traveling dress out of her trunk, and Franny assisted her in dressing. It was a bit wrinkled, but in the dim light of the setting sun filtering through the cabin porthole, no one would notice. The floor shifted as the ship swayed, and Lottie stumbled into her maid.

"Forgive me."

Franny pinched her lips not to smile, and she cast her gaze downward as if eye contact could cause sudden blindness.

"You think my lack of coordination is funny?" She smiled at her maid, who couldn't have been more than ten and six. "I would laugh too. I feel like a jug-bitten ostrich. All legs with the room spinning. It's taking all my concentration to keep my stomach from turning inside out."

The girl chuckled, and a spirit of victory ran through Lottie's chest. She'd make a friend yet. Lord knew she needed someone on her side during this voyage.

"This is a big adventure into an unknown world," Lottie said. "I admit, I'm a bit nervous."

Franny's gaze flicked to Lottie's for the briefest of moments.

"Edith said you're a good helper and to that, I now can attest. Although I miss Edith, I'm glad I have you with me."

Franny hid her smile under the fold of her collar.

A knock sounded on the door.

Franny hurried to hook the last few buttons on Lottie's dress. "There ya go, mum."

"Thank you, Franny." She walked her to the door "Tomorrow morning, I'll need help with my hair also."

"Yer hair is a fine color, mum. It would be my pleasure," Franny said to the wide plank floorboards before opening the door.

Nathan's tall frame claimed the entire expanse of the doorway. Franny bobbed several hurried curtsies and squeezed around him on her way towards the galley.

He leaned against the frame. His shirt front gleamed bright white beside his black suit and was as contrary as the man himself. He didn't need any frills or unnecessary décor to make him appear aristocratic. Even his relaxed stance exuded confidence.

If only she could own an ounce of his confidence.

"I assume you're finding the accommodations suitable?" He ducked to step under the low doorway.

The large room felt cramped with his presence. He moved about the cabin before his eyes settled on her. His business-like demeanor raised Lottie's guard. Was that a flicker of distrust in his eyes, as if she might make off with the silver? Or was it disdain? Lottie shrank back a half step, then stopped. She had cowered to her mother for eighteen years. Would she be setting the same precedent?

"Yes, the captain is very generous." The boat tilted and threw off Lottie's equilibrium. She leaned away to compensate, but the boat shifted again, pitching her toward the wall. Her hand grasped the bell pull for balance. To cover her misstep, she said, "And if I need anything, I'm to ring the bell, and someone will tend to me."

A muscle in Nathan's jaw tightened. "You may be accustomed to an assortment of servants and the finest of meals, but you're no longer in London. If you have any complaints, you are to bring them to me. Understood?"

"Quite." She forced a stiff smile, but her inner child curled into a ball and rocked back and forth.

"My crew is not at your beck and call. They are crucial in the running and maintenance of the ship to keep it afloat and protected from marauders. You might find them unconventional, but hospitable in their own way." His gaze wandered over her form, then jerked back to her eyes. "They're used to treating strangers like family. I expect you to do the same."

She started to respond, but he held up a hand. "No, I've seen how your family treats one another. Better for you to treat them as you would a dear friend, or better yet, an acquaintance."

The insult pierced her pride with a direct hit, but she refused to let him see her hurt. She grabbed the Bible and flipped it open again, but her tears blurred the page. "Is that all, Mr. Winthrop?"

Her throat tightened. He needed to leave—go away so she could cry out her despair at the disastrous mess she'd made of her life and weep over the horrid beast she was doomed to call her husband.

"No." He examined the room. "Captain Fielding will be joining us for dinner. Charlie will be along shortly to make preparations. I expect you to act as the dutiful wife." He slanted a brow. "That includes no childish fits of laughter."

Anger evaporated her tears, and her spine stiffened at the unprovoked attack. A true gentleman wouldn't throw her strained reaction to their forced marriage back in her face. She'd expect that of her mother, but she'd not tolerate it from a stranger. "Captain Fielding is welcome at my table, but you, sir, with your cutting remarks and demeaning looks can partake elsewhere."

He pulled back as if surprised, but then his eyes narrowed into slits. "Your table?"

She closed the Bible and held it against her chest like a shield.

"This is my table, and the people who eat here are at my invitation. I will not abide disrespect from my wife."

She was fed up with being a doormat for others to wipe their feet on. This marriage needed to begin with proper expectations. "Are you threatening me? Do you plan to starve me into becoming your obedient servant?" She stepped forward and raised her chin. "Do what you will, but I won't relent."

"Whoa, now. There will be no starving patrons upon my ship." Captain Fielding sauntered into the room.

Charlie followed, carrying a service tray stacked with dishes. The captain inclined his head, and Charlie began dressing the table with a setting for three. "At first I was hesitant to accept Nathan's offer of joining newlyweds for supper on their wedding night, but I can see a mediator may be necessary."

Lottie gripped the sides of her chair to keep her hands from going for her husband's throat. How dare he embarrass her in front of the captain?

"Charlotte was merely remarking on your generous accommodations." Nathan's gaze leveled on her. His face had the look of cavalier nonchalance, but his eyes commanded her acquiescence.

She wanted to close her eyes and block him out. Standing up for herself was what had trapped her in this travesty of a marriage, but if she didn't fight back now, he would belittle her for the rest of her life. She raised her chin. "Actually, when you entered, Captain, I was commenting on Mr. Winthrop's controlling nature, but I did express my appreciation for your hospitality earlier. Didn't I, Charlie?"

Charlie froze with a wooden plate halfway to the table. His gaze volleyed between Lottie and Nathan before turning to the captain. His shoulders visibly relaxed as if finding a haven. "Aye, Captain. She did."

Nathan's eyes flashed as if he'd just accepted a challenge, but it had been him who'd thrown down the white glove with his verbal attack.

"Well, it is my pleasure. Anything for such a beautiful lady." Captain Fielding smiled and pulled out a chair for Lottie.

After she sat, Nathan and the captain settled across the table from one another, and Charlie poured their glasses, ale for Nathan, and what the captain proclaimed as his best Madeira for the rest. Lottie's stomach protested against the acidic wine.

Captain Fielding held up his chalice. "To the happy couple."

"Indeed." A hint of sarcasm laced Nathan's voice. He lifted his glass, and a confident smile spread across his features. "To wifely obedience." He clinked Captain Fielding's glass and sipped his watered ale. The captain followed suit with his glass.

Must he try her patience? Lottie's fingers clenched her glass, envisioning it to be his neck. The dizzying lilt of the ship only added to her irritation. She lifted her glass, not to be outdone. "To an emboldened spirit and freedom."

Captain Fielding choked on his wine. Nathan's smile turned into a grim line. Lottie sipped from her glass. *Touché.*

Cook's dinner of roasted lamb shank with root vegetables showed the woman's merit, and discredited Charlie's complaints. The succulent lamb fell off the bone, but after such a grueling day, Lottie's stomach protested. She struggled to suppress her queasiness as Nathan and Captain Fielding discussed business, especially the challenges due to England warring with France and America.

On several occasions, the captain asked her questions about herself, but she kept her answers brief. Her stomach churned the small portion of food she'd eaten. She had one sibling, an older brother. She enjoyed the season. She did feel the weather was unusually warm.

Mostly, she listened to the two of them banter, allowing her further insight into their mysterious personas. The mere sight of the food on her plate threatened to gag her, so she averted her eyes to study her husband.

Nathan's regal nose was perfectly straight. Her brother Gerald's nose had been crooked ever since he broke it in a mock jousting tournament, and then again when he was in his cups and fell off his horse into the hitching post. Anthony Middleton also had an aquiline nose, though she wasn't sure why. Maybe Nathan's nose appeared overly straight because she'd adapted to hooked noses.

His lips contrasted with the sharp angles of his face. His bottom lip was especially full and usually drawn up in a sardonic half-smile as he conversed with the captain. He wore relaxed confidence like a cologne and extended his long legs under the table. She shifted her feet to the side so she didn't accidentally encounter his. Despite his casual state, passion lit Nathan's eyes as he became engrossed in the discussion on the safety of their crew.

Usually, men didn't converse about business in front of a lady. They retired to another room to deliberate such topics, but Nathan neither begged her pardon nor drew her into the conversation.

How utterly rude.

Finally, silence settled in the room. Nathan sipped from his cup and examined her over the rim of his glass as a locksmith would a keyhole. He maintained torque tension, keeping her ill at ease while his gaze maneuvered, poked, and prodded, hoping for a click, or in her case, a concession. Her jaw tightened, and she pushed a turnip root around her plate.

She wouldn't give him the pleasure.

He set his cup down. "I do believe our business ramblings have bored Lady Winthrop." He turned to her. "Is there another more suitable topic you'd like to discuss?"

"Actually, yes." She folded her napkin and set it on the side of her plate. "I was hoping you could tell me more about what to expect when we reach St. Kitts?"

"Splendid idea." Nathan issued. "Proper expectations should be set so you're not disillusioned."

Of all the egotistical...

"It is very different from England and from what people think they know of the island. Most of the sugar barons have made their fortunes and returned to England, letting their bankers and attorneys hire overseers to manage the properties. The land isn't producing as well now as it has in the past, so everyone on the island pitches in to work and do their part. It's not an easy life.

"The sun is strong, the heat saps a person's strength, and the fever runs rampant, taking people at will. English women are scarce, so don't be shocked to find freed mulatto women married to white men and some freed slaves intermarrying with Englishmen. Rum is poured freely, and men partake overmuch, becoming reckless." His eyes darkened, and he leaned over his wooden plate. "It's a demanding and dangerous place for a woman."

Lottie swallowed against the bile rising in her throat. "I'm certain there are some nice attributes about the island?" She despised the quiver in her voice.

Captain Fielding smiled. "Ah now, St. Kitt's is a beautiful isle —soft white sand and stretches of crystal-clear blue water. What's not a brilliant blue is a rich green. The cane ripples in the wind, beckoning with its wave, and the bayan trees rescue you from the sun with their thick canopies."

The tension tightening her shoulders eased. "It sounds lovely."

"Island folks are easygoing, unlike Nathan here." The captain chuckled and slapped Nathan on the shoulder. "The rum flows like the hot springs, but you probably won't be partaking of such, being married to this bloke."

She focused on Captain Fielding but could feel Nathan's eyes still on her.

Captain Fielding leaned in, resting a forearm on the table. "Nathan tells me you met when you asked him to dance?"

Lottie's mouth dropped open, and her gaze flew to Nathan. "I never—" How dare he misconstrue the truth.

Nathan lifted one of those thick sardonic brows. "I don't recall ever requesting a dance. Which means you asked me."

Lottie crumpled her napkin. "Ladies do not ask men to dance."

Captain Fielding's brow wrinkled. "You suggested a dance then—"

"That's not—"

"Yet, we partnered for the quadrille." Nathan pinned her with his stare. "At least confess to dancing. There are witnesses." His lips curled into a smug smile as if amused at her expense.

"We danced, but I did not ask you. We...we..." Lottie fumbled for words. "I didn't ask you, and you didn't ask me. We merely ended up dancing."

"If that's how you'd like to view it," Nathan said with a wry tone.

The captain snorted out a smothered laugh and covered the lower half of his face with his hand. His eyes glittered at their volley of words. "To think, a beautiful woman, whose dance card must have been full, decided to dance with the likes of you. Nathan, I believe that to be the utmost compliment."

The captain's eyes never left her, although he directed his comment at Nathan. Lottie pushed that same turnip root around her plate.

To her chagrin, Captain Fielding probed further. "I've always wondered how many dances a lady typically accepts in one night. It may be impolite to ask, but I beg you to forgive an old sailor and assuage my curiosity. The night you met Nathan, approximately how many dances did you partake in?"

Lottie closed her eyes. Would her humiliation follow her everywhere? When she opened them, the captain's eyes held a gentleness, but it didn't make the truth sting any less. She inhaled and, as if of their own accord, her spine straightened and her shoulders squared. Her mother would have found no fault in her posture as she answered. "One. I participated in one dance."

She didn't miss Nathan's flinch.

Captain Fielding issued Nathan a nod. "Wow, my friend, even more to your credit. Lady Charlotte is extremely selective, and you made the cut from among all the fine gentlemen in the room. Impressive."

Lottie clenched her teeth. Her husband's ego already filled the room. If it swelled any more, there'd be no room for any other on the ship.

"What was it that stuck out to you in regards to Nathan?" the captain asked. "His ravishing good looks, his dashing smile, the allure of a sugar baron?"

"None of those, sir."

The captain scratched his beard. "I can't imagine it was his cheerful disposition."

Nathan grunted and shifted in his chair.

"Why, then, out of all the men in the room, did you choose Nathan?"

Lottie squirmed under the captain's penetrating look. Nathan crossed his arms and also stared her down.

"Because he's an islander."

"So, you enjoy travel? You were looking for adventure?"

Lottie twisted her napkin into a rope under the tablecloth. "Not particularly."

"No." Nathan's voice dripped with scorn. "I was merely her escape plan. Are you certain the islands are far enough to transcend your mother's reach?"

Lottie ignored his question.

The captain leaned towards her. "Surely Nathan exaggerates?"

Her jaw tightened like a rusted trap, but she forced it to relax. Captain Fielding didn't intend to humiliate her further. He hadn't been there. He didn't know.

The overwhelming urge to defend her dignity pressed her heart against her breast bone. "The reason I only danced one dance was because people avoid me out of fear of facing the lash of my mother's tongue. The only reason Nathan danced with me was because he's a foreigner and doesn't know better. There." She rounded on Nathan. "Gloat in your triumph. Now you know the true extent of my humiliation."

Charlie had stepped into the room and silently moved about the table, collecting plates.

The captain pointed a finger at her. "Humiliation? Bah. I commend you for your bravery. While others cowered, you lived in the warzone. You suffered injustice and rebelled against tyranny. You embody spirit. Bravo."

The captain wasn't aware of the many hiding places she'd used to steal away unnoticed until her mother's ire cooled. He didn't know how hard she'd struggled for perfection in her imperfect body to spare herself another lecture. "I'm not a brave woman. Far from it, but thank you for your kind assessment."

"Intelligent, brave, and humble." He saluted Nathan with his raised glass. "Nathan, you are a lucky chap." He tipped back the rest of his drink. "Charlie, bring my best brandy. Tonight deserves a toast."

Charlie scurried to the wall above Lottie's trunk and pushed on a wooden panel. It fell forward to reveal a secret compartment. Charlie removed the stopper on a crystal decanter, and the smell of honey and strong alcohol filled the room.

He poured three glasses and handed one to the captain.

Nathan declined with a wave of his hand.

"I'd forgotten you don't partake of spirits." The captain

raised his glass to Lottie. "Lady Winthrop, will you have a toast with me, at least? It's not right for a man to drink alone."

Lottie's stomach squirmed. The sickeningly sweet smell made her want to wretch.

Nathan stared at the two glasses resting on the table with a furrowed brow. "Who had you been waiting for that evening?" His brows angled into a harsh slash. "Two glasses of brandy rested on the table. You were expecting someone."

Lottie felt the air around her change as his body tensed.

Yet his voice remained low and deadly calm. "I thought Middleton was planning to celebrate our deal, but it wasn't he who'd poured the glasses. It was you."

Lottie watched the tiny muscles around his mouth flex, and his eyes flared. She knew that look. It was the same angry expression her mother would display before exploding into one of her tirades. Lottie pressed back into the wooden slats of her chair.

"Who were you waiting for?" His blue eyes turned to ice.

Lottie's hand rose to her lips, and she nibbled on her index fingernail.

Nathan swiped her hand away. "Do not hide from me."

"P-Priscilla." She hated the quake in her voice almost as much as she hated him. "Priscilla and I were going to drink to my last night of freedom."

His eyes narrowed.

"It's true. Mama didn't like that I'd danced with you. S-she was forcing me to return with her to the country for the remainder of the season."

"So you'd been drinking."

She shook her head.

"Don't lie to me." His face reddened and a vein on the side of his head enlarged. "I told you spirits would addle your wits." He slowly stood and leaned across the table on his palms.

Lottie slid her chair back from the table. Her back dug into the wooden trim of the backrest.

"But you didn't listen, did you?" He sidestepped around the table.

She rose and scurried around to the other side of her chair, using it as a barrier to separate them.

His stance appeared deceivingly calm, but his eyes glowed with anger.

Lottie's stomach rose into her throat.

His eyes bored into her. "You're wrong, Captain. Despite her little show, my wife isn't brave. Her actions prove she doesn't have the guts to stand up to a field mouse."

Lottie stepped back.

"I was forced into marriage due to a cowardly act of drunken stupidity."

The furrow of his brow deepened, and he stepped forward. "Now it all makes sense. That's why you were swaying, why you closed your eyes and I had to steady you." His eyes blazed. "You were foxed."

She backed into the wall. The same feelings as that night returned. All those eyes boring into her. The stuffy hot air. The dizziness. *Don't faint.* It would only increase his contempt for her.

His face distorted with rage. "Because of your—your—lack of good judgment, I am now responsible for your life." A harsh laugh burst through his lips. "Do you know that I've witnessed over thirty deaths on the island? It's not a place for the meek or mild. I warned you."

Lottie backed up a step. "I...I didn't know."

Captain Fielding tried to interject. "Nathan. You're scaring her."

Nathan stepped closer until they were inches apart. "Because of you, my ships remain unprotected. The deal with Middleton was set. His military vessels were approved to provide escort for our ships to and from England to ensure not only the safety of the cargo from pirates, but the safety of the crew. All I needed was Middleton's consent, but he rescinded because of you." His lower jaw thrust forward, but his lips remained pinned together in a thin white line. With eyes that blazed, he jabbed a finger toward her chest.

Lottie tried to step back, but her foot bumped against the cabin wall. She was pinned, and she had to fight the panic welling inside her.

"Because of you, my ships and crewmen are vulnerable to attack. There are children who may never see their fathers again. Wives who are even worse off than widows because they don't know if their husbands are alive or dead. Families whose bellies will go empty because our supplies will be confiscated. They won't know where their next meal will come from." He ground out his next words in a harsh whisper, and they cut deep. "All because of your childish behavior."

"Nathan!" The captain's voice cracked through the air. "Enough. Your anger does you a disservice."

Nathan froze, but his eyes still bore into hers. Her entire body trembled, and sweat dripped between the cleft of her bosom. Her abdomen clenched. She tried to run, tried to push past him, but he was as solid as a boulder.

Lottie's stomach lurched, and her teeth began to chatter. She turned to face the wall and wrapped her arms about her waist, struggling to keep her food down.

Did her embarrassment know no end?

Nathan turned on his heel and, without a word, stormed out of the room.

Captain Fielding followed him, but stopped and turned back in the doorway. "Please forgive my colleague. Due to the weight of his responsibilities, his emotions run too high." With that, the captain left.

Lottie dashed to the chamber pot and cast up her accounts.

The violent heaves sapped her strength. She squeezed her eyes closed and covered her face with her hands, but another surge of nausea threatened. Hot tears streamed down her cheeks as Nathan's words rang in her ears. *Because of you...* Guilt compressed her heart as nausea clenched her stomach.

She'd never meant for anyone to get hurt. A sob escaped her throat.

Charlie scuffled about, cleaning up the remainder of the table.

Heaven help me. He'd witnessed her mortification.

He gulped down the brandy as if not to let it go to waste. "Shall I summon yer maid for you?"

Lottie rose as best she could and raised her chin, even though she still clutched the chamber pot. "Please do."

The door closed behind him with a click.

Her legs turned to jelly, and she placed a hand on the wood paneled wall to steady herself, but it wasn't enough. Her legs wouldn't hold, and her fingertips slid down the polished wood as she crumpled into a puddle on the floor.

Sobs wracked her body, and she wrapped her arms around her stomach as if the action might somehow hold her together. She dragged in another breath after the last sob left her devoid of air, and released a mournful wail into the silent room. The ship dipped and replied with its own sorrowful groan.

CHAPTER 8

Storm passed quickly. Warm and pleasant with a stiff
breeze. Rations are full. All is well with crew except for
one specific passenger who has taken to her cabin.
~ Recorded in the ship's log June 16, 1814

"*L*ady Winthrop?"

Lottie's heart folded in pain at Franny's use of her
new name. She didn't want to be that person. Neither
did she want to be Charlotte Etheridge.

Her stomach cramped, and she moaned.

She didn't want to be.

"I have some broth for you, and Cook is baking fresh bread."
She tapped on the door. "Please open. You need to eat. It's been
two days."

Lottie pulled a pillow over her head and groaned into the
mattress. How there was anything left in her body, she didn't
know, but the seemingly endless well of tears and nausea had
not run dry. She'd tried to rouse herself on several occasions,
but her blood had turned to lead, and her limbs were as weak as
kindling. There seemed little point in facing anyone. Nathan

would scoff at her weakness, and she couldn't demand to return to England.

She was a ship without a shore. Her father had been quick—too quick—to marry her off to a stranger, and certainly, her husband didn't want her. He'd made that abundantly clear.

Because of you...

Families would starve. Fathers and husbands wouldn't return. People would die.

Because of you...

She curled her legs into her chest and let the tears flow. Usually, she could find a positive, something to hold onto to get her through the day, but the only blessing she could count was that her wretched husband hadn't sought her bed. The idea of Nathan touching her only brought on another bout of sickness. She needed something to strengthen her courage so she could face the bleak misery that was her future. She didn't want to think these thoughts, but since her wedding night, it was as if a dark cloud had settled in around her, suffocating any hope she tried to grasp. Never had her sorrows penetrated this deeply. Never had she succumbed to such despair. She cried out to God, but the dark cloud mocked her. God wouldn't help someone so worthless.

"If you don't answer," Franny said, "I'll notify Mr. Winthrop."

Lottie stayed silent until she heard the shuffle of the girl's steps move away from the door. Then she cried harder.

~

*N*athan stood at the helm. Not a single ship in sight. So far so good. The sun cracked over the horizon behind them, illuminating the sails in a yellowish-pink light.

The exhausted night crew yawned and shuffled off to their hammocks while the day crew resumed their posts. The screech of the gulls disappeared as they trekked farther away from land.

Now, the only sounds were the gentle lapping of the waves and the flapping of the sails. Everything was peaceful, at least, compared to the drama before they'd boarded and directly thereafter. Nathan credited the serenity to the fact that his wife had sequestered herself below in the captain's quarters.

Nathan stood on the quarterdeck near Captain Fielding and stretched his stiff muscles. The sway of his hammock in the ship's hold helped him drift off to sleep, but the cramped position kept him from remaining asleep for long. He thought of the comfortable bed in which his wife lounged, and he grunted. She wouldn't appreciate the sacrifices others made for her well-being.

A salty spray cooled the heat of the sun's already-strong rays. It would be a hot one today, for certain.

"Napoleon's nose!"

"What's the matter, Cobble?" Captain Fielding checked over his right shoulder.

Cobble shaded his eyes with his gnarled hand and peered up at the mainsail. He turned to face the captain. "The stitches didn't hold. There was a tiny tear in the mainsail, so we had Charlie stitch it while we was on land, but last night's storm added a good five feet to the tear." As if in blatant mockery, the wind gusted, and the sound of ripping cloth split the air.

"Cannonballs and cutlass," Cobble muttered.

Nathan scanned the deck for Charlie. The lad might have nimble fingers, but he couldn't wield a needle if his life depended on it—which it did, along with the lives of the crew.

"Baby and Tucker!" Captain Fielding yelled. "Lower the mainsail before it splits in two."

The two large crewmen jumped to do his bidding. The sun gleamed off Baby's bald head as his plump fingers worked the knots holding the sail. Tucker untied the opposite side.

"Charlie!"

"Yes sir, Captain." Charlie jumped down from the rat lines and stopped below the helm where the line rested.

"For Pete's sake, Charlie." Captain Fielding turned his gaze heavenward. "It's the first lesson we taught ya. Never stand in a coiled rope. If the line goes tight, you'll find yourself upside down hanging from the rigging."

He quickly removed his foot. "Aye, Captain."

"Repair the mainsail, and fix it well this time."

"Aye, Captain." The lad's tone lost its enthusiasm.

Baby called after him, "Remember its tiny stitches like those flowers ya put on the handkerchief ya embroidered for yer ma."

"I don't embroider."

The whole crew laughed.

"Charlie."

"Aye, Captain?" He secured the line and hustled to stand at attention in front of the captain.

"How fares Franny with Lady Winthrop?"

"The lady hasn't been needin' her none. Franny's upset thinking she's not doing a good enough job."

Nathan sighed. He'd have to teach her a lesson about how one treats the help.

"But then I spoke to Cook." Charlie shifted his weight from one foot to the other. "And she told me Lady Winthrop has been refusing her meals."

Brilliant. His wife was throwing a tantrum. His sister used to pull a similar stunt when she was four. What was next? Was she going to hold her breath until she got what she wanted?

"She hasn't had a thing to eat since the night we set sail. Franny thinks she may be ill. She hears her crying, but when she asks if she can do somethin', the lady sends her away."

A pinprick of unease raised the fine hairs on the back of his neck. What if she was sick? No, she'd told him she didn't get seasick.

Captain Fielding turned a pointed look on Nathan, his message easy to read.

"I'll check on her. But if this is some sort of tantrum, I'm going to threaten her with swabbing the deck. A little hard work will take the wind out of her sails."

After descending the stairs, Nathan waited for his eyes to adjust to the dim light below deck. Pans rattled in the galley as Cook prepared supper.

"It's a bloomin' shame, that's what it is." Cook's voice resonated in between clangs. "It's been days, and he's not even come to the door..."

Cook and the lady's maid that accompanied Charlotte froze upon spying Nathan.

He eyed Franny. At least, the servant understood that everyone worked on a ship. He couldn't begin to understand the rational of his new wife, but if she wouldn't use her lady's maid, at least cook could benefit.

Franny wiped her hands on her apron and bobbed a curtsy.

Cook's bottom lip shook as if she might say something, but she grabbed a knife and chopped away at some carrots. The aroma of fresh bread was heavenly, overpowering the stench of sweat and unbathed men. Despite having broken his fast a few hours ago, Nathan's stomach growled.

"Smells delightful."

"I'm baking the bread fer yer wife," Cook said. "Hoping it will lift her spirits."

"That's kind of you, but she must adapt to being less pampered. She's to get the same treatment as the other crew members." He'd have to protect his crew from his wife's masterful manipulation. The new sailors Fielding hired to handle the cargo might be an exception, but the rest of the crew had sailed with Nathan since he was a lowly swabbie. They'd kept his neck above water through battles and rough seas. He wasn't about to let his wife turn his capable crew into cabin boys.

Nathan pulled an apple out of a bin and headed towards the captain's quarters.

"If we pampered her any less, she'd be dead," murmured Cook.

The comment raised another warning to Nathan, but he focused on the task at hand. He stopped in front of the oak door and beat on the panel with the side of his hand. "Charlotte, open the door. It's time to put an end to this little act of yours."

Nothing.

He jiggled the handle, and increased his volume. "Open the door. I command it."

A muffled whimper sounded as if from far away, but it must have been a squeak of the rigging as the wind shifted the pullies.

"Why must you be so difficult?" He dug into his pocket, pulled out the key, then shoved it into the lock. "You are to obey my orders. Do you understand?" It turned easily, and he pushed the door open. "I'd break the door down if I had to." He scanned the room, expecting to find her sulking or waiting for him with a defiant look on her face. Instead, he saw only a pitiful lump huddled in the far corner of the bed. It could have been another pillow except for the wave of red hair peeking out from under the covers.

He had a lot of work to do to toughen up his wife before they reached St. Kitts. "Do you have the mind to sleep the day away? On the island, we start work at the crack of dawn and consider laziness a sin." He walked over to the bed and yanked the pillow off her head. Her hands covered her face, and she groaned.

Nathan's jaw tightened. Traveling to the Leeward Islands was her own doing, and he'd have no patience for homesickness. She should have thought about the consequences before she decided to get drunk in a dark study. "There's no going back now, sweetheart. Better start getting used to the idea. Now, shake off your self-pity, get up, and eat something."

He stood over her with the pillow in one hand, but she didn't move. Tears splashed onto the already soaked mattress, and he realized the pillow in his grasp was damp. He leaned forward and peeled one hand away from her face. Her skin was pale, and deep purple circles surrounded her eyes. Her lips quivered, and her entire body shuddered in successive jerks as she sucked in a breath. She was still in the same traveling dress she'd worn the night of dinner, and her hair was matted.

Ice ran through his veins and seized his heart. "Are you ill?"

Her head gave the barest of shakes, then slowly nodded. Her voice cracked in a dry whisper. "Yes…maybe. It comes in waves when I least expect it."

"You must eat something." His voice pitched a bit high.

She squeezed her eyes shut and shook her head. "Don't speak of food."

With a slow, cautious movement, Nathan handed her back the pillow. She cradled it against her chest, once again burying her face.

He backed away, his steps wary until he reached the doorway. He turned and hastened back to the galley. Spying Cook he said, "What's the matter with her? Is it seasickness? When did this start?"

The image of Charlotte's pained expression couldn't be erased from his mind. What kind of husband was he? He should have checked on her sooner. Franny stopped stirring the pot on the stove and burst into tears.

"Franny, hush yerself. It's not catching." Cook flicked an end of a dishcloth in her direction.

Then Cook crossed her arms under her ample bosom and rounded on Nathan. "I'm not a doctor, but it looks to me like the girl not only is seasick, but has a case of melancholia."

"Melancholia? Are you certain?"

"It's worse than seasickness. She's real sad—bone-aching sad. My mother had the same disease after my papa passed. I remember the weeks she wouldn't get out of bed and wouldn't eat. She eventually succumbed to the sickness. They say she died of a broken heart."

His breath caught. Was Charlotte's life in danger? "Why didn't anyone inform me of her condition?"

Cook snorted. "One shouldn't have to tell a newlywed husband the condition of his own wife."

He flinched. Cook was right. Charlotte was his responsibility, and he'd let her down. "What can I do?"

"What worked best for Mama was when we got her out among people. Yer going to need to spend some time with her."

But there were navigational charts to discern, friendly and foul ships to be on the lookout against, and men to oversee, especially Charlie, who needed constant supervision lest he get caught in the lines. However, the same strong pull he'd felt when he agreed to marry her tugged on his heart now. Even though she'd gotten them into this mess, her life was in his care, and it was his duty in sickness and in health.

Cook wrapped up a piece of bread and a slice of cheese in a napkin. "Here. Give this to her and bring her above deck. The sun and the breeze will do her good."

He accepted the napkin.

"Franny and I will come with you to help make her presentable."

Nathan knocked gently on the door this time before opening it. Charlotte hadn't moved, but her crying had lessened.

Cook scooted around Nathan and pulled the covers off Charlotte. "All right dear, it's time to get you above deck."

"No." Charlotte stretched the word on a moan.

"Franny, hand me the hairbrush. We're going to brush your hair until it shines and get you into another gown. Then, you can take in the air above deck."

Charlotte's eyes flickered open for a second, but closed immediately.

Nathan stuffed his hands in his pockets, then pulled them back out again. He hadn't felt this helpless since... *No.* He wouldn't think about that.

"All right, here we go." Cook dug her arms under Charlotte's frame in a hug-like gesture and pulled her into a sitting position.

"I can't." Charlotte cried, and tears slid down her cheeks. "Mama warned me this would happen. Leave me be...*please.* I'm going to be sick."

She sounded so hopeless and defeated. Her reddened eyes met his with a penetrating sorrow that shook Nathan at his core.

"Yer not gonna be sick," Cook said. "Ya don't have nothing in yer system to vomit up anymore."

Nathan grabbed Franny's arm. "What does she mean her mother warned her?"

Franny couldn't meet his gaze and spoke to his shirt front. "I wasn't there, but it's said Miss Charlotte was frequently ill as a young girl and confined to a sickbed for most of her childhood. Her mother warned her not to overdo or she could relapse."

Egad. His wife was prone to illness? His blood solidified into thick sludge. The islands were rampant with disease. He ran a hand over his head and stared at Charlotte's gaunt face. What had he been thinking? He should never have married her. He should have fought harder to convince her parents of the dangers. He was to blame. His stomach twisted into a tight knot. If he was honest with himself, he'd admit he'd allowed his attraction to her to cloud his judgment. Before her death, his mama had encouraged him to find a woman and marry, but females were scarce in the islands. He hadn't been certain he wanted to be married, but if he had, he'd always known he'd have to find a woman in port and convince her to leave the luxuries and social life of England to live on a remote island.

The truth sliced through to his marrow. The scandal had made the decision for him. Marriage had been unavoidable, but also highly convenient. It allowed him to forego the wooing and courtship. He was returning with no effort on his part. He, too, had been selfish. However, now he knew the true consequences. By marrying Charlotte, he'd likely signed her death certificate.

"I didn't mean for anyone to get hurt." Charlotte's lips were as white as her pale skin. "I'm sorry. If I could trade places with them, I would."

A cold sweat broke on his forehead, and all the words he'd spoken rang through his mind. "They're my responsibility, not yours. I said things I didn't mean in anger."

Cook held her as Franny crawled onto the bed and began to work on Charlotte's hair.

"I'm gonna get her changed." Cook eyed him. "Yer free to stay or to go."

Nathan swallowed. "Uh…I'll go."

"Right then. Stay outside the door. I'll holler when we're ready."

He stepped into the hall and sagged against the wooden paneling. He'd put those thoughts into her head. He'd taken her vibrant sparkle and snuffed it out in his anger. In less than a week, he'd reduced her to a shell of a woman. This was his fault, not hers. He'd let his anger distort his opinion of her.

Nathan paced the hall. When Charlotte's father had stood in front of him and demanded an answer as to whether he would do the right thing by his daughter, Nathan had felt God nudging him to say yes. If God was for the marriage, then why hadn't Nathan been?

Yes, Charlotte had made an unwise decision by not making her presence known in the darkness of Anthony's study, but he'd made worse mistakes, and people had forgiven him. Yet, he continued to blame her. He wasn't the only one who'd sacrificed himself on the altar of marriage. She'd left her family, her friends, her home, her country, to live in a foreign land with a stranger. Shouldn't he have had some sympathy?

God, give me a chance to redeem myself in her eyes.

CHAPTER 9

Perhaps I haven't married an insensible ogre. Lord, give
me patience and help me remember we are all a work in
progress.

~ Scribbled within Lottie's prayer journal

*T*he soothing motion of Franny brushing her hair
settled Lottie's spirit and, to some extent, her stomach. When she'd been younger, her mother would take over the
task from her maid and brush her hair until it crackled. Funny
how she'd wanted to get away so badly, and now she missed
home so dearly.

She stood on her own as Cook and Franny eased a fresh
gown over her head. The effort exhausted her, for her arms and
legs felt as though they weighed a couple of stones each. They
propped her in a chair, and her eyes followed Cook as she tidied
up the cabin. Franny opened the door for Nathan, and his tall
frame strode into the room. For a moment, his dark eyes looked
remorseful, but why would he? He was the victim, she the
perpetrator. She dropped her gaze to her hands.

He crouched in front of her and dipped his head to look her

in the eye. "Cook said some fresh air and sun would do you good."

His eyes held a gentle kindness. She wanted to cling to the hope that something had switched and maybe they could be more amicable, but she didn't dare. She turned her head to the side.

He wasn't so easily deterred. Gentle fingers touched her chin and brought her head back around. "Charlotte, I spoke out of anger. I didn't mean the things I said. Yes, there are complications."

Tears welled in her eyes, and her lower lip quivered.

"But my mother used to say, 'Problems are the soil where the power of God blossoms.'"

The spigot of tears twisted open again and slid helplessly down her cheeks.

He wiped their tracks away with his thumb. "Please, don't cry."

He pulled her into his arms and lifted her, so he now sat in the chair with her cradled upon his lap.

She stiffened, but her muscles were too weak to resist for long, especially as he stroked her hair.

"Every miracle begins with a problem." He shushed her sobs. "So we're not going to cry. Mama would tell me we're going to rejoice at what the Lord is going to do."

She sniffed. "Your mother sounds like a lovely woman."

"She was."

Was. "I'm sorry. I would like to have met her."

A weak smile touched the corners of his lips, but pain left a hollowness in his eyes. "She would have liked to meet you too."

His warmth heated her skin as her head rested against the thin cloth of his shirt. The taut, sinewy muscles underneath revealed that her husband had not lived a life of ease. Only hard manual labor could sculpt a body so. Somehow that pleased her. Maybe if he'd worked hard to establish himself, maybe he'd work hard at their marriage. As she lay huddled in the warm cocoon of his protection, something stirred to life in her bosom, but it didn't dispel the dark cloud. However, the sleep, that had eluded her for the past two nights, crept in and slowly tugged down her eyelids.

~

A rumbling chuckle vibrated Lottie's cheek. The hazy fog of sleep lifted, and she stirred. The comforting scent of cedar and lemon oil filled her nose and reminded her of the trips to the parsonage when she'd accompanied Mama as a little girl. While her mother bent the vicar's ear, she would sit curled in the lap of his wife, Mrs. Simmons, who'd tell Bible stories. A hand stroked her hair in long gentle movements. The rumble sounded again, but the vicar's laugh wasn't so deep.

Her eyes sprung open. She wasn't in church. She wasn't snuggled in Mrs. Simmons's lap. She'd fallen asleep in Nathan's arms. *Good heavens!*

"You were a young lad back then, swinging from the riggings," said an unrecognizable elderly voice. "By His Majesty's madness, if someone said you couldn't do somethin', you'd do it just to spite them."

The din of the crew could be heard in the background, and a breeze ruffled the hem of her skirt around her ankles. She wasn't in the confines of her cabin. She was above deck, inappropriately snuggled in Nathan's lap. She pushed off his chest and blinked until her eyes adjusted to the sun. A crooked smile broke over Nathan's tanned features, and Lottie realized how close she was to his full lower lip. She jerked back and straightened her spine.

"Well, sleeping beauty has awoken."

Lottie twisted to see a man seated in a chair made out of a

barrel. His features were weathered by the sun, and his fingers curled with age, but he still wore the uniform of a sailor.

"Needed to catch a few winks, didn't ya?" His lips curled into a smile, and his face folded into a mass of wrinkles. "She's an out-and-outer, all right. A russet mane with da spirit to go with it, I'm sure. She reminds me of me wife, the lovely Maria."

Nathan let go of his hold on her to scoot himself up higher on the bench with his palms. Lottie used the opportunity to slide off his lap and sit next to him on the bench.

"Do you feel any better?"

The kindness hadn't left Nathan's eyes, and Lottie nodded. His niceness set her on edge. Would this state be temporary?

"Let me introduce you to my long-time friend, Cobble. Cobble, this is Charlotte Winthrop, my wife."

Did he hastily add the last bit, or was that her imagination?

"I'm honored to meet such a lovely vision as yerself." Cobble removed his tri-cornered hat and bowed. Tufts of white hair stuck out in all directions and blew in the breeze before he patted his hat back on.

"The honor is all mine." Lottie inclined her head.

"We were swappin' stories of when Nathan here first came aboard. Never seen a boy as hardworking as Nathan, but he thought he knew everything. Captain was a first mate back then and had to bring Nathan's hubris down a notch or two."

"That he did." Nathan nodded.

Cobble's eyes glittered as he eased himself back into his barrel seat. He laughed a hearty cackle, intermixed with a hissing *hee hee*. "Remember the time you thought you saw a pirate ship, and it turned out to be a flock of birds on the horizon?"

"I still believe it was a sloop. I saw the oars raise. You don't forget a pirate ship."

Cobble cackled even louder. "Bayonets and broad swords.

Gator woke every living soul on the ship. He even started filling the cannons. Captain was spitting mad."

"I'll say. I received ten lashes that night."

"All mates get a lashing at some point. It's good for ya. Puts hair on yer chest."

The normalcy of the conversation seemed too good to be true. She hesitated even to ask, but her curiosity won over. "You called him Gator. Why is that?"

"Ah, my dear, now that is a tale." He rubbed his hands together and leaned in.

"No exaggerating, Cobble." Nathan's voice carried a friendly warning.

"Our ship had taken a beating from a Spanish frigate. Even though we were friendlies, they mistook us for a pirate brigade. They sunk a cannonball into our hull, so we pulled into the Indian River down in the Seminole territory of Florida to make repairs. Nathan, being small and lightweight at the time..." His gaze rolled down the length of Nathan, and he winked at Lottie. "He certainly got big for his britches, didn't he?"

The corners of her mouth twitched in a feeble attempt at a smile. It felt strange, as if she'd forgotten how.

Cobble said, "We put him over the side and hung him there as he patched the hole and filled the gaps with pitch. At one point, he lost his balance. 'Bout took a swim, but he'd done what I'd taught him and wrapped his foot around the line. Good thing, too, because an alligator the size of me hauled up out of the water and snapped at Nathan dangling there like a worm on a hook. I'd been passing down a hammer at the time, and I've never seen a man scream so bloo—" Cobble paused and dropped his eyes. "Pardon my language. I'm not much in the presence of ladies, and I forget meself—"

"We can save the story for another time," Nathan said.

Cobble hung his head, and his shoulders slumped.

Lottie scooted forward. "Go on. I want to hear the rest."

Cobble's head snapped up. His eyes lit, and he cracked his knuckles across his chest. "Well, Gator here screamed loud enough to wake the dead. He climbed the line faster than any sailor ever to sail the Atlantic. Lieutenant Fielding hustled over to see what the fuss was about as Nathan reached the top. Except Nathan kept climbing. He reached the end of the rope, then climbed up Fielding like a monkey. There he sat, one leg swung over Fielding's shoulder and both his hands clinging to clumps of his hair still screaming like a banshee. His lungs grew two inches that day, and his mouth was open so wide we all got a glimpse of his breakfast down in his gut."

Lottie found herself nearly smiling again.

"Fielding was stark ravin' mad, but he didn't give you a lashing, now did he?"

Nathan snorted. "Much worse."

"He made Nathan not only finish fixin' the hole, but also paint the sides—of the entire ship. The devilish alligator stayed underneath the boy the entire time, hoping for a tasty Nathan morsel. Blasted creature tailed the ship all the way to the ocean."

Cobble's guffaws, followed by his raspy hissing, drew several of the crewmembers' attention, and they paused in their work of lowering the mainsail.

The contagious laughter lifted the corners of her lips, and she struggled to bring them back down, for she shouldn't laugh at her husband's expense.

"Ever since, Nathan hates gators—"

"Gator," Nathan said. "One particular alligator." He crossed his arms, but the lopsided twist to his lips showed he wasn't irritated, merely amused.

"Aye. He hates that gator with such a passion he won't do a single bit of trade in Florida, no matter how good the price."

"We can get perfectly good lumber from South America," Nathan said.

"Of course, the crew never let him live it down. They teased him mercilessly. Baby even carved out a log to look like an alligator. When most of the crew took to bathin' in a hot spring, Baby set the thing afloat right near Nathan." Cobble smacked his knee. "I know it's only Jesus who can walk on water, but that day Nathan came right close."

Lottie dared a glance at Nathan. His fingers picked at a small piece of thread on the inseam of his pants. The telling set of his jaw alerted Lottie to his irritation, but it was the reddish tint to his face that drew her attention.

Cobble pulled himself together enough to force out the rest of the story. "The most unfortunate part—or fortunate, depending on whose viewpoint you see it from—was that Cook was walkin' down to another section of the stream to clean up when Nathaniel ran by naked as the day he was born. We've called him Gator ever since."

"Winthrop, you're needed at the helm," the captain bellowed from his post.

"Duty calls." Nathan rose and faced her. "Will you be all right here with Cobble for a bit?"

She nodded and blinked at the genuine concern in his eyes.

"Saved from further embarrassment." He flashed a boyish smile, and Lottie's heart did a little flip.

The captain turned his head and yelled, "A good captain knows when a shipmate is in need of rescue. You are in my debt..." He paused for effect, and, with a wicked smile, added, "Gator."

Nathan walked over to the captain shaking his head.

"Hey, Gus!" Cobble yelled.

"Aye, Cobble?"

"How many arms does an alligator got?"

"Depends on how far down he's swallowed his lunch."

Raucous laughter sounded from the crew.

"Hey, Cobble?" Gus asked.

"Yeah?"

"What do alligators call Nathan Winthrop?"

"Supper!" Cobble shouted, and his eyes disappeared into the smiling folds of his skin.

Loud guffaws followed.

Cobble leaned in toward Lottie. "We're blessed to have an employer who'll let us joke at his expense, especially considering all he's been through. Nathan's a good man. Yer a lucky lady."

Nathan's linen shirt billowed in the breeze as he stepped up to the helm. He towered a couple of inches above Captain Fielding. Nathan's large muscular frame, paired with the stern expression he always wore, usually intimidated her, but today she'd seen a softer side of her husband. The same man who, several nights ago, had reduced her to a heap of tears, had only moments ago cradled her in his arms and gently stroked her hair.

Warmth spread through her stomach. Nathan was more complicated than she'd first thought. Perhaps he was more deserving of her respect. And, to hear the tales of him as a boy and see the way the men teased him, maybe he wouldn't be a horrid husband. She certainly enjoyed being on the receiving end of his smile. If only he did a little more smiling and a little less scowling.

She licked her lips and focused on the old man in front of her. "What did you mean by 'considering all Nathan has been through?'"

The criss-crossed lines of Cobble's face sagged. "That, my dear, is his story to tell."

He stared hard into her eyes for a long, awkward moment, but Lottie didn't dare look away.

"Ya have a kind heart, and it fills me with hope. I do believe God brought the two of you together."

Lottie's gaze dropped, and she shifted in her seat. The ship was small, and talk traveled fast. She didn't want her newest friend to be misled. "Cobble, we—"

"Oh, missy, love will come sooner than the changing wind." He puffed out his chest as if proud of himself. "Of that, I'll bet me right arm."

Then Cobble turned toward the deck and belted out a line from a sailor shanty about a one-armed pirate. "Oi knew a man who sailed da seas who thought he wuz quite clever."

Lottie startled at his unexpected bellow, but the crew answered with the next line in jovial harmony. "He had a lass in ev'ry port 'til his arm his wife did sever."

Cobble pushed himself up to stand and sang the chorus with his hat pressed over his heart and white tuffs of hair waving.

The entire ship responded. Men sang from the ratlines to the crow's nest. Even the captain and Nathan joined in from the helm.

*L*ottie might have enjoyed the singing and merciless teasing more if her stomach settled. She studied Nathan as he conversed with the captain and crew. He hooked his thumb into the pocket of his breeches and the breeze rustled his thick hair. His face grew dark with concentration, and the crease between his brows deepened as he listened to the concerns and suggestions of the lowest crewmember with the same intensity she'd seen in him as he'd conversed with lords of the peerage. He honored these men, and they respected him in return. Only the captain, who was probably used to being in command, appeared slightly put off by Nathan's authority. Captain Fielding solicited Nathan's counsel, but when he offered advice, the captain crossed his arms and leaned away.

Charlie pulled up another barrel seat and worked on mending a torn sail.

The wind fluttered loose tendrils of hair around her face, and she pulled a strand away from her lips with her index finger. She inhaled a deep breath, filling her lungs to capacity, then slowly exhaled. The fresh air acted as a balm to her ailing stomach, settling the constant churn to an occasional queasiness when the boat dipped substantially.

"Yer color's returned. I think sitting above deck appeals to you." Cobble fiddled with a pulley. He jammed a long tool into it and twisted. "You know what they say…"

When he didn't continue, Lottie shook her head. "What do they say?"

"Rough seas make great sailors." He disassembled the pully. "The first year I sailed, I slept above deck. T'was the only way my supper wouldn't make a reappearance. I found that keepin' an eye on the horizon helps too. Gives yer mind something to cling to until it can orient itself."

She surveyed the gray horizontal line in the distance as the ship rose over a swell and dipped. Although she couldn't discern a dramatic difference, her stomach didn't protest, and certainly Cobble must know of what he spoke.

"Ow." Charlie shook his hand, then sucked on his thumb.

"Yer gonna turn the sail red with all that blood." Cobble lifted his hat and ran a hand through his hair before plopping it back down. "And ya know what other passin' ships are gonna think when they see red. They'll start loading the cannons and preparing to defend themselves."

Charlie stabbed the needle into the sail. "I told you, I don't know how to sew."

"I'd help you, boy, but"—he held up his thick, calloused hands—"these fingers couldn't hold a needle, and my eyes would never be able to thread the blasted thing."

Charlie almost bent the needle as he turned it around to poke through the other side. "Ow! Confound it." He shook his thumb again.

"I know how to sew," Lottie said.

Both Charlie and Cobble peered at her and then at each other. Cobble shook his head. "A lady like yerself doesn't want to spend the day mending and toiling. Yer company is a gift in itself. We can't ask fer more."

"Nathan said everyone works on the island. I'd like to do my part." She nodded to confirm her words. "Besides, it would keep my hands occupied and be a good excuse for me to stay above deck."

Cobble's gaze flitted toward Nathan and the captain. He sucked on his bottom lip and released a breath.

"Please, Cobble. It would take my mind off the rolling of the ship. My stitches are tight. I can show you some of my embroideries to prove it."

She uncurled her feet from underneath her and made to stand, but her knees trembled from the exertion. Cobble stopped her with an outstretched hand.

"Only if ya feel up fer it. Anything would be better than Charlie's needlework, but if Gator asks, I'm tellin' him it was yer idea."

"Go right ahead." Lottie slipped the needle out of Charlie's grasp. "I don't give a fig."

Charlie and Cobble exchanged concerned glances.

She felt someone's gaze and looked up to see Nathan eyeing her instead of the seas ahead. The wind feathered his hair and pressed his shirt against his flat stomach.

She bent her head over her task.

Did she truly not give a fig, or had today changed her outlook?

CHAPTER 10

Dearest friend, how I wish you were by my side to
witness the liveliness of the crew and hear their shanties.
~ *From Lottie to Miss Priscilla Middleton*

*W*ith a task to give her purpose, the days melted
into one another, even though the nights below
deck continued to be long and torturous as her stomach reeled.
If only she could sleep above deck like Cobble once had, but
that would be indecent, so she suffered through.

Although their relationship had become less strained,
Nathan still didn't visit her chamber at night. Whether out of
consideration for her ill health or because he still held misgiv-
ings about their marriage, Lottie couldn't guess, nor did she
have any idea how to go about inquiring.

The crew accepted her and teased her as they would each
other. During dinner one evening, they even decided it was time
she receive a nickname.

"I say we call her Red." Baby smiled his toothless grin. "Cuz
of the hair." He spun a finger over the top of his bald head. The
men all stood as Nathan pulled out a chair for Lottie next to

him at the thick oak table in the crowded crew room. It had been converted into a dining area for the evening since a hard rain drove all but essential crew below deck.

"It's not very original, I'm afraid." Lottie sat, and Nathan pushed in her chair.

The men resumed their seats in the dim room. Save for a swinging lantern, the only other light emanated from a few candles set in bottles as a centerpiece. Over time, melted wax had glued the bottles to the tabletop.

The aroma of dried meats blended with the stale funk of sweaty men as Charlie brought in wooden trays of salted beef, sauerkraut, and hardtack. After setting down the food, he squeezed in to sit between Salt and Baby. The crew waited as Cook dished out portions for Captain Fielding, Nathan, and Lottie. As soon as Cook stepped back, the men dove for the rest of the food until nothing but scraps remained.

"How come she gets a nickname? I've been here longer." Charlie's brows lowered.

No one bothered to acknowledge him.

"How about Carrot Top?" Salt said through a mouthful of food.

"Nah, t'would make me hungry each time someone called her name." Cobble tugged off a hunk of the salted beef with his teeth.

"I know." Gus's face perked up. "We can call her Flame."

Nathan frowned.

"Or Candle?" Gus shrugged.

His frown deepened

"Matchstick?" Charlie's blonde brows raised.

"No." Nathan's dry tone sounded annoyed.

"Definitely not." Lottie squirmed in her seat.

Captain Fielding chuckled from the other end of the table. "What? Bring back bad memories?"

Nathan hit the captain with an icy glare, which only made him laugh harder.

Cobble pointed his carving knife in her direction. "Well, look at that glorious mass of hair. It's like a crown of glory."

Lottie's throat tightened, and tears pricked the back of her eyes. They spoke of her hair as if it were a blessing instead of a curse. She'd never known anyone to see it in that way. Why then did she feel like crying? The swarthy seamen grinned at her. How had she grown to care for the opinions of such an aberrant group of men?

"She's yer wife. What do you think her nickname should be?" Captain raised a brow at Nathan.

Lottie glanced at her husband lounging in his chair with one arm hooked over the back. His cravat hung loosely about his neck, and she couldn't help staring at the open expanse of tanned skin stubbled with the growth of a beard. His other hand absently spun his cup in a clockwise direction, and he studied her with more than mild interest. An undeniable current electrified the air between them.

"Titian."

He said the single word with such affinity that a wave of yearning crashed through her body. She sipped her watered ale to cool the heat flooding her cheeks.

"An ode to a redheaded warrior goddess. Well done, my friend." Captain Fielding lifted his glass in salute.

Charlie's head drew back until his chin almost aligned with his neck. "I can't be calling your wife a goddess. That would get me flogged for certain."

Cobble smacked the table. "The boy may have something in that head other than marbles." He wheezed out a chortle. "I know what we should call her." Cobble pointed a curved finger at Nathan. "Look at the way he's lookin' at her."

Lottie's eyes flew to Nathan's, but he quickly dropped his gaze and sipped from his drink.

"We should call her Boss because now we know who's truly behind the helm." Cobble raised his tankard.

The crew joined with shouts of "Aye," and "Here, here!"

Nathan avoided eye contact with her for the rest of the evening. Before long, plates were cleared, and the men refilled their cups. When they began to get a bit rowdy, Nathan rose from the table and offered Lottie his arm. She stood and bid everyone a good evening. The narrow hallway didn't afford them room to walk side-by-side, so Nathan pulled her through the turns and various rooms until they reached her cabin.

"Here we are," he said, stopping at the door. He didn't open it.

The nervous flutter in her stomach returned. It was the same as the night she'd boarded, but she refused to be sick again. He didn't move, only peered down at her. The lighting was too dim to read the look in his eyes.

"Nathan?" Her voice emerged barely above a whisper.

"Yes, Boss?" His lips parted revealing his white, even teeth.

She snorted out a giggle. "I daresay that nickname was the most ridiculous of them all."

"Why do you say that?"

She gaped at him. "Because I'm not at all like you. I don't exude authority." The boat rocked, and she leaned against the wall for support. "Who would follow my orders?"

"Plenty of people." He leaned against the opposite wall and crossed his arms over his chest. In the narrow hall, there was barely a foot of space between them. "People will follow you because of your kind and caring heart. You've already gained Cobble's and Charlie's loyalty."

"Charlie's merely glad I offered to take over his sewing duties."

"Exactly." He raised his brows. "And by doing so, you gained his utmost devotion. For in a way, you saved his life."

She wrinkled her nose. "How so?"

"You saw him with a needle. A man can bleed out from a thousand small pricks."

Lottie threw back her head and laughed.

Nathan chuckled along with her. His whole demeanor changed when he smiled. The intensity that cloaked him like a second skin melted into young and carefree. His gray-blue eyes held hers, and mirth shimmered in their depths. For a moment, it was as if they were a courting couple, flirting with each other at a party instead of in the hallway of a rocking ship.

Funny, she'd never noticed the dent in his chin when he smiled. An overwhelming desire to know these small details swelled to a pressing need. She knew so little about the man she'd married. She fiddled with her wedding band, sliding it around her finger. "Did you always desire to be a merchant in command of ships and their crews?"

He exhaled a whoosh of air and rested his head back against the wall. A shadow passed over his face, and he stared at the wood paneling above her. "Yes and no. I was a second son. My eldest brother was groomed to take over the plantation and gained most of my father's attention."

Lottie stilled her fidgeting. Nathan was revealing a part of himself, and she didn't want to interrupt the moment.

"It awoke a competitive jealousy in me. I strove to prove I could run the plantation better, and the crops I oversaw produced higher-quality sugar and in larger quantities. But my ambition caused a rift in the family."

His eyes grew distant and strained. Her hand twitched, wanting to reach out and comfort him. But would he welcome her touch?

"My parents sent me to the military academy where I learned naval skills. I was supposed to join the navy and fight for our island and mother country." His eyes shadowed as if haunted. "But my brother became sick with the fever and died."

Lottie's hand covered her gasp. "I'm so sorry."

"It's part of island life."

"That doesn't make it any easier."

"Indeed. He told me before he passed that…" Nathan's Adam's apple bobbed, and his facial muscles grew taut. "I was the better man to run the plantation. He told me to make him proud." Nathan peered up at the ceiling and blinked. After a long moment, he met her gaze with naked pain. "No matter what I've tried, the land won't produce like it once did." He cleared his throat. "But I couldn't let my family's inheritance dry up. So, I found another source of income in trade. Now I manage both."

Her heart ached for Nathan—and not only for his loss. She understood the pressure of wanting to measure up to someone's expectations, yet never quite reaching them. "That is a lot for one person's shoulders."

He shrugged. "I don't mean to scare you." His lip folded into a frown. "I may have said too much. You're used to means and fortune. I'm not as wealthy as some may believe, but I'm not destitute. I'll never allow you to lack." His eyes pierced hers with such a forceful intensity she had no doubt he would hold his promise.

She tried to lighten the mood with a teasing tone. "As you know, I didn't marry you for your money."

"No?" A lopsided smile lifted the corner of his mouth. "Why did you?" He closed his eyes and gave his head a little shake. "I admit, the night of our engagement is a blurry haze of yelling and angry faces."

"I married you for your fire-fighting abilities."

His eyes flew open and his lips quirked in a half-smile. "No doubt. I've been told it's my most attractive quality."

Lottie's cheeks ached from smiling so wide. She didn't want the moment to end, but she hadn't forgotten the lost men and their families. The suffering she would cause still ate at her. "I realize now how much you sacrificed that night. I'm sorry. I never meant for people to be hurt by my misdeeds."

"I know." His eyes held hers. "I shouldn't have placed the blame at your door. The fault was as much mine, if not more so."

Her lips parted. "You forgive me?"

One side of his mouth lifted, and he nodded.

The ship rocked, and she stumbled a few steps to the right. Nathan's arm curled around her to keep her from toppling. His firm hand slid across the sensitive skin of her stomach.

She drew in a quick breath.

The boat shifted again, and Lottie slammed into his hard chest. Her hands gripped his arms, and her forehead pressed into the top button of his waistcoat. The heat from the length of his body radiated through her thin muslin walking dress.

He stiffened, and his iron hands set her apart.

"I still haven't gotten my sea legs." She lowered her gaze, hoping he wouldn't see the flush that surely reddened her face.

"Good night, Lottie." He pressed his lips to the top of her head in a brotherly kiss.

Before she could return the sentiment, he turned on his heel and strode away. His arms swayed in rhythm with the click of his boots.

Once he rounded the corner, she let herself into her cabin and closed the door behind her. Her hand still on the latch, she squeezed her eyes shut and pressed her forehead against the thick oak panel.

How could the charming side of Nathan work her into a mass of nerves even more than his brusque side?

*T*he next few weeks passed uneventfully. Lottie assumed her usual spot in the shade of the mainsail behind the helm. During the days, she read the Bible and listened to Cobble and the crewman tell stories. At night, she joined the men for dinner. Nathan, in turn, would walk her back to her cabin. He'd kiss her good-night—if you could call his brotherly pecks kisses—but never asked to stay.

One night, instead of unlatching her door, she opened her mouth to question him, but he interrupted her.

"I know this has been a strange marriage thus far." He stepped closer and tucked a loose strand of hair behind her ear. His knuckle trailed around the curve of her jaw and along the tender skin of her neck, quickening her pulse. "I'd like to use the voyage to get to know one another and court you properly."

Lottie exhaled. That seemed a good plan. She still didn't know her husband well, and the idea of becoming more intimate broke her into a cold sweat. She nodded and bid him good night, and he pressed another kiss on the top of her head.

But over time, those kisses irked her.

Had she misread the desire in his intense eyes? She'd never been courted, but she knew brotherly pecks weren't how one went about it. Priscilla often spoke of stolen kisses and clandestine meetings. Lottie stabbed the needle into the fabric she was stitching in her seat above deck.

Cobble sat by her side and whistled. "You do a fine job. Neat little stitches, just like my wife."

"You're married?" She looked up at him.

"Don't sound so surprised that someone fell in love with an old seadog like myself."

Lottie pulled the thread. "No, I'm surprised a woman would put up with such a cheeky man as yourself."

"Whales tales and dolphin ears." He slapped his knee. "She could out-sass the salt off me. Whatever I gave to her she dished right back, but the woman had a heart of gold. She's in heaven now, God rest her soul, collectin' on all the rewards of living a good life."

Lottie paused in her sewing. "I'm sorry for your loss."

Cobble shook his head. "Don't be. She's in paradise." He pointed heavenward. "She's up there, probably singin' in God's choir and waitin' fer the day I join her."

Lottie grinned at the fond way in which he spoke of his wife. She knotted the thread and inspected her work. "I believe it's finished."

Cobble held the seam up to the light. "Well done, Boss." He stood and waved the captain over. "She did it. Sewed it up right."

Captain Fielding sauntered over and examined the stitches. He winked, then lifted his head and said loud enough for Nathan to hear, "Nice work, Boss!"

Nathan paused in sparring against Tiller to smile at her. Even with the distraction, Nathan was an excellent swordsman and didn't give up any ground. His fluid movements could easily best both her brother and Anthony. The breeze ruffled his hair, and he lunged at Tiller. The muscles in his back and arms strained against the confines of his jacket.

Dizziness swept over Lottie. Was she becoming seasick again? She stared past him to the horizon to orient herself, but her gaze was drawn back to Nathan's graceful assaults and virile presence.

"All right, men," the captain yelled. "Let's get this sail hoisted."

"Ship off the port stern, Captain!"

A jolt of alarm rushed through Lottie. The shout had sounded from Salt, the lookout in the crow's nest. The crewmen paused in their work and craned their necks to see. She stood and used her hand to block the sun. Sure enough, a speck of a ship sat on the horizon.

"Sink me!" the captain muttered. "Gus, man the helm." Captain Fielding grabbed his spyglass and held it up to his eye.

The fine hairs on her skin leapt to attention as she sensed someone's presence. She glanced over her shoulder to find Nathan standing beside her.

"Is it friendly?" he asked the captain.

"Aye, but that's what the crew of the *Amory* thought. We're dead in the water without a mainsail raised." The Captain turned on his heel and yelled to the men. "All hands on deck. Men, get the mainsail hoisted or some of you will be Roderick Random."

Organized chaos broke out as men scrambled to get the sail hoisted.

Nathan sheathed his sword and grabbed her shoulders. He turned her to face him, and the crease between his brows deepened as his eyes leveled hers. "You're to go below deck."

"Why is everyone running to their posts?" Her breath quickened. "Who's Roderick Random?"

"There's no time to explain. I want you to wait in your cabin, bar the door, and do not come up no matter what happens or what you hear. Do you understand?"

Lottie gripped his arms as her blood pounded in her ears. "What about you?"

"I'm needed. Every hand will count."

Captain shouted, "Smartly crew. We won't have much time." He lent a hand to Charlie, who struggled to hold the line. "Hold fast, boy."

"Bring Cook and Franny with you." Nathan spun her around in the direction of the hatch and gave her a push. "Be quick now."

Lottie fled for safety below deck and found Cook and Franny standing frozen in the small galley.

"What is it?" Cook's hand still gripped the knife she used to cut vegetables.

"A British ship."

Franny twisted her apron. "Why would we be worried about a British ship? We're British."

"It's not like that anymore." Cook pursed her lips. "The trade wars have tarnished everyone. You never know who's a friendly anymore."

Lottie grabbed Cook's arm. "Who is Roderick Random? Is he the British ship's captain?"

Cook shook her head. "It's a nickname for a person taken by a press gang." Even our own mother country's ships can impress our crew into naval service unless they have proper papers to prove they're from St. Kitts."

"Can we outrun them?" Franny's voice shook.

"The mainsail was down for repairs." Lottie's fingers moved to her mouth. "They're in the middle of hoisting a new one, but it's slowing us down. Nathan said we're to wait in my quarters and bar the door." She chewed a piece off her thumbnail.

Cook grabbed Franny's arm, and the three of them scurried to the captain's quarters and huddled together on the bed. They sat in quiet, listening to the shuffling of boots, the creaks of the deck and muffled commands.

Through the glass window, they watched as the faraway ship gained half the distance and doubled in size. Lottie could now see the British flag waving.

Cook closed her eyes. "We need to pray."

Lottie and Franny each took one of her hands.

"Heavenly Father," Cook said, "have mercy on us, the *Katherine*, and its crew. Help the men raise the sail and outrun the ship. Protect us from our enemies. Let no weapon forged against us prevail. Do not allow a single person on this vessel to be harmed or taken away. God, give our captain the wisdom needed for this situation."

The boat jerked forward.

"Hurrah! We're moving," Franny said.

Cook rose and inched back the curtain. "I hope we can pick up speed fast enough."

Each took turns continuing their vigilant prayers until a cannon blast shook the room. Franny screamed and ducked her head into the covers. Lottie stared at Cook. "Why are they firing?"

"It's a warning shot not to run." She squeezed Lottie's hand in a tight grip. "God will see us through. The captain knows what to do." Her voice sounded strong, but Lottie felt the telltale shaking of her hands.

The ship sailed close enough for her to count the mounted cannons. Fifteen on the port side. Their merchant ship was heavily outnumbered. Men in navy coats stood at the stern of the other vessel and prepared to board.

Wait. She recognized one of them. Standing at the helm as the ship drew up to their port side was Admiral Gainesboro. Her mother had introduced her to the man and his wife on several occasions. Beside him stood another familiar face, a friend of Anthony Middleton's.

She jumped to her feet. "I have an idea. Get me into my best gown and fix my hair. I must look my best."

Cook and Franny stared at her as if she'd sprouted horns.

"Smartly, ladies. Lives are at stake!"

CHAPTER 11

I daresay, I managed a fair impersonation. Truly her
blood runs through my veins.
~ *From Lottie written to her brother, Gerald Etheridge.*

*N*athan clenched his jaw tight to keep from spitting
in the haughty British commander's face. "As a
merchant ship from the islands commissioned to trade with
England, we are exempted from naval press gangs."

"Then I need to verify your men's citizenship papers along
with your protection documents." The man's polished brass
buttons shone in the sun as he strutted like a fluffed turkey
before Nathan and Captain Fielding.

"I showed you our protection documents."

The commander flicked his arm at a cluster of Nathan's
crew. "Yet, these men cannot produce citizenship papers." He
whipped into a ninety-degree turn and addressed his men. "Get
ready for onboarding. Take them to the hold."

Baby let out a growl and grabbed a soldier's wrist in a tight
twist. The man howled in pain, and his sword clamored to the
ground. The butt of a British musket slammed into Baby's face

with a sickening crack. The huge sailor teetered, then fell like a tall oak, shaking the floorboards.

Nathan stepped forward, but a British soldier met him with the point of his sword. He could go no farther. "You're making a grave mistake. The Society of West Indian Merchants will petition parliament over this. The prime minister will hear about your outrageous actions!"

"You." The commander turned back around and stepped within inches of Nathan, so close he could smell the coffee on the man's foul breath. His haughty eyes gleamed like a polished stone. "You think your nabob coin can buy your way into British amnesty? We're at war. Drastic measures and able-bodied men are needed to win the fight."

"Admiral Gainesboro, how lovely to see you."

Lottie's voice froze Nathan's blood. Icy tendrils of fear penetrated to his fingers and toes as she stepped above deck, dressed in the same gown she'd been wearing when she wed him. Her hair was swept up in an elaborate coiffure, as if she were about to attend a grand affair.

"Have you come to join us for tea?"

Nathan was going to throttle his wife for disobeying his command. White rage melted the ice in his veins as she sauntered up to the British commander and curtsied.

"Miss Etheridge." The Admiral bowed. "I never would have guessed you to be aboard. Are you traveling to the islands?"

She held out her hand, and he took it, lingering his lips too long over the back of her hand.

Had her bodice dipped that low the day they were married? Nathan itched to cover the smooth swell of her white flesh as the Admiral's eyes settled there. What did she hope to accomplish?

His gut clenched. Was it her plan to convince the Admiral to return her to London so she could be with Middleton? Had the last few weeks all been an act? Had he misread her feelings?

Could he have misconstrued their intimate glances, the shared laughter, his opening himself up to her, especially that night in the hall? If so, she'd played him for a fool.

"Yes, and it's been a pleasurable trip thus far."

Admiral Gainesboro cleared his throat and glanced around. "Is your mother...ah...traveling with you?"

"Not at the moment."

The admiral visibly relaxed. Even this man had learned to fear Nathan's mother-in-law. The thought almost made him smile.

Lottie tilted her head and gazed at the man through what appeared to Nathan as a sultry slant. Nathan's back tooth ached to the point of cracking under the pressure of his clenched jaw. "Shall I have my maid bring up the tea service?"

"Tempting as it is to enjoy the company of a beautiful woman such as yourself, I'm afraid duty calls."

"What duty brings you our way?"

"We need to enlist a few men to help us battle the Americans."

"Yes, yes. I do hope we put an end to this trade war soon. It's harming the merchant industry. We need American cotton for our gowns." A graceful hand fanned out the side of her skirt. "However, Admiral, I don't believe there are any Englishmen aboard from whom to choose. The crewmen are Kittitians, from the Leeward Islands."

Captain Fielding nudged Nathan's elbow. Nathan met his questioning eyes as he mouthed, *What is she doing?*

Nathan answered with a tiny shrug and a miniscule shake of his head. His fingers curled into fists.

"Half this crew doesn't have the proper paperwork to determine their nationality."

Lottie giggled. "You don't need paperwork to know their ethnicity."

She glanced in Nathan's direction. He leveled her with a glare he hoped would send her running below deck.

It didn't have the desired effect, but it did give her pause.

"You…only …" She tore her eyes away and focused back on the admiral. "Forgive me. I lost my train of thought. As I was saying, if you only listen to them talk, you can tell immediately they're islanders. Their accent is so strange." She shivered. "I haven't had a decent bit of conversation until you arrived, sir." She flashed him another smile. "I've heard them on several occasions take the Lord's name in vain." She turned to the crew. "Gus, go ahead and pronounce our Lord for the good Admiral."

Gus shifted his feet and glanced at the captain.

Captain nodded, and Nathan growled to himself. Now, the rest of them were joining in her foolishness.

Gus cleared his throat and in a deep, loud voice said, "Lawd."

"See." Lottie clapped her gloved hands together. "It's dreadful, isn't it? Listen to this." She waved a hand at Salt. "Salt, say the words *them* and *that* for me."

He stuck a hand under his hat and scratched his head. "Dem." He shrugged. "Dat."

"And Tiller, say sugar."

"Sugga."

Lottie's chin raised. "See. Kittitians. The entire lot of them."

"Their accent doesn't qualify as proof of citizenship. I need to see documentation. Now, if you'll excuse me. I must attend to the onboarding of these men." The admiral bowed and began to turn.

"One more thing, Admiral."

A rebellious glint shown in Lottie's eye. She stubbornly set her chin and peered into the man's face. Yet, remarkably, she looked down her nose at the admiral at the same time—exactly as her mother had done to Nathan.

"I'll need you to deliver a letter to my mother."

Admiral Gainesboro froze.

Lottie held out an open palm, and Franny passed her a notebook and quill. "It will only take a second. I'm going to ask Mama to pay your wife daily visits."

He spun to face Lottie, his eyes wide. "Whatever for?"

"She'll want to pray for your protection and the protection of your men." Lottie leaned back to peer around the admiral at the lieutenant. "Don't worry, Lieutenant Bixby. I'll have her stop by and visit with your wife also. Mama will happily keep vigil with them, especially when she hears the navy is in such dire straits that it needs to abscond with half of her son-in-law's crew."

The admiral stepped back. "Son-in-law?"

Captain Fielding leaned in and whispered in Nathan's ear. "I now understand your concerns about her mother."

"Oh, please forgive me." A becoming blush reddened Lottie's cheeks. "You see, I'm still growing accustomed to my new form of address. I should have corrected you earlier. It's no longer Miss Etheridge. I'm now Lady Winthrop."

Gainesboro's gaze flew to Nathan. His face mirrored Nathan's shock—although for different reasons—but Nathan found a bit of awe in the depths of the man's eyes. As if amazed anyone would willingly become son-in-law to Lady Etheridge. He muttered to the captain, "An ocean is not wide enough."

The admiral looked at the taut face of his lieutenant.

Lottie dipped her quill in the inkwell Franny held out for her and scribbled something onto the paper.

Both men blanched.

Gainesboro put a hand over Lottie's quill. "It won't be necessary. We wouldn't want to inconvenience you, Lady Winthrop. Please accept our congratulations on your nuptials and consider it a wedding gift. Good day." He bowed and marched over to the gangway. His men released Nathan's crew and turned to follow their leader.

~

*L*ottie's body trembled as she stared at the retreating backs of the officers' navy jackets. She dropped her gloved hand back to her side, unsatisfied with the taste of cotton instead of a pliable fingernail. Of all times to be wearing gloves. Her shoulders ached from remaining poised for the entire charade, but now she exhaled and let them slump. The only moment of doubt had come when her eyes met Nathan's. His dark scowl had almost caused her to duck behind the admiral for protection.

The entire crew watched in silence as the British man-o-war unhooked from the gunwale and sailed past. Only then did the *Katherine's* crew seem to relax in a collective sigh.

"Praise the Lawd," was murmured out of a few mouths. "It's a miracle."

Cobble's smile encompassed his entire face. Even his ears completed the U shape. "She's gone and saved the day." He danced a little hop-step. "Three cheers for Lady Winthrop. Hip! Hip!"

"Hurrah!" the crew answered as one.

Gus sung a shanty about a princess of the seas, and the crew joined in.

Two burly hands grabbed Lottie's arms and hoisted her onto Tiller and Salt's shoulders. She yelped and held onto the men's collars for dear life. They proceeded to parade around the deck, singing loudly enough for anyone within twenty nautical miles to hear. They jostled her about like a sack, and twice Lottie had to duck to avoid banging her head on the boon or catching her neck on the jib line. Their joy was contagious.

Lottie found herself laughing and joining in the chorus. Captain Fielding saluted her with an exaggerated bow and a bright smile. Nathan, however, tracked her with watchful eyes.

His face remained expressionless, except for a sardonic twist to his lips.

The song came to an end, and the men lowered her to the deck in front of Nathan. A tumult of carefully caged emotions flared in the depths of his eyes. Her smile faded, and a shiver ran through her body. His fingers curled around her waist and dragged her to his side. She placed a hand on his chest for balance and could feel the thundering of his heart beneath.

His lips brushed her ear as he muttered. "I don't know whether to kiss you or throttle you."

Her mouth opened in a silent gasp as his hand ran up her spine and gently brushed the windblown tendrils of hair off her neck. His strong fingers rested on the bare skin of her shoulders just above the back of her gown. Did those same fingers itch to close in a tight squeeze?

"Three cheers to Gator for having the sense to marry the chit," Cobble yelled, "Hip! Hip!"

"Hurrah!" the crew replied, then repeated their chant. Many shuffled over to pound Nathan on the shoulder with hearty appreciation.

Tiller stuck out his hand. "Fer da life of me, I couldn't figure out where she was going wit making me say sugga."

Nathan released Lottie to shake it.

Salt slicked his greasy hair back. "Ya sure saved our skins. Me wife an' kids will be greatly appreciative. When she finds out, she's gonna shower you wit baked goods. She makes da best pastries in all da islands."

Captain stepped around Salt. "You certainly got those lobsterbacks turning tail in a hurry. It makes me almost want to meet your mother to thank her in person for her part."

"I could arrange it." Lottie issued him a sideways glance.

Captain laughed and held his palms up. "Almost. I said almost." He gripped Nathan's shoulder and his expression sobered. "We're drawing close to land. Come and look at the chart. I'd like to avoid any more hostile territory. We don't want to tempt fate to see if Lady Winthrop can save our hides twice."

Lottie curtsied to the captain and started for the stairs, but Nathan caught the back of her gown in a tight grip. He reeled her back to his side.

"I want you to go to your cabin and stay there until we talk. Am I clear?"

She stiffened at the low growl in his tone. Of course, he'd still be mad. The rest of the crew was singing her praises, but Nathan would see it as a mark against her for disobedience. She straightened her shoulders and refused to glance in his direction. The last thing she wanted was for him to see her nervousness. When he released her gown, she dipped her head in a curt nod and walked away.

~

*T*he sun set low on the horizon, casting long shadows. Nathan stood at the bow of the ship staring at the darkening sky. He didn't want to believe it, but after so many incidences, after so much proof, it could no longer be denied.

He was cursed.

The obeah woman's harsh words replayed in his mind— taunting him. He'd been young. He'd been foolish in trying to impress the other planters. How could he have known the consequences would chip away at his life, piece by piece, until everything he loved was destroyed? First his family, then his men, and now he'd put Lottie in danger too.

He should have given her a thrashing for her little stunt, but she'd saved his crew. It was the most absurd thing he'd ever seen, yet a miracle. His timid wife had put herself in danger to save men she hardly knew. He exhaled and rubbed his stiff shoulder with one hand.

He squeezed his eyes tight against the *what if* scenarios

plaguing him. She could have been kidnapped, raped, or killed, and it would have been his fault.

A woman cleared her throat behind him.

Nathan whirled to find Lottie standing there, her hands clasped in front of her like a nun. Yet her loose vibrant hair flowed behind her like a Valkyrie.

"I instructed you to stay in your cabin."

"You also said we would talk. I waited in my cabin through dinner."

"I lost track of time." The night crew sauntered on deck to relieve the other men. "You shouldn't be walking above deck alone at night."

"I needed fresh air."

"I've known renegade men who obey my commands better than my wife."

She crossed her arms, and he glimpsed the creamy expanse of white skin above the bodice of her gown.

"It's my stomach that rebelled this time."

Nathan pulled his gaze away and swallowed.

She stepped next to him and gripped the rail. The sun colored her face a rosy-orange. "I've already hit my threshold of rebelliousness for a lifetime."

"I would have thought otherwise." The scent of lilac soap filled his nostrils, and he cautiously stepped aside, unable to trust himself at such a close distance.

"I know you're upset with me, and for good reason."

She gripped the rail tighter, and her eyes glassed over. She was going to cry. He clamped his arms to his sides to resist the urge to comfort her. She needed first to understand the danger. How frightened he'd been for her.

"I've never been so scared," she said, "but I couldn't stand idly by while they absconded with the crew. I had a plan. It was half-crazed but…" She smiled. "I didn't cower. I didn't stumble over my words."

Was she proud of herself?

"I merely pretended to be my mother, and they turned tail and ran."

He clenched his fists so he wouldn't strangle her. "It was a foolish thing you did."

Her smile faded. "I should have known you wouldn't understand."

She turned to leave, but he grabbed her arm. "Where do you think you're going? Didn't I just say not to amble about the ship alone? There are men with dishonest intentions."

"On this ship?" Her brow furrowed. "With their loyalty to you?"

He wiped a hand down his face. "I saw the way the British sailors looked at you."

She tilted her head in that adorable way of hers. "Me?" She blinked.

He released her arm and paced. "You're changing the topic."

"I'm not entirely certain what we're discussing."

"When the British boarded our ship, and you appeared in your... your... low-cut gown—"

"It's my best gown and the latest style."

"Your hips swayed."

She straightened.

"And your eyes... they ..."

She put a hand on her hip. "They what?"

The waves lapped against the ship as he struggled for the right word. "Batted." He bit the word, hating his jealousy as much as the thought of all those men ogling her.

"I did no such—"

He stopped her with a hand. "They outnumbered us. If they...if they had touched you..." His lips refused to form the rest.

Dusk illuminated her outline in an ethereal glow, and her blue eyes glimmered a bright teal. She implored him with a gaze that spilled over with questions he couldn't answer. He was getting too close.

Give her a brotherly kiss and send her below deck.

He didn't move.

Bid her good-night and turn around.

His lips didn't open.

He wanted to leave things uncomplicated. He couldn't bear to lose another loved one. He wanted to look away. He wanted …

She shivered.

Nathan shrugged off his jacket and draped it around her shoulders. She snuggled into its warmth, making him wish his hands still held the jacket—and her. The wind kicked up, catching her hair and sending it dancing like a red flame. His heart jolted and beat as erratic as a summer storm. He grabbed her hand and pulled her down the steps to the midship deck where the bow broke the wind.

He stopped abruptly and turned in time to catch Lottie before she crashed into him. He grabbed her delicate shoulders. Her silky hair tickled his wrists and teased the hair on his arms. "Lottie, what you did today…"

He lost his words as he stared into the eager-innocence shining in her wide eyes. What was the matter with him? He released her shoulder to run a hand over his face again. He needed to think. "You didn't know those men."

"But I did know Captain Gainesboro. His wife is on a committee with my mother."

He covered her lips with two fingers. "Shh." Instant regret filled him as his senses leapt to life. Her soft, full lips brushed his sensitive fingertips. Her lilac scent encased him in a heady bouquet. He longed to bury his nose in her fragrant hair. She was fresh air within a stale ship.

He forced his mind to focus on what he needed to say. "As your husband, it's my duty to protect you."

A light flickered in her eyes, and she swayed in his direction.

His mouth went dry. His hand caressed her cheek and slid into the gossamer strands at the nape of her neck.

"Protect you from men who want to do this." He crushed her to him. His lips covered her mouth, devouring its softness.

She melted into him.

The triumphant joy of a conqueror exploded in his heart. He drank her in, imbibing in the sweetness of her response. She let out a soft moan, and his blood caught fire. Passion sent his body up in flames. He couldn't get enough. She was a bud awakening. Since the first night they danced, he'd fought to dampen the desire consuming him, even though he yearned to be the sun that coaxed her into full bloom.

But there would be consequences...

He deepened the kiss to push the nagging thoughts away. She tasted like forbidden nectar. His hand slid under the jacket he'd given her and down a length of buttons before settling on her lower back.

They could do this. God's truth, she was already his wife. He wasn't doing anything wrong.

The curse will take her too...

CHAPTER 12

Oh, the sweetness! How it increased the mighty torment within me.

~ From Lottie to Miss Pricilla Middleton

*L*ottie reveled in the drunken ecstasy of Nathan's kiss. He cared for her. He must. She felt it in the possessiveness of his embrace, in the demands of his mouth. Something inside her awakened, bringing her world into focus.

She was the bone of his bones, flesh of his flesh, just like she'd been reading in Genesis earlier. They were united under God. She was his in body and mind. Let the storms come. They would weather them together.

She wound her arms around him and savored the power encased in his broad shoulders. The growth of his beard tickled her skin, but she reveled in it. She clung to his strength, yet at the same time, absorbed his vitality until she was uncertain where she stopped and he began. Her own eager response surprised her.

He pulled away, and the cool night air slapped her face. She blinked as the haze of her desire cleared, leaving behind an aching need.

His hands captured the sides of her face, and he rested his forehead against hers. She could feel his chest heaving and the pounding of his heart.

It matched her own. Their breath mingled with the mist of the night air.

"Lottie." His voice was a husky whisper.

It was the first time she'd heard him use her nickname.

"There's something I need to tell you."

A sprinkle of unease prickled her, but how could anything be amiss while he cradled her in the warmth of his embrace?

His arms fell away, and he stepped back.

She swallowed hard, hating the alarm sounding in her head. She had acted as a wanton woman. Was he put off? Did she disappoint? Lottie rubbed her arms to ward off the chill that crept into her bones. She stepped away, and her foot connected with something. A wooden pole whacked her in the back of her head. "Ouch."

His hand shot out and caught the pole before it fell. He flashed her a lopsided smile, "You all right?"

She rubbed the smarting spot until his hand covered it.

Nathan leaned in and dropped a brotherly kiss on her brow. "I'll speak to Charlie about putting the mop and bucket away first thing tomorrow." His hand lowered and encircled her waist. He escorted her in the direction of her cabin.

"In the next few days, we'll be drawing close enough to spot land." After that kiss, how could he suddenly shift to speaking of something so mundane? Or maybe this was part of the something he had to tell her.

Footsteps sounded, and Nathan stopped as the night crewmen inspecting the lines passed. Nathan's face darkened in the shadows, and the crease between his brows returned. Lottie tugged on the folds of her skirt, unable to tear her gaze away from the taut face that moments ago offered her a glimpse of paradise.

"Certain things have transpired in St. Kitts." He continued their walk. "Things that were set into place before our encounter."

He still thought of their first meeting as an unfortunate encounter? She swallowed around the lump forming in her throat.

"Emotions ran high in London. I didn't thoroughly recognize or weigh the consequences. I'm beginning to understand the danger, but it's too late. We're married."

She bit her bottom lip to keep it from quivering. Indeed, their marriage had been forced, but in the last few weeks, a fondness had developed between them. And what about the kiss they'd shared only moments ago? Pain tore through her heart as if he'd physically ripped it in two with his bare hands.

"I know now, I not only need to protect you from risks of living on an island, but also from the perils of being with me."

"Perils?" The word slipped out before she had a chance to debate her best response.

"You trust too openly and believe the best of people, but there's evil out there. I've seen it. I...I was young..." He closed his mouth and shook his head. "It's difficult to explain."

He guided her below deck, and she trailed to fit within the narrow corridor to her cabin. She struggled to order the burgeoning mountain of questions rising in her mind.

He stopped at the door to her cabin, not opening it as he usually did.

A lock of hair fell over her eye.

He raised a hand as if to brush it away, but hesitated. His fingers closed and dropped back to his side.

She tucked the loose strand behind her ear.

"Try to understand." His lips narrowed into a thin line. "I'm doing what I believe is in your best interest. When we reach St.

Kitts, which shall be in the next few days, you'll stay at the Cockleshell Inn."

"What?" She searched his eyes for a reason but the dim light shadowed his face. "Why?"

"My home is in no condition for a gentlewoman. It was partially destroyed by a hurricane a few years ago. I had planned to expand and renovate it, but there was no rush. I didn't expect to marry."

"Where do you plan for us to reside?"

"I'll remain at Calico Manor, my plantation, for there is much work to be done there."

"We won't...?" She hesitated to finish the question. Part of her wanted to throw care to the wind, wrap her arms around her husband, and beg him to make her his wife in every sense of the word. Heat rushed into her cheeks at such wanton thoughts. Did she really want to subject herself to more rejection?

He continued as if not hearing her. "The inn is owned by the captain and his wife. Mrs. Fielding and Franny will see to your every whim, and I'll frequently visit until better arrangements can be made. Do I have your agreement?"

She hesitated. It sounded like a terrible idea. She didn't expect the same luxuries as London. She'd be happy to sleep on a pallet on the floor as long as he was by her side, but the vulnerability haunting the shadows of his eyes stopped her from saying as much. She wanted to make him happy, and she could do so with one little word. "Yes."

The boyish relief in his expression coaxed a shy smile from her lips. His eyes flashed before his mouth lowered and brushed her lips with a kiss.

"Sweet dreams," he whispered before his hands gently tilted her head. He bestowed a brotherly peck on her forehead. His smile broadened, then he turned and strolled away.

Her lips tingled from the fleeting kiss, but the imprint on her brow pressed down like a anchor. If she never received another brotherly peck on the head, she'd be all the better for it.

~

"*L*and ho!" shouted a sailor from the crow's nest.

All heads swiveled toward the low-hanging strip of cloud on the horizon, and cheers sounded. As the ship drew closer, the spot tinged a bluish-green and began to appear more like land and less like a puff of mist. The men struck up a lighthearted ditty, and Charlie and Cobble even danced a little jig. Their enthusiasm grew contagious, and Lottie found herself staring into the horizon dreaming of the freedom of island life. At the same time, her stomach twisted.

Lottie resumed her usual spot next to Cobble and took up her sewing. After an hour or so, she noticed the men weren't at their stations. Instead, they stood in line as Baby draped one in what looked like an old sail and wrapped their faces in a steaming towel.

"Merciful heaven, what is going on?" she asked.

Cobble smiled. "A bunch of lovesick men are gettin' all cleaned up and groomed to impress their lady-loves."

Baby sharpened a double-edged razor on a pumice stone in quick swipes. Charlie unwound the towel over the captain's face and applied shaving soap in a lather. Lottie held her breath as Baby, with his big hands, tilted the captain's chin up and slowly dragged the razor down the side of his face. Charlie switched to holding a bowl full of water, in which Baby swished the razor to clean off the soap and hair.

Lottie turned to Cobble. "Where did Baby learn the barbering trade?"

"His papa was a barber," Cobble said. "But his brother assumed the business. It was all the better because, like most of us, Baby holds a restless spirit. Can't stay in one spot fer too long. Comes in handy though. We pride ourselves on being the best-lookin' seamen in the Islands." Cobble ran his hand over his beard.

"Are you getting a shave also?"

"Naw, no reason to now that my Marie's not around. I'll get a trim if there's time, but I let the young bucks go ahead of me. It's a tradition. As soon as the words, 'Land ho!' are uttered on our ship, the men jump in line to get their beards trimmed or shaved. Their wives will be seein' them for the first time in months. Keeps the flames of love burning brighter. Gator encourages it too. He believes a good woman will help keep riff-raff and horseplay off his ship." Cobble winked at her. "He's right too. Nothing like a good woman to make a man think twice about starting trouble."

"Good morning."

A clean-shaven Nathan stepped up beside them. Lottie smiled at the change in his appearance. Even though she'd grown accustomed to the growth of his beard, the clean lines of his jaw accentuated his handsomeness.

"You like it?" He rubbed a hand over his strong chin.

"I do, indeed."

A broad smile broke over his features. His eyes danced as they held hers.

Lottie returned his smile, but it felt bittersweet. In her periphery, she saw Cobble staring at them.

Nathan noticed it too and sent him a sideways glance. "What, Cobble?"

Cobble's eyes disappeared into a wrinkled grin so wide his lips almost touched his ears. He shook his head and licked his lips, but it didn't erase his expression. "'Tis nothing. Reminds me of my Marie, and the way we used to look at each other, is all."

Lottie's heart sank. Theirs was nothing like Marie and Cobble's marriage. Cobble had loved his wife dearly. Her dream of nightly dinners and reading the morning paper with her loving husband was slowly dying. She'd longed to manage the household by his side, but Nathan didn't want her near. He'd made that clear with his plan.

Nathan crossed his arms. "Don't you have something you should be fixing right now?"

Cobble winked at Nathan. "I'll let you two be. There's much to discuss before we weigh anchor."

Nathan leaned his hip against a barrel and watched Cobble swagger off.

Lottie swallowed. She and Nathan finally held a tenuous bridge of peace between them, but it could collapse at any moment. Would being on land help or hurt what they'd established?

"As you can see, we're close to reaching St. Kitts. I'm certain you'll be thrilled to step foot on land."

"I was just beginning to get my sea legs."

He chuckled. "I admit these last few weeks, your coloring has been a little less green." His eyes dropped to the wooden deck planks. "There's another thing I'd like to ask of you before we weigh anchor."

Impassive gray eyes honed in on her, and his arms crossed in a brusque demeanor. How did he switch from the teasing playful man who gave her hope, into the cool-eyed merchant who saw everything as a business transaction? Exhaling slowly, she fought to quell the alarm churning in her chest and raising the fine hairs on her arms.

"I want you to learn from Mrs. Fielding. She's a good woman to emulate. Strong, yet biddable. You'll like her. She and the captain are a love match, but I don't expect that."

The wind fled from her sails, leaving her heart hanging limply in the doldrums.

"She'll instruct you how things are on the island, and what you'll need to know to help run a plantation. It will be good for her to teach you how to avoid the riffraff of the island. You tend to see the good in everything and everybody, but there is evil on the island, including improper men who don't know how to treat a lady."

"When will I see you?"

"I'll ride into town every other day to join you, Fielding, and Mrs. Fielding for dinner if I'm not at sea."

"How often are you at sea?"

"I have some trade dealings in South America. So I'll sail out on my other ship, the *Amory*, when it comes into port in a few weeks."

They could have only a few weeks?

"It will give you time to adapt to island life," he said. "It's not as long of a voyage. If all goes well, I'll be back in under a month."

Once again, she was a bird being thrown out of its nest. "I see," she said, but she didn't.

"It's best to get one's bearings slowly. All will be well."

She gulped down the rejection that clogged her throat.

"Go and ready your things. By afternoon, we'll be on land."

CHAPTER 13

We have safely arrived. Have an account of the ledgers
ready upon my arrival.
~ *Missive sent by Winthrop to Mr. Marcus Tallant, overseer of
Calico Manor*

*L*ottie waved farewell to the crewmembers she'd grown
so fond of and, as they disembarked the ship, she
made them promise to call upon her before they set
sail again. She stayed above deck, staring at the luscious, green
mountain tops resting in the background like a sleepy dragon
curled up on a turquoise blue mat for a nap. Its smoky breath
collected about its humped back in a ring cloud. Was it a
friendly dragon accepting her as one of its children? Or would it
rear its head and char her to bits along with her future dreams?

In contrast to the peaceful landscape, stood the hustle and
bustle confusion of the docks. Bright, colorful storefronts
graced the center of Basseterre. She'd seen dark-skinned
Africans before, but not in such a large quantity. The lilt of the
French-creole accents drifted past her ears. The strangeness of
it all tightened her throat and squeezed the air from her lungs.

Nathan stood below on the main deck, his jacket tossed over a barrel beside him. The breeze ruffled his hair and billowed his shirt across his broad shoulders. He issued a command to a slave, who then rolled a hogshead of flour toward a dinghy. Nathan had said he needed to ensure their precious cargo arrived intact, and she was to go below deck and rest up. It would be a while before he'd attended to everything, and then he would disembark with her.

Yet she couldn't pull her eyes away from him in action. He wore confidence in every action, as well as the ease with which he controlled the group of men before him. Strangers bartered to buy his goods or for him to transport their hogsheads of sugar on to other countries for sale.

A stout man who wore buckled shoes and white stockings in a fashion from her parent's youth yelled out a price he'd pay now and another sum upon when Nathan's ship delivered his goods.

Her husband shook his head and called out a higher amount.

"Devil take it. How's a planter to make a profit at that cost?"

"Mr. Montgomery," Nathan hollered, "you may take your cargo elsewhere, but I'm willing to pay for the entire shipment now in full. No more waiting to see if the ship completes its voyage. No more hearing merchants tell you one-third of your shipment didn't arrive intact."

Mr. Montgomery straightened and his scraggly eyebrows lifted. He pointed his cane at Nathan's chest. "You mean to tell me you'll pay for all of the barrels in full before it sails?"

"Indeed, sir. We'll need to inspect the goods first, and then load it on the ship before the next sail."

Mr. Montgomery lowered his cane and shook Nathan's hand, pumping it with much enthusiasm. "By Jove, we have a deal."

"Speak to my man, Charlie, and he'll ensure there's room aplenty for your cargo."

Charlie stood by Nathan's side, tracking the inventory.

Occasionally, Nathan glanced her way. A pleased expression teased the corners of his mouth. Did that mean he enjoyed having her here? The thought warmed her more than the tropical sun and sparked a sense of hope. Maybe he could come to appreciate her, and over time even love her?

The afternoon sun shone brightly as Nathan finally waved off the planters and told them to come back the next day. Lottie assumed it was time for them to make their way off the ship, so she descended the steps to the main deck. A refreshing breeze whipped up, tugging her bonnet until it dangled loosely by its strings down her back.

One of the islanders elbowed another man, their tanned faces gawking at her. Nathan followed their gazes.

She froze under such scrutiny, and her fingers clutched the folds of her gown. But, it was Nathan's scowl that rooted her feet to the spot.

One man whistled a shrill, high pitched sound. "Look at her hair. It's brighter than a Caribbean sunset."

Her fingers squeezed the material of her dress tighter to refrain from hastily covering her head. She should have powdered it. Her mother was right. It was improper to have a mane so red.

"Name da price fer tat bit of goods." A mess of long greasy hair poked out from under the man's straw hat. "I'll pay da profits of a year's worth of sugar fer a chance wit da lady."

Nathan jerked the man up by his shirtfront. "You insult the lady. Now be on yer way, and don't step foot on my ship or..." His words trailed off, and his gaze flicked in her direction. "I won't be doing business with the likes of you." He shoved the man away.

The long-haired man backed up, his hands in the air. "I'm not lookin' fer a floggin'. I didn't mean any harm, gov'ner."

"Off with you now. All of you."

The men filed into a dinghy, each stealing backward glances at Lottie as if they'd never seen a woman with red hair before.

He rounded on her. "You should be below preparing your things."

The height of the steps held her at eye level with his blazing glare. She gripped the railing to keep herself from turning to flee. There was nowhere to hide on the quarter-deck. Besides, it was his ship. Where could she go?

She would not cower.

She fought to keep the quiver from her voice and raised her chin. "My things are ready. Franny is seeing that they are delivered properly to the inn."

"And you didn't go with her?"

"I thought you might want to be the first to show me the island." The words came out strong, and perhaps they held a bit of challenge.

He rubbed his chin. "Indeed." Resting his hands on his hips, he surveyed the landscape. His shadow blocked the sun and her view of the island. He sighed and focused again on her. "I apologize. You've been very patient."

Lottie's tension leaked out with his admission. She retied her bonnet tighter under her chin.

He shrugged on his jacket, donned his hat, and offered her his arm. "Shall we?"

She slid her hand into his crook, inhaled a deep breath, and nodded, ready to see the new place she would call home.

Nathan aided her out of the dingy onto the sandy shore. She inhaled the scent of the sun-warmed sand. Her boots shifted through its softness as he guided her up the path lined with seagrass towards the wharf. Small shells sprinkled the beach, and a larger one the size of her palm caught her eye. She bent down and picked it up.

"Look at this." She rubbed her fingers over the white grooved outside and flipped it over to admire the pinkish lavender color on the inside. "I've never held a shell before. It's beautiful." She raised it for Nathan to see. "How fortunate to find one in such perfect condition."

He stared at her with a strange smile. His eyes twinkled as if holding in his laughter. Heat rose in her cheeks, which were probably turning as pink as the inside of the shell. When she lowered the shell with an exasperated sigh, he opened his palm, asking to see it.

She placed it in his hand, but he barely looked at it. Instead, he continued to watch her.

Uncomfortable with his scrutiny, she turned to continue up the path.

"Look, another." She picked a similar shell with the bone-white bumpy side and a smooth pink inside. Down the path a bit, she discovered another and another. She swallowed her embarrassment at her earlier enthusiasm. "You must think me a veritable green. These are obviously common on the island."

He stepped closer, and the amusement in his eyes turned contemplative. "No." He held the shell up in the air. "You're right about this one." He pocketed it. "It is unique."

His tone made the words sound as though referring to something other than the shell. For the life of her she couldn't understand her husband's mysterious ways.

The dock was inundated with black men and women selling wares and goods, from potatoes and carrots to things she'd never heard of, like cassava roots. A few Englishmen who were dressed in a similar style to what she'd seen in London greeted Nathan and paused, as if hoping to introduce themselves. Nathan merely tipped his hat and kept walking.

Lottie was torn between peering into the colorful shops or staring down the white sand shoreline into the turquoise waters.

"A trifle different from what you're used to?" he asked.

"Those trees look like one of Mama's hats with the peacock feathers fanning out on top."

He threw back his head and laughed. The rich baritone plucked at the cords of her heart. "Those are palm trees."

"I've heard of them but never seen them in real life."

A man so dark he appeared to be a shadow in clothes approached with a monkey perched on his shoulder. Lottie couldn't help but stare. The creature screeched and bared its teeth as they passed. She reared back, bumping Nathan's shoulder.

"Easy." His arm encircled her, drawing her into the protection of his body. She inhaled his masculine scent, laced with salty fresh ocean air. "It's only a monkey."

She smiled at her reaction to the creature's affront. "I've seen one of those, once when the Middletons invited me to the circus."

He snorted. "Ah yes, the gallant Captain Anthony Middleton."

"Priscilla is my closest friend, and he was always good to me."

A muscle twitched in Nathan's jaw. Was he jealous of Anthony? No. He was still angry at Anthony's unwillingness to come to a trade agreement.

He released her and opened the door to the shop on their right. Strings of sea shells hanging near the door chimed, notifying the shopkeeper of their arrival.

Lottie entered the quaint boutique filled with rolls of lightweight colorful fabrics. Nathan followed.

A mulatto woman strolled out of the back room and smiled. Her light eyes contrasted with her dark hair and olive skin. "Bonswa, Mista Winthrop. Welcome home. We've been expectin' yer ship." Her gaze settled on Lottie. "But not an English woman. Who might dis be?"

"Good evening, Matilda." He smiled at the woman and

strode into the center of the room. Pausing in front of her, he flipped back the ends of his jacket and hooked a thumb into his waistband, resuming a wide stance. He reached back and pulled Lottie forward. "Lady Winthrop is going to be needing a new wardrobe. Something more suitable to the island than the heavy fabrics she's been wearing."

Matilda chewed her bottom lip as her gaze slid up and down, taking in Lottie's figure and stopping to stare at her hair. Whether due to the woman's scrutiny or the fact that Nathan had released her hand, Lottie would never know, but suddenly the ground shifted, and dizziness swept over her. She pitched to the left.

"Whoa now." Nathan gripped her upper arms to steady her. "You haven't gotten yer sea legs yet."

She lowered her brows. "But we're on land."

He flashed her a crooked smile. "It happens to even the best sailors. Your equilibrium will be off for a week or two, but then you'll be back to normal."

Matilda raised her chin. "I have just da thing. Several reams of fabrics I ordered arrived wit yer ship, a nice zephyr in a hue to match her eyes, and some cotton muslin. Come wit me." She motioned for Lottie to follow her behind the white sheet that hung as a door to the backroom. Matilda paused in the doorway and focused on Nathan. "Baby hasn't ben by me shop yet."

Nathan rubbed the back of his neck. "He's still unloading our manifest."

"You tell him I expect him to come callin'."

Nathan dipped his head. "Will do." His penetrating gaze met Lottie's through the open doorway, and her world tilted once again. She staggered to the right as Matilda dropped the curtain.

She could hear Nathan's deep chuckle as Matilda led her over to a small pedestal for measuring.

The heat in the back room was unbearable, even with the circulating fan overhead. Lottie removed her bonnet and placed it on a nearby chair. Two slave women drifted over, and each raised a hand toward her. Lottie couldn't help staring as she tried to make sense of what they were doing.

"Can dey touch it?"

"Touch what?"

"Yer hair. We've never seen the likes of it."

"Um, yes."

Their fingers patted her coiffure and tested the strands, feeling the texture. Even Matilda slid her fingers down a loose tendril. "An amazing color. My gowns will complement it, mek you stand out. *Trè bèl*, very beautiful."

"I was actually hoping to blend in."

Matilda snorted. "You are a woman on an island dat is mostly comprised of men. What you ask is *enposibe*." She shook her head and translated. "Impossible."

The women began taking Lottie's measurements.

Matilda peered at her through the large looking glass. "So, Mista Winthrop has taken a wife. Well, I'll be." She crossed her tanned arms. "He didn't seem bent on settlin' down. You musta changed his mind. I know a few hearts who're gonna be broke when dey find out, but don't you worry. There are men aplenty to go around. Dem ladies will justa pick demselves out another mista. Dey couldn't persuade Mista Winthrop to come up to scratch anyway."

Lottie lifted her arms so the slave woman could measure her bust.

"You musta be a real special lady to bring Mista Winthrop to heel."

Matilda's gaze met Lottie's in the mirror, and a weak smile wavered on Lottie's lips. If only they knew she wasn't anything special. Merely a clumsy woman who dropped a candle and caught her skirt on fire.

One of the ladies stuck a pin in the hem. "But what bout da curse—?"

"Hush, you chatabox." Matilda waved at the woman like she was a pesky fly.

The women continued their work in silence.

Lottie had heard island folk were superstitious, but it was all nonsense. Yet her curiosity got the best of her. "What curse?"

"Enough of dat talk." Matilda eyed each woman, and they shrank back. She waved a hand through the air. "It's nothin' but foolishness. I'm certain Mista Winthrop has nothin' to worry about."

CHAPTER 14

I appreciate you taking my newlywed wife under your
wing.

~ *From Winthrop to Mrs. Julia Fielding*

*A*n ocean breeze cooled Nathan's skin as they left
Matilda's shop. He'd long since taken off his jacket and
slung it over his shoulder. He pushed away the nagging weight
of his pressing responsibilities and let the relaxed island
atmosphere sooth his frayed nerves. The earlier bustle of
activity around the pier had died down. Now that the sun was
setting, the inns and taverns were aglow with boisterous
patrons filling their bellies with a warm meal and washing it
down with rum.

He called St. Kitts home, but it wasn't the same without a
family to come home to. He glanced at his wife on his arm and
drew her closer to his side. Things had changed, but in the past
year, happiness had been an illusion. Dare he trust it now?

The wind fluttered the loose tendrils of Lottie's red tresses
as she absorbed her surroundings. His chest swelled at the
wonderment in her expression. It was as if he was seeing the

island anew. Things he'd taken for granted, like the color of the ocean and common shells used in decorations, awed his wife.

His wife. The term floated easily through his mind. Maybe he was adapting to the notion. She'd surprised him already by surviving the voyage, even though it had been hard going for a while. His gaze drifted over her thin frame. She'd lost at least a stone, for she'd struggled to keep any food down the entire voyage. Her once fitted gowns now hung on her. His clothes would be big on him also if he only ate fish broth for two months.

He pulled open the heavy oak door to the Cockleshell Inn. Loud, boisterous guffaws met them from the taproom. The clerk recognized him and instructed a footman to escort Lady Winthrop upstairs to her room where a bath had been drawn.

He turned to face her. "Be back down by eight o'clock. We shall dine with the captain and his wife."

Wide blue eyes held his while she scratched at an edge on her index fingernail with the opposite thumb. She was nervous, and who could blame her being in a strange place? Was he doing the right thing leaving her here at the inn?

Her chest rose as she inhaled. With a curt nod, she turned and followed the footman up the stairs. He caught the sway of her hips and her hand moving to her mouth in that nervous habit of hers. Part of his heart ached to protect her, especially because of her timid nature. The other reminded him of the slim chance of her survival.

He poked his head around the corner of the taproom. Captain Fielding stood on the bar, spreading exaggerated tales of their voyage. The patrons hung on his every word and occasionally clanked their tankards.

Spying Nathan, he raised a hand in greeting and jumped down. "Winthrop, it's about time you joined us." He sauntered over and shook his hand. "The missus can't wait to meet our new guest."

"You explained my situation?"

"I did indeed." He issued him a skewed glance. "She believes as I do."

"She'll take her in?"

"Julia said she'd let you know at the end of the night."

"Good enough."

They sat at a nearby table and spoke of the ship's repairs, the next voyage, and the improvements that needed to be made to increase the vessel's speed and make it less prone to attack.

After a good hour, Fielding whacked him on the arm in a friendly manner. "Let's get some grub to fill our bellies."

Nathan sent a footman to fetch Lottie, who met them in the hall. She'd donned a fresh gown, and her maid had swept Lottie's thick mound of hair into some sort of loose top knot. The tendrils around the nape of her neck were still damp in some places. Her cheeks held a pink tint, but he couldn't be certain if it was due to a good scrubbing or her nervousness. If the way she twisted the tip of her stained glove was any indication, it was most likely the latter.

After Fielding greeted her, they followed him into the kitchen. Julia, as lovely as ever, stood overseeing the cooking. Her dark hair was pulled back into a tight bun, further adding tilt to her exotic eyes. She pointed to a boiling pot, and the worker immediately dumped handfuls of vegetables into it.

Fielding sauntered up behind her and planted a kiss on her neck. She stiffened and turned, a slow sensual smile spreading across her lips.

"*Mi amor*." He whispered into her lips before stealing a peck.

Nathan leaned in towards Lottie and inhaled the scent of damp hair and lilac soap. "That's Spanish for my love." His breath fluttered the small tendrils of damp hair resting upon her neck. "You'll hear him call her *my love* in various languages."

He felt her shiver, but in this heat she couldn't be cold.

Julia eyed them over the captain's shoulder. She pulled away, but Fielding tucked her hand into the crook of his arm and kept her close to his side.

"*Mon Amour*, let me introduce Lady Charlotte Winthrop, a recent newcomer to the island. Lady Winthrop, meet the belle of the island and my greatest prize, Mrs. Julia Fielding."

Julia fell into a graceful curtsy, and Lottie did the same.

"Welcome to St. Kitts, Lady Winthrop," Mrs. Fielding said.

"Please call me Lottie. It's what my friends call me, and I feel like I already know you from Captain Fielding's tales."

"I daresay he is prone to exaggeration." Julia ran a hand across her husband's upper back and affectionately patted his shoulder. "You may call me Julia."

Nate's fingers twitched. Would Lottie accept his touch as Julia did her husband, or would she pull away?

Julia turned to the workers, who'd stopped to watch the exchange. She spoke to them in Creole, and they went back to prepping the meals. "I'm certain you are hungry for some good food after a long voyage. I know the ship's cook is a good chef—she used to serve here at the inn—but even the best cook struggles to make food tasty with the meager rations invaded by mealworms. Follow me."

Fielding's hand slid around Julia's waist as if, even for a moment, he couldn't bear to be without her touch. Nathan appreciated the openly affectionate couple. His parents had been the same way. In the West Indies, wrought with illness and disease, life was too short to keep feelings bottled up and hidden, everyone waiting for the proper moment to express them, as they did in England.

Lottie followed Julia and the captain with her hands clasped demurely in front of her. Her glorious red hair, loosely knotted on top of her head, exposed her graceful neck. If he surprised her with a kiss on the neck as Fielding had to Julia, Lottie most certainly would have fainted dead away.

He rubbed his chin. Marriage to Lottie was the hand he'd

been dealt. Their marriage wouldn't be like that of his parents or Captain and Julia Fielding. He needed to protect his tender wife from the hardships of the island—the diseases that ravished people's bodies, poverty that turned English elite into white beggars pleading outside the markets, and the hollow eyes of death. He pushed the image of his sister's shadowed, unseeing eyes from his mind and glanced at Lottie's profile. To care for her meant keeping her away from him and ultimately the curse.

Perhaps it was for the best. God's ways were higher than Nathan's ways. Trade and shipping needed to be his priority. With the East India Trade Company losing their stronghold over the British government, new doors had opened for smaller merchant companies, and with Nathan's lands not producing sugar the way they did for his father, it was time to invest in a venture that could turn a profit. If Nathan buckled down and focused on growing profits, he could begin the Caribbean Sugar Trade Company and keep all the people who depended upon him employed.

Julia led them to a small room off the back of the tavern. The din of drunken ballads drifted from the next room, but the wall allowed for a measure of privacy. A large wooden table was set with fine china, crystal goblets, and silver. Tallow candles graced the center, and two long-stemmed candlesticks stood on either end. Their dancing light reflected in the glasses and dishes. Footmen scurried to pull out chairs, and Nathan settled into his place beside Lottie. They hadn't dined without the raucous accompaniment of his crew since the first night on the ship, the night she took ill.

Fielding asked for the finest mead to be poured, and a goat waterstew served.

Lottie's eyes flared a bit at the mention of goat. He expected her to balk, but to her credit, when the stew was served, she tried it, ate it, and even complimented the savory herbal flavors.

Julia put down her spoon and addressed Lottie. "Jere tells me you had a rough go of the trip."

Lottie blinked, and she stole a glance in Captain Fielding's direction.

Nathan inclined toward her. The lure of her scent enticed him to lean in closer until his lips practically touched her delicate ear. "Jere is short for Jeremiah, as in Captain Jeremiah Fielding."

Her lips parted, but it took her a moment to speak.

Did his nearness affect her as it did him?

She cleared her throat. "Indeed. The storm we encountered the first night turned my stomach inside out, and I daresay I felt its affects for the rest of the voyage."

"The sea isn't kind to some," Julia said.

"Once I took in the air above deck with more frequency, I fared better."

"What parts of the island did Nathan show you today?" Julia's glance flicked to Nathan, then back to Lottie.

"There wasn't much time after the ship was unloaded."

Fielding frowned at him and shook his head. "You are all business. Are there not others who can see to things while you show this lovely lady what St. Kitts has to offer?"

"You know as well as I," Nathan said, "that the men on that ship were raring to stretch their sea legs. What cruelness to hold them back from their families and ladies when I've had my wife by my side the entire return passage."

Fielding put down his spoon and leaned back in his chair with pursed lips. "Truly? By your side? Is that how you see it?"

Nathan was gearing up to tell Captain Fielding to mind his own business when Lottie said, "We had a lovely stroll. He showed me the main road right off the docks and was kind enough to order dresses more appropriate to the island climate. In this heat, I already find the thick fabric of my gown a bit oppressive."

Nathan was saved from further discussion of the topic by the arrival of the main course, comprised of mango chicken, peas, and rice.

As the night progressed, Lottie relaxed and participated more in the conversation. She tilted her head to the side and addressed their hosts. "You're aware of our unusual introduction to each other. How did the two of you meet?"

They issued each other a sideways glance, and Julia shrugged as if to say, *you tell it.*

"At a young age, even younger than our friend Charlie, I'd been impressed onto one of the ships run by the East India Trading Company." Fielding's eyes garnered a faraway look. "We sailed up the Hooghly River into Kolkata in Bengal to load up a shipment of spices." He chuckled. "I still smell the heavy scent of cinnamon and ginger even now thinking about it." He waved a dismissive hand. "Imagine my awe when I spy this fair lady"—he nudged his wife—"riding into town mounted on none other than an elephant."

Julia raised the crystal goblet to her lips and spoke over the rim. "I'd been born in India. Riding an elephant was as common as riding a horse." She sipped the mead.

"I knew it was love the moment I laid eyes on her, but she didn't give me a second glance. The first mate caught me staring and said she was the daughter of a nabob who'd moved from Bristol, England, and had been awarded a *jagir*, a land grant, on the outskirts of Bengal."

"My father was a good Englishman, but he was a poor overseer." Julia set down her glass, and her eyes darkened. "He treated the Indian people harshly."

Captain Fielding silenced Julia with a sideways glance. "The first mate granted me temporary leave from the ship. I used all of my meager wages and purchased a small bauble of a necklace—the most beautiful thing I could afford. A deep blue lapis stone hung on a silver chain. I had a slave child offer it to her.

She asked where he got it, and the child pointed to me in the crowd." He squeezed his wife's hand. "At that moment I knew I could die happy because she'd smiled at me."

Julia shrugged. "I told you he was prone to exaggeration."

"We set sail a few hours later, and I despaired thinking I'd never lay eyes again on my beautiful Indian princess. Fate had other plans, however." His expression sobered. "The sea hardened me into a man, and I moved up the ranks to take over the helm as a first mate. We received papers to return to Kolkata. The second we weighed anchor, I knew something was amiss. There was tension in the air. Much of the land had been converted to poppy fields because its sale as opium to the Orient held the greatest yield. It had taken a toll on the area, which I saw in the vapid stares of the people. Julia's father, too, had become an opium-eater, her home an opium den. It didn't take long for the slaves and workers to rise against their master."

Julia placed her hand over her husband's. "They slit the throats of my mother and father in their sleep. My maid helped me escape through the jungle and back to the main port. That is where Jere found me begging in the streets."

He glanced at his wife. "It was you who found me. I'd been overseeing the loading of cargo when a woman approached me. Even the dirt and filth that covered her body couldn't hide her beauty. She held up the necklace I had bought her ages ago." He snorted. "As if I wouldn't have recognized her. I persuaded the captain to allow her on board, and we were married as soon as the helm reached international waters."

I brought her back to England and set her up in a small cottage near the sea, but England was too cold for *mo ghrá*."

Julia shivered. "I could not get the chill out of my bones."

"My commission with the East India Company ended," the captain said, "and my grandfather reminded me about land in the West Indies where the climate was similar to the East Indies.

At the time, Nathaniel was investing in his first ship. He needed a captain to sail the vessel, and I needed a ship to take *il mio amore* to the Caribbean." He winked at Julia.

Lottie sighed. "Such a romantic story, and it's obvious the two of you are a love match."

Nathan swallowed. Did his wife wish for love? He sipped from his glass. If so, she would be destined for more disappointment, for he had none left to give. It had been buried in the graves of his family members.

Fielding nodded. "Indeed, but passionate people like ourselves have our share of spats that escalate into battles. Those fights always end in delightful reconciliations." He sent a rich smile to his wife.

Even in the dim light, Julia's tanned skin blushed a deep red, which only caused Fielding to laugh.

Silence fell over the group as the captain tipped back his glass and downed the rest of his drink.

"I fear for our island." Julia frowned. "I see similarities to what happened in India. The land isn't producing. The overseers beat their slaves to get more work out of them. Slave workers outnumber their absentee planters and grow in hatred toward white overseers. A rebellion is brewing. I don't want to be here when it takes place. I cannot go through it again."

Fielding grew serious. "Rightly so. On our next voyage, if we make good time, I'd like to scope out territory in Barbados. I hear they haven't had the same struggles, or perhaps in Louisiana. The Americans are not like the British Creoles. They came to America to stay and prosper. They're reproducing and are not outnumbered by their slaves."

His friend spoke the truth. Nathan loved St. Kitts. He had been born and raised here. It was his home, but even he couldn't turn a blind eye to the tragedies brewing. He ran a hand down his face. "The land is tired and ill at ease, but I can't give up on her yet."

A footman interrupted to serve coconut pudding. Nathan couldn't help watching his wife as her eyes closed while she savored each bite. Her pink tongue licked a dab of coconut cream from the corner of her lips, and his stomach flipped over twice. The image would surely keep him awake this night as he lay in his bed—alone.

"Indeed." Fielding raised his glass in salute. "You've kept hope alive by handing the plow to an overseer and taking to the sea."

Nathan sighed. "Even that is not without its struggles."

"Yes, but your husband here"—Fielding leaned over the table and peered into Lottie's face—"can evade any privateer in the Atlantic Ocean."

"Except for when the mainsail ripped from head to foot because Charlie's mending didn't hold fast." Nathan raised his glass to Lottie. He had to credit her courage, even if it might have been sheer madness. "It was Lottie's quick thinking that saved our crew from being impressed into His Majesty's service."

Captain Fielding retold the story from its start for Julia's benefit. Lottie flushed as he hailed her for her acting skills.

Guard yourself. Nathan already had grown too fond of the woman, but being among close friends made it easy to relax. He slid an arm over the back of Lottie's chair and brushed his thumb across the bare section of her shoulder under the puff of her capped sleeve. The rosy color of her cheeks heightened.

Captain Fielding and his wife exchanged a knowing glance.

"Ah, *mi cheri*, I do believe the patrons are becoming a bit too rowdy." He pushed back from the table, rose, and pulled the chair out for his wife. "Please do excuse us." They stole away into the next room.

Nathan stared at the beauty beside him. His fingers itched to pull her into his arms and see if her lips still tasted of coconut cream.

"Dinner was delightful." She filled the silence. "The food was nothing like I've ever tasted."

You are nothing like I've ever tasted.

She twisted her napkin in her lap. "Mrs. Fielding—er—Julia is as wonderful a woman as you described."

Not as wonderful as you.

Lottie swallowed and ran her fingers over the remaining silverware, straightening it.

His sister Katherine used to do the same thing. She loved to straighten things. He pictured her neatly folding her napkin and aligning the knife and spoon to perfect parallel positioning. She'd been so full of life, so sure of herself, and strong as any Kittian-born woman, but the fever had been stronger.

Nathan dropped his arm to his side and closed his eyes. The fever ravaged his beautiful, vibrant sister. He could still feel Katherine's body so light and frail in his arms as he held her until the wracking coughs subdued. His hands shook as he gently wiped the blood from her pale lips. He'd stayed by her side for days, mopping sweat from her brow until the light slowly dimmed in her eyes. Her body trembled as she expelled her last breath. He clung to her, sobbing into her hair, unwilling to let go. Nathan stared at his fingers resting on the edge of the table. Part of his heart deadened when he closed Katherine's unseeing eyes.

He swallowed. He should say something to Lottie to put her at ease, but when he looked at her, he saw her pale face lying in a cedar box. He grabbed his drink and downed it. He couldn't face that pain again.

He set his glass down and stared at his grip. His hands had been strong, but never had they felt so helpless. Fresh dirt from Katherine's grave had still been under his fingernails when he helped dig his brother's and mother's graves. He'd lost over twenty slaves and an overseer to the fever, and still had fields to plant and mouths to feed, but not enough workers to get the job done. Rolling up his sleeves, he'd once again dirtied his hands, this time to feed those who'd fought the fever and tended the sick alongside of him. They were his responsibility and he owed them as much. In a way, work had been a blessing. As long as he kept working, kept moving, he could stave off his despair. It had looked like they were going to have a good crop, even though they'd planted later in the season, but then a hurricane hit in the fall, washing out the lower fields.

He should have seen the signs then.

He rose with a sigh. "It's late and time for us to also retire."

She nodded, and he helped her rise. Her mouth quivered, and she licked her lips. "Would you see me to my room?"

His breath stilled in his lungs, and a sweep of emotions tingled the fine hairs over his skin.

She placed a slender hand on his chest and in a quavering voice said, "You need not go."

He swallowed down the lustful feelings he couldn't allow himself to feel. Instead of devouring those rosy lips tempting him, he raised her hand and kissed the back of it.

Her fingers quivered. It must have taken all of her courage to say those words.

"I must." He was a coward. "I'm eager to get back to the farm, for there is much that needs my attention, but I'll return tomorrow to show you more of the island."

He released her hand.

The shadow of disappointment clouded her eyes, and he lowered his gaze so he wouldn't have to witness the pain. He backed away a few steps, ignoring the clench in his gut that made him feel hollow, even after a full meal. He bowed and forced his feet to turn and walk out of the room. Once outside in the tepid island air, he rubbed his jaw to alleviate its tightness.

He was a cad.

She'd been as much a victim of all this as he. She was alone in a strange country, deprived of her family and friends. It would have been so easy to stay. God's teeth, it was his right as her husband. The closeness she desired was the one thing he couldn't give, because the closer he came, the more painful it would be to watch her slip away.

CHAPTER 15

Perhaps I shall paint you a watercolor. I sincerely doubt, however, that my abilities can capture the splendor of the island, specifically the delightful shade of the turquois-blue water.

~ *From Lottie to Miss Priscilla Middleton*

*W*hy had she asked him to stay the night? Lottie pressed the heels of her hands against her puffy eyes. She'd laid her heart bare, and he'd brushed it aside with a light kiss on the back of her hand.

Despite her weariness from travel, she'd slept fitfully in the strange bed. Shouts and revelry emanated from the tavern below until the wee hours of the morning. Their merriment awoke Lottie whenever she did fall asleep, and her mind hovered over each mountain of worry, unable to find a soft place to land.

Nathan neither desired her nor needed her. If it hadn't been apparent before, she could see that fact clearly now. She must either find a way to endear herself to him—love seemed too lofty a goal—or learn to enjoy the independence for which she'd always prayed.

She was grateful for her freedom. But why did she feel like she was still inside her sickroom watching the other children play, hoping someone would notice her and wave or perhaps ask her to come out and join them?

She didn't know the first thing about island life. After preparing for the day, reading a small pocket Bible she'd found in the drawer of the night stand, and breaking her fast, she'd wandered back to the room. What was she to do? How would she fill her days? The desire to be useful left her restless.

It grew worse when Nathan didn't come calling that day or even the next. He did send a note, apologizing for his absences and explaining how things needed dire attention on the plantation. On the third day, she'd had enough waiting around, and accompanied Julia to the market. She'd do some sightseeing around the island on her own.

The market bustled with merchants selling coffee, plantains, a root Julia said was called cassava, reams of cloth in a variety of bright colors, and even cotton hammocks. The blended smells of smoked meats, tropical fruit, and human sweat hung in the humidity of the open air. Slaves sold their wares on the outskirts where wild dogs, goats, and chickens lingered until someone shooed them away.

The footman who accompanied them didn't drift in the background like English servants did. The man Julia referred to as Paul stood at the point of Julia's elbow. He towered above them, his solid arms crossed over his barrel-sized chest. Paul might have been a slave, but he seemed to have an advanced position and acted as a sentinel standing guard over his mistress while she selected fresh mangos and papayas from a dark-skinned woman with no teeth.

The merchant woman kept staring at Lottie. Her breath quickened. Was it curiosity over a stranger, or had she spilled something down the front of her gown? She glanced down. No stains that she could see. The patrons and vendors alike stared as she passed or stole sideways glances while they conducted their business. Her hands itched to fidget. Lottie pulled her bonnet rim lower over her face and tried to stay next to Julia.

"It's your hair," Julia said. "Very few Islanders have seen a redheaded lady."

Lottie released a slow breath. "That's all it is? Thank God. I was beginning to feel like I had something on my face or stuck between my teeth."

The dark-skinned woman selling papayas extended her hand and nodded toward Lottie's hair. Paul stepped between them.

Julia pursed her lips as if annoyed. She sighed and shrugged a shoulder. "Might as well get it over with so they stop asking."

Paul moved aside.

Lottie smiled at the woman's wonder-filled eyes and removed her bonnet. The woman raised a timid hand, and Lottie nodded, encouraging her to feel the texture of her red hair. More women approached and asked to touch in their thick creole accents. Soon a crowd of women formed all around her, chattering in French, Creole, and English. They smiled brightly and offered her small gifts—a tiny cross made out of reeds, a necklace of tiny shells, and scraps of brightly colored fabrics.

She thanked them all as best as she could with the language barrier.

Paul crossed his arms and scowled at the gaggle of women.

Julia surveyed the excited group. "It seems you've already endeared yourself to the island women."

"I've never met people so easy to please. All I did was let them touch my hair."

"Ironic isn't it? They have so little, yet they are grateful."

Eventually, the women dispersed, and Julia continued to purchase the foodstuffs she needed for the inn. Her aggressive haggling with vendors jarred Lottie, but Julia reassured her it was what everyone did. As Julia engaged with a particularly stubborn vendor, Lottie wandered to the next cart filled with dyes for making cloth. Dark indigos, bright yellows, and deep pinks spread before her.

"Did you see the *Katherine* is back in port?" A deep voice caught Lottie's attention.

She could only see the shadow of two men behind the dyed indigo sheet hanging between the carts.

"Indeed. Did ya hear about the deal he's makin' with the planters? Payin' dem in advance fer their cargo."

"Unless he's God," said the Northern English accent, "I don't see how he can ensure the safe voyage of all his cargo. Mark my word, he'll be out of the shipping industry in under a year."

"I heard he struck a deal wit da pirate king trollin' these waters."

"Lafitte?" The Englishman coughed. "Is that of whom you speak, Jean Laffite?"

"Whyever not? Dey both were schooled here."

"Seems likely that Winthrop would do business with his old friend."

"Dere's gossips a plenty sayin' Winthrop is one of dem."

"A pirate?"

The islander's shadow nodded. "He and da Captain Fielding."

Pirates? Lottie chuckled to herself. Nathan was no more a pirate than he was the prince regent.

"Would ya care ta purchase some dye?" A young mulatto girl held out a tin towards her. "I got a pretty blue ta match da color of yer eyes."

"Thank you, but no." Lottie meandered away from the cart and peeked around the cloth to see who the men were, but all she saw was their backs as they strolled away.

Julia raised a hand to signal her. "It's time to leave."

Paul jostled several loaded sacks in his large hands down the sandy road.

Lottie fell into step next to her friend. "How long will Captain Fielding be with us before the *Katherine* sails again?"

Julia sighed, and her pace slowed. "A little longer than two weeks. Since we received word that the *Amory's* cargo was confiscated by the British navy, they must sail to Central America for more supplies and food."

"I don't understand," Lottie said. "Why would the British Navy take from its own ships? They impressed several men from the *Amory* into service."

"Some naval captains are privateers in disguise and keep the spoils for themselves. Merchant ships suffer the most during a trade war, but they also can exact a higher price because the risk of invading pirates and privateers is so great."

Lottie bit her lip. Should she tell Julia what she overheard? The rumor of Nathan being in league with pirates caused her stomach to drop. If the government believed the lies being spread about her husband, Nathan's life could be in jeopardy from hanging. *No.* She shouldn't tell Julia. She'd only be perpetuating the rumor. Nathan was not a pirate.

Images of him engaged in swordplay flashed through her mind. He was adept with a sword, even more so than her brother or Anthony, who'd attended Britain's Naval Academy. His hair and shirt had ruffled in the wind as he'd attacked and parried. His leg muscles strained against his breeches.

"Lottie?"

She shook her head to clear it.

Julia repeated her question. "Are you overheated?"

"No." Lottie fought the urge to press a hand to her cheek.

"Your color seems high."

Lottie's stomach dipped. "It's merely the tropical climate. I daresay, it agrees with me." She changed the topic. "Is Captain Fielding with his ship?"

"Indeed. He's overseeing some repairs."

They turned up the shell-lined path to the Cockleshell Inn.

"It's too stuffy inside this time of day." Julia fanned her face with her hand. "Would you care to sit on the porch? I'll have some lemonade brought outside."

"Sounds delightful."

Paul set the packages down and pulled out a handkerchief from his pocket. He dusted off the chairs before moving the foodstuffs inside to the kitchen.

They sat in the shade, and Lottie removed her bonnet to let the gentle breeze cool her hair. Julia did the same.

"Have you heard from Nathan?"

"Only another excuse about why he couldn't come calling."

Julia stared at her. Her lips parted, then closed as if reconsidering what she might say. She turned her gaze to the boats bobbing in the ocean, rising and falling like a steady breath upon the waves. "Do not be discouraged." Her brown eyes returned to Lottie's. "There is an overwhelming number of tasks to be supervised on a plantation. Especially when one is gone for more than two months at a time."

"You don't believe he's avoiding me?" Lottie hated how insecure she sounded, but she needed to know the answer. Franny was too young and inexperienced to offer her any sound advice. Julia, however, was married and worldly. Lottie picked at a snag. "Nathan didn't wish to be married. I'm afraid he sees me as an added burden."

"Very few men wish to be married." Julia's lips curled in a haughty sneer. "Until we convince them otherwise."

Lottie sighed. "There are times when I catch him looking at me with warmth in his eyes. It fills me with hope that maybe we can grow to love one another."

A woman arrived with a tray of lemonade. She handed a glass to Lottie and another to Julia.

Lottie sipped the sweet-and-sour liquid. "Other times, it's as if he's given me the cut direct. He behaves detached and aloof, as if he wants nothing to do with me."

Julia turned her head, distracted by a customer entering the inn. Her graceful silhouette instilled the impression of royalty.

Lottie raised her chin and straightened. She'd been taught the same posture, but it felt forced, unlike Julia who managed a natural look.

Gulls glided over the waves, crying their wails of longing.

A drip of condensation from the glass dampened Lottie's fingers. "I know nothing of marriage other than my parent's example."

"Every marriage is different." Julia's eyes grew distant. "Jere and I were fire and ice, or yin and yang as the Chinese would say. We were passionate with youthful ardor, but also naïve and stubborn."

"I see." Lottie hid her disappointment by sipping her lemonade. The brotherly kisses Nathan pecked on her forehead could in no way be described as youthful ardor. Maybe talking to Julia about this had been a bad idea.

"Initially, you stumble around as you learn about each other, blundering as often as succeeding. But eventually, you fall into understanding."

"How am I to learn about my husband when he's not around?"

Julia arched a brow. "Maybe you must first learn about yourself?"

Her words hit their target. Lottie had always been under her mother's wing. Now she had her freedom, and what had she done with it? At the tiniest struggle, she'd reverted to her old ways of hiding. She'd hidden in her cabin seasick, and now that they'd landed in St. Kitts, she'd remained holed up in her chamber at the inn waiting for her husband to come calling. A beautiful tropical island lay before her, yet until today, she'd confined herself to the security of her room. She'd been fearful of venturing out on her own.

Maybe God wanted her to learn she didn't need to be reliant

upon any one person. All her life she'd been dependent upon her mother, and now she'd acted as if Nathan was supposed to take over the role. A light dawned in her mind. She didn't need Nathan to be her mother, nor did she want him to be.

"There is something I think you should know." The cords on Julia's slender neck grew taut. "I had hoped Nathan would have explained this to you, but it's obvious he didn't."

Lottie's chest clenched, and the men's voices from the market echoed in her mind. *He's doing business with a pirate king.*

"I think when you hear this, it will put some of the pieces together."

Lottie held her breath.

"Nathan is a very private person. I may be betraying his trust by telling you this."

Lottie swallowed, and her stomach twisted.

"As you know, the island can be ruthless at times, and Nathan has seen the worst of it. His father moved here back when King George the Third began his reign. He married Miss Rebecca Lawton of Bristol and brought her to the island. They had three children, Amory, Nathaniel, and Katherine."

Lottie smiled. "He named his vessels after his siblings."

"They were a very close family. Hardworking, but jolly people. They teased each other mercilessly, but it was all in fun."

"I'd like to meet them." She smiled at the thought of Nathan jesting with his siblings.

"If only you could. I do believe they would take to you instantly."

Lottie's smile fell. "What happened to them?"

"The fever. Katherine came down with it first, followed by Amory and Mrs. Winthrop. Each was a painful passing."

"I had no idea." Lottie shook her head and bit her lip to keep it from quivering. Poor Nathan watched one loved one die, only to have to go through the entire heartwrenching scenario a second and then a third time.

"Nathan's father turned to the bottle to numb his despair. Six months later, he died when his wagon rolled over on him."

Lottie gasped.

"Nathan became the sole provider for over thirty slaves and the caretaker of over three hundred acres of damaged crops. He worked day and night to bring the cane back and get the land to produce. Because of his efforts, not one of his slaves went hungry."

A servant appeared at the door. "Miz Fielding? There's a guest who'd like ta have a word wit ya."

"Tell our guest I'll be right with him." Julia rose, and Lottie did the same.

"Thank you"—she forced the words around the lump in her throat—"for telling me this."

"I wanted you to know so you'll understand." Julia's eyes darkened. "Nathan's staying away because he's afraid he'll lose you too."

Tears burned behind Lottie's lids, but she dared not cry and appear weak. "Do you mind if I stay out here a bit longer? I need to sort out some things." A thunderous wave crashed in the background. "Maybe I'll go for a stroll on the beach."

"If you do, take Paul with you."

"I have Franny. Today was her morning off. She went to the docks to visit with Cook, but she should have returned by now. I don't want to tie up your servants."

"It's best to have male accompaniment to be safe."

"As you wish." Lottie flashed her a wobbly smile.

~

*T*he fresh air and invigorating walk were exactly what Lottie needed to clear her head. After hearing Julia's words, Nathan's rejection no longer stung. If she'd been through all he'd suffered, she'd be afraid to allow her heart to love again too. Time was what he needed.

In the interim, she would no longer keep herself hidden away. She didn't know how many days God had determined for her life, but she certainly wasn't doing herself or God any good staying confined in her room.

Paul and Franny hung back a few paces to allow her space, since very few people roamed the beach. A dark cloud hovering overhead seemed to keep most folks away. She picked up a few shells to keep and listened to the rhythmic crashing of the waves. She stopped at the marina to see Cobble and a few of the *Katherine's* crewmembers, including Charlie, but he spoke mostly to Franny. A light rain shower cut their visit short.

Her bonnet had dampened by the time they entered the side door of the inn. Julia called to Paul from the kitchen, asking him to assist a servant in the stockroom. He excused himself from Lottie and Franny and headed in the direction of Julia's voice.

The steps to her room stood before her, but Lottie couldn't force her legs to climb them, not after her taste of freedom. There had to be somewhere else she could go. Julia had mentioned a study where she could find books to read.

She ambled down the hall, Franny on her heels, peeking into open doors until she found a room with a large desk and, behind it, shelves of books. They stepped inside. Franny waited by the door as Lottie scanned the embossed titles. She ran the pad of her index finger down the leather spines of several books. *The Pirate's Treasure* stood out among the titles. How funny to discover the same book she'd opened the night she'd been in Anthony's study. She pulled it out and skimmed the first page. It truly was the same novel. This time there was no candle, no glasses of brandy, and she was already married, so nothing could go wrong.

Lottie waved for Franny to have a seat before she pulled out a chair and sat down to read. She was deep into chapter four when a burly man's voice raised her head.

"Well, what have we here?" The man's frame filled the doorway. "Two lovely ladies sittin' pretty."

His beard held bits of bread caught in the scruff, and she could smell the spirits on his breath. He sauntered into the room, and another thinner man followed him in.

Lottie's heart picked up its pace, but she calmly set the book aside. The lean man smiled at Franny, and several of his teeth were missing. Franny scooted closer to the wall.

Lottie rose, keeping her back straight, and pointed to the hallway. "Gentlemen, the tavern is the next doorway on the right."

"Oh, we're not lost. We had to stop when we saw such beauties idlin' the day away. I couldn't help but wonder if you were lookin' for some entertainment?"

"I don't believe my husband would appreciate my cavorting with another man."

The man's brows raised. "And who might your husband be?"

"Nathaniel Winthrop."

A loud raspy guffaw rattled in the man's chest, echoed by the hissing laughter of his companion. "Winthrop hasn't taken a wife. I've seen him working his fields every day since the *Katherine's* arrival. A warm-blooded man doesn't hole his woman up at an inn. If he had a wife, he'd have her by his side. Keep her under lock and key, especially a fine white woman." He put a hand to his chest. "Name's Cyrus McCurdy, and this here is Jack Reid. I'm the estate manager down at the Swanson plantation in Sandy Point, and Mr. Reid is its overseer."

Lottie kept a chair between, issuing them a curt nod.

"May I say what a pleasure it is to meet you." His gaze roved over her form.

Mr. Reid scooped up Franny's hand and kissed the back of it. Franny tugged it back, but the man held firm.

"Unhand my maid." Lottie's voice boomed in true Lady Etheridge fashion.

Mr. Reid froze and released her maid's hand.

A flash of movement caught her attention behind the man, and the long tip of a saber slid by his neck to tap the underside of his chin.

"Mr. McCurdy and Mr. Reid." Julia stepped forward and spoke in a deadly calm voice. "You will unhand my guests and leave them be."

Mr. McCurdy raised his palms. "We were only havin' a bit of fun. We weren't causin' any trouble."

"You, gentlemen, must be leaving. I don't want you in my sight."

"But ya have the best scotch in all the islands." McCurdy's brows angled together. "And what will Mr. Reid do without his whiskey?"

"He should have thought about that before he laid his grimy fingers on my friends. Now be gone before I have Paul toss you out on your ear."

Paul's dark frame shadowed her in the hallway.

The two men slithered past, and Paul watched until the front door closed behind them.

"Are you unharmed?" Julia swept her gaze over Franny, then to Lottie. The woman had remained so calm—so strong.

No wonder Nathan wanted her to be more like Julia. She licked her dry lips. "Just a bit shaken."

Julia handed the sword to Paul, who sheathed it and left. "Some islanders have poor manners."

Lottie eyed the doorway where Paul disappeared. "Can you teach me how to defend myself with the sword?"

Julia's chest rose and fell with her sigh. "Fencing is a challenging sport, especially for a woman who can be overpowered. I don't have the time or patience required to teach you."

Lottie's chest fell. "I see."

"What you need is to learn how to shoot." Julia arched a brow.

"You know how to shoot? You'll teach me?"

"I'm an excellent markswoman, but, no, I will not teach you."

Lottie's brow furrowed.

"Nathan will." She issued a crisp nod and swept from the room.

CHAPTER 16

I fear he isn't pleased with me and that is the reason he has stayed away. Lord, must I always fall short of other's standards? Thank You for loving me for whom I am.
~ *Scribbled in Lottie's prayer journal*

A footman knocked on the bed chamber door as Franny brushed Lottie's tresses up into a simple twist. She allowed some curls to fan out on top like a fiery bouquet. Lottie pinched her cheeks for color and peered into the looking glass one last time. The pale blue gown that had arrived yesterday with the others fit her perfectly and amplified the blue of her eyes.

Would Nathan notice? She inhaled a steadying breath. "He's here." She squeezed Franny's hand. "Say a prayer all goes well."

Franny's dimples flashed. "I will, mum."

Lottie itched to run down the stairs. Instead, she lifted her head and straightened her spine with as much poise and grace as she could muster. Her stomach somersaulted with each step.

Nathan stood over a table in the taproom with a large map spread out before him. He pointed at a spot, and Captain

Fielding leaned in closer to inspect. Nathan's light tan jacket hugged his shoulders. The light from the window illuminated his profile, and the crease between his thick brows suggested he was deep in thought.

She hadn't realized how much she'd missed him. His air of authority, ruggedness, and vital power all drew her like a shelter from a storm. Funny how he had become her comfortable sense of familiarity in this new strange world.

"The pirates probably hid behind San Dominique, raided the ship, and sailed to Barataria to auction the cargo."

Lottie stepped forward and folded her hands in front of her.

He glanced up and spied her. A slow grin spread across his face as if he were pleased to see her. His gaze swept down her figure and back up again. "You look lovely. Matilda knew exactly the right fit and colors for you."

Exhilaration swept through Lottie. She'd send Matilda flowers later for her excellent work.

He inhaled and released a breath with a puff of his cheeks, his face losing its pleasure. Whatever was wrong? Her hair? Her gown? Was she not standing straight enough? Out of habit, Lottie hid her hands among the cotton folds of her dress.

"You're a bit overdressed for what I was thinking."

Her pale blue walking dress wasn't an evening gown. It seemed perfect for strolling the streets of Basseterre or even the beach. She raised her brows. "What did you have in mind?"

"A shooting lesson."

She inhaled a gasp. How had Julia worked such magic this quickly?

He extended a hand. "We shall make do."

Her fingers slid over his calloused palm. She shivered, not out of disgust but because of the sheer masculinity of him, a man who worked with his hands. Her fingers felt like fragile twigs in the coiled power of his grasp.

He tucked her hand into the crook of his arm and escorted

her outdoors. The evocative scent of last night's heavy rainfall mixed with the salty tang of the ocean air.

Paul stroked the horse's nose and held the reins as Nathan aided her up into the seat of the two person gig. He strode to the other side, climbed aboard, and accepted the reins from Paul.

Nathan spurred on the horses, and their small gig bounced down the road away from the crowded streets of Basseterre. He glanced her way. "It seems you've taken to the island air. You've a bit more color and a glow about you."

His words spread warmth through her chest. "It's more likely due to the fact that the floor no longer rolls beneath my feet, and my breakfast stays in my stomach." She lifted her face to the sun peeking out from behind the clouds. "St. Kitts is beautiful. Have you ever seen a sun so bright, waters so blue, or even fields so green?" She gestured to some wild orchids growing alongside the road. "Even the flowers are more colorful here. Julia took me to the market, and the people there were delightful. They made me this." She held out her arm for him to admire her bracelet of tiny strung seashells.

Nathan slowed the horses as they crossed over a section of washed out road.

"I'd like to prevent other run-ins like the one you had the other day with McCurdy."

She smoothed her skirt. "Julia told you about that?"

"Captain Fielding, but Julia sent him."

"I don't know if Mr. McCurdy meant us any real harm. We were, after all, in an open room well within hearing range of the rest of the inn, which is how Julia became alerted. Most people on the island have been very kind and mostly curious about my…" She pointed to her red hair.

Nathan exhaled. "Most islanders are well-intentioned, but emotions run high in St. Kitts. Men are starved for a woman's" —he glanced at her, and his neck flushed—"affections. Add to it that rum is easier to obtain than a cup of tea. And, with the land not producing, islanders are on edge. We're under constant pressure to bring in a good crop to put food on the table, not only for us but also for our workers and slaves. Many slaves have threatened to revolt, and they grow bolder by the day."

She eyed some slaves wielding their machetes in a nearby field. Were they dangerous? What would they do in an uprising, attack their owners and burn down the houses? Would they then move into the town and burn it to the ground?

He must have read the fear in her expression. "I don't mean to scare you. I merely want you to understand how a friendly encounter can turn on you when you least expect it." He locked eyes with her. "You should never go out unescorted. Take Paul or send for me, but one of us should be with you at all times if you venture outside the inn."

"Send for you?" Despite the open air, a tight band constricted her chest as if her stays had been pulled too tight. It was the same sensation she'd had as a child whenever her mother was around. Had she sought her freedom an entire ocean away only to have it ripped from her hands? She would no longer stand and watch from the window. It was time to live. Didn't making it this far prove she wasn't weak? If he desired a strong woman like Julia, she would give him strong.

"As if you would come." Lottie rounded on him. "And I hardly think it is possible for me to always be accompanied. You're busy with the work at Calico Manor, and Paul has duties at the inn. Am I supposed to remain a prisoner in my room?"

His jaw tensed. "You don't understand the dangers. There's no sense of honor when a man is in his cups." His grip tightened on the reins. "I am trying to protect you."

"How can you protect me when you're not around?"

"There are others who depend upon me. I've been over-seeing my fields."

Unshed tears burned in her throat. "Indeed, too busy to remember you have a wife."

A muscle in the side of his face twitched. "I can't be traipsing about assisting you on shopping trips when there are mouths to feed. I have responsibilities beyond you."

His words hung in the air as Julia's remarks echoed in her mind. *Because of his efforts, not one of his slaves went hungry.*

She understood the weight of his burden. He was a good man, of that she had no doubt. The wounds from the deaths of his family members were still fresh. He protected his heart by keeping others at a distance, including her. She was sorry for his pain, sorry for all he had endured. Sorry that he was stuck married to her.

She started to apologize. It was what he expected, and hadn't she always done what was expected? The words stuck in her throat. She wouldn't let him off the hook for this. If he could be responsible for all his workers and their families, how much trouble could one more woman be?

The sea breeze rustled the coarse grasses.

She could remain the timid little mouse he'd met back in England, or she could find freedom and, for the first time, discover who Charlotte Winthrop really was. Did she walk with her red hair held high? Did she laugh and put people at ease? Or, did she confront problems with a pistol in hand? Maybe she would do all three.

If he didn't want the new her, then she'd survive or die. But in the process—for the first time—she'd truly live.

Nathan stiffened and a muscle twitched in his jaw.

The weight of her silence blared between them.

He exhaled a long breath and his shoulders sagged. "No. You're right. Your ire is well deserved. I should make myself more available to you."

Lottie blinked. Her lips parted, but she was too stunned to speak.

"I'll endeavor to come around more often. You have my word."

"Thank you." She worked to keep herself from stammering. Never in her life had her mother apologized. She might be congenial the day following an unkindness, but never would she admit to any wrong.

"I don't mean to add to your burden." Lottie dropped her gaze and fiddled with her glove. "It's simply that I cannot stay cooped up at the inn. I spent most of my childhood watching the world go on without me. While other children laughed and played, I read, perfected my embroidery stitch, or practiced the pianoforte. Mama was too worried that I would be injured or become ill again."

"She wanted to protect you." Nathan snorted. "Maybe your mother was wise."

Lottie swallowed her initial reaction. If Nathan started behaving like her mother, they were in for some trouble. "I understand your concern, but I didn't travel across the Atlantic to a distant island to watch the world pass me by again. I could very well become sick. I could very well suffer an injury, but watching the world through a window isn't living."

"And it's not that I'm not scared. I'm frightened that I could die tomorrow, but it would be a true tragedy if I died without ever having lived." She removed her bonnet and tilted her face to the dazzling sun. "The night we danced was the first night I started living. I might have gone about it all wrong, but I don't regret it."

The gig slowed to a stop.

She opened her eyes to find his locked on her. She swallowed her fear and spoke the truth. "I will never regret marrying you."

"Lottie, I—"

"You don't have to say anything. I've been an unexpected intrusion in your life. I merely hope that maybe someday, we might be able to..." *Love one another.* She couldn't say the words. Not out loud. "To become friends."

His eyes clouded as they searched hers. For an endless moment, all she could hear was the thudding of her own heart and the chatter of the birds in the underbrush.

He gently ran the back of his fingers down the side of her face. He opened his mouth to speak, but one of the horses snorted. He briefly closed his eyes and gave his head a tiny shake. "Just promise me you'll not go out alone. The sooner we teach you to shoot, the better."

Silence returned between them. He continued to stare as if seeking some form of agreement.

She finally nodded. She could only pray she wouldn't regret it later.

CHAPTER 17

Remind me never to challenge anyone to a duel. Not
merely because it's improper, but more importantly,
because I am a terrible shot.

~ *From Lottie to Miss Priscilla Middleton*

I *will never regret marrying you.*

Lottie's words pervaded Nathan's thoughts as she
smiled at him during their drive. Her expressive blue eyes
wondered at each new sight. He summoned every ounce of his
strength to abstain from pulling her into his arms and kissing
her as a husband should.

He shouldn't think these thoughts. He should remember the
feeling of desperate hopelessness he'd experienced as Katherine
had expelled her last breath. But it was hard to focus on death
when Lottie found such excitement over the smallest things.
Things he'd taken for granted, like the little geckos climbing on
tree trunks and the graceful egrets roosting among the
mangrove trees. At the sight of a large iguana sunning itself on a
rock, she dug her nails into his arm, yet leaned out for a closer
glimpse.

Finally, they arrived at Frigate Bay away from the military forts. Best to avoid any chance of the militia mistaking their practice for the island being under attack. Nathan grabbed his satchel resting on the floorboards and tied the team to a hitching post.

He aided her down from the carriage and unbound the straps of an empty barrel he'd fastened to the back of the gig.

"Follow me." He carried the barrel down the sandy path, but stopped when he noticed Lottie wasn't behind him. He glanced back to find her balancing precariously on one foot with her kid boots in her hand. She pulled off her stocking with the other.

"What are you doing?"

She stuffed her stockings into her boots and ran to catch up with him. "I wanted to see how the sand felt under my feet."

He bit back a smile. "And?"

She beamed at him. "It feels lovely." She lifted her skirt the tiniest bit and wriggled her toes in the sand.

Nathan stared at her slender feet and trim ankles, and his mouth grew dry. He closed his eyes. *Lord, take these feelings from me. I cannot go through the pain of losing someone else.*

He opened his eyes and found Lottie had shut hers.

"The sand is so smooth and warm."

Her long lashes lifted, and he yearned to be part of the childish delight that sparkled in the depths of those crystal blue eyes.

"You really must try it."

He snorted. "I grew up walking barefoot in the sand."

"But you've not stepped on this very sand in this very spot before."

He didn't know whether her rosy skin glowed with excitement, or if that was simply the reflected sunlight off the sand. The sight of her stirred a whimsy he hadn't felt in a long time, not since he and his siblings played in the surf and created stories about mythical creatures.

But he couldn't let himself be bogged down in fancies. They had to get started. The boiling room still needed draining, and the north field must be inspected.

She sighed as if sand between her toes were pure ecstasy. Her eyes dared him to comply.

Just this once. He set down the barrel and tugged off his boots.

The sand cradled his instep with its soft warmth.

Lottie stared at his feet.

His were large and tanned. Hers slender and pale. The intimacy of the moment jarred him into stepping back.

She blushed a pink that rivaled an island sunset. "How does it feel?" She lifted her blue eyes to meet his.

Soft, warm, but not as delightful as you feel in my arms. Nathan cleared his throat, along with his thoughts. "Sandy. It feels sandy." Leaving his shoes, he lifted the barrel and headed for the shoreline.

The sand squeaked beneath her feet as she scurried to catch up with him.

"You can stay right there. I'm going to set this down and come back."

In a bit of shade provided by a cluster of mangrove trees, he set down the empty barrel. Tiny monkeys babbled in the canopy as they munched on the fruit the trees produced.

Lottie wandered over and stared at their playing. Why did it not surprise him she disobeyed his order to stay put? She raised up on her toes to observe one sitting on a nearby branch.

"Careful, they bite."

The monkey chose that moment to open its mouth and screech at Lottie.

She jumped back, tripped over the hem of her gown, and landed on her backside in the sand.

Nathan threw back his head and laughed. He couldn't help himself.

"Do they? Truly, do they bite?"

He strode over and helped her up.

She backed away from the creature a few more steps.

"They've been known to on occasion, if you get too close."

He waved her back to the copse of trees. "The mangrove will provide shade."

She inched toward him, keeping a leery eye on the monkey.

He removed his flintlock pistol from his satchel. "Have you ever used a pistol before?"

She shook her head.

"This is a Queen Ann flintlock." He displayed the weapon, which was only slightly larger than his hand. "It's small enough for you to keep on your person. However, you only have one shot before reloading, so you must make it count." He removed a small sack of powder and a slug. "To load the weapon, you're going to unscrew the barrel like so." He twisted the end off of the pocket pistol. He pulled the tie on the small sack of gun powder with his teeth and poured the black power into the opening. "Place the round slug on top and screw back on the barrel."

She stood so close, the scent of lilacs enveloped him.

He leaned in closer until their arms brushed.

Her pink lips parted.

He forced himself to concentrate. "Cock the weapon by pulling back on the hammer until it goes no further. To aim, hold your arm out." He pointed the weapon toward the barrel. "Position your body like so." He turned sideways with his head facing the same direction as his arm. He widened his stance. Brace yourself for the recoil and pull the trigger."

The gun exploded with a bang, startling a gasp out of Lottie.

The monkeys bolted off, running down the beach.

He lowered the weapon. "See how it shot straight through the center of the wooden barrel?" He raised his voice to compensate for the ringing in their ears.

She rubbed her ear and stared at the target.

"Don't fret. The ringing will cease shortly. Now it's your turn." He unscrewed the barrel of the gun gingerly, for he hadn't allowed much time for it to cool. He handed her the powder bag, and she poured in the black substance until he told her to stop. "Now the slug."

Her delicate fingers placed the tiny ball on top, and he screwed the barrel back on.

"Now, cock the weapon."

She pulled back on the hammer.

"Aim the pistol by looking straight down the barrel at the target."

She lifted her arm to eye level.

"Position your body."

He hesitated before resting his hands on her slender waist and turning her body to the side. Just this once, he allowed himself to enjoy the feel of her in his arms.

Just this once. For practical purposes.

His hand shifted to the flat of her belly, and he leaned in closer to see her line of vision.

By Jove, she fit nicely in his arms.

A tremor ran through her. She swayed, leaning back against his chest.

His heart thundered. Could Lottie feel its thumping? Could she hear its pounding in her own ears? Did it move in rhythm with her own?

His head tilted down until the tendrils of her hair tickled his lips. His tenuous hold on his self-control was slipping. He longed to lean in, to kiss the skin behind her ear, to nuzzle the sensitive skin on her neck. He needed to focus, but his whole body felt as if it were on... "Fire," he whispered.

Her finger squeezed the trigger. The blast jolted and she yelped. Her arms flew back and her elbow hit him in the gut.

He grunted and stepped aside.

Her eyes sprung open.

"Were your eyes closed?"

"No… Well, maybe." She peered up at him from under her long lashes with a contrite frown. "Yes…but it was an accident."

He chuckled and shook his head, thankful for the distraction. "Rule number one—keep your eyes open when you shoot."

He loaded the weapon again and handed it to her. This time, he stood back a bit. "Brace, now aim. Fire."

She pulled the trigger, and the recoil knocked her backward into his chest.

He steadied her with his hands. "Keep a wider stance. It's a small weapon, but it has a big kick."

"Did I hit the barrel?"

They stepped up to the target and inspected its surface, but there were no holes other than Nathan's initial one.

Lottie frowned. "Let me try again."

She attempted several more shots, but left no marks in the barrel.

"You're trailing a little to the left." He positioned her body and arm. "See if this helps."

Still no holes.

Her lips pursed and her eyes narrowed. Three more shots. Still no holes.

"Try moving closer."

She stepped toward the barrel.

"Take your time."

Her chest rose as she inhaled a deep breath. She released it and fired. This time, only her forearm raised from the recoil. She peered over her shoulder at him, and a brilliant smile lit up her face. "I think I did it that time." She passed him the gun and scurried to examine the target.

Nathan didn't move. Her hopeful expression set the pit of his stomach tingling. Beyond their target, something surfaced in the water. Its scales flashed in the sun.

"I thought for certain I'd hit the target that time." She frowned at the barrel.

"You hit something." He strode past her and waded into the surf. The water splashed up onto his breeches, soaking him up to his mid-thigh. He scooped up a dead sunfish. Sure enough, a hole bored straight through the fish's middle.

He waded back to the beach and held it up for her to see. "Brilliant shot. The fish didn't know what hit him."

She paled, and her lips parted, but slowly they curved into a smile. She pinched her lips to keep from laughing, but merriment leaked out her nose in snorts. She covered her mouth with her hand to no avail. The giggles overwhelmed her, and she leaned against the barrel.

He peered at the fish and burst with laughter.

It was all the encouragement she needed. She stopped fighting and allowed her glee to overtake her.

Her laugh was musical, light and warm. Katherine would have adored her.

The thought sobered him, and he tossed the fish back into the surf. He inhaled a deep breath, but a smile lingered on his lips.

"Pass me the powder and another slug." Lottie held out her hand. "I'm getting closer. This time I *will* hit it."

He shook his head. "I'm afraid that was the last of my supplies. We'll try again another day."

Disappointment shadowed her eyes, but she flashed him a smile with a determined glint. "I'll redeem myself. Mark my words."

"Of that, I have no doubt." She was full of surprises. When he'd taught Katherine how to shoot, she'd complained about the pain in her arms, yet Lottie had held up well today for such a delicate woman. He tucked the pistol and powder bag back into his satchel and hefted it onto his shoulder. Balancing it with one hand, he offered her his other arm. "It's time we head back."

She looped her arm through the crook of his elbow.

His steps slowed, and he was surprised to find he wasn't eager for their time to end. On a whim, he said, "There's much still to see before we lose the light."

Her eyes sparkled. "Truly?"

"It's about time I showed you your holdings, Lady Winthrop."

He heard her light intake of air.

They reached the gig, and he set down the barrel. Then he collected their shoes from where they left them at the start of the path. Both of them sat on the barrel to dust the sand off their feet before donning their stockings and boots.

Out of the corner of his eye, he could see her delicate pink toes. She glanced at him, but he quickly looked away. He helped her into the gig, and she settled into the seat.

An air of excitement raised the fine hairs on his arms.

"Do I look presentable?" She straightened her gown and fiddled with her bonnet.

He needed to set her expectations properly. "Now, mind you. It's a humble holding, especially the main house."

She nodded and bit her bottom lip, but the corners still curved into a shy smile.

He flicked the reins, and the horses trotted away. He turned them back the way they'd come.

Lottie's neck craned. "Is that part of St. Kitts, or is that another island?"

He followed her gaze. "That's our sister island, Nevis. See the clouds that hover around the top of the mountain? It got its name, the Spanish word for snow, because the clouds make it appear like a snow-capped mountain. There's only a strip of inlet called the narrows that separates us. It's tricky to navigate a boat through because of the tide and strong currents."

She tilted her head back, allowing the sun to spill upon her face. "Smell the tropical breeze." Her eyes fluttered closed, then opened again.

It smelled like home to him.

"It's so wild and free. There are colors and life everywhere."

And death.

"It's what I imagine the Garden of Eden must have been like."

An image of Lottie with her long red hair unbound, biting into an apple with only fig leaves... He shook his head to clear his errant thoughts, but a part of him screamed. *She's your wife. Remember Song of Solomon? You're supposed to be enjoying the fruits of your youth.*

Her wide eyes locked on him. "What was it like to grow up on the island?"

He ran a hand over his lower jaw. How could he explain? "Much like living in the countryside of England, but a little more lenient on social standards and propriety. When people have a greater risk of death from disease, their priorities change. We have our own assembly, which governs and reports back to England. We have churches and schools. In fact"—he pointed up to a stone arch on the mountainside—"I attended both church and school at that very spot. That was, until I was shipped off to attend Eton."

She gaped at him. "You attended Eton in England?"

His jaw tightened at her obvious surprise. "Are my manners so uncouth?"

"No, it's not that."

She placed a hand on his arm, and a tingling sensation spread up into his shoulder.

"I'm only surprised because it's a far journey, especially for one so young. How old were you?"

"Age eight."

"Were you scared to travel to a country you'd never seen?" Sympathy shone in her eyes. After all, she had just undergone the same.

"To me, it was an adventure. I took to the ship and its crew immediately. I followed the captain around like a shadow the entire voyage. It might be why I was so drawn to the shipping industry."

"Did you enjoy Eton?"

"Not particularly."

"Because of the conditions? I heard the food is dreadful."

"I'm not certain the mush they fed us could be considered food, but it didn't bother me."

"Was it the strict rules?"

He grinned. "Indeed, that was a part of it."

"I've heard the schoolmasters can be harsh." She crossed her arms. "Especially with punishments."

"I'd say my punishment was fair. They sent me down to rusticate."

"Expelled!" Her mouth dropped open. "Truly? May I ask what you did?"

"I rode the school master's horse."

"Well, that doesn't seem a crime fitting enough to be rusticated."

His smile grew parting his lips. "It is when you use the horse to leap over the headmaster's dining table."

She cupped a hand over her mouth, and her eyes widened into two large liquid pools.

"While the headmaster was still sitting at it."

Her hand lowered. "How did you...? I can't believe... Why would you attempt such a feat?"

"I was dared."

"You risked rustication for a dare?"

He shrugged. "My honor was at stake."

She stared at him as if waiting for an explanation.

"Children can be cruel, especially to a foreigner. They teased me, betting among themselves that I ate pepper pots while sitting on the floor. They mimicked my accent and imitated my

LORRI DUDLEY

loose gait and how I dangled my arms. I was young. For the most part, I ignored their comments, but when they bet I couldn't seat a horse, I decided I'd had enough." He glanced her way.

"Seeing the looks on the other students' faces as I wheeled the horse with perfect control was well worth the lashing I endured later. My father wasn't happy with my return, but I'd like to say I kept my honor and earned the respect of my peers." He rubbed a hand across his chin. "I can still picture the headmaster's face, his eyes wide as he dove out of the way. He had nothing to fear. I easily cleared both him and the table."

Lottie burst out laughing. If only he had a million stories so he could make her laugh like that every day. She held her stomach and had to wipe the tears from the corners of her eyes. "Merciful heavens. At least, you were better at rebelling than I was. I should have asked you for pointers on confidence. Maybe then I wouldn't have gotten nervous and dropped the candle." She chortled out a sigh. "I too can still see a face—my mother's. Her expression still haunts me. In all my life, I'd never seen Mama so upset that she lost her capacity of speech."

Nathan forced a straight expression. "I'm glad you said something, for I wake up screaming at night because of the same memory." He shivered. "Gives me the chills." His lips twitched.

Another round of mirth swept over Lottie. This time she didn't bother to wipe away the tears that coursed down her cheeks. "Please stop." She wrapped her arms around her middle. "My stomach aches."

They bumped along the road, and Lottie swept a shy glance his direction.

"What?"

"It's silly really." She waved a hand as if to push away the thought. "Did you ever…?"

He glanced at her quickly. "Did I ever what?"

180

"There was talk in the market." She raised a gloved finger to her mouth, frowned, and dropped her hand back to her side. "Merely something I overheard."

He braced himself and focused on the road ahead. His smile faded.

The curse.

CHAPTER 18

*I shall be joining my brother, Pierre, in the American
state of Louisiana, but I shall not forget the debt I owe
you. If ever you are in need of a favor...*
~ From Mr. Jean Lafitte written to Nathan seven years prior

"Of course, I found the gossip absurd." Nathan watched
Lottie adjust her bonnet as she spoke. "You being
friendly with a pirate. Ridiculous, really."

The tension melted from his body. Maybe she hadn't heard
he was cursed? "They were probably referring to Pierre and
Jean Lafitte."

Her eyes widened. "So you are acquainted with them?"

"I attended the military academy with Jean. Pierre is a few
years his senior." Would his past friendship with Jean lower her
opinion of him?

"Pirates attend military academies?"

"Jean Lafitte did not plan to become a pirate."

"You know him well then?" Surprise laced her tone.

Honesty was the best recourse, but he searched her face for
any hint of disdain. Even though he found none, he shrugged to

make it seem commonplace to befriend a pirate. "We sailed aboard the same ship as recruits. He set his hopes on being a privateer, but there were signs even then. Jean always had a daring side. His quick temper got him into trouble on more than one occasion, but his charisma and wit made him a natural leader."

"Isn't it dangerous to associate with pirates?"

"I haven't crossed paths with either Lafitte in years, almost a decade." A slow grin parted his lips as a memory resurfaced, and he chuckled. "Not since I saved his hide."

"How so?"

"We'd finished running a drill. The weather had been particularly hot that day. There wasn't a bit of breeze, and the sun beat down as we finished dueling practice. We were eager to cool off with a swim. The ocean beckoned us like a siren. Lafitte conned another fellow into finishing his duties and made a big show of diving into the water first. I had an entire deck to swab and had to listen to him taunt me with how good the water felt. He bobbed in the waves and teased us heartily. The other men groaned and fussed. We all had at least another hour's worth of grueling work until we could join him.

"After a while, we all tuned him out, but then he became too quiet. I peered over the rail, expecting to see him relaxing in the water. I can still see his hair flowing like seaweed. I kept thinking he'd surface at any moment and mock me for still having work to do, but he didn't. Never had seconds felt so long. Something had to be wrong. I jumped overboard from the upper deck and swam to him. I grabbed his arm. Instantly, my hand burned."

"Burned?"

"Lafitte had been paralyzed by a man-of-war."

"What's a man-of-war?"

"It's a large jellyfish with tentacles that can stretch longer than a man's body. Its sting burns like the dickens and can momentarily render a man immobile."

"Were you frightened?"

"There wasn't much time to think about it, but afterward I shook like a leaf."

"Had he been under the water long?"

"Thankfully, no. Lafitte coughed and sputtered as he surfaced, but touching him transferred the burning sensation into my own body. I lost function of my hand, and he submerged back under the waves."

"Oh my." Her fingers splayed over her chest.

"I was able to tread water with my legs and good arm while I called for help. A rope was thrown to us, but I couldn't dare touch Jean lest I suffer his same fate. I had no choice but to reel him in by his hair."

"Heavens." Her eyes widened.

"I looped the rope over him, and the crew hefted him over the rail. As I climbed aboard, the poor bloke lay on the deck, writhing in pain." He struggled to suppress his smile.

"Are you laughing?"

"No." He shook his head. "At least, not at his discomfort. It's merely that…" He hesitated, challenged by the delicate phrasing. "There is a known remedy on the island to ease the pain of a jellyfish sting. It is…well, it may not be appropriate for a lady's ears."

"But I must know."

"Let's just say that, as I pulled myself onto the deck, the crew stood around Lafitte…er… relieving themselves."

She gasped and covered her mouth with her hand, but he caught the hint of a smile before she did so.

"Lafitte's temper flared. His words made even the most foul-mouthed man appear civil. Burly men blushed like maidens."

"Under the circumstances, I daresay, he deserved a little grace."

"He settled down and even thanked me later for saving his life. He promised to repay the favor someday, but shortly thereafter, we were assigned separate commands."

"It's probably for the best, considering his decision to become a pirate."

"Indeed."

They continued down the narrow road back through Basseterre and past the Romney plantation. Whenever Nathan glanced her way, he found her smiling. Having her by his side chased away the heavy cloud of his burdens. His shoulders felt lighter and his chest...hopeful. His waif of a woman had the fortitude of a weathered sailor. Only a brave woman could survive living with Lady Etheridge, and it couldn't have been easy to stand up to her mother the night of the Middleton party. She had the courage to leave her family and sail across the Atlantic with a near stranger, and then she'd survived the worst episode of seasickness he'd ever witnessed. Many men with hopes of becoming sailors never sailed again after suffering lesser bouts. Maybe he'd underestimated her.

The vibrant color of her hair suited her passion for life. The way her expressive eyes—fringed with those long lashes—widened with delight at the smallest of things, sprouted new growth in his dead heart. He loved the soft feel of her skin and how she was the perfect height. He could tuck her head under his chin and wrap his arms around her narrow waist.

"Is something amiss?"

He blinked and shook his head.

"It's merely that you keep looking at me with such a strange expression."

Desire. It's called desire. She wouldn't know anything about that. *But maybe...*He gritted his teeth. What about the curse? Would he bring the curse upon her too? He couldn't bear to watch the vibrant light within Lottie extinguish.

He turned the team up a dirt road lined on both sides with

the long reeds of sugar cane. The roofline of Calico Manor rested on the hill. Had this been a wise idea?

In the fields ahead, his men hacked away at the cane with machetes, while the women bundled it. They sang as they worked, cutting the reeds in rhythm.

Lottie sat up higher in her seat. "Listen to their music." She raised a finger and tapped the tempo in the air. "So soulful and rhythmic."

Her excitement peeled away his doubts. If only he could harness her enthusiasm.

The workers spied them pulling up the lane. Their singing ceased abruptly, but they continued working.

"Why did they stop? It was so beautiful."

"Planters don't encourage their heathen customs and songs. Many believe it will lead to uprisings and rebellions."

"And what do you believe?"

Nathan shrugged. "I haven't thought about it much."

She stared at the laborers as they passed, and if any of them dared to make eye contact, she smiled. "It looks like exhausting work. I do believe I'd need a little music to keep going."

"We're coming up on the main house." He slowed the horses. Would she see the dilapidated building and the unfinished kitchen and beg him to return her to England? Even as he perspired under the hot sun, regret chilled his skin. "I need to warn you. It's unfit for a lady. The house I grew up in was bigger, but a tropical storm destroyed a wing and most of the second floor. I've rebuilt, and it's sound, but if Mama were alive, I would have restored it in its entirety."

Lottie rested a hand on his arm. Her gaze filled with compassion. "I'm so sorry about your family."

The too familiar stab of sorrow seized his chest, but the warmth of her hand kept his focus on the living. He nodded.

His overseer, Marcus, was headed back up to the main

house. Lunch would be served shortly, and everyone would soon gather.

He pulled in front of the cottage house in which he'd been raised, and saw it now from a stranger's eyes. Gone were the brightly colored shutters. He'd replaced them with plain white. Mama's neatly laid flowerbeds had been choked out with weeds. The stone foundation had been raised to encompass the first floor because stone better withstood storms. The second floor was comprised of wood, a material easier to replace than stone after a hurricane. It had been replaced four times already, three before he was born and once after. The roofline extended out on all but one side to provide additional shade and terraced porches. On that one side, a stone wall, which used to be the foundation for the rest of the house, led to an outdoor fireplace, which was formerly the kitchen.

Adana, their cook, huddled near a large pot hung over the fire and used a large spoon to ladle rice and fish onto wooden plates. Chickens scratched the ground in the side yard outside their coop, and a goat neighed out back.

He jumped down and turned to assist Lottie. When she was steady on the ground, he said, "Welcome to Calico Manor."

She surveyed the grounds with a hint of wonderment in her eyes and a small smile. Her chin tilted up as her focus followed the fields of cane halfway up Mount Misery, then lowered as her gaze swept over the house. She paused on the large twisted branches of the Saman tree. Some of its low limbs reached down as if to steady itself. "This is where you played as a boy?"

"I spent many hours in that tree."

She held his gaze, perhaps searching for the boy within. An easy smile swept across her lips.

He reached out to pull her in and kiss that alluring mouth. It teased him with its softness, but he stopped. Instead, he slid his hand around her back and escorted her over to where Marcus now stood at the hand pump, drying his hands after washing off the grime.

"Lottie, may I present to you Mr. Tallant, overseer of Calico Manor, it's land, and holdings."

Marcus passed the drying rag to Adana and strode in their direction.

Lottie bobbed a curtsy.

"Mr. Tallant, this is Lady Charlotte Winthrop…"

With one hand Marcus tipped his straw hat midstride.

"…my wife."

Marcus missed a step, but recovered quickly. His dark eyes met Nathan's with questions. Had Lottie noticed his surprise? The last thing he needed was for Lottie to think he was hiding their marriage. *Blast.* He should have mentioned he'd married earlier. He'd had plenty of time, but he was still adjusting to the idea. And with the unrest among the slaves and the problems with the cane, he'd been distracted. Now, he'd have a lot of questions to answer after Lottie returned to the inn.

"Delighted to meet you." Marcus passed a quick sideways glance at Nathan. "I knew Winthrop would someday spy a lovely Englishwoman in his travels and carry her to the altar."

Lottie giggled. "That's not exactly how it came about, but thank you for your kind words."

Marcus raised his brows. "Ah, I smell a tale." He gestured toward the outdoor seating area under the fans on the porch. "But sit and eat first. Winthrop can divulge how you made each other's acquaintance while we fill our stomachs." He flashed Nathan a sideways glance. "You know how I love a good story."

⁓

*L*ottie relished the feel of Nathan's strong hand pressed against the small of her back as he guided her up the few steps to the porch. They strolled to a small teak table, and Nathan pulled out a chair for her. Her heart pounded as she tried to absorb everything around her.

This would be her future. It wasn't the same as what she imagined with Anthony, but it felt intimate and just as thrilling. They would break their fast on the veranda. He'd watch his ships sail into port through the clearing as she read him letters from home. She'd have a warm bath prepared for when he returned from a long day in the field, and his favorite meal cooking over the outdoor hearth.

There was still so much she didn't know about him. Maybe she would find the answers she sought here. Maybe if she came to know and adore the things he knew and respected, maybe he could learn to love her. Maybe if she proved to him she could be a proper and dutiful wife, he'd bring her here to be with him.

Lottie unfolded her napkin and placed it in her lap, enjoying the cozy atmosphere of eating outside in the open breeze, much more than the stuffy formality of dining with her parents, each seated at the far ends of the table.

The midday meal consisted simply of rice and fish and was served by a slave woman named Adana. Her cocoa skin held a natural glow, and there was an exotic beauty about her wide dark eyes, prominent cheekbones, and plump lips. Her course hair was tied back with a rag, but she exuded an air as if this were her domain. The woman's dark eyes met Lottie's and held for a long moment until Lottie looked away.

The laborers poured in and sat under the Saman tree and anywhere else they could find shade to eat. Nathan motioned for Mr. Tallant to join them. The man assumed a seat across from Lottie with a gracious nod. He spoke to Nathan of the progress of harvesting the cane, and it was easy to see the two men held a mutual respect for one another.

Mr. Tallant sipped his drink and focused on her. "How have you liked island life so far? I'm assuming Mrs. Fielding is hosting your stay at the inn?"

Lottie dabbed at her lips with her napkin and set it in her lap to stall. "Captain and Mrs. Fielding are a lovely couple and most generous hosts, but I'm looking forward to residing here."

"Much work is needed in the main house to make it acceptable." Nathan shifted in his seat. "It may be quite a while."

"Knowing your anticipation to become the mistress of Calico manor, I shall endeavor to hurry things along." Mr. Tallant raised his glass to her in salute.

Nathan cleared his throat. "We must first focus on the harvest. I have buyers waiting."

As the two men went back to talking about shipments, Lottie took the chance to admire the similarities between them. Both were dark haired with tanned skin from the sun, and they carried themselves in a confident, but relaxed, manner. However, Nathan held an air of intensity, whereas Mr. Tallant seemed a bit more easygoing. He had a quick smile and a friendly manner.

As Adana approached to clear the table, Mr. Tallant complimented her meal and drew a smile from her lips. She'd seen a few stolen glances between them. Perhaps something was brewing between the pair, or would be soon. Adana cleared Mr. Tallant's and Nathan's plates, then turned to take Lottie's. The woman stilled as her eyes fell on her. She grasped a small sack dangling from a string around her neck and whispered something in Creole.

Nathan stiffened.

Mr. Tallant half rose out of his chair. "There's more work to be done in the kitchens. See to it."

Nathan turned a lethal stare on Mr. Tallant.

He raised his hands in front of his chest and rose from the table. "I'll speak with her." He bowed to Lottie, but there was a sympathy in his eyes she hadn't noticed earlier. "Lovely to meet you."

Nathan stared at the man's back until Mr. Tallant caught Adana's elbow and drew her aside.

"Come." Nathan rose and ushered Lottie from her chair. "Let me show you inside."

The pressure of his hand on her lower back didn't give her time to overhear Mr. Tallant's discussion. She turned to study her husband's face as they walked. "What was that about?"

"It's nothing." His face masked any emotion.

Lottie frowned, but let the matter drop so she didn't spoil her first glimpse of the house. As they stepped inside, she immediately fell in love with the cozy atmosphere of its whitewashed walls and unpolished wooden floors. The paint had worn from the top of the newel post where hands gripped it to turn the corner. Furniture was sparse, and it needed a woman's touch, for there were no rugs or curtains, but it held a quaint feel. The salon that would normally be used for receiving callers held only tables, which were strewn with various maps and navigating tools. The dining room off the back housed the same. Upon the large dining room table fit to suit over fifteen guests, rested more maps and ledger books spread wide open. Amazingly, Nathan's study was neat and tidy, except for the water stains on the wallpaper. They ascended the stairs to the second floor.

Nathan kept a marked distance between them. His hand didn't stray to her lower back to guide her through the house as it had earlier. It seemed as if a wall had been erected between them. She would have to find out what the words meant Adana had spoken.

"When I was a child, there were four chambers and several dressing rooms, but two of the rooms were destroyed in the storm." He pushed a door open wider to reveal a dresser and single bed, neatly made. "This is my chamber."

Lottie peeked inside, and his scent of salt, ocean air, and clean linen filled her nose. The bed rested against one wall, and across from it sat a writing desk with a neat stack of ledgers. A nearby antique umbrella stand, instead of holding umbrellas, was filled with rolled maps.

He nodded to another door but didn't open it. "The other room was the master chamber. It was badly damaged during the storm and is currently being used for storage."

Her lips parted to ask why he'd chosen to sleep in the smaller room and not the master, but she closed her mouth tight. Of course, it would be too painful to sleep in the room his parents had once occupied.

"As you can see, I never intended for a woman to live here."

She shrugged. "It could use a woman's touch."

"A touch?" He feigned serious. "I'll have to cancel the ship full of British designers I'd requested."

His teasing relaxed her stiff spine, and the glitter in his eyes summoned an inner shout of *Huzzah.*

She gestured to a door on the right. "And where does that door lead?"

He sobered and pulled it open to reveal a soft pink chamber. "This was Katherine's room."

She stole a quick peek and expected a twelve-year-old girl to come bounding from the dressing room at any moment. Nothing had been disturbed since her passing.

He gestured towards the stairs, and they both descended.

Outside, the laborers were finishing their midday meal. The women collected the dishes to be scrubbed down by the stream. They paused as Lottie passed, and each grabbed the pouch hanging around their necks.

Mr. Tallant raised a hand to stay them and sauntered over to speak to Nathan. While they discussed an irrigation matter, Adana peered up from her accumulated stack of plates. Keeping her gaze on Lottie, she leaned closer to another servant and whispered the same Creole words she'd said earlier.

A shiver trickled down her back. Nathan might not like it,

but if this was going to be her home and these women under her direction, she needed to know what was being said about her. At a break in the discussion, she addressed Mr. Tallant. "What did Adana say to me?"

The man's tan face paled around his hairline, and he flicked a glance at Nathan.

Nathan's hand grasped her elbow in a firm grip. "It's time for us to go. I have much work to do."

He pulled Lottie back a step before she planted her feet and refused to budge.

Mr. Tallant's gaze slid to Nathan. "Slaves are a superstitious lot."

"Truly." Lottie pulled her arm away from Nathan. "I'd like to know if our cook has a grievance with me so that we might get it cleared up." She attempted to add some humor. "I wouldn't want to find out later she's been spitting in my soup."

Mr. Tallant swallowed, and his Adam's apple bobbed.

Nathan reclaimed her elbow. "It's a cultural thing. Nothing to worry your head about."

Lottie ignored him. "I don't mean to insinuate Adana would do such a thing," she kept her gaze locked on Mr. Tallant, "but it is better for all when the lady of the house keeps in good standing with the cook." She hit him with bold confidence.

The disappointment she'd seen earlier in Mr. Tallant's eyes changed into a glint of respect. She touched his arm. "Please tell me. I'd like to know what I've done."

"It is nothing you've done."

"Then what is it?"

Mr. Tallant peered at Nathan.

Nathan sighed and his head sagged. "Tell her."

His eyes darkened with deep sorrow. "Adana sees the spirit of death upon you."

CHAPTER 19

Lord and Lady Carlton request the honor of your presence to dine at Montview Estate...

~ Invitation to Mister and Lady Nathaniel Winthrop

$\mathcal{L}$ ottie's blood turned to ice, and she fought to mask her surprise. Raising her chin, she pretended the words hadn't stunned her to the core. "Adana could probably say that about half the people on the island." With a careless shrug, she added, "We're all going to die someday, Mr. Tallant."

"It's time to go," Nathan's head bowed, and he rubbed the back of his neck. His other arm hooked through Lottie's.

She barely got out a farewell to Mr. Tallant before Nathan tossed her up into the carriage. He jumped in beside her and snapped the reins. The horses jolted and sped off down the lane.

Silence screamed between them. Did he believe Adana's words? "You don't believe in silly superstitions, do you?"

Nathan's knuckles turned white on the reins, but he continued to stare straight ahead as if he hadn't heard her.

Lottie dropped her gaze to her folded hands in her lap. "I don't believe Adana can foretell the future. Only God knows when my time is up, and even if it is to be soon, I'm not scared of death. I know I'll be in heaven with my Savior and Creator." She glanced at Nathan's rigid profile. "I refuse to be a slave to fear. I will live my life and entrust my future to the Lord."

Nathan remained quiet until he stood in the front foyer of the Cockleshell. He bid her goodbye with his usual peck on her forehead, and she withheld a weary sigh. Hadn't today changed their relationship? She turned and mounted the stairs before he saw the disappointment she could no longer mask.

"Lottie."

Her breath hitched. She'd only ascended a few steps when her name rolled off his lips. She paused, one hand gripping the carved railing, and faced him.

"I almost forgot." He stood in the doorway. "Be ready tomorrow at six. I will pick you up in the evening. We've been invited to the Carltons' dinner party in Sandy Point. Wear your best gown."

She pinched her lips together, but she couldn't hold back her smile.

His eyes held her as if memorizing the look upon her face. He paused a long moment before he tapped the doorframe and exited the building.

∼

*L*ottie slid a white satin glove up to her elbow while Franny pinned the last few curls of her hair. Nervous energy fluttered through her midsection and tingled in her extremities.

"There, miss." Franny stood back to admire her work. "You look splendid."

Lottie rose from her chair, her skirts swishing in a graceful cascade of silk. Franny held the looking glass up for her to see. The pale blue fabric of her gown matched her eyes and appeared to heighten the rich color of her hair. Franny had piled it high on top of her head in a mass of curls and ringlets as bright as a lighthouse beacon warding off ships from danger.

"Maybe I should wear a cap." She didn't need to draw unwanted attention, especially after yesterday. Did others believe as Adana does? Were they all waiting for her to succumb to death? Was Nathan? She could understand his concern after his family's deaths, but would he put any stock in a superstition?

Franny gasped. "No, my lady. A cap would spoil the effect."

"But it's so red." She lifted her hand to chew on a nail, but caught herself and dropped it back to her side. "It must be the teal color. I should change gowns."

"The teal makes your eyes sparkle." Franny lowered the looking glass. "Forgive me if I speak out of turn, but I believe it's simply nerves. You look stunning."

Lottie bit her bottom lip and squeezed Franny's hand. "I don't know what I would do without you." She pressed her hands against her churning stomach. "I'm being silly. It's merely that I want tonight to go well, and I'm afraid I'll do something to ruin it."

"I have faith in you, my lady." Franny held the mirror up in front of Lottie. "Look at the woman before you. With her striking hair and incomparable beauty, Mr. Winthrop won't be able to take his eyes off you."

Lottie stared at her image in the mirror. Her skin was pale, but her color high, and her red hair stood out like a flame. Her mother hated her hair, but it was proof of the courage of her ancestors. She was of their lineage, which meant boldness ran in her blood.

"Indeed. Tonight, I will woo my husband's guarded heart. And, if that doesn't work," she flashed a teasing smile, "then perhaps I can incite his jealousy."

She'd given Nathan plenty of time to adjust. Yes, he hadn't wanted to marry her, but it was time he made the best of it. She couldn't be imagining the spark between them. Yesterday had solidified it in her mind. The day had been magical. They'd spoken to each other and teased one another like longtime friends—until Adana had ruined it. But Nathan was beginning to care for her. She knew it. She willed it to be so.

"It's time he made me his wife in the Biblical sense."

Franny giggled.

Drat! Had she spoken that out loud?

Biblical. "That's it, Franny." Lottie paced the short length of the room, organizing her thoughts. "I don't know why I haven't done this already. I've prayed for Nathan, for his crew, for safe travels, and for myself, but I haven't prayed for our marriage."

She grabbed both of Franny's hands and pulled her down to sit upon the bed. "Will you pray with me?"

"Of course."

They closed their eyes, and Lottie prayed, "Heavenly Father. Your Word says a man shall leave his father and his mother, and cleave unto his wife, and they shall be one flesh. Let it be so with our marriage. Bless it and let it be fruitful. Let tonight be the start of a new beginning. In Your name. Amen."

As Franny echoed her *amen*, a knock sounded upon the door.

"Lady Winthrop." A servant called, and Franny jumped up to answer. "Mr. Winthop awaits her ladyship in the foyer."

Franny informed the footman Lady Winthrop would be right down.

Inhale, exhale. Lottie sucked in a deep breath and released it. She felt as nervous as when she'd been presented at court. *Please God, let this go well.* She nodded to Franny and strode to the door she held open. "God has been with me thus far. I have nothing to fear."

She swept out into the hall with her chin high. Laughter rose from the tavern below. She paused partway down the stairs to inhale a steady breath, but instead spied Nathan's well-defined profile below. He studied a painting on the wall of a naval battle between British warships and the Spanish.

He appeared so much as he had the first night she met him at the Middleton ball, that her heart doubled its pace. His snowy-white cravat contrasted against his tanned skin and dark waves of hair. He stood tall with one hand pushing back the side of his jacket to rest comfortably on his hip. Nathan easily commanded a ship and a ballroom.

Her chest swelled. He'd kept food in the bellies of his laborers after the loss of his family. He'd purchased a small fleet when the sugar crop showed signs of slowing. He established trade relations with Britain, Central America, and South America, and displayed the business intuition that drew the respect of his peers and the peerage.

This man was her husband.

Her blood surged. Would she please him as much as he made her proud?

He leaned in closer to the painting.

Her satin slippers made no sound as she descended. She repeated the mantra, *God is with me. He is with me.*

The last stair squeaked under her weight, and Nathan's eyes snapped in her direction.

She froze.

His bold gaze raked over her from head to foot and slowly back up again. A glint of satisfaction lit his eyes, and a slow smile spread across his lips.

Her fears melted as he strolled over and lifted his hand. She placed hers in his. Even though his touch was light, the firmness of his grasp hinted at the reserve of harnessed power.

He bowed and brushed a kiss on the top of her satin glove. His gaze bathed her in admiration. "You are a vision."

His words flowed through her, tingling from her scalp all the way to her extremities.

Quiet settled over the adjoining taproom as the constant din of laughter and drunken joviality died. Lottie glanced over her shoulder to discover all the patrons of the tavern staring unabashedly at her and Nathan. She gripped his hand and tried to hide behind his large form, but he shifted out of the way so she faced the room of dram drinkers.

He lifted her hand. "May I present Lady Charlotte Amelia Winthrop, *my wife.*"

He said the last words with such vehemence that cheers rose from the room, and the men lifted their glasses in salute. One man's voice shouted over the rest. "Sign me up to be a sea rover if it means I can share in those sort of spoils."

Lottie's cheeks burned hotter than the tropical midday sun.

Nathan ignored the man's comment and tucked her hand into the crook of his arm. Captain Fielding, dressed in his formal captain's garb, led his wife down the hall. Julia wore a dark indigo gown trimmed in lace that set off her exquisite form perfectly. Together, the couples exited the building.

The sun hovered over the ocean in a blaze of color when they stopped to await the carriage. Nathan glanced at the horizon, then at her. He leaned in until his lips brushed the tiny curls dangling near her temple. "Look, the sun is attempting to emulate the rich color of your hair. I believe nature is jealous."

Her stomach flipped, not merely from his remark but from the intimacy of the moment.

The footman brought around a barouche open carriage, and the gentlemen aided the ladies up. All the while, Lottie's heart thumped in her chest. She licked her lips and mentally thanked God. It seemed she'd been granted a prompt answer to her prayer.

As Nathan settled in next to Lottie, his clean fresh-air aroma billowed around her. Captain and Mrs. Fielding sat across from them, then Paul assumed the reigns and drove the team through the narrow streets.

"You are in for a treat, Lady Winthrop." Captain Fielding

draped his arm over the backrest and ran his thumb down Julia's arm. "These dinner parties used to be frequent on the island, but alas, have become fewer as of late."

"And why is that?" Lottie asked.

"Absentee planters." Nathan shifted in his seat and tugged on the knees of his breeches. "Very few planters live here anymore. Most made their fortunes and returned to England, leaving their holdings in the hands of attorneys and overseers."

Captain Fielding crossed one leg over the other. "The Carltons returned after they discovered both their attorney and their overseer were pocketing more than their share."

"Good help is hard to find on the island." Julia pursed her lips. "But tonight, we shall forget about island politics and enjoy ourselves." She patted her husband's leg. "Right, my love?"

"*Sim, meu amor.*" A jaunty smile lit the Captain's lips, and his hooded eyes slid a sensual gaze over his wife.

Nathan scratched his nose. "Portuguese?"

Captain Fielding nodded.

Deep in her heart, Lottie sighed. Would she ever experience a love like Julia and the captain's? She stared at her folded hands, afraid that if Nathan glanced her way, he'd see the yearning in her eyes and either become more reserved or scoff at her childishness.

Julia arched a brow at Lottie. "Are you ready for all eyes to be on you?"

Lottie stiffened. "What do you mean?"

"The island is small and word travels quickly. Everyone is going to be buzzing about the redheaded Englishwoman Nathaniel Winthrop has made his wife." She eyed Nathan. "There will be plenty of questions asked and unasked. I hope you are prepared."

Lottie could sense the coil inside Nathan tighten. Was Julia trying to get a rise out of him?

He merely shrugged. "As always, my affairs are none of their concern."

His affairs? Was he speaking of their marriage? His words seemed laced with secrecy. They had only been recently married, but what else could he be referring to? The voices of the men in the market echoed in her mind. *I heard dat he may be chummy wit da pirate king, Jean Lafitte.*

Julia nodded towards the water. "Look, the sun is setting." A gentle breeze off the ocean ruffled their gowns.

The foursome watched as the yellow ball melted into the ocean, changing the sky from orange to a pinkish-coral. The captain nestled Julia closer to his side. Their closeness made the hand's width gap separating Nathan and Lottie feel like the size of a British frigate.

A glow among the jungle trees caught Lottie's eye. The carriage turned toward the mountain, and Lottie gripped her seat tighter due to the sharp incline. The light dwindled as the jungle canopy blocked the remainder of the sunset.

In the dimness of dusk, Lottie could barely make out Nathan's silhouette next to her. Paul steered the team to the left. The canopy opened, returning the light, and the ground leveled off. Tall palm trees lined either side of the lane leading to a large plantation house with its windows aglow. Violins serenaded, and the sound of laughter drifted across the grass. As the carriage pulled in front of the house, Lottie could hear her mother's voice ticking off a list of commands. Instead of smoothing her skirts, checking her hair for any loose tendrils, and straightening her shoulders to appease her mother, she did so because she was a lady.

Nathan stepped down and turned to aid Lottie out of the carriage.

Despite the heat, her hands felt ice cold. He placed one on his arm and strolled through the entrance of the Carlton's plantation as proudly as a duke gracing the home of the peerage.

He passed his card to a footman, who didn't read it before announcing, "Mister and Lady Nathaniel Winthrop of Calico Manor."

Lottie might have walked into any house in the English countryside. The Carltons' plantation house was decked with the finest wood moldings, fabrics, furniture, and paintings. Twenty or so people milled about in their finery as footmen passed out drinks and finger sandwiches.

Julia's prediction had been correct. Many a gaze traveled their way. Some groups stopped their conversations. Others leaned in to begin speaking.

Nathan ushered her straight to their hosts. "Lord and Lady Carlton, thank you for the honor of being your guest this evening." He bowed his head. "Please let me introduce you to my wife, Lady Charlotte Winthrop."

Lottie curtsied.

Lord and Lady Carlton dipped their heads in return. "Delightful to finally meet you, Lady Winthrop." Mama would have approved of Lady Carlton's decorum. The woman held herself in a regal manner. Tiny lines creasing the sides of her eyes made her appear of a similar age to Julia. "I must admit I have been curious to meet the woman who returned with Mr. Winthrop on the *Katherine*. He had not made it known he was seeking a wife."

"Lady Winthrop is the daughter of Lord and Lady Etheridge," Nathan said.

Lady Carlton reared back. "I-I'm acquainted with your mother." For a brief second, she lost her polite composure. "She is an—er—unforgettable lady."

Lottie bit the inside of her lip to keep from smiling. "Indeed."

"Quite so." Nathan didn't hold back his wry smile. "However, please let it be noted that my wife takes more after her father's side of the family."

"How delightful." Lady Carlton visibly relaxed, and then

noticed her gaffe. "For your father, I mean. I'm certain he's quite proud."

"He was reluctant to see her go." Nathan nodded to their hosts and pulled Lottie further into the house, pausing to introduce her to people as they passed.

The room was heavily weighted towards the men. Several military lieutenants and sergeants were present, their bright red coats standing out among the crowd. As the drinks flowed, some younger corporals gawked openly at her as if they hadn't seen a female in years. Nathan rested a possessive hand on top of hers.

"Good to see you back, Winthrop." An impeccably dressed man with a tightly trimmed beard clapped Nathan on the arm. Nathan introduced her to the man, who he said was a planter from Sandy Point. The fellow inquired about business and dealings before turning his attention upon Lottie.

"And how did you fare on the long sea voyage, Lady Winthrop?"

Lottie's heart skipped a beat as she searched for a proper answer.

"Lady Winthrop found the open sea air refreshing."

Nathan's creative response welled up a fit of giggles in the back of Lottie's throat. His dry sense of humor heightened his appeal, drawing her like a ship into shore. She turned her head, pressed her cheek against his shoulder, and feigned a cough in an attempt to smother her laughter.

A footman jingled the dinner bell, and the guests made their way into the dining room.

Silver tiered candelabras illuminated the room and sparkled off the crystal goblets and silver flatware. Footmen dressed in livery pulled out their chairs and placed silk napkins on their laps. Soups were ladled into fine china bowls, and rum punch flowed freely. Lottie chatted amicably with a man from Bristol, Lord Sperry, who'd recently returned for the harvest. He prattled on about who they knew in common in London, and Lottie, surrounded by the comforts of home, almost forgot she wasn't there.

Nathan's presence by her side and his clean tropical scent returned her to her senses. He relaxed into his chair, and his arm brushed hers. That slight touch invigorated her senses. He regarded the lieutenant with relaxed indifference, as if only half paying attention, but he was qualifying every word the man spoke. The realization spread warmth through her chest. She'd come to know her husband's slightest nuances. For the first time, she truly felt like a wife.

Nathan, Captain Fielding, and one of the lieutenants discussed the slave revolts in Jamaica and the costs of Britain, once again, waging war with America. Each time Nathan commented, his baritone voice enlivened a part of her brain, and she found herself politely disengaging from Lord Sperry. Nathan's masculine baritone flowed over her skin and reverberated through her.

"If Britain wants to win this war, they must first take New Orleans." Nathan lifted his dark gaze to the lieutenant.

"New Orleans is already in His Majesty's pocket. The area is a conglomerate of French, Creoles, and Spanish. They hold no loyalty to America. They will happily step aside and let our royal troops take control to avoid a bloody battle."

"It may prove to be more challenging than that." Nathan cleared his throat. "It will depend upon where Lafitte's loyalties lie."

"What influence could a dastardly pirate hold? Not enough to battle a fleet of frigates."

"Bah." Captain Fielding waved a dismissive hand. "You forget Lafitte was trained at our military academy here on the island." Captain Fielding inclined his head toward Nathan. "Isn't that right?"

Nathan answered with a single nod.

Julia set down her glass, and her lips curved into a shrewd smile. "Isn't there a rumor of Lafitte putting a reward out for Governor Claiborne's arrest?"

The lieutenant, whose face had become red with drink, perked up. "Indeed, I have heard of this tale regarding the Louisiana statesmen."

"Of course." Captain Fielding smiled wide. "Lafitte is a wily one."

Eyes all over the table stopped and stared at the captain.

"Governor Claiborne wanted to put an end to Lafitte's smuggling." Captain Fielding met the eyes of each of the guests to ensure their attention. "So he posted a five hundred dollar reward for the capture of Jean Lafitte. Lafitte strolled down the main street, carefree as a wren and confident as a falcon in flight, and stopped to read every posted proclamation nailed to the lampposts. Each time, he grinned like a thief and chuckled to himself."

The lieutenant swigged his drink and hissed out a bout of laughter. "'Tis the very truth."

The captain glared at the man, apparently irritated by the interruption. Then he continued. "The next morning, all the notices were torn down and new proclamations were posted stating a fifteen hundred dollar reward for anyone who captured William C. C. Claiborne, the Governor of Louisiana, and delivered him to Grand Terre."

The few women present gasped. Several men appeared indignant, but most of the men raised their glasses and saluted the pirate for putting one over on the American government.

A crooked smile curved Nathan's mouth, but he didn't participate in the toast.

Several more tales were told about Lafitte before the topic turned to the blight of pirates and privateers increasing their business in the area. Although owning slaves was condoned, slave trading had become illegal. Unfortunately, its ban brought an entire underground trade to life. The term *black ivory* was spoken in hushed tones during several conversations. Lottie deduced from gathering snatches of conversations that it meant the smuggling of African slaves. Nathan remained quiet during the night's conversation until dinner finished and the guests streamed outside for a bit of dancing.

Nathan's firm hand guided her down the steep torch-lit path toward the beach. Seagrass brushed against the edges of her gown. Rich notes of the orchestra serenaded as they approached, having already relocated to a gazebo near a small dock in the inlet. A footman stood where the beach began and collected their slippers or shoes so they could dance without sand filling them.

Lottie peered up into Nathan's shadowed face. "If this is common for all island parties, then you truly did grow up barefoot in the sand."

The brilliant white of Nathan's smile reflected the light of the full moon. "Come along now." He pulled her toward the place where couples had gathered on a makeshift dance floor. "I've been longing to dance with you again since the night we met."

He'd longed to dance with her? Tingles ran under her skin and settled into the pit of her stomach.

He pulled her into the closed stance of a waltz. Couples swirled around in the sand, the soft floor not hindering their dancing at all. Nathan held her a bit closer than what would be considered appropriate in an English ballroom. However, Captain Fielding held Julia the same way, and even their hosts enjoyed the relaxed stance. Mother would never approve. But Lottie didn't care. The thrill of being in Nathan's strong arms, his focus solely on her, was a heady sensation.

Couples traded partners for the next set, and Lottie danced with Captain Fielding, then the two lieutenants, and Lord Sperry. With such a shortage of women, it only seemed kind to partner as many dances as possible so that every gentleman could get a turn. The other women of the group appeared as flushed as Lottie felt.

A younger man in uniform she'd been introduced to earlier bowed and requested the next dance. The potent smell of spirits reeked from his person, and he could barely lift his gaze to her face under weighted lids. She opened her mouth to excuse herself for refreshment, but Nathan stepped beside her and explained the dance was already taken.

Winded from previous dances, but unwilling to miss out on another dance with Nathan, Lottie accepted his arm.

A group of slaves dressed in livery lined up on either side of the gazebo. The two on the ends carried long drums. The orchestra paused, but Nathan continued to pull her toward the dancing area.

The drummers struck a beat. One lifted what appeared to be a cowbell and joined in.

Lottie hesitated. "I haven't heard this sort of music before."

Nathan gripped her in a closed hold. "It's common on the islands of Trinidad and Tobago. The planters there allow their slaves' special privileges to perform. Lord and Lady Carlton stopped there on the return voyage and found the music so splendid, they purchased a Trinidadian slave to teach theirs to perform. It has become an island favorite."

"I'm at a loss as to the steps."

"You merely need to move to the rhythm. It's a slow four-beat instead of the three rise and fall beats of the waltz."

He must have felt her hesitation for he said, "Relax and follow me."

He promenaded her on his arm, and she quickly picked up the four steps. The dancing went against everything she'd been taught. Instead of a stiff carriage with her back straight and her chin high, they moved with relaxed grace. Instead of the quick high steps and jetés, the steps were slower, looser, swaying her hips. He moved her into several spins, smiling as she mastered them.

If only her mother could see her now. She'd faint dead away.

The song ended, and the drummers began another beat. Nathan guided her toward a servant passing out refreshments and handed her a drink. A gentle breeze picked up, cooling Lottie's warm skin as she sipped.

Nathan leaned in close enough that she could feel his radiating heat. His breath swayed the loose tendrils of hair and tickled her ear, reminding her of the night of their first dance.

"You must be overheated. Let's take in the air and enjoy the breeze."

She nodded as she sent him a cautious smile and followed him as they escaped farther down the beach. The moonlight reflected off the waves, and the cool sand softened their steps. He laced his fingers through hers, and they strolled hand in hand as if they were a love match. A vast canopy of stars twinkled above their heads, and Lottie whispered *thank you* to her maker.

"Are you enjoying yourself?" Nathan's husky voice reverberated above the ebb and flow of the nearby surf.

"Immensely." She didn't bother reining in her smile. With the exhilaration of her fingers encased in the warmth of his strong hand, it would have bubbled up in one way or another.

"I thought it might remind you of home." His steps slowed. "Have you been missing...?" He rubbed the back of his neck with his other hand. "Rather...have you been homesick?"

"Not when I'm with you." Her breath hitched at the boldness of her statement.

He stopped.

She searched his face for any hint of what he was thinking, but the dim light shadowed his face.

His hand cupped her cheek.

She leaned into its warmth. Even in the darkness, she could feel the weight of his gaze upon her.

"Lottie, I…"

Something crawled over her foot.

She screeched and jumped forward into Nathan's arms. Her feet danced a lively jig until they rested on top of his. Her fingers dug into his arms. "There's something in the sand."

CHAPTER 20

My wishes I beg you to gratify, for the pang of your
absence is too great for me to bear. I simply must see you,
tonight.

~ *Note secretly delivered to Franny*

*L*ottie clung to Nathan as he gripped her elbows and
steadied her, then inspected the ground. A large
white-toothed smile flashed at her before Nathan
chuckled. "They're sea turtles—newly hatched." He crouched
down, pulling her with him, for a closer look.

Little flippers flicked up sand as the tiny turtles strove to
drag their round bodies to the ocean. There must have been ten
or fifteen of them scrambling about the beach.

One waved its flippers in the air and pushed its head against
the sand.

"Oh my. I overturned it." She moved to flip it over, but
Nathan stilled her hand.

"He's got it. Watch."

Sure enough, the little guy craned its neck, pushing its nose into the sand, and righted itself. It sat dazed for a moment before working those flippers once again.

"It's such a far trek to the ocean. Should we help them?"

"The struggle is what gives them the strength to face even greater dangers later."

She squeezed his arm to keep her balance in her squat position. "They're cute little things aren't they?"

Nathan nodded, but his gaze remained on her and not on the adorable little creatures.

"How amazing to see nature making a way. How do they know what to do? Which way to go?"

Two more flicked past their ankles.

Nathan picked up one with his index finger and thumb and held it up for them to examine. Its little fins rowed the air. He set it back down facing the other way, but the turtle steered back towards the ocean. "The hand of God must guide them."

The ocean washed over those in the lead. Several of them rolled over with the tide. The ones that landed on their backs righted themselves and kept moving.

Watching these vulnerable, tiny babies doggedly fight their way to the place they belonged was truly special. Something she'd be lucky to ever witness again in her life. And she'd gotten to see it with Nathan.

One turtle toppled down a ridge in the sand and lost the ground it had worked so hard to gain. She couldn't resist aiding it along. It moved towards the water, eager to catch up with its brothers and sisters. Lottie dusted the sand off her fingers and straightened, then turned to glance at her husband.

Nathan's gaze stole her breath.

He watched her with such intense longing her breath caught. He grabbed both of her hands, and lowered his head until their foreheads almost touched. "I'm sorry for not being around more, and I apologize for sorely misjudging you. You're kind-hearted, and you hold a zeal for life that I and many others envy. You're stronger than I first believed."

Her heart melted at the sweetness of his words, and she swayed toward him. Her eyes lowered to his strong chin and chiseled mouth. His arm snaked around her back, drawing her close until there was only a breath between them.

Was he going to kiss her? Was this the moment for which she'd prayed?

Laughter sounded from the guests, breaking the spell.

Nathan pulled away. "The hour is growing late. We need to return." Nathan slid his hand down the length of her arm to grasp her fingers. Her chest tightened for it meant an end to a spectacular evening, but she allowed herself to be led back over the dunes and seagrass towards the party. She yearned for his kiss, and not merely a peck on the forehead, but a true measure of the passion he restrained. For the moment, she'd settle for her hand wrapped in his. A few guests had dispersed, but many were merely getting started as more glasses of rum circulated to cool their thirst and overheated bodies.

His protective arm drew her closer to his side. The reflection of the torch flame writhed in the dark pools of his eyes.

He nodded to the captain, but the captain waved him off. "Julia and I are reluctant to leave. You two run along. Lord Carlton offered to have his coachman return us."

They extended farewells and gratitude to their hosts, then hiked up the path to the house and waited for the groomsmen to bring around their carriage. Without the dancing to keep her blood pumping, Lottie's skin quickly cooled. Although the air temperature was still tepid, the night breeze lifted the hairs on her arms and sent a shiver along her skin.

"Are you chilled?" He shrugged out of his jacket and placed it around her shoulders.

Its warmth enveloped her, and she snuggled into the lingering scent of him.

His carriage arrived, and he aided Lottie up into her seat. Instead of taking the seat across from her as was customary when riding as lone male and female, he settled into the cushion next to her. The fabric of her gown shifted tingling her skin like a caress.

"Are you still chilled?" he asked.

She shook her head the barest amount, but he must not have seen, for he slid his arm around her shoulder and drew her up against his side.

Other than the one time on the ship and the lesson in shooting, he'd never held her this close. She fit comfortably against the firmness of his side, and she even dared to lean her head a bit against his chest. Was that his heart beating so profoundly, or was it her own?

"Did you enjoy yourself this evening?"

"It was lovely." A sigh slid from her lips. "I don't want it to end."

"I figured you'd be dead on your feet after all that dancing."

"I'm certain I'll pay dearly in the morning."

"You wanted to linger longer to socialize?"

"Oh, no. I do believe I spoke with everyone."

"If it wasn't the dancing or the socializing, what didn't you want to end?"

She closed her eyes and breathed in the salty air and the clean scent of his soap. "This." Her voice barely registered above a whisper. "I don't want this to end."

He stiffened beside her, and remained so for what seemed an age. When he finally moved, he shifted away from Lottie.

Why had she laid her heart open for the slaughter once again? Hadn't she learned her lesson the last time?

Without his heat, her body ached to reach out and draw him back toward her, but if he needed more time—more space— perhaps she should respect his wishes.

"Lottie." Her name rolled off his lips like a caress. "Look

at me."

She opened her eyes to discover his face within inches of hers. Even in the shadowy light of the moon, she could make out his firm chin and finely molded lips.

His hand rose, and his strong fingers slid around the soft skin at the nape of her neck. She could feel the light scraping of his callouses, but she didn't mind. They were a testimony to his resilience.

"You deserve the moon and the stars, but I don't have the moon nor the stars to give. All I can offer is problems."

"You said problems are the soil in which miracles grow," her voice trailed into a whisper.

Moonlight glinted off the white of his slow smile. "My mother used to say that phrase. I wish I had its optimism." His thumb caressed the sensitive skin of her neck. "I haven't witnessed many miracles."

Although the light was scarce, she sensed the intensity of his gaze boring into her soul.

His thumb stilled. "Unless I count you."

Lottie's lips parted as she inhaled a wispy gasp.

"At first, I wanted to protect myself from you, but now..." He swallowed. In the glint of silvery moonlight, his profile shifted and a muscle twitched in his jaw. "I find the need to protect you from me."

The rawness of his words tore at her heart, and a delicious shiver swept over her. His lips brushed hers, teasing like the summer breeze. She tilted her head back and offered her mouth to him. Her heart thundered, surprised by her own daring.

He swooped down and captured her lips in a strong but gentle kiss. She tasted the salt on his skin. He gathered her closer, and she clung to the front of his shirt. His drugging kiss deepened. Her fingers slid up the hard surface of his chest and wound around his neck. She'd waited for this moment for so long—it seemed her whole life. She reveled in the feeling of his warm velvet lips, the strength of his arms enfolded around her, and the thoroughness of his kiss as if he was memorizing the moment—savoring it.

$\sim$

*T*he change in the sound of the horses' hooves as they moved from packed earth to the cobblestones of the dock area awoke Nathan from his passionate haze. Lottie's soft curves fit all too well against him, and broke loose a tumult of emotions he'd struggled daily to suppress. How many nights since their first dance had he awoken aboard his ship or in the small chamber of his room dreaming of holding her, kissing her soundly? The intoxicating effect of drinking in her sweetness left him craving more, much more than he'd ever anticipated in his dreams.

Male voices rose above the sound of the surf. Nathan pulled back from the luscious redheaded titian so soft and tempting in his arms. Her slight moan of disappointment drew his smile. He leaned his forehead against hers, reluctant to let her go. He fought to even out his breathing. She appeared to be as affected as he, for the white expanse of her skin rose and fell in rapid succession, straining against the bodice of her gown.

He gently pulled down on her arms still entwined around his neck. "There is passion hidden behind that compliant façade."

Lottie lowered her gaze and rolled her lips. Even in the dark moonlight, he knew a becoming blush stained her cheeks.

He trailed a knuckle down the side of her face. "You're a most pleasant surprise." It took everything in him to pull back completely and settle in his seat. "We're almost to the Cockleshell."

He chuckled as her hand flew to her hair, trying to right the damage done by his fingers.

The space between them returned some of his sanity. *How*

many more mishaps do you need to prove you truly are cursed? How can you provide for her when your shipments continue to be looted by pirates? What would it take for you to accept your life is destined for ruin—the loss of the plantation? A ship sinking?

Lottie's death?

Nathan shook off the wretched thoughts. He draped an arm over Lottie's shoulders and drew her closer to his side as if her sweet nature could chase away his demons.

"Nathan?"

His pride swelled at her use of his given name.

"I don't want to be your wife in name only."

His heart leapt, but quickly recoiled. She didn't know what she was asking. She didn't know the truth of it all.

"I want to be your wife fully. I want to bear your children and be by your side. It doesn't matter if the house isn't suitable. I'll make do. If it means sailing the seas, then I will stay above deck until my stomach adjusts. Or, if it means digging together in the dirt, I will happily do so. I merely want to be with you."

The tenderness of her words pierced his defenses. No matter how he tried to shield his heart, her light illuminated the dark places. He ran a hand over the lower half of his face. "My only intention has been to protect you."

A cloud shadowed the moon, and other than the faint glow of the oil lamp posts along the road, they were shrouded in darkness.

"Protect me? From whom? From what? How can you protect me when you're not around? Wouldn't it be simpler if I were near you?"

"I'm protecting you from me."

He felt her stiffen. "I don't understand."

"No, you don't. I haven't been forthright with you." He felt for her hands and scooped them into his own. "I desire you, more than you know, but..." His stubborn side resisted, but she deserved to know the full truth. "I'm cursed."

Anger at the injustice of it coursed through his veins. It was difficult to hear the words spoken. "And if you're close, I fear harm could come to you."

The breeze pushed the cloud along, and the moonlight spilled on her upturned face and reflected off her glossy curls. Her eyes were liquid pools, and her full lips tempted him to lean in for another kiss.

She shook her head. "That's ridiculous. Why would you believe such a thing?"

Most women would pull away from him, but Lottie stayed put.

"I didn't at first, but then the tragedies started."

She squeezed his hands. "You're not the cause of your mother's and siblings' deaths. They died of the fever, as many others have."

"There have been countless other events, but their deaths were the most tragic. I did everything I could to save them." His voice cracked, and he swallowed the familiar gnawing ache of their loss. "But they died anyway."

Lottie's tears splattered like the first drops of rain upon the lapel of his jacket.

He closed his eyes and summoned the strength to regain control over his emotions. "And that was only the beginning. My father died in a carriage accident, the land stopped producing, our sugar profits dropped by half. I worked the fields alongside the laborers. I had promised my brother, Amory, I'd turn the land around. We had one good crop, but the next year, we were hit with a blight. I could no longer count on the land to provide. I was still in denial. I hadn't put two and two together, and I lashed out at God. How could he take so much away from me?

"Thankfully, I had saved the profits from the previous season, so I purchased a ship. Things seemed to improve. My earlier schooling paid off, and we made enough of a profit to purchase a second ship. But then, one night, a storm came and tossed the boat around like a toy. The waves crashed over the bow. We'd have sunk if it hadn't been for Captain Fielding being at the helm. It was then I realized I truly had been cursed."

"Bad things happen because the earth is cursed, not you."

"You don't understand. A curse was cast upon me." His throat constricted as if the witch herself gripped his neck, but he needed to get the words out. Lottie must understand that he was the danger. "I saw her and heard it with my own ears."

"Who would do such a thing?" Her voice shook with either fear or outrage.

"The slaves call them obeah women. They practice black magic."

"How did you run into a woman like that?"

He released her hands and massaged the tight knot in his shoulder. "I'm not proud of my actions. I was naive, hotheaded, and barely a man. It all started when I visited a neighboring plantation to see how they prospered. The owner had purchased a group of slaves fresh from the auction. He was breaking them in when two tried to run. The overseer yelled to catch them. I sprinted after them and was led on a vexing chase, but the woman stumbled. I tackled her to the ground. She struggled, and I got an elbow to the nose. Blood gushed everywhere. She continued to fight, and I had no choice except to pin her, but then she spit in my face."

He closed his eyes. He hated himself for what he had done. "I hauled her up and handed her to the overseer." He swallowed back his shame. "She didn't even flinch, but her eyes hardened, and she muttered strange words under her breath."

His palms grew slick, and he wiped them down the length of his thighs. The events of that day still churned his stomach. "The overseer yanked her to a post by her hair. He said he'd show me how they treated rebellious slaves. He tied her hands to a stump and ripped the shirt off her back. I don't remember him pulling out the whip or even how many floggings she received. All I see is her dark eyes staring straight into me as she screamed. The overseer held nothing back. I couldn't stand there and watch a human be brutally tortured, so I seized the overseer's arm. The woman raised her head and cackled with delirious laughter. She yelled in plain English, 'I curse you.' I don't know how she even knew English or those words, but she said them clear as day while she peered over her shoulder directly at me. Later, she died from her wounds. The other slave escaped into the mountains."

The night air suddenly left him chilled. Lottie held completely still. Was she in shock? Did she hate him as much as he hated himself? Was she wishing she'd never married an unmerciful, cursed man? If only he could go back and undo all the horrible events of that day.

He tried to keep the tremor out of his voice. "I had blocked the entire incident from my mind. Even after the fever took my mother and sister. It wasn't until the night of the storm. Something someone said triggered the memory. The captain reacted the same way you did. He laughed and asked if I believed in black magic. I said no, but my mind started a running log of suspicious events. As they continued to add up, I had a harder time believing it was nonsense."

"Maybe my mind is slipping." He sighed. "Maybe I should be locked up in Bedlam, but since then, two of my ships have been plundered by pirates, and one was boarded by a British press gang. Part of its crew was impressed into His Majesty's Navy, and two of my men were killed. Then I was caught in an assignation upon your character, which destroyed my chances of establishing an agreement with the British Navy to sail with us as escort. It's impossible to have all these situations pile up and not start to question whether the slave woman's hex was real."

"You tried to intervene."

"I didn't try to early enough."

Lottie shifted in her seat to face him and placed her hands on his upper arms. "You are not cursed, Nathaniel Winthrop. I don't believe it, and I *won't* believe it. Indeed, you had a string of awful and unfortunate events, but life this side of heaven isn't going to be easy. Jesus said we will have trouble, but to take heart because He has overcome the world. Living in fear isn't living. I should know. I lived in fear of displeasing my mother all of my life. You may have considered it bad luck to have been caught together in that room, but I now see it as an answer to my prayers."

He raised his brows. "You didn't believe it a blessing when you begrudgingly walked down the aisle." He chuckled. "As I recall, you forced your vows through tight lips."

"I was afraid. Being forced to marry was not how I envisioned God answering my prayers, but God sees what I can't. He turns all things around for His good, even my mistakes." She sighed. "Especially, my mistakes. All this has taught me to trust Him. He is greater than my fears, and He's more powerful than the curse of a slave woman."

She reached up and her full lips captured his in a persuasive kiss. Then she pulled back enough to say, "I'm not afraid anymore."

His mind reeled from the heady sensation of her soft mouth. When had his wife become so brave? If only he held the same confidence. He backed away and cupped her face in his hands, memorizing the way her eyes revealed everything she was thinking. "I don't want anything to happen to you."

"I could live to be one hundred, or I could die tonight. Only God knows when my time is up." She placed her hands over his. "Until then, I want to live life and live it to the full."

The carriage stopped in front of the Cockleshell. Boisterous laugher rang inside.

He wavered, his mind weighing the arguments. Did he dare believe her? Did he dare take a chance? "Lottie, I—"

"After all you went through with losing your mother and siblings and father, would you have preferred never to have known them? Was the pain so great you'd wipe them from your memory?"

Certainty wrapped around the old familiar ache. "Never."

"Then, please, don't wipe me from yours. Give me a chance. Give us a chance."

Paul unlatched the carriage door and pulled out the steps.

Grateful for the chance to gather his thoughts, Nathan alighted and helped her descend. Her fingers trembled, and her eyes were shimmery pools. Her words sounded so sure, her argument sound, yet her hands quaked. Was she nervous or frightened? Of him? Of the curse?

Her mere presence drove him to distraction. How was a man to think clearly?

He escorted her into the inn and hesitated in the front lobby. The crowd in the taproom had dispersed, except for a few men slouched over their pints of ale. She peered at him with wishful eyes. Their vivid blue held a calm reassurance that wiped away his doubt. She was a miracle. His heart clenched. Had God blessed him, and he'd been too blind to see it? Lottie had been honest with her feelings, and now here she stood, her soft mouth beckoning him. A tiny sliver of her pink tongue moistened her lips.

His decision was made. "I'll walk you to your room."

Her brilliant smile was reward enough, but he had much more in mind. He only made it to the steps when his self-discipline slipped. He scooped an arm around her waist and pulled her into an alcove behind a bookshelf. His hands plunged into her thick hair, and his mouth claimed hers in a searing kiss. She melted into him and responded with reckless abandon. Pins scattered about their feet as he trailed a path to her earlobe for a nibble and then down the tender skin of her neck.

She was his. She was his wife. His miracle. And he was never going to let her go. Tonight he would do what he should have done the first night they were together. He would unite them.

He released a low growl and pulled away, only to hurry her up the stairs. He felt young again. The weight of his problems fell from his shoulders, releasing the vigor of a young lad. She slowed at her door and fumbled for the key tied on a ribbon around her wrist.

She yanked it off. The metal key slid out of her shaky fingers and fell to the floor.

It was taking too long. He reached down and snatched it up, but before sliding it into the lock, he pressed her back against the door and kissed her speechless.

A female voice sounded from within the room. Blast. He forgot about her maid. How quickly could he send her on her way? Without ceasing their kiss, he lined up the key and inserted it into the lock.

A thump sounded from within Lottie's room, followed by a murmur. A murmur that came from a man's voice. Nathan froze mid-kiss and pulled back. The baritone voice spoke again. Lottie stiffened in his arms. A man was in Lottie's room. An intruder?

Nathan pushed Lottie behind him, turned the key, and slammed the door open. It hit the wall with such force that it shook the frame.

Franny screamed, and her fingers dug into the back of a young male nibbling on her neck as they sat on the mattress. The young man straightened and stood with his hands raised. He slowly turned, eyes wide.

"Char-lie." Nathan hissed out his name one syllable at a time through clenched teeth. He lunged to strangle the boy, but his fingers curled into balled fists near Charlie's face. He closed his eyes and hunched over, battling to subdue his anger. Of all the ill timing. He raked his hands into his hair. He'd seen the long glances Franny and Charlie cast one another on the

Katherine. He should have suspected. He should have said something.

"Franny, what in heaven's name is Charlie doing here?" Lottie stepped around Nathan into the center of the room. "Do you understand the repercussions of your actions?"

Lottie's eyes flashed, and her anger helped to quell his own.

Franny burst into tears.

Charlie lay a hand on Franny's back. "Franny is not to blame. I came to the door hoping to find her here. I convinced her to let me in." He tried to look Nathan in the eyes, but couldn't quite meet his gaze. "I'll suffer whatever punishment you deem acceptable, but please don't dismiss her. She needs the work."

"Maybe you should have considered that before you planned this clandestine interlude." Nathan's voice barely concealed his anger.

Charlie visibly shook but stood his ground.

"We'll discuss disciplinary measures on the way home." Nathan pointed to the hall. "Have my carriage brought around."

Charlie hesitated and peered at Franny, who was weeping as she sat on the bed.

"Get out of my sight now!" Nathan barked.

Charlie jumped and bounded into the hall.

Franny sobbed into the palms of her hands.

"I'll deal with her." Lottie's eyes shone her disappointment.

He stepped forward and placed a quick kiss on her cheek. "I have business tomorrow in Nevis, but I'll come by the day after. I promise."

She nodded and saw him to the door.

In the hall, he bid her goodnight with a stiff nod. Had it only been minutes ago he'd pressed her against that same door? Indeed, his lips still burned from their kiss.

Lottie flashed a remorseful smile before she closed the door and muffled the sound of Franny's weeping.

Nathan spun on his heel and stomped down the stairs. He

exited the building and spied Charlie, pale and sullen, sitting in the raised seat and holding the reins. He stiffened as Nathan climbed up beside him.

"You are too young to be playing the part of a libertine."

Charlie's mouth quivered. "I...I'm not... We're in love."

"You are too young to understand the complexity of love."

"Perhaps." He looked Nathan straight in the eye. "But, maybe I know a boon when I see one. A young lady like Franny is hard to come by. I'd hate to let her slip through my fingers."

Nathan gritted his teeth. He didn't need a lecture, especially not from the young man who caused this night's boon to slide out of Nathan's grasp. "You're on deck duty for the rest of the year. Any free time will be spent attending to my wishes. You'll be too busy for your thoughts to stray where they shouldn't. Am I understood?"

Charlie's shoulders slumped, exaggerating his bony frame. "Aye, sir."

They rode in silence along the dark lane with only the thumping of the horse's hooves and the distant thundering of the waves crashing onto the shore.

He forced thoughts of Lottie from his mind, but their kiss had opened Pandora's Box. No matter how he tried, he could no longer suppress his feelings for her, nor his thoughts, especially of what they might have been doing this very moment if Charlie and Franny hadn't ruined it with their own lustful desires.

The carriage hit a deep hole in a washed-out section of the road. A loud crack sounded and a jolt shot through him.

The axle.

The seat beneath them tilted. Nathan grabbed the side of the carriage with one hand and gripped Charlie's shirt with his other just as the lad pitched over the side. Nathan strained with everything in him to hold the boy as he dangled over the edge, dangerously close to a deep gorge that dropped off the side of the road.

The broken axle dug into the ground, yanking the wagon and horses to an abrupt stop. The animals strained into their harness, and Nathan released his hold of the wagon to grasp Charlie's arm with both hands as he pulled with all his strength. He braced his legs against side of the wagon before they both toppled down the steep precipice. Charlie clung to Nathan's sleeve as a lifeline while his feet pedaled air.

Blast it all.

Nathan heaved a final pull and hauled Charlie back into the carriage.

The lad lay half across the seat as he gasped for breath. "You saved me."

Nathan wiped his brow with a shaky hand and tried to calm his ragged breathing. "You're not hurt?"

"Thanks to you."

Nathan nodded, and the two of them climbed over the other side of the wagon to safe ground.

"I didn't see the hole." Charlie gripped the wagon as though his legs weren't strong enough to hold him. "Honest, Mr. Winthrop. It's too dark even with the oil lamp. I can see only a few feet in front of my face."

Nathan unhooked the oil lantern swaying on the carriage pole, then leaned down and surveyed the damage.

He should have known. Here he'd allowed himself to hope again, but happiness eluded his grasp. His opportunity to be with Lottie had been thwarted and Charlie almost lost his life. It was too dark to fix the broken axle, and they didn't have the right supplies or tools with them. He and Charlie would have to unhook the horses and ride them home. He'd come back in the morning to deal with the carriage.

A gust of wind rustled the leaves.

Nathan swallowed and tried to block out the sound of haunting laughter hissing among the swaying palm branches.

CHAPTER 21

I hope you and papa are faring well. Saint Christopher's Island is beautiful and the people are much like those in England. The horrid picture of a disease-infested isle was undoubtedly over exaggerated.

~ From Lottie to her mama, Lady Etheridge

*M*ama had always warned her not to befriend the staff because they would take liberties. Now Lottie understood. After staying up several hours lecturing Franny about morals and propriety, Lottie had spent the following day and a half comforting her.

"But we love each other." Franny broke down crying while she fixed Lottie's hair.

"You're too young to understand true love." Her words sounded hollow. Did she understand love herself? Her heart leapt when Nathan was near, but was that love? Or was it the deep ache she felt when she wanted to take away the pain of his past. Or perhaps the victorious joy that swept through her when he smiled.

"You don't understand." Franny wiped her tears away with her apron. "We spent so much time together on the ship. With you being ill, I had no one to tend, and Charlie would sneak away from his duties. We spent hours together each day."

No wonder Nathan was always searching for Charlie.

"Since we reached St. Kitts, we've barely said a word, only a secret wave in passing. I thought I might die from longing. But then he sent me a note and arranged for our meeting. We were so delighted to see each other, we got carried away."

"Indeed."

"He's sailing out in a week. We didn't know if we'd see each other again before he left, and then he'll be gone for a sennight. I shall die pining for him."

"You most certainly will not die from pining." Lottie inhaled a slow breath and prayed for patience. Her face felt warm, probably from irritation, for her tolerance wore thin of Franny's drama.

As Franny pinned up the last curl, a knock sounded at the door.

Lottie rose from her chair, and Franny opened it a crack to see who it was. Franny's head bowed. "Good morning, Mr. Winthrop," she murmured into her chest and backed away, opening the door as she did so.

He strode into the room, tall and confident, but in that relaxed way of his. He wore the island style—light cream-colored breeches with a matching cream jacket.

"Are you ready for another shooting lesson?"

"Indeed, I am." She grabbed her bonnet from the table and tied its ribbons under her chin.

"Very well." Nathan tucked her hand into the crook of his arm.

Lottie peered over her shoulder at Franny. "Stay here, and no visitors while I'm gone."

"You'll have nothing to fear." Nathan started for the door. "Charlie has a mound of work to keep him out of mischief until the *Katherine* sails."

Franny's shoulders slumped.

Lottie felt sorry for the poor chit, but it was for the best.

Nathan gestured for her to go first down the narrow hall, but he took her arm as they descended the main stairs. Julia and Captain Fielding were entertaining patrons in the tavern already, and Nathan nodded to them as they passed. A footman swung the door wide, and Lottie stepped into the sunshine. The streets bustled with carriages and wagons as vendors sold their wares at the market.

"It's a beautiful day." Nathan peered up at the sky. A few scattered clouds provided relief from the powerful sun's rays. "There's a good breeze by the ocean. I thought a walk on the beach might be nice." He shaded his eyes from the sun and pointed between some buildings to a cluster of rocks up the beach. "We can do the lesson there."

He turned back, and their eyes met. His gaze held a sensuality that hadn't been there before the Carlton dinner party. His lips curved into the barest of smiles, and she remembered their velvety feel.

Dizziness washed over her, and she exhaled to clear it. "A walk sounds lovely."

Nathan waited for a carriage to pass before guiding her across the street. He veered toward the short pier, and Lottie called to Baby and Gus, who were loading supplies into a rowboat. They removed their hats and waved them in the air as a salute.

"They're preparing for the next voyage."

"They leave in a fortnight?" Lottie picked at her fingernail.

"Indeed."

"Will you be aboard?"

He sighed. "I probably should be, but Captain Fielding can

manage. It's a short run to pick up goods from San Antonio, but the gulf is a rough area, full of privateers who attack British ships."

He led her down a sandy path, and the sound of the crashing waves grew louder.

"You can trade with a Spanish colony even though they fought for years over control of St. Kitts?"

"It's hard to fathom, but a peace treaty was signed between Britain and Spain. We can't trade with America nor the French. If we couldn't trade with the Spanish colonies, many of the slaves on the island would starve."

"The wars have taken their toll on the people of St. Kitts."

"Very much so. There was a time we could only trade with our mother country. I was young, but I remember us not being able to afford tea. There were times even our sugar jar was empty."

"I'm sorry."

He shrugged. "That time has passed. If only the land weren't so tired, we'd be flourishing once more."

He stared out into the ocean. "How did you fare with Franny after I left?"

Lottie released a heavy sigh. "She believes she's in love with Charlie and the world will end if they're separated for too long."

Nathan chuckled. "Charlie is much the same. I sent him to the ship to peel potatoes because I could no longer stand his deep sighs and sulking about."

They drew near the crop of jutting rocks and entered the cove.

"What are we to do with their young love?" Lottie sighed.

"Part of me wants to wring his neck, but another part of me, one that is new to all this, sympathizes with the lad."

Lottie's breath caught. *Was he implying he was in love with her?*

He stopped in a secluded area in the shade of the rocks.

Propping his foot on a black stone, he unbuttoned his jacket and scanned the area.

His chiseled profile held the confidence of a man commanding a ship. He turned her way, twisted an arm around her, and pulled her close.

She gasped at the suddenness of his move, but his gaze was a soft caress of silent expectation. He tucked a loose tendril of hair behind her ear. "I'm beginning to understand his despair at being parted."

Her pulse leapt, and her stomach swirled wildly.

His lips gently brushed hers, coaxing a response.

She rose onto her toes and slid her arms under his jacket.

He crushed her against his body, as if to weld her into his being. His kiss deepened, and Lottie lost herself in the dizzying whirl of heady sensations.

Nathan softened the kiss and pulled away. "This is not the place. Boats and fisherman often cruise through this cove."

She nodded even as her head spun. She clung to him for support, but her world still tilted. Her hand moved to the nearby rock to keep her from toppling over.

"Are you all right?"

"Lovely."

A smile split his face. "Time for a lesson before I throw caution to the wind and chance being spotted."

She inhaled a deep breath, and her equilibrium returned.

"Do you see the washed-up bow of a ship right there?" He inclined his head to the half-buried side of a boat, its wood damp and covered in moss and algae. "I want you to hit it."

She nodded. This was a much bigger target than the wooden barrel. She could do this.

He passed her the pistol. "You remember how to load the chamber?"

Lottie unscrewed the barrel and loaded the powder and the shot.

"Very good. Now, let me see your stance."

She stepped one foot forward and braced her legs.

He peered down at her skirts. "Your knees are slightly bent." Nathan stood behind her, and his fingers slid over the sensitive skin of her wrists. Her pulse fluttered and quickened its pace. *Could he feel it race?* She inhaled a breath and released it to slow her heartbeat.

"Let's try using both arms, one to support the other." He raised her hands and showed her how to hold her wrist to steady her other arm.

He stood so close she could feel the whisper of his breath against her temple. The dizzy sensation of being enveloped within his clean masculine scent caused her to sway against him. He didn't push her away. She relaxed and focused on her target, but the ground wouldn't hold still. It must be his nearness. Not only did he make her world spin, but he set her body ablaze. Her neck and ears burned, and beads of perspiration broke out on her forehead.

"Aim and fire."

She closed her eyes and opened them again. The broken ship came into focus. Her finger clenched the trigger. The explosion drove her deeper into Nathan's chest, and her ears rang.

"I believe you hit it. A splinter of wood ricocheted." He released her and strode toward the ship. "Indeed. You nicked the top." He ran his finger over the notch and turned back to her with a wide grin.

She returned his smile, but his faded. His brows lowered, and he strode back toward her. "Are you sure you're all right? Your cheeks are flushed."

She lay a hand against her cheek. It indeed felt warm. How mortifying for him to see the effect his nearness had on her. She couldn't blame it on the sun or the air temperature because they stood in the shade of the rocks and enjoyed the ocean breeze.

"I'm fine." She pushed down her bonnet in hopes it would

cool her face. "I'm merely excited to have finally hit the target." She busied herself reloading the weapon.

He resumed his place, and she resumed her stance.

"This time, focus on the center of the ship, right above the waterline." He raised her arms into position and ducked his head to check her aim. He straightened, but didn't move away. "Fire whenever you're ready."

The breeze picked up, cooling her damp forehead. A chill ran though her body, and she shivered.

"Don't be nervous." He slid a hand around her waist and splayed his fingers across her stomach. "You were so close last time. This time it's certain to be a direct hit."

She swallowed her dizziness and pulled the trigger.

Sand sprayed against the wood. Nathan backed away but didn't move toward the target. "Try again."

She almost dropped the bag of powder because her hands were trembling. How could they be this cold midday?

Nathan stood behind her, but not as close this time, for which she was grateful. Maybe she could focus better without the distraction of his touch.

She braced her legs and raised her arms, but weariness sapped her strength, and the dizziness returned tenfold. The target blurred before her, and she swayed on her feet. A dull throbbing started in her head. She forced her finger to squeeze the trigger. The gun slid from her hands, and she staggered backward.

"Lottie?" Nathan grabbed her before she fell. His strong arms supported her weight.

"Maybe we should try this another time," she said. "I seem to be coming down with a bit of a headache." She closed her eyes against the distant waves. The receding tide wreaked havoc on her equilibrium.

Nathan guided her over to a rock and helped her sit. He kneeled in the sand, an act that would soil his boots and cream-colored breeches. He didn't seem to think of it though. Lines of concern dug deep grooves in his forehead.

Her dizziness eased a bit, and she ached to erase his worry lines with her fingertips. "I merely needed to sit for a moment. I do believe the late nights and Franny's dramatic episodes have taken a lot out of me."

He pressed the back of his hand to her forehead. His face blanched, and his eyes narrowed on her. "You're burning up. We should head back."

She waved away his hand. "I'm actually a bit chilly, but nothing a walk in the sun won't cure." She rose, but the ground was unsteady beneath her feet.

Nathan grasped her elbow.

As much as she hated to end their time, she might not be able to go much farther. "Maybe you're right."

He escorted her to the road where the ground was flatter. It helped her wooziness, but with each step, her legs grew heavier, as if her slippers had turned to leaden boots. Her breaths became short, and she grew winded. Maybe she'd fallen ill, but so suddenly? The last time a fever came on so quickly, she'd been a small child. Was she relapsing? *No, God. Not now.* Not when Nathan was beginning to develop feelings for her. Would he believe it could affect her ability to bear children as Mama insinuated? Could it?

A wagon approached, and Nathan raised a hand to halt the conveyance.

"Truly. I'm feeling much better." She released her hold on Nathan's arm and strolled down the road a few steps. "I'm fine." She turned to peer at him over her shoulder. The wagon stopped, and Nathan spoke to the driver. "You'll need to catch up—"

Dizziness hit her like a hurricane. Darkness seeped into her periphery, swallowing her vision.

God, help me.

"Lottie!" Nathan's voice called to her.

She forced her gaze in his direction and attempted to smile to reassure him, but the tiny effort commanded the strength she would have needed to move Mount Misery.

Before she could move again, darkness consumed her.

CHAPTER 22

Thank you for your sentiments. I shall keep you abreast
of her condition. I dare not leave her side. Please pray for
her recovery. I fear the worst.

~ *From Nathan to Mr. Marcus Tallant*

*N*athan knew the signs. It started with the fever,
followed by chills. Her skin radiated heat, and
sweat beaded on her face, but her body shivered uncontrollably.
He held her in his arms in the back of the wagon until the driver
stopped in front of the Cockleshell. Paul rushed to aid him.

"I'll take her." Nathan jumped to the ground, then scooped
Lottie into his arms.

Paul leapt up the few steps and held the front door open.

"Inform your mistress of Lady Winthrop's condition and
have extra sheets, wash towels, and broth brought up to her
room." Nathan ascended the stairs, holding her head close to his
chest, careful to not bump against the walls or railings.

He reached her room and yelled, "Franny, open the door."

The young maid's eyes were puffy and red from crying, but
her face paled upon spying her mistress. She pushed the door

wide and scurried to the bed to turn down the covers. "My lady, whatever happened?"

"She's fainted and can't hear you." Nathan gently laid her upon the mattress and tried to set her in a comfortable position.

Franny removed Lottie's bonnet and slippers and pulled up the sheets. "What's the matter?"

"She's fallen ill, most likely with the fever."

The maid gasped and burst into tears.

Nathan grabbed her arm. "You must get ahold of yourself. Lottie needs you. We are all she has right now."

She nodded and wiped the tears from her eyes with her fingertips. "How can I be of service?"

"When her body shakes, we will need to keep her warm. When her fever rises, we must keep her cool." His mouth said we, but the fear seizing his heart had him wanting to bolt from the room.

But Lottie was his wife. No matter how terrified he might be, she was his responsibility. It was his duty to stay. "If God's favor shines upon us, the fever will break in three to four days. In the meantime, we need to keep her as comfortable as possible."

A knock sounded on the door, and Julia strode into the room, followed by servants carrying the sheets, towels, and a tureen of broth. She pointed to the dresser. "Set it down over there."

The help did as she commanded and ducked out of the room.

"When did the fever start?" Lines creased Julia's forehead.

"It came on suddenly while we were out strolling the beach. One minute she was smiling and laughing, and the next she was dizzy and feverish."

"Has she vomited?"

"No. No, she hasn't, but she did complain of a headache."

Julia inclined her head to Franny. "You should get some broth in her as soon as she wakes. Whatever she'll keep down."

Franny prepared a bowl from the tureen. Nathan scooted Lottie up and stuffed pillows behind her back to support her in a half-seated position.

Julia laid a hand on Nathan's shoulder, and he met her solemn gaze. "We knew this might happen. We shall hope for the best over the next few days." She moved to the door and paused in the open frame. "If there is anything she needs, you know where to find me." She mustered a sad smile. "This is not your fault."

Nathan closed his eyes and nodded, but he could still see the witch's wide mouth and hear her bark of laughter. *I curse you.* When he opened his eyes, Julia was gone and the door clicked shut.

Lottie's face was as pale as the white pillows upon which she lay. Her eyes were shadowed, and the fever had already colored her lips scarlet. Adana's face appeared in his mind's eye as she clutched the satchel hung around her neck to ward off spirits. *The spirit of death is upon her.*

Nathan rubbed his face with both hands. This was his fault. He shouldn't have kissed her or allowed her near him. *Blast.* He never should have married Lottie. She was here because of him. She was ill because of him. She was cursed because of him.

~

*L*ottie's body ached everywhere and her head pounded. A warm liquid dripped over her lips and down her throat. Some of it ran down her chin, but a soft cloth gently mopped it up.

Franny. Franny must be taking care of her.

"Water," Lottie whispered through chapped lips.

The feel of cool porcelain parted her lips, and fingers lifted her chin. Water flooded her mouth, but stopped before she choked. The cold liquid soothed her parched throat. For someone so young, Franny was a natural caregiver.

Lottie struggled to open her eyes, but it wasn't Franny she saw.

Nathan. His face appeared haggard, with dark circles under his eyes as if he hadn't slept all night. The stubble of a beard darkened his chin. He must be the one who had cared for her. Her eyes closed of their own accord, for she didn't possess the energy to keep them open.

"Rest, darling. You need to reserve your strength."

"How long have I been asleep?" Weariness from speaking left her limbs and head feeling heavy.

"Three days."

Her lids opened and fluttered back closed. *Three days? Nathan cared for her all that time?* But the fields and his ships? He shouldn't be away from his work for so long. Her joints ached and complained, but she slid her arm towards him and covered his hand with hers. She may have squeezed. She wanted to, but she was so weak her fingers didn't seem to cooperate.

Her lids wouldn't open, but she forced her lips to move. "Thank you." She had meant to say, *Thank you for staying by my side. I know all you're sacrificing to be here. I love you.* But exhaustion set in, and she was dragged back into nothingness.

～

Lottie's feet sank into the sand. Water rushed around her ankles and saturated the hem of her gown. The tide was coming in. Another wave crashed, pushing her back a step until the undertow dragged her forward. She strained against the water, trying to break away from its grip. The sky grew as dark and stormy as the sea. She shouldn't be out during a storm. She needed to find shelter. She scanned up and down the beach, but there were no houses, no people, not even a single boat.

"Help. Someone, please help me." Maybe someone would hear her cry.

Her foot slid in the sand, and she almost fell into the water. A large wave rolled in, splashing water up to her knees, and her gown became the weight of several stones. She panted from the exertion of merely holding her ground. She needed to get away, out of the water, away from the waves sucking her to a horrible death. She struggled harder, but only lost ground.

Thunder crashed as another wave barreled into her, knocking the wind from her lungs. Her foot caught on her gown. She fell to her knees and staggered to get up. The rushing undertow flowed over her back, soaking her hair. Her heels dug into the sand as she turned to face the next onslaught.

An ocean wave rose higher than any she'd seen. It towered above her, foaming at the top and preparing to crash down on her at any moment. The wind rippled the water into the shape of a woman. Seaweed laced the woman's hair, and the ocean was her native garb. Her fluid hands spread her skirts wide, and strange words poured out of her mouth, like fish spilling from a cut net.

Frantically, Lottie flailed her arms and legs, fighting against the ocean's current. "Help! Please help!"

The woman leaned down and lowered her face to within a foot of Lottie's.

Lottie cringed and raised her hands as a shield.

The woman's mouth opened, and a blast of rain and wind beat against Lottie's face.

"Curse you," she shrieked. "Death is upon you."

The wave of her body crashed over Lottie, knocking her backward and somersaulting her under the water. Rushing liquid sounded in Lottie's ears as her elbow and chin scraped against the sand at the bottom. She gained her footing and pushed back up out of the water, sputtering to catch her breath.

The ocean water pulled back, reshaping the wave-woman's body even larger.

"That's a lie." Lottie spat salty water from her mouth. She struggled to keep her footing, even though her soggy skirts weighed her down. "I will not believe you."

The wave woman threw back her head and laughed a harsh gurgling sound.

"You're a liar." Lottie rose as tall as she could, straightening her shoulders the way her mother taught her, and screamed. "I have built my foundation upon the rock of Jesus Christ, not upon sinking sand. My Lord will see me through."

The woman's eyes darkened, and she stirred up the ocean by thrashing the waves. She raised her arms until the crests loomed high over Lottie, threatening to sweep her away with one swoop.

The undertow dragged Lottie in until her feet stumbled on a firm foundation. A rock. She shored herself up. "I am not afraid. Jesus is with me. I won't be moved." She raised a hand and pointed at the woman. "I rebuke you in the name of Jesus."

The wave woman roared and lunged at Lottie, but a warm wind blew, and the wave fizzled out. A few other waves, like greedy hands, tried to pull Lottie off her rock, but her feet stayed secure. The tide receded and left Lottie on the shoreline.

"Thank you, Jesus." She repeated the mantra with each heavy breath and fell on her knees. Drenched and battered, her hair dangled around her face, and salt water dripped from her nose and chin.

The sky cleared, and the bright sun emerged. She lifted her face to warm her skin and squinted into the light.

Pray. The word was loud and clear, but it wasn't audible. It entered into her heart, vibrant and distinct. *Pray,* it repeated, and again, *Pray.*

"I will," she said to the light. She rose to her feet. "Pray, that is." She smiled. "I shall pray."

$\sim$

*N*athan awoke to the sound of Lottie moaning. His eyes cracked open, but his lids felt weighted by anchors. Several nights of sporadic slumbering in a chair left his muscles stiff and achy, and he arched his back to ease the tightness. He grabbed the wet towel in the wash basin near his feet and wrung it out.

Lottie's brow furrowed, and her pale cracked lips murmured something, but she showed no sign of wakening. He wiped her flushed face with water to cool her feverish brow. Days three and four had passed with only a slight reprieve before the fever burned again, this time worse than before. She'd begun thrashing and murmuring incoherently in her sleep. He mopped her brow and closed his eyes against the pain of the truth. He was going to lose her.

She groaned and turned her head. Strands of stringy red hair stuck to her face. He brushed them away with his finger and leaned in, hoping maybe just once he'd understand her words.

"Pravb," she mumbled, but it easily could have been a gasp of breath.

Nathan stilled and focused on her lips.

"Pray."

Her voice was hoarse and weak, but he distinctly heard the sound and saw her lips form the word. "I will, darling, I have been, and I still am. Don't give up. Keep fighting. Please, darling, for me."

He kissed her palm. Tears burned the back of his lids. "God, please don't take her. Wasn't my family enough? Haven't I paid enough for my sins?"

A shudder ran though Lottie, and he raised his head to find

her convulsing. He scrambled backwards, uncertain what to do. When he hit the wall, he opened the door and stuck his head out. "Franny! Come quickly."

His hands and lips trembled. This was it. The shadow of death had come. He moved to her side and pinned her arms and legs with his own, as if he could keep her from slipping into death if only he held her tight enough.

Her eyes rolled back, revealing the yellowing, a sign that the fever was winning the battle.

"No!" Nathan released her. *No, not again.* His heart squeezed to the point of bursting. He'd seen that same look in Katherine's eyes, in Amory's eyes, and in his mother's eyes before the fever took them.

I can't watch Lottie die.

He'd witnessed enough death. He wouldn't give it the satisfaction of watching the torment on his face or hearing his weeping. His lungs struggled to drag in air. He needed to go... somewhere, anywhere, far away from the cold gasp of death.

He closed his eyes and fumbled for the door. "I'm sorry, darling. So sorry," he whispered.

Franny ran past him into the room and knelt by her mistress's side. She burst into tears at the sight.

Nathan turned and fled.

CHAPTER 23

Our signal shall be the raising of the French flag.
~ *From Captain Fielding to his contact on Grand Terre*

*H*e was a coward.

Nathan's heart twisted until he could barely breathe. Lottie had paid for his selfishness.

A spray of salt splashed over the bow of the *Katherine* and misted his face, but Nathan continued to stare out into the swirling ocean water.

He should have been there for her. He should have held her hand until she breathed her last breath. He'd owed her that. She'd come here because of him, and she died here because of him. He hadn't even had the decency to stay by her side.

Death wasn't pretty. He'd heard it said people pass in peace, but he'd witnessed Katherine struggle for her last breath as her lungs filled with blood. There had been no peace in it.

"You look like you're contemplating a swim." Fielding interrupted his thoughts as he sauntered closer. "I wouldn't recommend it in these rough seas."

Nathan's fingers tightened on the rail. Death by sea would be too good for him. It wasn't slow or painful enough. He wouldn't burn with fever for days, nor vomit and cough up blood. A few minutes of struggling for air while he sank to the bottom of the ocean would be too easy.

He'd hoped sailing would take his mind off Lottie, but with each day, his guilt corroded his soul, and he grew frustrated with himself and his actions. Now he only wanted to get back to St. Kitts.

She'd be buried by then.

A fresh stab of pain sliced his heart. *God, please have Franny and Julia present for her funeral. Please don't let her be buried alone.*

"We're making good time. Should arrive in Galveston in a couple days."

Nathan couldn't trust his voice so he merely grunted.

"Listen." The captain lowered his gaze. "I know you think the curse has struck again, but what does a slave woman know? Her tribe may believe in her black magic, but we're Englishmen. We know better."

"I was born an islander."

"By golly, you're right, but English blood runs in your veins." He clapped Nathan on the back and sauntered off.

Movement caught Nathan's eye. Cobble was checking the rigging near the foremast. He peeked up and met Nathan's gaze. The weather-beaten man's face sagged, and he swiped his tricorn hat off his head.

"I'm awfully sorry about yer wife. She was a bonny lass with a sweet spirit. Reminded me of my own missus. We were blessed having known her."

"Thank you, Cobble." He nodded his acknowledgment and walked away. "If only she'd been blessed to have known me."

Cobble's rough hand gripped Nathan's shoulder and spun him around. Nathan jerked away from the elderly man.

"You've got a few attics to let if you believe she wasn't blessed to have known you." Cobble crossed his arms over his chest. "I understand if yer feelin sorry fer yerself, but I heard it straight from her rosy lips. She was grateful you rescued her, not only from her mama, but also from a life of exile due to a tarnished reputation."

"At least she would have been alive."

"She didn't believe so. It didn't matter that she cast up her accounts for most of the trip. Lady Winthrop reveled in the freedom and the opportunity to see the world. Don't ruin her memory. The last thing she'd want is for you to become bitter."

Nathan's shoulders sagged. "You don't understand."

"I know the world is cursed. Bad things have happened since Adam ate that apple, and cuz we're in the world, we're cursed, too." He waggled a finger in the air. "But Jesus took the curse on himself. Lady Winthrop taught me that." Cobble reached into the front of his shirt and pulled out a worn leather book. "She got me back readin' and seekin' God's truth. Turn to your Heavenly Father, and He'll ease yer pain."

"I believe in God." Nathan rubbed the back of his neck. "I just don't believe God is going to help me."

"If you turn yer heart away and believe in witches and put other things above God, then He cannot bless that life." Cobble clapped Nathan on the shoulder. "Ya have to choose faith and choose life. No matter the hardships, Lady Winthrop chose to see the best. She chose life."

Nathan gritted his teeth. "She's dead, Cobble. Her life was taken from her. How is that not a curse?"

"Once she realized her life was a gift, she lived it to the full. She touched my soul and influenced many on this ship. I believe she'd say that was why we're put on this earth—to give hope and run God's race through to completion. I wish she'd been around longer, but I know she'd tell me her death was part of God's bigger plan."

An awkward silence fell between them, and only the sound of the bow plowing through the waves could be heard. His family had believed the same, but so much had happened. When it came to the Winthrops, God, it seemed, had looked the other way.

"I appreciate what you're trying to do, my friend." Nathan sighed and stepped away. "But I don't deserve it."

Cobble turned and let him pass. "None of us do. That's the wondrous love of Jesus."

~

*L*ottie's head pounded, and her throat felt like she'd swallowed sand, but she was awake and, although exhausted, felt better than she had in days.

She cracked her eyelids open. The blinding sunlight streaming in the window sent a stabbing pain through her skull. She quickly closed them and shifted to face the wall. That action, too, intensified the throbbing.

Footsteps sounded in the hall, followed by the jiggling of the latch and the squeak of the hinges. Probably Franny coming to check on her.

"He ruined the plan by sailing."

It was Julia's voice. A second heavier pair of footsteps entered the room.

"Should you be speakin' so freely?"

Lottie recognized Paul's deep baritone voice.

"It's been several days, and she hasn't awakened." Julia's hand shook Lottie's shoulder.

She wanted to answer, to turn and let them know she was awake, but her exhausted body wouldn't obey her command.

"She's holding on longer than I would have guessed." Julia released her shoulder. "Considering what a frail thing she was."

Was? Past tense?

"Her odds be slim." Paul's voice drew closer. "Her colorin' is mighty yellow."

"It won't be much longer now."

"I'll start makin' arrangements for da funeral."

Lottie flitted in and out of consciousness. Images of the past and present merged within her dream state—Nathan's smile, Julia dancing with Captain Fielding, women from the market touching her red hair, Paul's dark scowl, Julia's folded arms.

Shoes clicked toward the door. "It's a shame the fever is taking her." Julia's voice reverberated in Lottie's ears as if echoing in a windowless chamber. "She turned out to be a boon. Winthrop would have stayed on the island, but with her ill, he's already back aboard."

Nathan left? He was sailing on the *Katherine*? Was he so anxious for her to be gone?

Paul's voice grew louder. "Don't be forgettin' yer promise."

Julia exhaled a deep sigh. "Jere is gifted at pitching the gammon. He'll find a way to gull Winthrop into believing it was privateers. Before he's the wiser, we'll have sold Winthrop's cargo and settled into our manor in Florida."

Florida. Nathan hates Florida. No, Gator hates alligators. One particular gator...in Florida.

"Don't fear," Julia whispered. "If this run goes well, you shall gain your freedom for your assistance."

Lottie held completely still, fighting to grasp the bits of thoughts and snatch the pieces of conversations as they floated past her ears. Her heart and head throbbed in rhythm. Was she conscious or dreaming? Fielding...Julia...smugglers? Shamming Nathan? *God. Protect. Him.*

Julia's boots clicked down the hall. The hinges squeaked, and the latch on the door clicked. Paul's heavy footfalls followed her.

Captain Fielding...lying rogue? Julia his jade? Weariness washed over her, and any clear thought danced out of her reach. *Nightmare?* Sleep took her.

She awoke again later to the swish of skirts and struggled to roll over.

"Franny. Bring some bread and broth. Our patient is awake." Julia brushed a strand of hair off Lottie's face.

She peered into Julia's warm eyes as the woman helped prop up her head with pillows.

"Lady Winthrop." Franny rushed to her side and knelt. "You're awake. Praise God. We were beginning to think the worst. You've been unconscious for days." She held up a spoon. "Do you feel up to eating?"

Lottie nodded. She needed something to bring her energy back.

"Mr. Winthrop will be so pleased." Julia rose and offered Franny her seat by Lottie's bedside. "He stayed by your side day in and out." She tilted her head towards the chair to her left. "He slept for a whole week in that very chair. It's a wonder he could even move. That seat is not very comfortable, as I've discovered since he left."

Lottie's heart clenched, and she closed her eyes. His business was everything to him. He felt responsible for so many people, and that was an honorable trait. She shouldn't be disappointed he'd left, but her heart wouldn't listen to her head.

Franny tilted the spoon, and the warm broth ran down Lottie's throat. "I think you scared him when you turned for the worst. He hollered for me, and when I got here, you were in a sorry state. I dropped to my knees and prayed. I thought your time had drawn near, and so did Mr. Winthrop. Charlie came to wish me farewell before they shipped off. He said Mr. Winthrop was not himself. Charlie said he was as skittish as a newborn colt." A sad smile touched the lips of her hopelessly romantic lady's maid. "I believe he left because his heart was breaking."

"He had business..." *to attend. Nothing more.* She finished the sentence in her head, for speaking the words required too much energy.

"Eat and then rest." Julia opened the door. "I'm going to

check on the staff and let them know the good news. They'll be delighted. I'll come back in a bit."

Lottie swallowed several more spoonfuls of broth before her eyelids slid to a close.

Praise God, it had only been a nightmare.

CHAPTER 24

Much to my dismay another splendid catch is off the
market. The Duke of Linton has returned from hiding,
but announced his engagement to Miss Georgia Lennox
in the papers. If you recall, she's the woman who always
dressed in the color pink.

~ *From Priscilla to Lottie*

*L*ottie's appetite had finally returned in full. She donned
a chintz day gown with tiny pink flowers and
descended the steps to the dining room.

In the last two weeks, she'd made tremendous progress
towards a complete recovery. Between naps, she read her
Bible and spent time in prayer, thanking God for second
chances in life and claiming the same for her marriage. Her
strength had been the last to return, but even that showed
promise. Yesterday, she'd strolled to the pier and back. Each
time she pressed herself to walk a bit further. The fresh air
had felt wonderful, and the sunshine worked magic on her
constitution.

Julia was already seated in her usual spot by the window, and she raised a hand when she spied Lottie. Paul pulled out the chair in front of her, and Lottie sat.

"There's color in your cheeks today, and your eyes don't appear as hollow. You've made a miraculous recovery."

"Praise God." Lottie leaned back so Paul could pour a her glass of lemonade. "He still has plans for me yet."

Julia leaned in. "We all thought you were on your way to kingdom come. We've seen a lot of people, way too many for my taste, come down with the fever. Once their eyes and skin assume the yellowish tinge, very few come back. You're a strong woman, Lady Winthrop."

Lottie smiled. "I have been called a lot of things, but strong has never been one of them." She examined her arms. "I've always been thin and frail, and now it's even worse. I daresay I haven't a bit of meat left on me."

"I shall endeavor to fatten you up." Julia signaled for their dinner, and Paul carried in a large tray of sweetmeats and cheeses. "Give her a double portion."

Lottie laughed, but an odd feeling niggled to the surface as an image of Julia and Paul standing over her sickbed flashed through her mind.

"I've enjoyed dining together." Julia unfolded her napkin and set it on her lap. "I must confess, I grow lonely when Jere is away. It's nice to have someone who understands."

"Nathan and I haven't been together as long as you and Captain Fielding have, but I do miss him, and I hope one day he will look at me the same way the captain looks at you."

Julia sipped her drink and eyed Lottie over the rim. Despite Julia's aloof demeanor, Lottie had on occasion been able to coax a smile from her.

"And that he will also call me his love," Lottie added. "He doesn't need to say it in various languages, though. English will do."

Julia pressed her napkin to her lips and her dark eyes flashed with pleasure. "He started learning different languages when I shared with him my dream of opening an inn in every port. He only remembers how to say *my love*, but he claims that is all he needed to know."

"And, look." Lottie held out her open palms and peered about the room. "You've already started on your dream." Lottie laid her hands on the table and leaned in. "So, where is your next one to be established?"

A dimple appeared in Julia's cheek as her smile twisted into a cynical grin. She shook her head. "It wasn't meant to be. The Cockleshell has never brought in enough profit to warrant the establishment of a second, not to mention one in every port." Her face hardened with cold dignity. "So Jere went back to sailing the seas."

"And you stay here to run the inn instead of sailing with him. Do you ever wish to travel alongside your husband?"

"No." Her tone was firm. "My constitution is stronger than yours, but I despise the constant queasy sensation of an unsettled stomach. I sail when I must, but otherwise, I keep my feet on dry ground."

Lottie raised her glass. "To dry ground."

Julia clinked her goblet against Lottie. "To dry ground."

Lottie lowered her glass first. "You shouldn't give up on your dream. Who's to say an inn wouldn't do better on another island, or even in America? I've heard more and more people are settling in the west and in the gulf. They will surely need an inn for visitors. Your experiences here have taught you what to do and not do for your next venture."

"We've considered the Spanish territory of Florida, but you, my friend, are overly optimistic. Do you ever have a negative thought?"

Before he's the wiser, we'll be settled into our manor in Florida. Lottie blinked away the remnants of her fever-driven nightmare and didn't answer Julia's question.

Franny rushed into the room waving letters above her head. "My lady, a ship arrived with mail from home."

"How splendid." Lottie put down her fork.

Franny set three letters next to Lottie on the table, and Franny herself kept one.

Julia finished chewing her bite and wiped her mouth with her napkin. "Please, do not wait to read them on my account."

"Go ahead and read yours also." Lottie nodded to Franny. "Letters are a special treat. If you don't open them now, the suspense will distract you, and you won't hear a word I say."

"It's from my mum." Franny tore open the letter and devoured its contents.

Lottie was a bit more careful and used the edge of her knife to slice the top fold. She recognized Priscilla's loopy script and skimmed it, reading a few of the highlights out loud for Julia's benefit. "She says everyone is atwitter with the return of the Duke of Linton. It turns out all this time he'd been residing right here on our sister island of Nevis." Lottie glanced at Julia over the pages. "Were you aware of this? Did you ever see him?"

Julia shrugged. "People can hide in these parts if they keep to themselves, which he must have, because word of a duke would have spread quickly."

Lottie scanned the letter further. "She says by the time we receive this letter, the Duke will have married Lady Georgia Lennox. They fell in love when she visited her father on the island." She folded the letter closed. "How romantic."

"Lennox." Julia tapped her bottom lip with her index finger. "I do know that name. I believe her father was a planter. I think Winthrop had some dealings with him. Shipped his barrels of sugar to England."

The next letter she knew to be from her mother. She placed it next to her on the chair to read later. Even though she longed to know how her family was faring, it would be best to read that one from the privacy of her room.

She didn't recognize the handwriting of the third letter. The nonchalant, slanted script could only be from a male hand, but it wasn't her father's nor her brother's. Most curious. She opened the letter, and her gaze fell on the signature at the bottom.

Anthony.

Her head drew back. Why would Anthony write her? She scanned the brief contents. His ship would be anchoring at St. Kitts to deliver some recruits to Brimstone Hill, and he would like to pay her a visit during his brief stay to see how she was faring.

"You look puzzled." Julia raised a questioning brow.

"It seems my friend's brother will be arriving in St. Kitts, and he would like to call upon me."

"Oh." Franny glanced up from her letter. "Does it say upon which ship he is sailing? I saw a British frigate coming into port. I believe it was the *Fortitude*."

"It's the very one." She turned the pages and pointed at the name scribbled on the page.

Franny clapped her hands. "He'll bring more news of home. I know just how I will dress your hair for such an occasion."

Lottie's stomach rose into her chest, but whether from excitement or anxiety she couldn't determine. Would this merely be a friendly visit to wish her well and see how she'd gotten along? What would she tell him, knowing word would certainly get back to her family?

~

Two days later, the knock she'd known had been coming sounded on her door.

Franny opened the door, and Lottie heard Paul's voice. "Please tell Lady Winthrop a Captain Middleton awaits her in the foyer." He passed the card to Franny.

Franny thanked him and shut the door. She flipped the card over. "It's him, my lady." She moved to the wardrobe and pulled out a royal blue gown. "This one will go nicely with the color of your hair."

Lottie shook her head. "No. It's much too bold. The plain lavender day dress will do. I'm not trying to court Captain Middleton."

"Very well, my lady."

Franny quickly aided Lottie in dressing and re-pinned a few of her curls. In no time, she was descending the stairs to the foyer, her stomach in knots. Would seeing him bring up old feelings? She couldn't fight down the worry that she was somehow jilting Nathan, even though Anthony was an old family friend. It was logical for him to pay her a call. Why then was she wishing more than ever that Nathan were here?

Anthony studied the maritime picture on the wall, just as Nathan had done before. Except Anthony with his smaller frame, didn't fill the room with his presence like Nathan had. Nor did her heart flip at the mere sight of him as it had when she'd spied Nathan.

Sucking in a deep breath, she settled her stomach. Anthony turned, and she greeted him with a smile.

"Miss Etheridge—er—I beg your pardon—Lady Winthrop." He bowed. "Do forgive me. Old habits are hard to break." His gaze held hers. "As ever, you are a sight to behold."

"You are too kind." She looped her arm through his and gestured toward the adjoining salon. "Please come and sit. I'll ring for tea."

She rang the bell pull before she settled into a tufted chair, while he sat on the green brocade sofa. "Anthony, we've known each other since Priscilla befriended me. You may call me Lottie as you always have done."

He chuckled. "Indeed, when Priscilla sets her mind to something, nothing can change it, and in this case I'm glad."

"She seems to be faring well with the season. I received her letter two days ago, along with yours."

"I'm glad my letter found its way. I thought perhaps I might be taking you by surprise."

"Even if it hadn't, your visit would have been a nice surprise." A spark lit his eyes.

Lottie stiffened. "I mean, it's always good to visit with a friend." She added emphasis to the word friend, and the spark in his eyes faded.

He glanced at the whitewashed walls and the Bombay writing desk. "I would be remiss if I hadn't checked in on my dear…friend." He drew out the word with equal emphasis and a hint of derision. "How are you and Mr. Winthrop faring?"

"Quite well. Thank you."

"And whereabouts is your husband?"

The terseness of his tone set her on edge. "He is seeing to business at the moment."

"So, it's true he's holed you up here at an inn?" Anger flared in his eyes, and his face grew splotchy. "He hasn't the decency to bring you into his house. Your mother was correct. The man is a scoundrel. Even in England, if a man isn't happy in his choice of a wife, he brings her into his home to keep up appearances. He wouldn't dare set her up *carte blanche* in an inn as he would his mistress."

Lottie tightened her jaw to keep her mouth from dropping open.

"Winthrop doesn't deserve you." He pushed forward to the edge of his seat, but his eyes never left hers. "I always wondered if that night had been a tragedy of errors or if he'd staged the act to force your hand."

Lottie opened her mouth to refute his statement, but he continued.

"I should have said something in the church. I should have stood and called out his blackguard ways." His fingers pressed lines into his breeches as he rubbed them over his knees. "Island gossip says you had separate cabins upon the ship, and he hasn't stayed the night here at the inn. Instead, he stays on his plantation, probably laughing at the prospect of getting even with your mother by never giving her the pleasure of a grandchild."

Nathan would never do something so malicious. "His—*our* house is under construction." The excuse sounded inadequate even to her. She'd seen his home. It seemed suitable enough. She'd suspected he needed time to adjust to having a wife, but surely he'd done so by now.

"Has he even taken you to his bed?" The hiss of his words sliced through the air.

Lottie gasped. A gentleman would never pose such a question.

He scooped up her hands and pinned them between his own.

"I apologize for the shocking nature of my question, but I must demand an answer for your own good."

She jerked her hands away. "I will not justify your rude question."

"Lottie, don't be embarrassed. As you said, I *am* your friend. It's most unfortunate you were forced to marry a cad, but all may not be lost. You are not responsible for his actions or inactions, but if the answer is what I believe, then I will speak with my captain and find room aboard the *Fortitude*. When you reach England, you can appeal to the Prince Regent and have your marriage annulled."

"This is Mother's doing. She's trying to control me from across the ocean, and you are her pawn."

"This is Winthrop's doing." Anthony's face flushed, and malice flashed in his eyes. "His business is failing, so he decided to abscond with a daughter of a viscount's dowry."

"You are mistaken. I was supposed to meet with Priscilla that night so we could say good-bye before I was sent to the country. She was delayed because she hoped to return with you and play matchmaker. However, Nathan entered the room instead. I hid due to my fright, and it was I who dropped the candle. He saved my life."

"He must have seen you enter the room alone. He saw an opportunity and took it with the intention of seducing you. He poured brandy hoping spirits would loosen your morals." Anthony snorted. "He even tried to convince me my sister poured the drinks."

Was Anthony truly here out of concern for her well-being? His words sounded as such, but his movements and facial expressions appeared rancorous. "I poured those glasses. It was another act of rebellion against my mother and another poor choice on my part. Nathan doesn't drink spirits."

"No matter." Anthony's eyes hardened. "The man is a scoundrel. Now, answer my question."

Anthony wasn't in love with her. He didn't look at her the way Nathan did, as if he could never get his fill of her. Anthony was in love with precepts and principals. He was allowing his sense of justice to be tainted by revenge.

"I love my husband. I made my vow before God, and I will honor it."

A harsh laugh rose from his lips. "You were always the optimist, but you are delusional if you think a man if his ilk will love you in return. There will never be a happily-ever-after with a man like Winthrop."

Her anger rose. Nathan may not love her, but he was her husband. Anthony, on the other hand, never had the fortitude to pull off what he was suggesting. She needed to be clear about the truth to dispel any future doubts. "Are you proposing if I leave with you and beseech the Prince Regent for an annulment, that you will marry me?"

His eyes widened. "I-I cannot subject my family to such a scandal. Think of my sister. Her marital options would suffer."

"Just as I thought." A sense of relief surged through her. "You

never loved me. You may have fancied me, but it was not love."
She leaned forward and placed a hand on his arm. "Anthony, I
hope someday you'll be blessed to experience love. Only then
will you understand why I cannot leave."

"How can you believe yourself in love with such a man?"

"I don't believe, I know, and deep down, I believe he'll come
to care for me in return."

"The humidity has made you daft. When a man loves
someone, he doesn't treat her like a kept woman."

"He also wouldn't sit idly by and watch her marry another."

The muscle in Anthony's jaw clenched. "Fine, remain here.
Let this island slowly kill you. Don't think for a minute I haven't
heard of your illness or noticed the dark circles under your eyes
and how your gown hangs on your frame." His nostrils flared.
"Your mother will certainly hear of this. Mark my words, she'll
be on the next ship over."

Lottie straightened her shoulders. "The island hasn't killed
me yet. I daresay, it has only made me stronger." She rose. "I
appreciate your concern, Anthony. You are, and have always
been, a good friend. I will always think of you as such, but I do
believe it is time for you to go."

He stood and yanked down on the bottom of his navy coat.
"I will give your regards to my sister."

"Please do. I miss her companionship." She curtsied, and as
he walked by, she placed a hand on his sleeve.

He paused and peered down at her over his shoulder.

"It was good to see you, Anthony. Truly. I wish you all the
best."

He nodded before he strode away.

Lottie drifted back to her chair and sat, reeling from the
conversation. She laid her head against the back of the chair and
closed her eyes.

A knock sounded on the door frame, and Lottie opened her
lids to see Julia in the doorway.

"Mind if I come in?"

Lottie gestured to the sofa.

Julia swept across the room and lowered onto the couch in a graceful flutter of skirts. Mother would have loved how Julia sat with stiff-backed dignity. Mother would have insisted Lottie be more like her.

"I couldn't help but hear your conversation."

Lottie groaned. "I believe my mother has planted ideas in his head."

"What he said about Winthrop isn't true. In all of our dealings, he has been nothing but ethical and honest." A deep sadness filled her eyes before she lowered her gaze. "I know your arrangement here hasn't been ideal." She peered up at Lottie. "But you've brought about a change in him. He seems... happy, and it's been a long time since I've seen him that way. You both deserve it. To be happy, I mean." Julia cleared her throat. "I must be getting back to the kitchen. There's much to oversee." She rose and swept from the room.

"Julia?" Lottie called.

She paused in the hall and turned.

"Thank you." Lottie tried to muster a smile.

Julia's lips curved into a shy smile before she turned back and pushed through the kitchen door.

Lottie was cracking Julia's tough exterior, and she would crack Nathan's also. There was hope. She wouldn't listen to her mother's or Anthony's nonsense, nor the doubts in her head. She'd become her own woman. With God's guidance, she'd keep forming her own opinions and allow Him to direct her steps.

CHAPTER 25

It grieves me to bring this to your attention, but you should be aware of your daughter's predicament.
~ From Captain Anthony Middleton to Lady Etheridge

"What's the meaning of this?" Nathan stepped up behind Baby's large frame.

Baby jumped at the sound of Nathan's voice. His thick fingers froze on the rope, one hand over another. The half-lowered British flag snapped in the wind.

"Who told you to lower our colors?"

Baby continued to hold the line with one hand, but pivoted on his heel to face Nathan. "Capt'n Fielding's orders, sir."

"Why on earth would he give that order?"

"I'm merely guessin', but I do believe it's because we're entering the gulf—Lafitte's territory. Our red ensign is a boon for pirates and French privateers."

"Sailing without the protection of our flag would attract them even more."

Baby yanked a length of fabric out of his vest pocket. The

tricolor red, white, and blue of the French flag unfolded before him. "He told me to raise this." Baby held the flag up.

Nathan's jaw tensed. It was treasonous. Their home country was at war with France. What had gotten into Fielding? He couldn't have been in his right mind when he'd made the order. Men bustled about their duties, climbing ratlines, belaying ropes, and caulking timbers. Captain Fielding stood at the helm next to Gus on the sterncastle deck.

"Give me a moment with Captain Fielding," Nathan inclined his head at the flag Baby clutched in one hand. "Do not raise that unless you hear from me."

"Aye, sir." Baby stuffed it back into his vest.

Nathan hoisted up the ladder stairs.

Fielding handed the helm over to Gus and met Nathan halfway across the deck. "Mornin', Winthrop."

"What's the report?" Nathan asked.

"The good news is we passed the Isle of Hispaniola early last night. We should spy the coastland of Florida this afternoon. The bad news is Muzzer found spilled sugar in the hold. He thinks the rats might have chewed through one of the barrels."

"Blasted rats. Have him see what can be salvaged." Nathan pushed back the lapels of his coat and rested his hands on his hips. "Has there been activity on the seas?"

Fielding shook his head. "So far we've had clear sailing."

"No sign of other ships?"

"No, but one can't be careful enough in these waters."

"Is that why you ordered a French flag raised? You're worried about privateers?"

"Aye." Fielding raised his chin a notch. "Not only are the Americans friendly with the French, but so is the pirate Lafitte. We lower our risk of being boarded by raising the French flag."

"Raising a French flag is treason. It would risk our British trade contract. Without the mainland to sell our sugar, what would you have us do?"

"The crown will never know."

Nathan glared at his friend. "I would know."

"You're making much out of a trifling matter." Fielding's gaze drifted as if done talking about the issue.

"Committing treason isn't insignificant."

Fielding shrugged.

How could he be so flippant? Did he care nothing for his country? The law? "I cannot allow it. Not now, and not when you're sailing without me. Are we understood?"

The captain crossed his arms, but nodded. "Don't forget the risks of sailing under a British flag. Many American privateers prey on ships like this."

"Indeed. That is why I hired the best captain to outrun them."

Fielding smiled, but his eyes remained shadowed. "And so we shall."

Just open your mouth and tell her. Lottie pushed the food around on her plate, working up the courage to say what she needed to.

Julia paused with her fork half-way to her mouth. "Are you not hungry?" Her thin brows drew together into jagged angles. "You're not becoming ill again, are you?"

"No." Lottie set down her fork and drew her hands into her lap. "I'm well." She sighed. "It's merely that Anthony's visit brought up some good points."

Julia swallowed the bite of food and frowned. "I don't recall anything worth repeating coming from his mouth."

"Captain Middleton is not a bad fellow. He may be a coward, but his intentions are honorable."

Julia snorted.

"I truly appreciate your hospitality in allowing me to stay

here at the inn, and I so enjoy our daily shared meals. Your friendship means a lot to me, and that is why this is so difficult." Lottie chewed on her lower lip.

Julia leaned back in her chair.

"I believe it's time for me to settle in at Calico Manor."

Alarm widened her dark eyes. "But the house isn't suitable yet. The work has barely begun." She shook her head. "It would be best for you to stay here."

"I know, but Anthony is right. I must be careful of appearances. I'm only harming the Winthrop name if people believe I'm a kept woman and not fully his wife."

"Appearances be hanged." Julia pursed her lips. "This isn't London. Things are lax on the island. People are forgiving."

"Indeed. But I will not knowingly continue to damage my, nor my husband's, reputation if it can be helped. Franny is upstairs packing my things. I believe it's best if I leave after high noon tea. It will give me time to settle in with the staff before nightfall."

"You will only be in the way on a sugar plantation." Julia's back straightened into a stiff line.

Lottie didn't take offense. She knew Julia only said that because she didn't want her to leave. "I'm good at finding ways to become useful. If nothing else, I can help with the mending, and I can ride into town and do the shopping." She reached out and squeezed Julia's hand. "It will give me an excuse to visit at least twice a week."

Julia's shoulders relaxed a bit, but the tension remained in her face. "It's in your best interest to stay put."

Warmth filled Lottie's heart. As much as Julia conveyed herself as a strong woman, she craved friendship as much as Lottie did. "I will need your advice on decorating and what furniture to purchase. Do you think you'd be able to spare a few trips out to the plantation?"

"Of course, but..." Her chest heaved with a deep sigh. "No one could keep me away."

"Good. I was counting on it."

~

*B*y early afternoon, Lottie and Franny reached Calico Manor. Julia had arranged for Paul to escort them by carriage.

The house was quiet as they pulled up, the full workforce tending the upper fields. Paul brought up her trunks and set them in the room beside Nathan's. Lace curtains hung in the window above the bed, and homemade dolls sat in a chair in the corner. She tiptoed over to the dresser with the porcelain wash basin and fingered a silver hairbrush still entangled with silky strands of blond hair. The letter *K* was carved into the back of the handle. Katherine. This had been Katherine's.

She bowed her head and prayed that the memories of Nathan's lost family members wouldn't be forgotten. She also thanked God for Nathan, who cared so deeply for his family. It filled her with hope that a man who could feel such love might find room to love her too.

Guilt ate at her for invading his dead sister's space. In England, men had their own chambers and wives an adjoining suite, but she had no idea how married couples handled sleeping arrangements on the island. Disturbing his sister's untouched room unsettled her nerves. Lottie straightened. She'd sleep in her husband's bed. It would keep her closer to Nathan, and if he objected, they could discuss a better solution later.

Lottie entered Nathan's room. She'd had a chance to see it before, but not the opportunity to linger. His bed was neatly made with tightly folded corners, and appeared way too small for such a large man. She should speak with Mr. Tallant about building him a larger bed with leftover wood from the addition. A watercolor of the island of Nevis hung above the headboard, the scene similar to the view from the beach at Frigate Bay. Upon closer inspection, she spied the initials *A.W.* Was Amory a painter? Was this his handiwork? If so, he'd been quite good. Did Nathan share his brother's talent?

A breeze waved the long gauzy white draperies dangling from the window, and Lottie inspected the top of Nathan's dresser. A golden compass rested next to his wash basin. She placed it in the palm of her hand and turned until the arrows came into alignment. She flipped it over. Inscribed on the back were the words, *To help you always find true North.* A gift then. From his parents? A friend? A woman? A spark of jealousy flared, but Lottie snuffed it out.

On the other side of the basin rested a silver bowl full of small shells. Each of them was unique. One looked like a tiny baby's ear, and another was shaped like a small fairy's top hat. It also held a small conch shell, and the smooth flat shell of a clam fanned open like a butterfly's wings.

Her breath stilled as her fingers came upon the ridges of a scallop shell. She pulled it out. This was the very shell she'd found on the beach the day they'd arrived. It had the small groove on the outside as if a worm or something had nibbled on it. She flipped it over to reveal the pinkish-lavender color underneath. He must have thought her green to have held it with such reverence.

Next to the bowl lay a dried white rose like the one she'd placed in his buttonhole after they were married. Could it be coincidence, or had he kept that flower? And, if so, did these items hold sentimental value for him?

She licked her lips. She wanted to believe she meant something to him.

Lord, please make it so.

A door banged shut below, then footsteps sounded on the stairs. Franny must have already settled into the small room under stairs and was coming up to tend to her mistress. Lottie smoothed her skirts and opened the door, only to come face to face with an unknown servant. The African woman shrieked as if she'd seen the dead. She spun to flee, but Franny stood at the bottom of the stairs peering up. The woman screamed again and clutched a small sack hanging around her neck with one hand. She squeezed her eyes shut and muttered something in a foreign tongue.

Adana ran into the foyer, holding her skirts in one hand and wielding a wooden spoon above her head in the other. She skidded to a halt at the sight of Franny. Her head jerked in Lottie's direction. She lowered the spoon and snapped at the frightened woman on the stairs. "Ya da not see a ghost. Master Winthrop's woman still lives." She glanced back up at Lottie and murmured, "Fer now."

Lottie stiffened. "I assure you I am very much alive, and you will be seeing much more of me, for I will be taking my rightful place here at Calico Manor."

Adana's hand also rose to hold the tiny sack hung around her neck.

Lottie ignored the gesture and addressed Franny. "Please bring up some clean water to freshen up."

Franny bobbed a curtsy and scooted down the hall.

"What is your name?" Lottie asked the woman on the stairs.

She opened one eye to peek at her. "Olufemi." She dropped into a curtsy from an awkward position on the stairs. A duster she held swung, feather side up, as she bobbed. "But on da island, I am called Lu."

"Pleasure to meet you Lu. I'm Lady Winthrop, your mistress. I didn't mean to frighten you. You may proceed with your duties."

The slave dropped her gaze and started up the stairs.

267

"Lu, you are needed outside in da kitchen."

Lu hesitated. She looked at Adana, and then back upstairs before turning to go down them.

Was Adana trying to supersede her mistress's authority, or was there truly a need in the kitchen? She didn't want to stir up any animosity on the day of her arrival, so Lottie merely asked her, "When do the workers return from the fields for supper?"

"When da sun is a hand above da horizon." Adana held up her palm as if measuring it.

"I see." Lottie rested her arm on the newel post. "When you see Mr. Tallant, please let him know of my arrival and set a place for him across from me on the porch. We have much to discuss."

Adana's lower jaw protruded, but she made no complaint. She bobbed a curtsy before she strode back outside to the kitchen.

Franny carried a pitcher of water up the stairs and poured it into the wash basin in Nathan's room, where Lottie waited.

Lottie dipped her hands into the cool water and splashed it on her warm cheeks. Something about Adana always got her heated.

Franny seemed to feel it too. "Something doesn't sit right in my spirit about that woman." She handed Lottie a dry towel.

"I heard the same thing happened to Lady Irving when she married and became mistress of Fennel Park." She patted her face dry. "Lord Irving refused to remarry for such a long time, and the housekeeper had been the sole woman in charge for over a decade. You can imagine the adjustment it must have been to report to the new Lady Irving, barely even of age." Lottie handed Franny back the towel. "It's probably the same with Adana. I must do my best to make her feel comfortable with my authority. It's important things go smoothly. I need to prove I can be an asset as lady of the house. I don't want Nathan to be disappointed."

Franny pulled the pins from Lottie's hair to remake her coiffure. "I do hope you're right, my lady." She re-twisted Lottie's mass of red hair back up into a knot. "But something tells me the woman is going to cause trouble."

CHAPTER 26

Heavenly Father, watch over Nathan and provide him
with safe passage back to me.
~ *Penned in Lottie's prayer journal*

"Ship at nine o'clock off our starboard bow, captain!"
shouted Salt from the crow's nest.

Men paused to glance over their shoulders.

A series of clicks sounded as Captain Fielding extended the
telescoping spy glass and held it up to his eye. "Aye, it's out
there."

He passed it to Nathan, who peered through the lens. Sure
enough, a speck of a triple-masted ship sailed on the horizon.
Nathan's hair rose on his arms.

A frenzy broke out among the men as they set to work.
They'd practiced this drill a hundred times. Nathan felt for his
pistol on his left side and his cutlass on his right. Captain
Fielding barked commands. "Raise the headsail. Cut us forty-
five degrees into the wind. Man the guns. Salt!" he yelled to the
young man high above. "Get an eye on what type of ship we're
up against."

"Looks like another schooner, Capt'n."

"Blast!" Fielding rounded on Nathan. "It must have come off the western coast of Cuba. Our ship has a full belly. It's going to be challenging to outrun them."

Charlie hung from the ratlines, checking the rigging. Baby and Cobble loaded the cannons. These men were counting on Nathan, and he'd put them in danger.

"Prepare to gybe," Gus called to the crew.

Shouts of "Ready!" echoed from around the ship.

Captain Fielding grabbed Nathan's arm. "This is not your fault." His eyes softened. "I know you think it's the curse, but this is typical for these waters."

The curse.

He shouldn't have come. When would the curse be satisfied? The death of his family hadn't been enough. As soon as a semblance of happiness returned to his life, the spell took Lottie too. Would it not stop until it devoured the lives of his crew? His friends? Would it destroy everything he held dear?

"It's not too late to raise French colors." Fielding's eyes bore into his, awaiting the answer.

The memory of Lottie's smiling face appeared before him. He wouldn't tarnish her memory by becoming a traitor. He wouldn't betray her home. "No. We'll only fly our flag." He grabbed Fielding's lapel. "I shouldn't have sailed with the ship."

"Sails are trimmed, Captain." Gus appeared at Fielding's side. "We're at seven knots, but they're gaining on us."

"Bring her on her beam ends."

"Aye, captain." Gus's voice boomed out to the crew. "Bring her to beam ends!"

Winches cranked, and booms swung into position. Men braced as the ship heeled starboard until it was almost on its side.

Spray from the waves splashed over the deck, drenching the crew.

Gus wiped the end of his spyglass with the underside of his shirt and held it up to his eye. "She's still on us, sir. Less than one league."

Charlie yelled from his position. "They're hostiles, Captain. Preppin' ta board. If I had ta guess, I'd say pirates."

God, don't let them die because of me. A myriad of nautical strategies Nathan learned in school rushed through his mind, but none would save them with a full hold. He may have been a liability, but he'd do everything in his power to keep his crew safe.

"They'll be on our broadside in less than five clicks."

Broadside. A scene played in his mind. It might just work. Peace settled over him. *God, let this be you.* Nathan grasped the Captain's shoulder to gain his attention. "I have a plan, but it will be a challenge to pull it off."

The captain's eyes lit. "What kind of challenge?"

"I'll need to take the helm."

Fielding's brows inverted into a *V*. "You want control of the ship?"

"I want to keep my men alive without us getting boarded." Nathan's gaze swept across the deck, reviewing the plan in his mind.

Fielding squinted. "Our chances might be best if we let them board and strike a deal with 'em."

"If they board our ship, we don't hold any of the cards. We'd be at their mercy. They could take our cargo and burn our ship with us in it. It's too great of a risk."

"But you schooled with Lafitte." Fielding waved an arm in the air. "Surely we could negotiate something."

"What makes you so certain this is Lafitte's men?"

The captain's lips opened, and for a moment no words came out. "I ..." He shrugged. "There's no way to know for certain."

A warning shot pierced the air.

Nathan pulled the spyglass from the captain's fingers and

held it up to his eye. The opposing ship outgunned them by at least double. They must take a head-on approach.

"Bring her around for a faceoff," Nathan instructed Gus before he turned to Charlie. "Help Cook bring all the bottles of rum above deck and pass them out to the men."

"You're going to give a rum toast at a time like this?" Captain Fielding gaped at Nathan.

"Do it quickly!"

Charlie dashed below deck.

Nathan turned to Fielding. "Have all our men grab a rag and an oil lamp and take cover in the stern of the ship. Have them lie down on the deck if need be." He raked a hand through his hair. "You too, Captain. I don't want anyone in harm's way. I want them to stuff the rag into the bottle of rum. When I give the command, have them light the fiery cocktails and sling them at the other ship."

A second cannon boomed.

Nathan had no plans to slow the ship. "Hurry. Get everyone in position." He assumed the wheel as Gus sought cover.

Cannons roared as they took on raking fire. One missile flew past Nathan, splintering a hole in the forecastle deck and scattering debris. Nathan covered his face with his arms, but a stabbing pain pierced his leg. A splinter of wood the size of a stake protruded from his thigh, and blood oozed through his breeches. Another cannonball busted through the railing and rolled across the deck and down the stairs.

Nathan gripped the wheel tighter, forcing himself to ignore the pain in his thigh. His crew lay flat on the deck. All eyes were on him.

The other ship drew closer.

Hold fast.

Closer.

He could see the swarthy pirates waving their hooks to board, cutlasses ready for a fight.

Only a boat's length remained between the two ships. Nathan spun the wheel, and the ship veered off to the left.

"Now!" he shouted. The men rose and bombarded the pirate ship with their assault. Fiery cocktails crashed onto the deck. Stunned, the pirates ducked to shield themselves. Many abandoned their posts to put out the fires.

"Stations!" Nathan yelled, and his crew rushed to their positions to trim the sails for a fast getaway.

A thunderous boom shook the air and the ship. The pirates recovered a cannon, and its blast pounded the *Katherine*. The boom cracked, but fortunately, the spar was left intact. The sail now flapped in the wind, its lines whipping and snapping like the stinging bite of a snake.

Orange flames licked the pirate's sails as the crew rushed to lower them. A much-needed distance grew between the *Katherine* and the pirate ship. Nathan breathed a sigh of relief, but kept the vessel at full tilt until the other boat was only a dot on the horizon. Only then did he turn to survey the damage.

"And here everyone thought *I* was the crazy one." Fielding clapped Nathan on the shoulder.

Nathan gritted his teeth against the pain throbbing in his leg. "We didn't come out as unscathed as I would have liked, but at least the crew is alive."

"Indeed. We can make some repairs, but a broken boom is like a limping soldier." The captain shook his head. "Maybe you're right about the curse. What will it strike next?"

CHAPTER 27

Now that you will be mistress of your own house, it's important that you set proper expectations immediately. The staff shouldn't be fraternizing, and stiff punishments should be applied for gossip and tongue wagging.
~ *From Lady Etheridge to her daughter*

"What a delight to see you, Lady Winthrop." Mr. Tallant pulled out her chair to dine with her in the coolness of the porch. He sat across the table from her as dusk settled around them. The field workers settled on the ground and stone wall of the outdoor kitchen, where Adana prepared the dishes to be served. "Glad you're hale. Not many survive the fever. You are most fortunate."

"I am grateful God pulled me through." Lottie draped her napkin over her lap. "And for those who tended to me."

Mr. Tallant cleared his throat. "Your husband has faced death too many times for one soul to bear. I beg you not to believe ill of him for leaving."

"Have no fear, Mr. Tallant. I don't fault him for..." A deep nagging cut off her sentence. Did she fault him? He'd not cared for her as he would have his mother and sisters. One person could only bare to witness so much death. But she was his wife. Shouldn't he have stayed by her side, at least to make proper arrangements after she died? Instead, he'd passed the task off to Julia and her slave.

"I've been informed you're taking up residence here at Calico?"

She shook off the thoughts. "Indeed." She leaned back as Adana filled her cup with watered ale. "I'm overdue in assuming my wifely duties."

"We have begun the rebuild, but progress is slow. I must agree with your husband. The manor isn't suitable for a woman of your station. Every available pair of hands is in the fields. It will be hard to afford you the necessary servants."

A fire burned in her belly. She was tired of people assuming her to be weak, telling her what she should do and where she should go. "I will make do."

"If Winthrop were here, he'd agree with me."

Lottie set her jaw. "It's most unfortunate he cannot be consulted."

"Then his last advisory should stand."

"Many things have happened since his last advisory, Mr. Tallant. I have prayed about this and sought God's counsel. This is where I should be, and I shall remain until my husband returns and says otherwise."

"You are not accustomed to the daily hardships of living on a sugar plantation." He settled back in his chair and crossed his arms over his chest. "There will be no one to provide you with high noon tea or prepare for entertaining guests."

"Forgive me for speaking so boldly, Mr. Tallant." Lottie set her hands on the edge of the table and leaned forward. "But I do believe I will muster through without high noon tea."

"You've cheated death once, but it will be on *my* head if something happens on my watch."

"I understand your concern." Lottie smiled over clenched teeth. "But I refuse to stay locked in a tower. Every person on an island works, and I can be of service. If we are agreed, then we shall get on well together." She dragged in a deep breath to calm her ire.

A broad smile swept across his face. "I didn't believe Winthrop when he claimed you were spirited, but now I see he spoke the truth."

A mix of emotions meshed in her stomach—horror for appearing as a veritable shrew, pride for standing up for herself, and pleasure that her husband had called her spirited.

A scream split the air around them. Mr. Tallant jumped from the table and raced down the porch steps. Lottie did the same. One of the slave workers ran in a circle, shrieking and shaking his arm.

"Calm down, Percival." Mr. Tallant grabbed the man's shoulders to still him. "Let me have a look."

"S-s-skòpyon!"

Lottie stopped a few feet away from Mr. Tallant and the flailing man. "What's the matter with him?"

"He's been stung."

Lottie's shoulders relaxed. "By a bee?" She'd been stung several times before. It hurt like the dickens, but wasn't life-threatening.

"Not a bee. A scorpion."

As if to prove the point, the man shook his arm, and out of his sleeve flew a small yellow insect. It landed at Lottie's feet and angled toward her with its pinchers held high. Its segmented tail curled back, ready to strike. She recoiled with a gasp.

Mr. Tallant's boot slammed down on the disgusting creature, crunching it beneath.

A shiver ran through her at the nauseating sight of the crumpled spider-like critter. She'd never seen anything like it, but the thought of it crawling up her skin caused Lottie to scan the area for any of its friends.

Percival held his arm as if it burned, but his screams turned to groans.

"Is he going to be all right?"

"Scorpions are poisonous, but usually not fatal." Mr. Tallant waved to Adana, who rushed over. "Make him a poultice."

She nodded and ushered Percival off, still clutching his arm.

"Are scorpions common around here?" Lottie forced herself to breathe.

"There are a few of them." He pointed to the stone wall upon which Percival had been sitting. "They like to hide in rock crevices and dark places. Best to shake out your shoes before you slip your foot into them."

Lottie's stomach twisted.

"Blast." Mr. Tallant pursed his lips. "Percival could be laid up for a week, and we need every hand."

Lottie fumbled for a response, but had none.

Silence fell between them until Mr. Tallant said, "Shall we finish our meal?"

With a light hand at her back, he escorted her to her seat and once again held out her chair. The rest of dinner proceeded better, with Mr. Tallant explaining the process of harvesting cane and how it was made into molasses at the boiling houses. His descriptions fascinated her, but the slightest movement drew her attention. Her gaze frequently panned for any creepy crawlies. Did she have the fortitude for plantation life? Did she have the resolve? If she wasn't cut out for living on a plantation, did it mean she wasn't cut out for a life with Nathan?

Lord, help me stay strong.

She excused herself after dinner and retired to her room for the night, but it was several hours before she climbed into bed. She and Franny scoured every inch of Nathan's room for unwelcome guests before even thinking about sleeping.

~

*T*he next morning, Lottie arose early after a fitful night. She'd dreamt of a scorpion infestation at Calico Manor that poisoned the crops and crippled Mr. Tallant and the workers.

She washed her face in the basin, still trying to shake the impact of her dream, and felt for the small Bible inside the pocket of her gown for solace. She must return it to Julia on her next trip into town. She'd grown so accustomed to carrying it with her, she'd forgotten to take it from her pocket before leaving.

The light of the sun rising over Mt. Misery drew her to the window.

The door to Adana's hut swung open, but instead of the surly woman, Mr. Tallant exited. His hair stuck out on one side, and his shirt hung half tucked. He sneaked back to his cottage, but paused at the side door, where he glanced toward her window. He stiffened.

Lottie stepped back. Had he seen her? She ventured another peek, but Mr. Tallant had already disappeared inside. A few seconds later, Adana emerged from her hut. She tied her apron behind her back as she strode to the house.

What was going on under her husband's nose? The few times she'd caught Mr. Tallant's arm touching the cook, the long looks he'd given her now made perfect sense. Should Lottie confront them about their indiscretions? Adana already didn't like her. Dare Lottie stir up more hatred? She despised the idea as much as standing against her own mother. Adana made for a similar foe.

Heaviness weighed her down, the same heaviness that had fallen on her in her dream.

God, I need wisdom.

She pulled out the Bible and cracked it open to Deuteronomy. She skimmed to the passage she'd glazed over yesterday, chapter thirty, verse nineteen. "I call heaven and earth to record this day against you, that I have set before you, life and death, blessing and cursing: therefore choose life, that both thou and thy seed may live."

Blessing and cursing. Choose life.

Lottie rested her head in her hands and prayed. *Lord, help me choose life. Help me be bold to do Your work and live as You would have me live. Please return Nathan safely to me. I ask for Your wisdom to be a good wife and a proper sugar baroness to the staff and slaves. Infuse me with Your strength for whatever lies ahead.*

As she prayed, the heaviness lightened.

Franny entered, helped her dress for the day, and pulled her hair back into a tight chignon. Lottie grabbed her gloves, then hesitated. They were too hot for this climate, but they kept her from biting her nails. If she was going to be bold and courageous, she couldn't continue to chew on her manicure. She wavered, rubbing the satin material with her thumb. She had to face Adana, Mr. Tallant, and a staff who all believed an evil curse would drop her dead at any moment.

Her hand raised to her mouth at the mere thought. *No.* She lowered her fingers and draped the gloves over the back of her chair. She would trust God.

Silverware clinked and voices murmured from the porch as Lottie descended the stairs.

"Curses aren't catchable." Mr. Tallant's voice floated through the open window.

Lottie paused at the foot of the staircase and peeked around the curtain.

"So, yer now da expert on dis?" Adana dished rice and beans onto his plate. "I'm tellin' you. She married him, and it's in her now too. Look at Percival, and den last night, Hawley burned hisself in da boiling house."

"It was a minor burn." Mr. Tallant put down his fork.

"On his face. He be scarred da rest of his life."

He shrugged. "You may be right, but what can we do? She's our mistress, and we *will* serve her."

"I don't have ta like it."

Franny peered over the railing. "Do you need something, my lady?"

Lottie let the curtain drop and turned to Franny. "I was merely checking the weather before I stepped out." She opened the front door and strode onto the porch.

Adana stepped back from the table.

Mr. Tallant rose. "Good morning, Lady Winthrop."

"I couldn't help but overhear your conversation."

He blanched and flicked his gaze to Adana, then pulled out a chair for Lottie.

She sat. "Please." She gestured to his chair. "I think it's best to talk about these things openly."

He sank into his seat.

Adana scooped some rice and beans onto Lottie's plate.

"I'd like you to hear this as well," Lottie said to Adana. "I realize that some incidents have happened." She pulled her Bible from her pocket and laid it on the table. "The Bible says that in this world, we will have trouble. Not *might* or *may*, but *will* have trouble. But we are to take heart because Jesus has overcome the world."

She met both Mr. Tallant's nervous gaze and Adana's defiant one. "I know there are rumors about my husband being cursed, and I overheard you arguing about whether I am cursed as well. I want you to know that it doesn't matter if you believe in a curse or not. My God is greater than any curse or any obeah woman's powers, and He will prove it. Just you wait. Woe to the person who attempts to thwart His plans."

Adana's eyes widened, and Mr. Tallant cleared his throat.

"I don't want to hear any more talk of curses. Instead, we

will focus on how God has delivered us and provided for us. We are going to choose *blessing*. Am I understood?"

They both nodded.

"Splendid." Lottie unfolded her napkin and slid it across her lap. "Also, I wrote Rev. Kirkland and asked him to send us a chaplain this morning so we can worship together. Mr. Sanders should be arriving anytime now."

"But the workers are needed in the boiling houses." Mr. Tallant's brows pushed together. "We can't afford to lose a day."

"It's the Lord's day. I'm certain you will find the workers even more efficient on Monday after a day of rest."

Mr. Tallant frowned and scratched the back of his head.

Lord, show them Your faithfulness in this matter. Squash their doubts.

~

*M*r. Sanders arrived an hour later and preached under the shade of the Saman tree. The workers sat on blankets or stood under the palm trees. The distant ocean shimmering in the sun, combined with the words from Second Corinthians chapter four, gave Lottie hope.

"'We are troubled on every side, yet not distressed,'" read Mr. Sanders. "'We are perplexed, but not in despair; persecuted, but not forsaken; cast down, but not destroyed.'" He peered up at the congregants. "And why don't we despair? Why don't we lose hope and give up?" His gaze shifted among the small crowd. "Because God knows what we do not. God sees what we cannot. Verse eighteen says, 'While we look not at the things which are seen, but at the things which are not seen: for the things which are seen are temporal; but the things which are not seen are eternal.'"

Afterward, Mr. Sanders joined Lottie and Mr. Tallant for lunch. He congratulated Lottie on her marriage and spoke well of the people of St. Kitts. Before he climbed into his carriage, he offered to return the following Sunday.

Adana washed the plates, and Lottie carried a handful of glasses to her.

"Ya don't need ta dirty yerself. Lu will get da rest."

"I don't mind. Besides, she's retrieving more water." Lottie set the glasses in the wash bucket. "I'd like for you to collect mending from the workers. I may not be able to help in the fields, but I can mend clothes."

Adana paused in washing the dishes, but didn't look at Lottie. "Do you believe what Mr. Sanders preached today?"

"I do."

Adana didn't say anything else, merely continued scrubbing the plates.

Lottie inhaled a steadying breath. "I know about Mr. Tallant's visits to your hut."

Adana twisted around. Water dripped from her fingertips, and she eyed Lottie with wariness etched in her taut features.

She silently prayed for courage and wisdom. "I can't condone these actions when you are my responsibility." Was this a taste of the burden Nathan felt for his workers?

"Are you gonna have me whipped?" Adana's mouth remained partially open.

"Of course not, but I want you to understand that you are deserving of God's best. When you have a relationship with a man who is not your husband, you intentionally walk out from under the shield of God's protection."

"Dis is not England. Yer God doesn't care 'bout us islanders."

"Yes, He does." Lottie smiled. "You are His daughter, and He cares for you."

Adana turned back around and stared into the bucket water.

Lottie's hands shook, so she hid them in the folds of her gown. Would Adana understand Lottie's intention was to help her, and not judge her?

She left Adana to her thoughts and meandered near the garden. A breeze tugged at her bonnet strings. This time of day, the house would be stifling. She wandered up the same path the workers traveled. As she did, she held out her hands over the growing cane and prayed for God's provision. She hummed the hymn they'd sung earlier. A couple of the slaves heading to the river to wash glanced up when they heard her. She smiled at them and encouraged them to sing along. Many were hesitant at first, but slowly they joined in, mumbling through the lyrics they didn't know while they walked.

Over the next days, the prayer walks became a daily ritual for Lottie. By the end of the week, the workers knew all the words to several hymns and bellowed the verses in harmony. The young slave children followed Lottie, mimicking how she held out her hands and moving their lips in prayer. She stopped to help the youngest ones over any big rocks or up sharp inclines. Due to the steepness of the path that led to the north field, she wasn't able to walk the full extent of Nathan's lands, but a sense of satisfaction filled her each time she returned to the house.

Adana presented her with baskets full of mending, and Lottie started sewing. The slaves thanked her, and Mr. Tallant confessed that with Sundays off, the slaves were more productive, and their output hadn't slipped in the least.

A few days after Mr. Sanders' visit, Lottie stopped at a large rock overlooking the ocean. It had become her favorite spot to sit and soak in God's presence while she prayed for Nathan's land and for his safe return.

A loud ruckus erupted from the boiling house about a hundred yards up the path leading to the south field. She stood and squinted in that direction. The rock allowed her extra leverage to see above the cane to where three men carried a screaming worker toward the sick house. Lottie jumped off the rock, hitched up her skirts, and scrambled to see what was amiss. She caught up with the men, one of them being Mr. Tallant, before they reached the sick house.

The slave's face contorted with pain, and he wailed in agony. The scent of molasses emanated from his body. His pants dripped with the sticky liquid.

"What happened?" Lottie caught her breath and yanked open the door to the hut.

"He slipped into one of the vats and was burned from the waist down." Mr. Tallant grunted as they carried the man inside and laid him on a cot. "We got him out quickly, but it's not the burn we have to worry about as much as the infection."

The men left with their hats in their hands and shaking their heads.

Adana's footfalls sounded behind them. "I heard da commotion and came runnin'." Her chest heaved, and she stopped beside them. She swallowed hard as she glimpsed the man's injuries. The taut cords of Adana's neck told Lottie the woman struggled to keep her face emotionless as she dug through a basket of bandages and ointments. "Excuse us, Lady Winthrop. Dis is not a sight fer a lady." Adana removed the shears from her basket and bent down to cut away the man's pant leg.

Lottie stepped outside and tore off the ragged edge of her index fingernail with her teeth. She stopped herself and folded her hands in prayer as she paced outside the hut. Eventually, the man's cries stopped, and Adana stepped out.

"He's restin' now. I gave him something for da pain and ta mek him sleep."

"Is there anything else we can do for him?"

Adana shook her head. "Pray." She spit out the word as if it were a curse. "Pray to yer God. Nuthin' else can be done."

She regarded Lottie for a minute before striding back to the house. Lottie followed in her wake, the heaviness in her heart growing with every step.

Despite Adana's best efforts and Lottie's diligent prayers, the slave died three days later. His body was buried on the hill, and a small memorial was held. As the workers departed, returning to their work in the fields and boiling houses, Adana paused in front of Lottie.

"Where is your powerful God now?" Grief shadowed the woman's eyes.

Lord, what do I say? Lottie ached to comfort her, but she had no words.

Adana lowered her head and stalked back to the main house.

The next morning, Lottie arose early to do her prayer walk. As she walked, she gave voice to her ache. "Why God? Why would You allow him to die when it would only cause them to doubt You?" Her shoulders drooped and tears rolled down her cheeks. Mr. Sanders' preaching resurged in her memory.

God knows what we do not. He sees what we cannot. His ways are higher than our ways... We are troubled on every side, yet not distressed; we are perplexed, but not in despair; persecuted, but not forsaken; cast down, but not destroyed.

On her way back up the path near the slave quarters, the door to Adana's hut opened and Mr. Tallant inched out. Lottie's steps slowed.

"Are you a coward?" Adana's voice hissed from inside. "You fear her wrath more den mine?"

The man paused in the doorway, still looking inside. "Lady Winthrop is right. We can't continue to meet in secret. It doesn't feel right having to hide all the time. Winthrop being at sea made it easy, but with our mistress living here, it's opened my eyes. Having to sneak around and hide all the time. I've met with Mr. Sanders, and he's set me straight. God does not approve of this." Mr. Tallant stood in the doorway. "I'm sorry."

"Git!" Adana pushed him out the door. "Ya blackheartman!" She slammed the door behind him.

Mr. Tallant hung his head and trudged back to his abode.

Lottie froze and wished she could blend in with the sugar

cane. Adana would be riled by Mr. Tallant's stance, but it was for the best. Their actions would only rob them of blessings. *God, please help her to understand.*

Adana opened her door and strode to the main house, her expression as angry as the clouds rolling in over Mt. Misery. She paused, as if feeling Lottie's eyes on her, and turned. Their gazes met. Adana inched up her chin and glared, before spinning back around and marching to the house.

CHAPTER 28

Captain Fielding requests a rendezvous at the Cock-leshell upon his return.

~From Mrs. Julia Fielding to Captain Phelps of the Amory

*N*athan hobbled toward the helm. He could still feel the burn of the needle where Charlie stitched his thigh. He kept his pace slow because he couldn't afford to pull any threads loose and re-open his wound. Charlie may have the nimblest fingers, but Nathan had witnessed how well Charlie's sewing of the main sail had held.

Salt stood with the spyglass pressed to his eye. "We have another problem, Capt'n." He scanned the horizon. "A blow is forming in the west. The clouds are black as night."

"Sink me!" Captain Fielding slapped his hat on the rail. "We can't take another hit."

"Can we outrun it?" Nathan asked.

"Not with a cracked boom and flappin' mainsail. We might as well be dead in the water."

Nathan raked a hand through his hair. *Why God? Why have*

You abandoned me to this curse? Will You let it strike me down until I'm destroyed along with my ship and its crew?

"Batten down the hatches," Fielding yelled, and men scurried in all directions. "Secure the hold. Prepare to reef the sails."

The storm bore down on them in less than thirty minutes with a drenching rain. Soon after, the gales picked up and the rain turned into pounding pellets of hail.

The men ducked and did their best to take cover. Captain Fielding steered toward the flatter spots between waves, but they still pounded the side and washed over the deck. The boat rolled, and Nathan grabbed hold of a man before he washed over the rail. The *Katherine* righted, only to pitch again.

"Are you all right?" Nathan yelled. The pounding rain blurred his vision.

The lad nodded but appeared pale and shaken.

A mix of ocean water and raindrops splashed into Nathan's mouth and down his shirt. "Hold fast to something until the storm passes."

"Yes, sir."

The *Katherine* groaned against the battering surf as his men struggled to keep her afloat without slipping on the water-logged deck.

As quickly as the storm arrived, it passed, but not without spoiling the sails and further damaging the decks. Nathan surveyed the wreckage and tallied the cost—more than the entire load of cargo he'd sold. They might make it home, but the *Katherine* may never sail again.

~

*L*ottie leaned over the porch railing and spied Mr. Tallant approaching with a few workers in tow. She scurried down the stairs and into the mud, not caring how it might ruin her boots. "How fared the fields?"

"I can't believe it." Mr. Tallant shook his head. "All the neighboring fields were decimated. Whatever cane still stands is riddled with holes."

Lottie halted. The blood drained from her face, leaving her lips and nose tingling. How would Nathan take this news?

"However," Mr. Tallant said, "our fields are fine. Only the north field sustained some damage."

Her hand flew to her heart.

"It's a miracle." Mr. Tallant smiled. "A complete miracle. It's as if God drew a line at the path where you do your prayer walks. One side of the line, the cane is perfectly healthy. The other side is ruined."

She whirled around to where Adana, Lu, and Franny stood on the porch, awaiting the news. "It's fine. God protected our fields. We'll still have a harvest."

A cheer went up, and the ladies hugged each other on the porch.

Mr. Tallant stepped forward and better projected so all the women could hear. "There is damage to the north field, but some of it is salvageable. Our neighbors are going to need our help. The storm was not as kind to them."

Lottie stepped forward. "What can we do?"

Over the next few days, everyone pitched in, sifting through the damaged plants—Adana, Franny, and even Lottie. Long hours were spent fertilizing the salvageable cane and gathering the broken to take to the mill.

A week after the storm passed, Lottie set down her machete and stretched the aching muscles in her back. The sky blazed with pinks and oranges, and the sun lowered to less than a hand's length above the horizon. "I think it's time we called it a day."

Adana rose and wiped the sweat from her brow. She dusted off her hands. "Best ta get back and get supper on the coalstove."

They turned in their machetes and bundles of cane to the

neighbor's overseer, who thanked them again for their kindness. Weary and worn, the two women trudged back to Calico Manor, knowing they still had supper to prepare before the sun set and the rest of the workers returned, craving food to fill their bellies.

Adana cast her a sideways glance. "Many now believe yer God is stronger den any obeah or black magic. Dey want to worship da God who can hold off da storm. Deh is no mistakin' da areas you prayed over were spared."

Lottie's heart warmed. Problems truly were the ground in which miracles could grow.

"I don't know 'bout da storm. It may be a coincidence, but I've seen your faith and da kindness you've shown our neighbors and da grace you've given ta me. Dat is no small thing. Most folk would have me whipped or send me off deh land. If yer God taught you dat, den I respect dat God."

~

When they finally docked at St. Kitts, Nathan oversaw the last of the cargo unloaded and purchased supplies to begin the long list of repairs needed for the *Katherine.*

The men bid him farewell and left to see their women and families. He watched until the last of them disappeared before he limped over the weathered boards of the wharf. He'd never felt so alone and so empty.

At least on the ship, he'd had work, shipmates, and danger to keep his mind occupied. But back on St. Kitts, it seemed memories of Lottie were everywhere. Her amazement at the blueness of the ocean, and her look of wonderment as she held up the scallop shell, thinking the trinket was a rare treasure.

She'd been the treasure.

Her death was on his shoulders. He should have protected

her, thought of her well-being, not his desire. He should have stayed away. If he'd kept his distance, maybe she would still be alive. Maybe there'd still be a little more joy left in the world.

Paul passed him on the road, carrying a sack of flour back from the docks. He greeted Nathan with a nod.

Nathan stopped. He didn't have the heart to walk into the inn and talk to people. All he wanted was to visit Lottie's grave to pray for forgiveness.

He signaled to Paul and hobbled over to him. "Where can I find her...?" His voice trembled. "Where is she...?" *buried.* He couldn't force the word past his lips.

"Calico Manor," Paul said in his gruff way.

Nathan nodded and hailed a hack to take him home. As the wagon bumped down the road, Nathan dropped his head into his hands.

It's better for her to be buried there. With my family.

The thought only tightened the vise squeezing his heart. He didn't deserve solace. This was his punishment. His curse to bear.

He passed fields of cane broken and punctured with holes. *Hail.* The storm had hit here too. Most likely Calico Manor had been demolished. Without a harvest, he'd have no money to fix the *Katherine*. Without the *Katherine*, he couldn't import or export. He'd have no money to pay his men or feed his workers. People would starve. He'd starve. His ruin and the ruin of everyone in his care was complete.

He arrived home in the dim light of dusk and wandered up to his family's plot on the hill. A freshly dug grave rested with the slaves' graves. Tears blurred his eyes. They should have buried her next to his family. Guilt shredded whatever remained of his heart. Add this to the list of reasons why he never should have left.

"I'm sorry." A sob clogged his throat. "I'm sorry I left. I'm sorry I never told you how much I loved you." Tomorrow he'd ask Adana where he could get flowers for her grave. Orchids. Lottie loved those. He'd heap them on her grave, as many as he could find.

Dark shadows appeared on the horizon as his men returned from the field. He started back down the hill toward the house. His slaves must have put in a long day trying to salvage what they could.

It would never be enough.

Adana wasn't cooking in the kitchen. Had she left? Did she predict the horrors to come and escape before it was too late? Nathan sighed and trudged up the front steps. He grunted, putting too much weight on his bad leg. He lit a candle inside the parlor and sank into his favorite chair.

Lilacs. Lottie's scent haunted him. His voice was but a whisper. "God, if only You'd tell her I'm sorry." His throat constricted. "So terribly sorry."

A potted orchid sat on the end table. Adana must have put it there. Lottie would have loved it. Her face had lit up when she'd first seen its delicate flowers. She marveled at everything. Nathan's chest constricted as memories surfaced—her standing too close to the monkeys in the mangrove trees and her astonished expression when he showed her the fish she shot by accident.

He ran his hands down the sides of his head and stared at the ceiling. "Why, God? It should have been me. I mean nothing to You. You've forgotten me. At least tell her how precious she was to me. How much she meant..."

His throat closed, and he blinked away tears.

The front door opened, and a woman's form stood in the entranceway. Not just any woman.

He blinked. It couldn't be. Lottie? Dirt smeared her face as if she'd clawed her way out of the grave.

He froze. Was it the curse? Could her soul not even rest in peace?

"Nathan?"

She smiled at him and her blue eyes lit with joy. She may have been an apparition, but his heart swelled at the image. He didn't care. He only wanted to see her again.

The apparition stepped closer.

She looked so alive—so real. He blinked to clear his vision, but she remained.

"Thank God you're back." She crossed the room and put her hands on his cheeks.

She felt real. He lifted a hand and rested it upon hers. Her skin was warm.

He rose. "Lottie? Am I dreaming? Are you...? How?"

Tears shimmered in her blue eyes.

He crushed her to him. One hand dug into her hair while the other rubbed her back and caressed her arms. He needed to feel every inch. *She was alive. Lottie was alive.*

He drew back just enough to see her face. His fingers clutched her gown in a tight grip. "How?"

"God wasn't done with me yet." Her eyes bathed him in warmth, and she stroked his hair.

"But I..." He squeezed her tight and blinked away tears. "It's a miracle. I must be dreaming."

She pulled back and touched his face with a gentle stroke of her fingers. Her gaze melted into his. "I'm here, and I'm not going anywhere."

"You..." He shook his head. Truly, it made no sense. "You were in the final stages. People don't survive... Your skin was yellow and your eyes..." He crushed her to him once again. His heart filled his chest until it pressed against his ribs aching with joy. His lips trembled and his hands shook as he kissed her temple and her forehead. "The fever didn't take you?"

He felt her smile. "I'm here."

For now.

His heart recoiled and fear iced his veins.

The curse.

He shouldn't be near her. He couldn't risk her dying. He released her as if she'd burned him. "I-I can't be near you." He stepped away.

Hurt clouded her eyes.

"I should have told you this before. I should have told you…I love you. I love you, and that's why you must go." He couldn't resist coming back to brandish her lips with one last kiss. After a painfully short press, he raised his face. "Something will happen if you stay. You must return to England. I'm sending you on the next ship."

"No." She shook her head. "I won't go. The fever was not your fault."

"God has given me another chance to save you." He stroked her cheeks. The confusion marring her beautiful face ripped open the hull of his heart. "At least I got to say I love you."

"If you love me, you won't send me away."

"I'm cursed. As long as I kept you far from me, you were safe. As soon as I started to care for you, as soon as I stayed near you, you contracted the fever." The constriction of his throat changed his voice to a raspy whisper. "Lottie, you hung on death's door. You miraculously recovered when I left. What more proof do I need?"

She frowned at him. "You're being ridiculous."

"I'm a plague." He backed away, holding up his hands to ward her off. He was a contagious leper. "Stay back." His dead heart, for a brief moment, had come back to life, and it cried out for more sustenance, but the blaring of his mind screamed he was tainted—cursed. His entire being was ripping apart, but this time he would sacrifice himself for her. "Stay away. I couldn't bear it if something happened to you again. Please believe me. It's better this way."

She stepped forward. "No, I won't let you. You can *choose* blessings. You don't have to be cursed. Do you doubt God's greatness? He's more powerful than some black magic woman who murmured words to scare a young planter's son."

He stepped back farther, his leg aching. "God is punishing me. I should have said something to stop them—to save her. Instead, I stayed silent while he beat a slave to death."

Her voice was soothing, gentle. "God's grace holds no bounds. He will forgive you."

"God doesn't want anything to do with me."

"That's a lie. He loves you, and He's not punishing you. He put our punishment on Jesus's shoulders so we don't have to bear it. God wants you to come back under His protection, but you must renounce this curse. It has no hold over you."

He bumped against the wall, and the plates rattled in the cabinet.

She stepped closer. Her eyes locked on his, begging him to believe. Her fingers brushed the stubble on the side of his face.

He jerked his head away as her touch tried to burn through his resolve. His emotions splintered like a mast struck by lightning. He ached to draw her close, to feel the softness of her curves against him, to sink his face into her silky hair and inhale her womanly scent. But he couldn't. He couldn't risk her being punished for his sins.

"I'm not afraid." Her gaze bore into him.

"I can't." He gripped the edge of the cabinet. The tips of his fingers dug into the wood enough to leave a mark. "I'm responsible for you."

Tears glistened in her eyes. "I'm responsible for me, and I'm trusting God."

"You don't understand. I prayed." His voice broke. "I prayed and I prayed, but God didn't save them. Katherine died. I held her in my arms. They died because I was there."

Lottie's eyes flashed, and an angry flush stained her cheeks. She poked a finger into his chest. "That's what the devil wants you to believe." Her chest heaved and her fingers clutched the front of his shirt. "Remember the baby turtles striving to get to the ocean? The struggle is what makes them stronger. We can't stop living. If we do, then the devil wins. You can choose to face troubles with God, under His protection, or you can face them on your own. Nathan, please, choose life. Let God show you the abundance of His blessings."

"I want to believe." He wanted to with all his heart, but the risk... Could he leave her life in God's hands?

She smoothed out the wrinkles her grasp had created in his shirt and his muscles clenched in response to her touch. "I don't believe any of this came by accident. I was meant to be with you, Nathaniel Winthrop. Despite all of our mess-ups and how we've misconstrued things, God meant us to be together as man and wife. He chose us for each other. I could have convinced my mother and father if I had wanted to, but my heart knew long before my head caught on. I chose this life. I chose you, and I wouldn't change one moment."

Mr. Tallant strolled into the room and spied Nathan. "Welcome back." His gaze drifted to Lottie's hands on Nathan's chest, and he stilled. "My apologies. I didn't mean to interrupt your reunion." He quickly backed out of the room.

Lottie continued to peer at Nathan with those wide blue eyes filled with expectation.

He needed to think, to clear his head, to determine the best course of action. "Hold up, Marcus," Nathan called after him. He stepped aside and refused to look at the disappointment he knew he'd see in her face. He wanted to trust God the way Lottie did—to believe God would forgive him, but the commandments clearly said, *thou shall not murder*. Yet, he'd handed the woman over and watched her be murdered. He might as well have held the whip in his own hands.

297

CHAPTER 29

I praise you, Lord, for Nathan's safe return. You are so faithful, but now I must ask for You to reveal to him your power. Have him know You are greater than the hold of any curse.

~ Written in Lottie's prayer journal

*L*ottie flipped back the covers. She couldn't sleep, not when her husband lay in Katherine's room, and not in his own bed—not next to her. Two days passed since Nathan's return, but instead of talking things through, he chose to work it out in his own mind and had avoided her completely.

She set a place for him at her table, but he stayed too busy to eat and had supper brought to his room after everyone retired. She knocked on the door to his office, but he wouldn't answer. She followed him into the fields, but he had Mr. Tallant send her away. He claimed to be protecting her, but the walls of his fortress were suffocating her. It was as if she were living her nightmare where the sea-witch tried to drown her. The harder she fought against the current, the more she was pulled out to sea.

But the sea-witch didn't get you.

Because she'd prayed.

Exactly.

She bowed her head. *God, how can I get through to him when he keeps me at a distance? Please, speak to his heart. Reach him, because I can't.*

She prayed until she had no more words before lying back down to sleep. Yet sleep wouldn't come. If she wasn't going to slumber, at least she could get some mending done. She lit a candle and crept down the stairs. Light fanned out from under the dining room door. Who else could be up? Her breath hitched. Could it be Nathan?

She was in her night clothes, but what did that matter? He was her husband. She pushed the door open a crack, hoping to catch him unaware so he couldn't turn her away.

Adana sat alone at the table.

Tamping down her disappointment, Lottie entered the room. "Mind if I join you?"

Adana's head jerked up, and she pushed back from the table.

"Don't get up. I didn't mean to disturb you. I couldn't sleep." She eyed the large slice of bread and the hunk of cheese on the plate in front of Adana. "Did you not get enough at dinner?"

Adana's eyes lowered. "I guess I couldn't have kept it a secret any longer." She twisted her apron. "I'm going ta have Mr. Tallant's babe."

Lottie's breath hitched, but she forced her expression to remain neutral as she sat.

"It's one of da reason's I became so angry wit you." She lifted her gaze. "But I should have been thankin' you. He has decided ta mek an honest woman of me. Wit Mr. Winthrop's approval, we shall be married by da end of next week."

"How splendid." Lottie leaned forward over the table. "I'm truly happy for you."

"It's because of wat you said. He got right wit God." She broke off a piece of bread and offered it to Lottie.

"No, thank you. You're the one eating for two."

Adana smiled, and they discussed the wedding and the baby arrangements. Mr. Tallant, in his free time, was building a crib, and Lu was sewing some tiny clothes. Lottie offered her help also.

"You should be sewin' clothes for yer own child."

It was Lottie's turn to lower her gaze.

Adana's hand squeezed hers. "Deh isn't much dat stays a secret. I know Mr. Winthrop hasn't been visiting yer room."

Anger heated Lottie's neck. It wasn't her place to speak so plainly.

"I only say dis because you did me a favor when you spoke tough to me."

Lottie's anger evaporated. "He fears the curse more than he loves me."

"He fears da curse *because* he loves you."

"I can't live in fear. Living in fear isn't living."

"Den why are you down here?"

Lottie blinked at her.

"Show him a taste of what real lovin' is."

Her prayer before the Carlton's ball echoed in her mind. *Your word says a man shall leave his father and his mother, and cleave unto his wife, and they shall be one flesh. Let it be so with our marriage.* It was still the prayer of her heart, but could she make herself vulnerable and face rejection again? She rubbed her face. Shouldn't Nathan come to her? *God, I'm not brave enough.*

I did not give you a spirit of fear.

Lottie straightened.

Love perseveres.

Adana pointed to the door. "Go, Dage. God is wit you."

Lottie rose. She could do this. "You're right." She strode to the door but pivoted back around. "Why did you call me Dage?"

Adana smiled, her white teeth illuminated by the candlelight. "It means *takes a firm stand.*" She nodded towards the door. "Go, for you are courageous and yer faith is strong. Yer God will bless you for yer boldness."

Lottie patted the door frame. "God loves you too, you know."

"I'm beginin' ta understand."

Tears filled Lottie's eyes. "You are a wise woman. Thank you, my friend."

Adana rolled her lips, and she looked away, but not before Lottie caught the shimmer of tears in the woman's eyes.

Lottie strode into the foyer and placed a steady hand on the stairway railing. *Ready or not, Nathan, here comes Dage.*

∼

*N*athan woke and fought to gain his bearings. The floor didn't sway and the moon's rays outlined a pair of frilly curtains above the window. Katherine's room. He thought sleeping here would further solidify his resolve to stay away from Lottie, but the persistent ache that penetrated deep in his heart hadn't lifted. It didn't help that every time he drifted off to sleep, he dreamed of Lottie. Especially tonight. He rolled onto his back and stretched. His hand bumped something... something warm... something human.

Nathan jerked upright. "Who's there?"

"It's me." The female voice wavered. "Your *wife.*"

Knowing who it was didn't lessen his panic. Why would she speak as if he wouldn't recognize her voice, as if he didn't know her—as if she hadn't permeated his thoughts every minute of every day since the moment she asked him to dance. Didn't she understand the danger? "Why are you here?"

Her hand touched his chest. His muscles tensed, and he retracted. Her fingers slid up and cupped his cheek.

He grabbed her hand. "What are you doing?"

"I'm being a wife."

Her tone radiated confidence, but her hand trembled. The satin strands of her hair brushed over his skin and wafted the scent of lilac under his nose. Her soft lips pressed against his.

He tried to pull back, but her hands slid around his shoulders and down his back. Her mouth coaxed his, and the heat of her body lured him into an intoxicating trance. Her soft curves met his bare chest, and he grew fully aware that the only thing separating them was her night shift.

A warning surfaced in the fog. He broke their kiss. "Don't." His voice sounded harsh to his own ears.

"I am your wife." She matched his tone. "It is not right for you to turn me away."

"You don't understand."

"Oh, but I do."

"The curse will kill you."

"The curse holds no power over me. It can never take my hope." She pressed a kiss on his shoulder. "I may be hard pressed from every side, but I cannot be crushed."

Nathan sucked in a breath.

She brushed a kiss on his temple. "I may be perplexed, but I will not despair."

His fingers curled into fists as he fought to resist his desire.

She kissed the hollow of his neck between his collar bones. "I may be persecuted, but I will not be abandoned."

She was his wife. She wanted him, and he wanted her.

She kissed the corner of his mouth. "I know I can be struck down, but I will not be destroyed."

God help me. I am a weak man. He loved her more than life itself. "Keeping you alive is my one chance to redeem myself. I can't add to my list of sins."

She backed off, and Nathan inhaled a shattered breath. *Thank you, Lord.*

Stillness fell over the room except the sound of the distant waves.

Lottie didn't leave. "Why do you believe you're unforgivable?"

"I told you." He swallowed. "I allowed a woman to be beaten so horrifically she bled out and died before my eyes when I could have stopped it."

"You tried."

"I didn't try hard enough." His voice slashed the night air.

Silence, once again, stretched between them.

"Did you know Moses beat an Egyptian to death?" Her soft voice cut through the silence. "He ran and hid in the desert afterward, but God forgave him. He sought Moses out and made him one of the great forefathers of our faith."

His mother had shared a Bible story of a baby found in a river. Moses was raised by an Egyptian princess, and he later freed the Israelites from slavery through many signs and miracles. But Nathan had never heard the story Lottie spoke of.

"Did you know King David had one of his mighty men killed in order to cover his own sin of adultery? Yet, God still called David His beloved."

He knew the story of Bathsheba, but he'd never correlated it with himself.

"One of the psalms David wrote says God knows all of our thoughts. He's familiar with all of our ways, and there is nowhere we can go where He isn't present. Even the darkness cannot hide us from His love."

She cupped his face and peered deep into his soul. "God forgave you before you were even born. Your sins are covered by Jesus's blood, and God chooses to remember them no longer. You must do the same. You must decide whether you want to keep managing your guilt and pain at the sacrifice of our marriage—of me." Her voice cracked. "Or you can relinquish it to God."

His body quaked as if stretching to reach something just out of his grasp. "I don't know how."

"Pray with me." She folded his shaking hands between hers. "Lord, forgive me of my sins. Come into my heart and take control of my life. I relinquish it all to you. Show me your unconditional love."

He sucked in a deep breath and whispered, "Yes, Lord."

"Nathan."

He opened his eyes.

"We are stronger together." Love shone in her eyes as she trailed her fingertips along his jawline. She slowly pushed off the bed as if to leave.

God, I'm entrusting Lottie—myself—our marriage—into your care. He gripped her hand.

In the still of the darkness, God answered.

The same peace he'd experienced the moment he'd agreed to marry Lottie filled him now, settling his mind and spirit, scattering his doubts. He pulled her to him and devoured her mouth, making her flesh of his flesh and bone of his bone. She clung to him as he laid her among the scattered blankets and pillows and loved her the way a wife should be loved.

~

In the morning, Nathan awoke feeling more alive than he had in a long time. Maybe ever. He understood now why the rooster crowed and why the lion roared. The first rays of sun crept in through the window, illuminating Lottie's hair in a reddish-blond halo. He stroked the silky strands between his fingers. The fans of her long eyelashes rested against her rosy cheeks.

She was his. He could never have guessed how well they would fit each other, or imagined the love he'd feel for her, or known how much he needed her. She was a blessing.

He was lucky…

No. He was cursed.

He squeezed his eyes shut to block out the invasion of his thoughts.

Now, so was she.

"What's the matter?" Lottie's blue eyes were open, and they searched his. She propped her head up on her elbow. The blanket draped around her and made her look like a Greek goddess.

"I didn't mean to wake you." He shifted onto his back and stared at the ceiling. He could feel her patiently waiting for an answer. "It's always when life feels too good to be true that the doubts cry out even louder."

She slid her hand over his and laced their fingers. "There will be troubles. No one is denying that, but God will turn them around for our good. I count it a blessing that I was sick as a child, because it made me appreciate my health. I count it a blessing to have had a domineering mother because she taught me how to be strong and instilled in me an appreciation for healthy relationships. I'm blessed to have come to this beautiful island because it strengthened my faith and taught me who I truly am. I'm blessed by you." She leaned over him, and smiled. Waves of red hair cascaded over him. "You have shown my heart what it is to love."

She was right, but he couldn't release the knot of tension in his chest.

"Life is only a breath, a fading morning mist. You can waste it living in fear." She folded his hands in both of hers. "Or we can face it together. But you must make that choice. I can't make it for you."

Her face shone with strength. Her blue eyes glistened with steadfast love. He leaned into her faith, absorbing it as his own as he encased her in his arms.

"I choose blessing."

CHAPTER 30

On your morning off, meet me by the fishermen's rocks.
I shall not sleep until I look upon your bonny face.
~ *From Charlie, sent in secret to Franny*

*L*ater the following morning, Lottie had a worker drive she and Franny to the Cockleshell. She waved the driver off after they disembarked. "We'll be several hours, so enjoy your morning and check back after the noon meal."

Franny had the morning off, so they parted ways in front of the inn. "Give Charlie my regards," Lottie said before the giddy girl crossed the street to the dockside. "And tell him he'd better conduct himself as a gentleman, or I'll have him placed back on deck-swabbing duty."

A blush tinged Franny's cheeks, but she muttered, "Yes, mum."

Adana had given her a list of items she needed from town, so Lottie used it as an excuse to call upon Julia and return the pocket Bible.

She missed her friend. A visit was long overdue. She bit her lip to keep from smiling as she mounted the steps to the entrance. She couldn't wait to tell Julia the wonderful news about her and Nathan.

The wind chime shells jingled as she opened the front door and stepped into the dim foyer. The smell of spirits hung in the air, and a faint muttering came from the few men who nursed their aching heads after a night of drinking.

A mulatto woman greeted her.

"Is Mrs. Fielding in?" Lottie asked.

"She's in the back hall dining room," the woman said. "You may follow me."

The sea shells chimed again. Another customer opened the front door, and the mulatto woman hesitated, in case the person needed assistance.

"I know the way. I'll see myself there." Lottie stepped past the woman and avoided walking through the tavern. The familiar scent of mango chicken and rice caused her stomach to growl. Maybe she could join Julia for an early dinner.

The door to the dining room stood closed, which was odd. It usually remained open. She lifted her hand to knock, but hesitated when she heard a voice within.

"Winthrop won't know we're smuggling black ivory."

Captain Fielding's voice stilled her hand.

"If this run goes to plan," he said, "we'll have proven ourselves, and then they'll let us transport slaves, and we'll be in on the dealings where the real profits lie."

"How are you going to smuggle slaves under Winthrop's nose?" The tenor voice was too high to have been Paul's.

Lottie's breath stilled. Captain Fielding was a smuggler? How could he betray Nathan like that? Reminders of her fever-induced nightmare surfaced. Had it not been a dream? Was Julia part of this? Her feet itched to run back to Nathan, but the need to know the full truth kept her legs planted.

"The same as how we got rid of Skitter and Knuckles."

Lottie jolted. The men who'd been killed?

"The *Katherine* holds steady shippin' sugar as our pretense." Fielding cleared his throat. "We'll start movin' black ivory with the *Amory*. Leave the *Katherine* until Winthrop's loyalists meet with one disaster or another."

Lottie's blood stopped flowing. Did he mean Cobble, Baby, Salt, and Cook? Did he intend to kill them? *Please, Lord, no.*

She turned to leave, but two men emerged from the taproom. Their backs were to her as they said their farewells, but she recognized the voices of Mr. McCurdy and Mr. Reid from the incident in the study. She wouldn't be able to get past them without them causing a ruckus. She'd have to wait until they left.

But instead of leaving, they struck up another conversation and blocked her path to the front entrance. Perspiration broke out on her palms.

"Every time something bad happens, we blame it on the curse," Fielding said. "I played it up real good to the point he won't dare set foot on deck for fear of the curse sinkin' his ship."

"His ships mean everything to him," the other man said.

"That they do, and he can't afford to lose them. They're his only chance of saving his father's legacy. He won't come aboard."

"Lottie's a God-fearing woman. She stopped the practice of black magic at Calico Manor. She won't be hearing any talk of curses."

Lottie recognized Julia's voice. She quickly cupped her hand over her mouth to muffle her gasp. Julia was in on the deception. They were stealing from Nathan and planned to kill his crew. Her heart stung as if Julia had run her through with her rapier. How many lunches had they talked and laughed with each other? Had those been part of the deception?

"You were supposed to keep a close eye on her to keep things like that from happening," The captain sneered.

There was no response.

"What if Winthrop rallies because of her?" The tenor asked. "How long can you keep up the charade with her around?"

Captain Fielding's voice dropped to a low murmur, and Lottie pressed her ear against the door. "She should have died of fever. It would have been better for all of us, especially her."

A shiver ran through her body.

Julia spoke. "Maybe we should leave them be. We have enough to build a fine house in Florida. Let's cut and run."

She might be willing to steal their last shilling, but at least Julia didn't want her dead. Lottie pulled back from the door. Could she slip past McCurdy and Reid? She needed to get to Nathan. He must know the truth. He wasn't cursed. He was being deceived, and their friends were in grave danger.

Fielding growled in a deadly tone through the closed door. "I will have justice. Henry Winthrop stole my father's inheritance, and I won't stop until I've taken every penny away from the Winthrop family."

"Winthrop died, along with his wife and two of his children," Julia said. "Don't you think they've suffered enough?"

"Not yet." The captain's voice rose. "I should have been the sugar baron's son, reaping a harvest and using the proceeds to buy ships, not toiling in the service of the East India Company like a third child of a poor wretch."

"Lower your voice before someone overhears," the tenor said. "Listen, I'm in, but I want a third, no less, and I'll leave the problem of the wife to you."

There was a long pause.

"Agreed." The captain said. "Paul, see to Lady Winthrop."

Paul must have been standing nearby for his baritone voice answered. "Consider it done."

Leave. Run!

She stepped back from the door and collided with a servant carrying a tray of empty glasses. They crashed to the floor, sending glass and the smell of spirits everywhere. The two men at the end of the hall swiveled their heads in her direction.

The door swung open, and Captain Fielding's eyes leveled on her.

She grabbed her skirts and sprinted through the glass remnants. She only made it five steps before a hand clamped on her arm. She screamed, but the captain muffled it by pressing her face into his chest.

"How delightful to see you, my dear."

A sharp point jabbed into her side. It pierced the soft cotton of her gown, went through her stays, and poked her flesh. She winced and shifted away, but he held her tight.

"Try anything, and I'll cut out your innards," he hissed in her ear before releasing her from his chest. He pushed her into the room with Julia, Paul, and the tenor.

"It has been a long time, hasn't it?" The lilt in Fielding's voice was such that she could imagine him licking his lips and sneering a villainous smile, as if she were a rabbit and he a wolf. "Julia, aren't you happy to see your good friend again?"

Julia's face paled when she spotted Lottie. "Indeed," she said to the floor.

Lottie stared, willing Julia to meet her gaze so her eyes could question her, but Julia's focus remained averted.

"How kind of you to spare us the time of fetching you." Fielding wrenched her arm in an awkward position behind her back, and Paul tied her hands together.

The captain yanked his handkerchief from his pocket and nodded to Paul.

Paul's fingers pinched her backside. When she gasped from the pain, the captain shoved the handkerchief deep in her mouth. She gagged at the awful taste of the rag, but Paul looped a rope over her head. He jerked it tight in her mouth and tied it off behind her hair. No scream could get past her lips without it being muffled by the cloth. The deep-wedged cotton reeked of his strong cologne and dried out her tongue.

"What are you going to do to her?" Desperation rang in Julia's tone and intensified the icy fear penetrating Lottie's bones.

Fielding leveled his wife with a scathing look. "We'll take her aboard the *Amory* and sell her at auction for a pretty penny."

He yanked off Lottie's bonnet. Her neck stung where the string broke. "Winthrop will believe the curse has struck again when we show him this and tell him she met with an untimely accident."

Lottie struggled against her bindings. She had to warn Nathan. They couldn't get away with this.

"No!" Julia's eyes blazed.

Lottie jumped at her shout.

"You can't sell her like chattel." Julia clutched her husband's arm. "You know what they'll do to her. She doesn't deserve that."

"Fine." Fielding flipped his cutlass around and offered it to his wife. "Why don't you do the honors? It's time you got some blood on your hands."

Julia stared at the knife in horror. "There are other options."

"No, there aren't." Fielding nodded toward the back door. "Take her to where the row boat is stashed and lock her in the *Amory's* cargo hold."

"What if someone spots her?" The tenor voice asked. A tanned young man dressed similarly to Captain Fielding stepped forward.

"What of it?" Fielding snorted. "Do you think Winthrop's going to come after her? Leave his fields in prime harvesting time? Is he going to disrupt his trading to come looking for a wife he never wanted in the first place?" He clapped the man on the shoulder. "Captain Phelps, you overestimate a woman's hold over a man." Captain Fielding pushed Lottie towards Paul, but her boot caught in her skirt and she tripped. Fielding jerked back on her arm to keep her upright, and a shot of pain jolted her shoulder.

Julia stepped in front of them. "I won't let you do this. I won't let them do to her what was done to me."

"Stand aside, *meine liebe*."

Her defiant gaze held fast.

Hope sparked in Lottie's chest. Even though Julia had betrayed her, it didn't stop Lottie from wanting to hide behind the woman's skirts like a child behind its mother. She was a force of strength.

The sound of his fist slamming into Julia's jaw stole Lottie's breath and weakened her knees. Julia collapsed in a heap. Her arms covered her face as she cowered from her husband.

"You needed a reminder of who owns you, *mon amour*."

Julia's eyes darkened with such malice, Lottie shivered.

The captain either didn't notice or didn't care. He thrust Lottie through the doorway into Paul's waiting hands.

Paul shoved her through the kitchen. A few workers glanced up, but turned away quickly, continuing their food prep as though they'd seen nothing. Paul pushed Lottie through the back door, and she stumbled down the few steps onto a sandy path. Her knees quaked and her balance teetered, unable to steady herself with her hands tied behind her back.

Please, Lord, help me. Her chest heaved as if she couldn't draw in enough air. If she could gain someone's attention... She glanced over her shoulder at the inn, but Paul shoved her hard enough to send her to her knees. Sand sprayed in her face, and she blinked it out of her eyes. He wrenched her back to her feet and half-pushed, half-carried her over the rocky descent to the water.

Paul kept her close to the sand dunes and out of sight of any beachcombers trolling the surf until they reached the very alcove in which Nathan had held her in his arms. The piece of wood she'd nicked with a bullet rested a few yards away. A row boat lay over-turned in the sand. If Paul got her in the rowboat, it would be over. She wouldn't be able to warn Nathan or have a means of escape once the *Amory* set sail.

Julia's words haunted her. *I won't let them do to her what was done to me.* What did that mean? Would she be sold into slavery or become a lightskirt working for a petticoat-pensioner? *God, help me.*

Paul knocked her to her knees as he lifted the side of the rowboat to turn it over. This might be her only chance. She jumped to her feet and sprinted for the docks. The tip of her boots caught the hem of her skirts, tripping her up, but somehow, she kept her balance. If only she could gain Cobble or Charlie's attention.

The gag muffled her screams, and her kid boots sank in the soft sand. The thud of Paul's footfalls drew closer. The impact of the large man's body knocked the breath out of her as he tackled her into the sand. Her lungs screamed, and her muscles cried out from pain. Fine grains of sand stuck to her face and slid into her bodice.

He spit on her and cursed her in several languages. When he pushed to his feet, Lottie curled into a ball, waiting for him to pummel her. Sharp pain wrenched her head as Paul dragged her back to the rowboat by her hair. Her scalp burned, and her feet scrambled to get traction to alleviate some of the pain. He yanked her to her feet and tossed her into the boat.

Something white flashed against the black backdrop of the volcanic rocks. Was that a shirt? *Someone? Anyone?*

She hit the wooden seat of the rowboat hard with her shoulder, and a jolt of pain sliced down her arm and up her neck. Dizziness swept over her, but she fought it while she struggled to right herself. Once she did, she stayed low and whimpered like a wounded animal. If Paul thought she was injured, maybe he'd believe her to be less of a threat and leave her alone. He dragged the boat the few feet to the ocean. When he peered in the direction of the *Amory,* she dared to glance back at the rocks.

Charlie stared at her, wide-eyed, half-hidden behind a large boulder. He clutched Franny to his side, one hand over her mouth to keep her from screaming.

Charlie. Was he friend or foe? Lottie didn't know the difference anymore. Did he have Franny hostage? No. He loved her. She'd witnessed their young love. Most likely they'd come to this secret spot for stolen kisses.

God bless Franny. For once, Lottie could kiss her for disobeying an order.

She turned back, not wanting to draw attention to them.

Please, God, let them warn Nathan.

CHAPTER 31

I shall be departing on the next ship to ensure with my own eyes that my daughter is being treated in a fitting manner.

~ Letter from Lady Etheridge, lost in transit and never received by the Winthrops.

"She and Miss Franny rode into town." Adana passed plates full of saltfish and the bitter greens of callaloo to Nathan and Marcus.

Nathan released a deep breath he hadn't known he'd been holding. He kept remembering the feel of her next to him and the warmth in her eyes. He'd fallen in love with his wife. Her optimism was a light in the darkness, and he was drawn to it, craved it, desired it. Last night, he'd wrapped himself in her hope as if he could absorb her confidence. He wanted with all his being to have the strength of her faith.

"I have something I need to ask you." Marcus stared at his plate.

The muscles in Nathan's back and neck tensed, waiting for bad news.

Marcus met Nathan's gaze. "Adana and I want to be married."

Nathan relaxed, and relief brought a smile to his face. "When did this happen?"

"We've been…" Marcus squirmed in his seat. "Ah…visiting with each other, until Lady Winthrop straightened us out and helped us see we were cheating ourselves of God's best plan for us."

Lottie?

Marcus relaxed a little. "Your wife is a good woman. She changed a lot of things around here in the brief time you were away."

"Truly?" Why was he so surprised? She certainly had turned his life upside down in a short time.

"After we'd finished planting, there was a hail storm."

The same one had pummeled his ship and poked holes in his sails.

"A lot of planters had to start over. They lost several months like we did in the north field."

Nathan rubbed his temples. He'd seen the damage—another costly expense. "How is that proof of making a difference?"

"We should have lost it all. The neighbors to the right and left of us lost everything." He leaned in toward the table. "You see, Lady Winthrop was doing these strange walks every morning, talking to herself while she went. She walked the perimeter as some sort of prayer vigil, but the north fields were too far and too steep."

"It's not easy terrain," he said, "as most of it's straight uphill."

"Which is why she couldn't pray over the north field. I'm telling you, I wouldn't believe it if I hadn't seen it with my own eyes, but I stood right there. On one side of the path—the part she'd walked—the plantings stood healthy and strong. Less than a foot away on the other side, the part she hadn't prayed over, the plants were torn to shreds. It was a blessed miracle. Next day, several workers asked her what to pray. Several got up before the day began and walked the north fields in the dark, covering it in prayer before the sun even rose."

Nathan would never have believed it if the healthy cane crop didn't stand before his eyes, swaying in the breeze.

"Lady Winthrop wanted to know how she could help," Marcus continued. "I didn't know what a gently bred lady could do, but she offered to help with mending the workers' clothing. Said you had mentioned the poor condition of their clothes. Said you'd paid a pretty penny for bolts of cloths, but they were lost when the *Amory* was raided."

He squeezed his eyes shut to block out the reminder of the curse. "I did." But now, all was going to be well. He was forgiven.

"She got right in there and started mending, and the other women helped, too, when they weren't in the fields. Changed the whole attitude of the men. Lifted their spirits. I've never seen a field get planted so quickly. She transformed my opinion of your new way of planting. I'm sorry I'd been so resistant earlier. It really is a much better way.

"She showed me how it worked in the kitchen by designating specific tasks to specific women. They prepared our meal right quick. I implemented the same technique in the boiling houses. We finished each day with time to spare. People are even singing again."

Nathan frowned. "Singing their homeland songs?"

"Naw, hymns. They've been singing hymns. Helps them enjoy their work."

So that was the music he'd heard the other day. But when he drew close, the people had quieted.

"It reminds me of old times when there was joy here at Calico Manor."

But Nathan had returned, and with him the curse. "Don't get your hopes up, my friend. In this life, we will have trouble."

"But we take heart because Jesus has overcome the world."

Marcus puffed out his chest. "Learned that from this Sunday's sermon."

"That's true but…"

"Lady Winthrop's has us saying what we're grateful for each night during supper. She says we should be counting our blessings, not our problems." Marcus snorted. "I tell you, before she came, all I saw was the negative. But dash it all if I don't now see how blessed we are."

Nathan sat taller. Marcus's words and the memory of last night shoved the inkling of doubts pecking at him back into their dark corner.

"It certainly has changed my thinking for the better. And I'm as stubborn as they come." Marcus glanced toward the outdoor kitchen and smiled.

Adana smiled back at him and handed another plate of food to the staff.

"It's a wonderful feeling." Marcus leveled him with a knowing look. "Maybe you should try it." Marcus leaned in, resting his arms on either side of his plate. "Choose to be blessed and not cursed."

"Indeed. I've decided to choose—" The sound of a carriage rumbling up the lane cut Nathan off.

He squinted against the sun to see who it was. A stiff-backed woman sat next to Cobble as he pulled up in front of Calico Manor.

It couldn't be. Nathan squeezed his eyes closed and re-opened them. The sight dropped his stomach straight to his toes. The woman issued commands to Cobble, who shrank back as if under attack. It couldn't be, but it was.

Lady Etheridge.

*L*ottie climbed up on top of the stacked crates in the locked cargo hold. After Paul rowed her out to the *Amory*, she'd been roughly hauled aboard and half-dragged, half-thrown into what now served as her locked cell. She cupped her hands around her mouth and screamed once again toward the ceiling, "Help! Someone, help me!"

Could they hear her? Would anyone care if they did? Was the crew aware of the captain's misdeeds? Were they in on the deal, paid for their silence?

Lottie sat on a crate in the cramped space of the hold. There were no windows, and the stale air smelled of mold, mildew, and rot. The bars that had once imprisoned Africans to be sold into slavery now confined her to endure a similar fate.

If Captain Fielding had his way, the *Amory* would once again find masses of human cargo in this very hold, fetching a hefty price for the black ivory. Boards creaked above her as more cargo was loaded on another deck.

Lottie shook each bar once again, pushing and pulling with her entire body, but to no avail. She tugged at the lids of each crate until her fingertips bled. A rat stopped and sniffed the air in her direction before scurrying away. Lottie's entire body revolted with a shiver.

She dropped her face in her hands. "God, I'm scared."

I did not give you a spirit of fear.

"Nathan will believe it was the curse. He won't learn the truth, and Captain Fielding will keep doing evil."

Don't let your heart be troubled. Cast your cares on Me, for I care for you, and I care for Nathan.

"Lord, I need to get off this ship. Their plans are evil."

Fear not. I am with you. I will strengthen you. I will uphold you with My righteous right hand.

Lottie lowered her hands and fought to settle her troubled heart. "You're right. I will trust You."

The muffled sounds of someone barking commands drifted from above, followed by the thumps of crates being dropped . How long did she have before they set sail?

"Pssst. Lady Winthrop." Charlie peeked around a barrel on the other side of the cell bars.

"Charlie." Lottie jumped down from her crate. She grasped the bars, pressing the sides of her face against the cold metal. "You've got to get me out. We must warn Nathan."

He crept closer, but stayed crouched out of view behind the barrel. "I don't have the key." He yanked on the lock, but it didn't budge.

"Who would have a key?"

Charlie's face fell. "Only the captain."

Her spirits plummeted.

He searched the hold and found a wooden shim. Holding it in one hand, he dropped to his knees and used the piece of wood as a chisel to pick apart the wood at the base of the metal bars.

Bits of wood splintered, but she couldn't tell if it came from the floor boards or from the shim. "How did you get here?"

"When I saw Captain Fielding's man handle you rough-like, I knew something was amiss. I swam up and climbed aboard unnoticed." A smug smile flittered on his lips. "It's not the first time I've boarded an enemy ship. It's merely the first time I've boarded one of our own ships."

"Where's Franny? Is she safe?"

His hair flopped into his eyes, and he shoved it back with his hand. "I told her to stay hidden under the pier. She'll be safe."

"You've got to help me get out. Captain Fielding and Captain Phelps have been stealing from Nathan. They're the ones who planted the idea of the curse so they could smuggle his cargo and blame its disappearance on pirates."

"Hound's teeth!" He paused in the chopping motion and peered at her.

"I overheard them talking about it. They plan to sell me on the black market to keep me from warning Nathan."

Charlie hacked faster at the boards and shook the metal bar. Streaks of lighter wood appeared, but the shim snapped with a loud crack. "Blast."

Two boisterous voices sounded outside the hold. Were they coming this way?

"Go." Lottie pointed towards the door. "Go quickly. Tell Nathan what they're conspiring to do."

Charlie hesitated. "I can't leave you—"

"Don't worry about me."

"But they're prepared to make sail. The ship might leave before we return."

"God will protect me." She reached through the bars and grabbed his shirt sleeve. "It's more important for Nathan to know the truth."

"But—"

"Be careful. Don't let them see you."

The voices outside the hold grew distant.

"Hurry." She commanded, shoving him towards the exit.

He scrambled to do her bidding.

Lottie stepped back from the bars and harrumphed. Turned out she had a lot of her mother in her.

~

*N*athan fought to keep his face pleasant, despite the unpleasant sound coming from the chair across from him.

"I sailed the Atlantic to see my daughter, but you have yet to produce her." Lady Etheridge's lips thinned into a straight line as she sat in the parlor. Her assessing eyes slid over the contents of the room.

Thankfully, Lottie had already added some feminine touches

to make the salon more presentable. A planter sat on the end table with a delicate orchid in bloom, and some of his mother's china had replaced his rolls of maps in the casement, making for a much more appropriate display.

He'd spent the last three hours inundated with Lady Etheridge's demands. He'd shown her the house and pulled workers out of the fields to make her accommodations presentable. The staff bumped into one another, rushing to do her bidding. He offered to pay for a room at the Cockleshell Inn, but she refused. She demanded to see up close how her daughter was faring and under what conditions.

"I knew I should have come sooner." She pursed her lips. "I can see this place is in desperate need of renovations. The kitchen isn't even attached to the house."

Nathan exhaled slowly to calm his temper. "The kitchens are built separate to keep the heat away and to reduce the chance of fire spreading to the living areas."

"Well, Charlotte is too delicate to live so"—her eyes drifted around the room—"simply."

A muscle in his jaw twitched. "Your daughter is stronger than you think."

"Charlotte may not have the boldness to say it, but if you cannot provide for my daughter, then I shall insist you take the money I offered, or else return to London. You can run your merchant business from there."

He spoke through clenched teeth. "I never wanted, nor will I take your money, and an annulment of our marriage is out of the question."

"That's the response I had hoped to hear." Lady Etheridge smiled. "It's the reason why I implemented such a preposterous plan."

"What?" His eyes shot open. "Are you saying you never expected me to keep my hands off your daughter?" Nathan rose from his chair. "Are you denying you wanted to keep Lottie as your personal servant so badly you offered to annul our marriage?"

Adana passed by the doorway and eyed him.

Splendid. He'd shouted it loudly enough for all the staff to be in the know. He lowered his voice, but his tone turned deadly. "Lottie deserves better than what you would offer her. She deserves better than you, and she deserves better than me." He closed his eyes, and silence fell over the room.

"Indeed."

A tremor ran through him. He opened his eyes and glared. "Madame, I do not care for your sarcasm."

Lady Etheridge's eyes issued him a challenge. "I'm not being sarcastic. I'm in wholehearted agreement. I understand full well the wonderful qualities my daughter holds, and I'm glad to hear you've discovered them as well."

He rubbed his temples. He must be losing his mind. If it wasn't him, then Lady Etheridge was certainly a madwoman.

"When you first met Lottie, she'd been going through a rebellious phase." She sighed and glanced heavenward. "Most wouldn't have thought much of it, but I know my daughter very well. I spent day and night for months on end by her side. I'm sure she told you what a sickly thing she was when she was younger."

He found himself nodding, despite the ridiculousness of the moment.

"Her expressive face also gives away her every emotion."

He grunted his agreement.

"I recognized the signs well before Charlotte did."

Where was she going with this?

Lady Etheridge's lips curved into a reminiscent smile. "It started when I instructed her to wear the lavender gown. Instead, she donned the pale green. I'd find her embroidery stitched in the opposite corner from where I told her to place it." She crossed her arms with a haughty air. "And then, she stopped powdering her hair."

Nathan's patience ran out. "What are you trying to say?"

"Whatever I told my daughter not to do, she was going to do it, merely to spite me." Lady Etheridge raised her chin a notch. "If I'd told her to love and obey you, she would have given you the dickens. So instead, I made her believe I didn't want the two of you together."

Her lips pinched into a smug expression. "I saw the way you eyed each other. It was the same way Lord Etheridge and I gazed at each other in our prime." She rested back in her chair, as if finished. "I long for grandchildren. My reckless son will take years to settle down."

She sighed. "If I hadn't intervened, I'd be an old woman, unable to bounce them on my knee, before I had any. Heaven knows, Lord Middleton certainly wasn't going to come up to snuff, and I daresay, I wouldn't want his weak-minded children tainting our bloodlines anyway."

"But you'd farm your daughter out to a complete stranger?"

"You are not a stranger. Your mother was the sister of my brother-in-law. My sister married your uncle. I've known about you all your life. I know you were set down from Eton for jumping a horse over the headmaster's table. I know you broke your left arm from an unsuccessful attempt to gather coconuts. And I know you devoted yourself to your family." She arched a brow. "I'd ruled you out as my son-in-law merely due to your inconvenient location, but then my daughter had that foolish incident with the candle."

Nathan blinked, completely at a loss for words.

"What I don't understand is your ridiculous belief in a superstitious curse."

"You don't know the things that have happened—" *Wait a minute.* He raked a hand though his hair. She knew his mother? She knew about the curse?

The pounding of horse hooves dragged Nathan's attention away from the tangle in his mind.

Thank heaven, Lottie was back. He couldn't bear another minute with his mother-in-law. She'd completely muddled him to the point that he wasn't certain if up was down or down was up.

"That's probably Lottie now." Nathan stood and bowed to his mother-in-law.

"It's about time she returned." Lady Etheridge rose. "I was beginning to wonder if you were stalling."

Nathan excused himself and stepped outside. He raised his hand to shade his eyes from the glare and made out Charlie's figure on horseback galloping, Franny clinging to the saddle for dear life in front of him.

A jolt of fear shot through him. Franny and Lottie had ridden into town together.

The strained look on Charlie's face warned something must be wrong. Where was Lottie?

Lord, please, no. Not Lottie!

Nathan broke into a full sprint and skidded to a halt as Charlie slowed the horse and jumped down.

"They've got her." Charlie gasped for air. His hair was damp and so were his clothes. "They're gonna sell her at auction."

"What? Who's got whom?"

The door slammed behind him. Charlie's eyes darted to the woman descending the front porch stairs. Nathan grabbed Charlie's soaked lapel, tempted to strangle him if he didn't reveal what he knew faster.

"Captain Fielding and Captain Phelps." Charlie shoved his hair out of his face.

"What about them? Someone's got them? Where's Lottie?"

"No." Charlie heaved another breath. "They've got Lottie."

He couldn't make sense of the words. Fielding was his

friend. What would he do with Lottie? Charlie must be mistaken. "Are you certain?"

Franny broke into sobs and lowered her head into the horse's mane. Miraculously, Lady Etheridge remained silent behind him.

Charlie held his hands up. "They've been using you. Sellin' your goods and blaming it on pirates. Captain Fielding's behind it all, and he's got Lottie in the hold. I boarded the *Amory* and saw her locked up there myself. I couldn't get her free."

Lady Etheridge gasped.

Darkness encompassed Nathan's periphery until his vision consisted of a narrow tunnel. At the far end, Franny wailed and Charlie awaited his next command. "It's the curse." Dazed, he staggered a few steps. "I told her to stay away from me. This is my fault."

"Yer not cursed." Charlie grabbed his shoulders and shook him back into the light. "The Captain talked up the curse to scare you off so he could steal from you." His grip tightened. "It was a lie, not a curse." Charlie released Nathan's arm and pressed his hands against the sides of his head. "They have her, and they're getting away."

They have Lottie.

His life leapt into focus. "Saddle my horse!"

The stable boy ran to do his bidding.

Nathan darted back toward the house, brushing past a stunned Lady Etheridge.

"It's too late," Charlie yelled.

Nathan skidded to a halt on the porch and pivoted back around.

Charlie's shoulders slumped. "They were already settin' sail before I even got off the ship. What are we going to do?"

"The *Katherine* is still under repairs." Nathan raked a shaky hand through his hair and fought the panic seizing his brain. "It's in no condition to sail, and even if I recruited twenty men, we'd be delayed at least a week. Lottie could be as far as Santa Domingo by then."

"I know of a ship we might borrow," Lady Etheridge said.

Charlie and Nathan rounded on her. Even Franny stopped sobbing and straightened.

Charlie tipped his head toward Lady Etheridge and mouthed, *Who is she?*

"You may refer to me as Lady Etheridge." She peered down her nose at him.

"Winthrop's mother-in-law."

Charlie paled, and his Adam's apple bobbed.

How the woman heard Charlie's silent question, Nathan didn't have time to fathom, nor did he have the time for introductions. "What ship?"

"I do believe Captain Anthony Middleton's ship is in port."

"A British frigate?" Charlie's mouth dropped open. "The British navy isn't going to loan out a warship."

"Then we'll board it." Nathan set his jaw.

Charlie pushed his hair out of his eyes. "We're gonna steal a warship?"

"Borrow." Lady Etheridge arched a single brow. "And don't think for a minute you will do this without me. She's my daughter. I'm going with you."

Nathan didn't have time to argue and, judging by the determined set of her jaw, it would have been fruitless anyway. "Charlie, have a carriage brought around for Lady Etheridge and Franny, then meet me at the docks and help me gather those I know we can trust. Only crewmen who've been with me from the start—Cobble, Salt, Baby, Tucker, and the like. I'll be right back."

He burst into the house and bounded up the stairs two at a time. In his room, he removed a key from his dresser drawer and slid a box out from under the bed. He jabbed the key in the lock, turned it, and lifted the lid. The deed to Calico Manor and its lands lay neatly folded among the contents. It was his only bargaining chip. He knew where Fielding would take her. There was no doubt in his mind. Fielding had slipped Lafitte's name into too many conversations for him not to be smuggling goods to Grand Terre, but would this absurd plan work?

His hands shook as he removed the deed and returned the box under the bed. He'd entrusted Lottie to God, and now she'd been kidnapped by someone he'd believed to be his friend. He wanted to blame the curse, but the curse was a farce.

What would Lottie do in this situation?

She'd pray.

The answer filled his mind without any hesitation. Nathan tipped his face up to the ceiling. "Lord, protect Lottie. Don't let a hair on her head be damaged. Make a way for this plan to work and help us be swift in our rescue. Amen."

He jumped to his feet and scrambled back down the stairs. As he exited the house, the stable boy steadied the horse out front. Nathan mounted it. The horse sensed his urgency and danced underneath him. With a click of his heels, the mare broke into a full gallop. Nathan's fingers dug into the leather of the reins. Despite the heat, a cold sweat broke over his body. His blood pounded in his ears, and every square inch of him screamed *faster*! His heart continued to cry out to heaven.

Help us, Lord. We must reach Lottie in time... Oh, God, please...

CHAPTER 32

Men, I am in need of your services in this dark hour. The voyage may be perilous and I cannot ensure your safety.
~ From Winthrop to specific members of the crew of the
Katherine

*N*athan crept over the rail and sneaked up behind Anthony Middleton. Middleton had left his crew and now relieved himself over the rail of the ship. The loyal crewmen of the *Katherine* clung to grappling ropes over the sides of the British frigate, just out of sight of Middleton. Charlie swung to the right just in time to miss the stream.

Lady Etheridge gasped, but Baby elbowed her as a reminder to keep quiet. At first, she'd balked at the indecency of climbing on a man's back, but after learning it was the only way she'd be coming along, she begrudgingly accepted her fate. If Nathan hadn't been so worried for Lottie, he might have savored the moment.

His men followed Nathan's lead, boarding the ship with the same stealth. He signaled for them to spread out.

Middleton staggered back toward his British naval men,

who were all gathered on the main deck. Loud peals of laughter filled the air as someone won a hand of cards. Bottles clanked, followed by silence as they each imbibed, only to resume their gaiety. Nathan skulked closely behind Middleton. The man reeked of rum and stumbled twice, but caught the rail for balance. Nathan laid a hand on his shoulder before he reached full-view of his sailors.

"Bloody—" He whirled around and would have fallen if Nathan hadn't steadied him.

"Winthrop! You blackguard. What are you doing here? Remove yourself before I arrest you and lock you in our gallows."

"I'm in need of your ship. Mine has been rendered unseaworthy."

Middleton burst out laughing. "You jest." He leaned his hand on the sidewall of the quarterdeck. "This isn't a fishing boat. You don't borrow a British frigate."

"Lottie has been captured by pirates. I need your ship to bring her home."

Middleton's laughter dwindled.

Behind Middleton, the frigate's crew crowded around a sailor dealing out cards. The men each scooped up their stacks and squinted over their cards at their opponents faces. No one noticed the additional pairs of eyes creeping up behind them.

"'Tis a pity, but I have my orders to follow." He turned to walk away. "For what it's worth, I hope you find a ship and see her returned." He waved a dismissive hand. "See yourself out the way you came."

"I'd hoped to do this with your consent."

Middleton froze and slowly swiveled back around. A haughty smile curled his lips, and he snorted. "You're more of a fool than I thought."

Nathan unsheathed his cutlass and pointed it at Middleton's

throat. "That may be, but either way, I'm taking your ship to save Lottie. With or without your consent."

"My men will hang you for treason." His Adam's apple bobbed.

"Not if you tell them about your new set of orders." At the edge of Nathan's vision, the British sailors raised their bottles in a toast. "Look past your men, and you'll see you're under siege. We have you surrounded, but my men won't act unless I give the signal. I'd hate for this to come to blows, especially when your men are at a disadvantage, being so fuddled on island rum."

Middleton's face noticeably paled, even in the moonlight. "You'll pay for this, Winthrop." A muscle twitched in his jaw. "With your head."

Nathan held Middleton's gaze. "I'd give that and more to see Lottie safe."

∿

*L*ottie landed on her hands and knees at the booted feet of Captain Fielding. His younger version, Captain Phelps, dusted off his hands. "The hold's a mess. At least three of the crates are ruined, covered in vomit. And yer not gonna get the pretty penny yer wantin' with her lookin' like a slattern and smellin' like a rotting corpse."

She removed a splinter of wood embedded in her palm. She didn't doubt she looked a fright. The intermittent bits of sleep she'd received in the last week had been in a seated position, perched up on top of a stack of crates with her head resting against the hull of the ship. The first night, the crates shifted as the ship crested a big wave and toppled her chamber pot. Its sickly contents seeped back and forth along the floorboard beneath her.

"We don't have time to give her a proper cleanin'." Captain Fielding puffed out a sigh. "Have yer man do what he can to get her presentable before they board." He stared at her with menacing eyes. "Yer marriage came as a surprise and a boon." He jabbed a finger in her direction. "You were supposed to keep Nathan at home in yer bed, but you couldn't even do that right. Yer not worth the trouble you make. I'll be glad to be done with ya."

A hand clamped around her arm and yanked her to her feet. A burly man with a jagged scar across his face hauled her up two flights of steps to the main deck. She squinted against the bright sun, but couldn't resist lifting her face to its warm rays. She hadn't seen daylight in seven days. The sails snapped in the wind. A flash of red and blue waved above. A French flag? Was Captain Fielding sailing for France?

Men scurried about, and she peered into each of their faces. Had Charlie made it off the ship, or was he hidden among the ship's crew, or worse, locked up below in another hold? *Please, God, let him be with Nathan.*

"Bring to!" Captain Phelps commanded his men to slow the ship to a stop.

The burly man with the scar released her, and she rubbed her upper arm.

Off the port bow, another ship neared to almost within boarding distance.

A crewman with a faded scarf tied over his balding head belayed a nearby line.

Lottie stepped toward him. "Please, help me. I'm being held captive. I'm Lady Win—"

A barrel of water hit her with the force of a wave. She screamed as it drenched her gown and soaked her hair. She sputtered, spitting out the dirty salt water that had probably been used to swab the deck. The burly man and the crewman cackled with laughter as she wiped the water from her eyes.

The sky darkened as the *Amory* fell under the shadow of the other ship. A shiver raised the hair on her arms. She swallowed against the rising panic that gripped her throat and threatened to suffocate her. On the other ship, grisly-looking men tossed ropes over the *Amory's* rails to secure the sides, then raised planks to connect the two ships.

Captain Fielding was going to sell her to these men.

Lord, I need a miracle.

God spoke Nathan's words into her heart. *Problems are the soil in which miracles happen.*

A plank slammed against the rail, and Lottie jumped back. The man with the scar across his face clutched her upper arm to keep her from running. Three men stepped up onto the planks from the other ship. In a feat of balance, they crossed over to the *Amory* like cats on a rooftop ledge.

Captain Fielding's voice boomed behind her. "Welcome, friends. We have many dealings to do this day."

CHAPTER 33

I never meant it to come to this, I can no longer justify
my husband's actions.
~ *Missive from Julia Fielding to Winthrop*

A nudge jarred Lottie awake. She lifted her head off of its
warm cushion. The burly man snarled down at her.

Merciful Heavens. Had she drifted off to sleep while standing
up? And, leaning against the man's arm, no less?

The sun had been setting when Captain Fielding and the
pirates went below deck to inspect the barrels of sugar,
molasses, and other cargo stolen from Nathan. Now the stars
were bright in the night sky. Her barely-damp hair whipped
about in the breeze. Captain Fielding and Phelps emerged from
below deck, followed by the three pirates.

The shortest one, as thick as he was tall, laughed and wacked
Fielding on his back. "Your best bottle of port and finest meal
won't persuade me to go against Lafitte's orders. He's bloomin'
mad about the damage you did to Beluche's ship, and he'll be
speaking to you in person about it."

It might only be the moonlight, but Captain Fielding's face appeared deathly pale.

"Is this the woman yer sellin'?" The thick pirate pointed at her and stepped forward.

"Indeed." Captain Fielding nodded and stood behind the pirate. "This lady-bird is a mite timid, but clean her up a bit, and she'll warm any man's bed."

The pirate held his lantern high over Lottie's head and nodded.

The burly man's fingers squeezed Lottie's cheeks so hard, her mouth opened with a gasp.

The pirate shifted her head this way and that. "She's got all her teeth and is fair of face, but not everyone likes red hair."

Burly-man released her, and Lottie rubbed her cheeks.

"What'll you pay for her?" Captain Fielding crossed his arms over his chest, and the frill of his cuffs hung down.

Each battle prepares you for the next one. Lottie lifted her chin and faced the pirate the way she'd always wanted to confront her mother, and with the same bravery she'd used to confront Nathan. "I demand to see Jean Lafitte." Her voice echoed in the night air.

Stunned silence fell over the crew, and all eyes peered in her direction. Only the sloshing of the waves against the ships could be heard.

The pirate rested fisted hands on his hips. "And who might be asking to speak with our leader?"

A plan came to her in a flash, and the words flew out of her mouth before she could consider the repercussions. Lottie's spine straightened, and she pulled her shoulders back into the best imitation of her mother. "Tell him Lady Winthrop requests his presence, daughter of Lord and Lady Etheridge and wife of Nathaniel Winthrop. He will remember his friend from their schooling at the military academy."

Captain Fielding stepped forward. "Pay her no heed. She's a conniving actress."

The pirate raised a single brow. "Or is she a timid mouse? Which is it, Fielding? She certainly seems spirited, and if she's an actress then, by Jove, she does a good impression of the English quality."

The loathing in Captain Fielding's gaze fell upon her like a hangman's noose, but Lottie's spine locked into position, ready to battle. Would her plan work?

"She's coming with me." The pirate turned and ambled away.

Lottie glanced over her shoulder at the rough pirates manning the other ship. Had she caused her situation to go from bad to worse?

Lord, protect me.

Fielding blocked his path. "You haven't paid for her yet."

The pirate's assessing gaze roved from Lottie's head to her kid boots. The all-too-familiar feeling of not measuring up to her mother's expectations weakened her resolve. She hid her hands in the folds of her skirt.

"I daresay, she'll have more fitting accommodations on my ship. I will not allow her to be touched until we can get this whole thing sorted out with Lafitte." The pirate raised a brow. "Stand aside, Captain."

Fielding's face twisted into a snarl, and he reached for his cutlass.

Five pirate men drew their swords faster than Lottie could blink and aimed the tips at Fielding's throat.

Captain Fielding's crew wasn't at the ready and struggled to pull their swords.

"Stand down." Fielding told his men as he stowed the weapon. He raised both hands. "Have it your way."

Two men each flanked Lottie like sentinels. The pirate leader stopped at the planks and helped Lottie up over the rail. He backed toward his ship with both her hands in one of his.

The breeze whipped her skirts and tossed her hair about her face. The plank swayed as the ships bobbed in the swirling black waters. Her stomach lurched, and her fingers clamped down.

"I gotcha now. Fielding gets off too easy if you become shark bait. I'd like to keep you around a while longer, if nothin' else than ta watch Fielding have an apoplectic fit." He walked backwards down the plank toward his ship, tugging her along after him.

A splash sounded below, and she looked to see the white crest of a wave as it curled and dissolved against the side of the ship. Her heartbeat quickened to double time. Dizziness swept over her, and she teetered on the plank. A high-pitched squeak sounded in her throat.

"Keep yer eyes up here." He pointed two fingers at his own eyes. "It will help with yer balance."

She nodded. Her hair stuck to her lips and occasionally blocked her vision, but she focused on the man. God was her protector. He'd been faithful. He wouldn't let her drown, and if He did, then she'd trust it was for a greater plan.

In the lantern's light, the man's leathered face appeared harsh, and his tone was gruff, but a spark glowed in the depths of his eyes. "The name's Captain Dominique You, but my crew calls me Captain Dominique."

She inched the soles of her boots down the wooden slat.

Captain Dominique reached the other side and reeled her in.

She stepped onto the pirate ship rail and exhaled a relieved breath. "Pleasure to meet you, Captain. I wish it were under better circumstances."

He grinned a wicked smile. "Rendezvous with danger makes for a well-lived life."

"Indeed." She'd survived crossing the Atlantic, the fever, a black magic curse, and so far, being captured. All these things, had strengthened her faith. Captain Dominique's words reinforced that God was protecting her. "I'm not in danger with you, am I?"

"Yer either spirited or nicked in the nob." His brows drew together. "What makes you say such a thing? Men three times yer size quiver with fear in my presence."

"I prayed for a rescue, and here you are. God sent you to be my champion."

Captain Dominique threw back his head and guffawed with deep, bellowing laughter. "Did you hear that?" He glanced over his shoulder at his men anchoring the plank. "I'm a knight in shining armor."

Lottie dared him with her eyes to disagree. "Am I wrong?"

"That's for Lafitte to determine, not me, but Cap'n Fielding wears his emotions. I'm not sure what you've done to wrong him, but there's nothing but malice in his eyes." His gaze shifted over her shoulder to the *Amory*. "Be prepared. You haven't seen the last of Fielding yet. He'll be following us to Barataria."

He aided her down onto the main deck. She could smell the salt on his skin. The scent was similar to Nathan's when he was at sea. A pang of longing twisted her heart. Would she ever see him again? *Please God, let Charlie be with him. Let him convince Nathan he isn't cursed.* Maybe now, God could redeem his heart and heal him of all his undeserved guilt.

"Well done. You'll be scaling the rat lines in a fortnight." Captain Dominique laughed with a wheeze like Cobble. He passed her to a pair of meaty hands, who grabbed her upper arm. She peered up at a massive man who made Baby look like a child.

"This here is Shorty. He'll show you yer accommodations."

The irony of his name raised a bubble of mirth to her throat. She pinched her lips together to force it back down.

Captain Dominique whacked Shorty on the shoulder. "I believe she's findin' yer name amusing."

Shorty glared at her as if she were a bug he considered stepping on.

The captain eyed the man. "Keep watch at her door. No comings or goings or funny business. She's requested a meetin' with Lafitte."

Shorty nodded. "This way." He spoke in a deep voice and added a wave of his platter-sized hand.

Lottie followed him past the leering eyes of the crew and below deck. A man in the galley whistled at her as his eyes lingered over her form. He spoke with jeering lips what she assumed was a lewd comment, but his accent was so thick she didn't understand enough to be offended. Shorty silenced the man with a growl.

He ushered her into a room and ducked his head to make it through the doorway. Lottie peeked around him. The chamber was sparse in furnishings. A desk was nailed to one wall and, above it, a painting of a scantily clad woman peered down at her with a coy smile. On the opposite side, an overly long bed spanned the length of the room.

Only a very tall person would need a bed so large. She raised her gaze to meet Shorty's. "Is this your chamber?"

He didn't answer, merely glowered at her.

She released the sides of her gown and placed a hand on his sleeve. "I'm sorry. I don't mean to put you out."

He shrugged, but the creases in his frown lessened. He shuffled his feet and wiped his hands down his sides. "Captain's dinner is at eight."

The coolness in his eyes reminded her of Adana. She, too, had protective walls and a toughness to her, but when Lottie looked closer, she saw a desperate need for acceptance. "Thank you. Perhaps at dinner you may tell me how you received the nickname Shorty."

He didn't respond.

"I bet you can't guess what nickname they gave me on the *Katherine?*"

He crossed his arms, and he grunted. "Red."

"No."

"Flame."

"They considered that, but no. It was *Boss.*"

Shorty's face cracked into a slow smile. He turned and strode out of the room, but before he slammed the door shut with those meaty hands, Lottie heard his chuckle.

She sighed and resisted the urge to nibble out her nervousness on her fingernails. Instead, she folded her hands in prayer. *All right God, now we only need to meet the infamous Caribbean pirate, Lafitte, win his favor, and convince him to provide me with passage back to St. Kitts.*

She sank onto the bed and peered out the small porthole window.

Problems are the soil in which miracles flourish.

CHAPTER 34

We've acquired an interesting guest. She has requested an audience with you, and you may know her husband, Nathaniel Winthrop.

~ From Captain Dominique You to Captain Jean Lafitte

*T*he hazy morning sun warmed Lottie's face as she strolled above deck. The ship had slowed, and the wind no longer whipped loose tendrils that had escaped the piece of twine she'd used as a hair tie.

A strip of land emerged above the fog off their port bow. Her stomach flipped like a leaf before a rainstorm. They'd reached Barataria. She gripped the rail tighter. Galileo may have proved the earth was round, but the sensation of her life sailing off a precipice persisted.

She set her shoulders. God was with her, and if The Almighty was for her, who could be against her? She was stronger now. The Lord had seen her through so much already.

Captain Dominique and Shorty stood at the helm, deep in discussion, occasionally peering back at the shadow of the *Amory* trailing in their wake. As if sensing her presence, Captain

Dominique tipped his hat and nudged Shorty. Shorty frowned, but raised his hand in a gentle wave. The beast of a man was as shy as they came around women, but Lottie had worked hard to set him at ease.

Despite the circumstances, her voyage with Captain Dominique and his crew had been far better than her treatment under the hands of Captain Fielding. She'd been allowed her freedom to roam the ship during the day, but Captain Dominique had explained that, for her safety, she needed to stay in her room at night. The crew grew raucous after supper when the ale freely flowed.

Unfortunately, her stomach protested against the confines, and she fought to keep her supper down. Her mind swirled with the unknowns of her future and speculated on the horrors of a pirate's lair. But worst of all, her heart ached to look on Nathan's face one last time. She should have told him what he meant to her. Now she may never have the chance. Remorse dampened her pillow each night.

In the wee morning hours, after her tears ran dry, after the crew had their fill of rum and the laughter and songs died away, the belly of the ship moaned.

Captain Fielding's words rang in her ears. *If we prove ourselves, then they'll let us deal in black ivory.* Slaves. Their woeful cries raised the hairs on her arms. This was a smuggler's ship, and although Captain Dominique had been hospitable, the early morning wails were a reminder that her escorts were dangerous men with wicked reputations. If she hadn't been fair of skin, if Nathan hadn't schooled with Lafitte himself, would she be sharing their fate?

Might she still? It was yet to be determined.

God's plan is bigger than my fear. He's bigger than Lafitte.

"Would ya like ta have a look, mademoiselle?" Captain Dominique lifted the spy glass in the air and raised his heavy brows.

She nodded and stepped up to the helm.

"We're still a ways from Barataria, but welcome to what the French named Louisiana." The captain handed her the spy glass.

It was heavier than she'd anticipated, and the end dipped in her hands, but Shorty helped her balance it. Lottie raised the piece to her eye and peered through. A strip of beach and a brackish inlet loomed before her. She stepped back.

Shorty chuckled at her reaction.

"Laugh at my expense again," she studied the speckling of islands, "and I'll switch the alligator emblem you requested embroidered on your shirtfront to a bouquet of flowers instead."

Shorty stiffened.

Captain Dominique let out a hearty guffaw and pounded Shorty on the back. "Now I understand how she got her *nom de guerre*. Boss is perfect for such a formidable lady."

Thick waves of green sea grass covered the rich delta soil. She scanned the shoreline where fingers of rivers emptied into the gulf, culminating in a maze of little isles and fertile land masses. "Shorty, you never did tell me how you received your nickname."

He released his hold on the spy glass, and she could hear his feet shuffle as he shifted his weight.

"Ah, now that's a simple tale." Captain Dominique's deep voice hinted at a grin. "You see, the crew here, when they have to divvy up an unfavorable task on Barataria, they hold up a fistful of reeds or sticks. One is cut shorter than the others, but you can't tell by how it sits in a man's fist. Each one chooses a reed. Whoever gets the shortest one loses the draw and has to take on the unfortunate chore. Shorty, here, notoriously drew the shortest one every time, earning himself the nickname."

"Truly?" Lottie lowered the spy glass and blinked at Shorty.

Shorty stared straight ahead and adjusted the wheel as if it took all of his concentration.

"It was either Shorty or Unlucky." Captain Dominique stuck a fisted hand on his hip. "No one loses that many, but no one could prove foul play."

"But his hard work paid off." She peered through the spy glass once more. "He's now the first mate."

Shorty nodded with a grunt.

"That does put a nice spin on it." Captain Dominique rocked back on his heels. "The crew didn't see it that way. They joked about a port woman putting a hex on him, which probably contributed to Shorty's fear of women."

Lottie dropped the spy glass to her side. "It's that kind of gibberish that got me into this predicament."

"Superstition weighs heavy in these parts."

She raised the spy glass, but this time she swung the wide end south toward the *Amory*. Captain Fielding stood at the helm with Captain Phelps. Fielding flung his hands in the air. The frill of his cuffs swung back and forth under his wrist. His lips curled as he hurled words at the younger captain. His sharp movement filled Lottie with courage. If Fielding was nervous, wouldn't that be good for her?

"I can see yer still worried about Fielding." Captain Dominique gently tugged the spy glass out of her hands.

Lottie sucked in a deep breath and released it. "The Lord is my defender. 'God knows what is going on in the home of the wicked and heaps disaster upon them.' I read that in Proverbs twenty-two this morning."

"You are *une femme courageuse*," Captain Dominique said. "Means a brave woman. I wouldn't be surprised if that husband of yours turns hell upside down looking for you."

She shook her head. "My husband's ship was badly damaged by a hailstorm." She heaved a heavy sigh. "He will not be sailing anywhere, anytime soon."

"I think you underestimate your appeal." The captain raised a brow. "If he has anything sittin' between his ears, then like I said, he'll turn hell upside down searching for you. He'll find a way."

"You are too kind." She forced a smile.

"It's time to prepare to disembark." He shooed her away. "Go collect yer personal items and fill yer stomach. We'll be loading the pirogues and rowing to Barataria within the hour."

~

"Mademoiselle, what do you think of Grand Terre?" Captain Dominique's lips twisted into a grin.

Lottie sat in the flat-bottomed boat next to him while another crewman rowed them to the island. Before leaving the ship, she had bid Shorty farewell and thanked him for the use of his cabin. He would accompany her no further, for his services were needed to oversee the unloading of the slaves, who were being taken to what the men referred to as the Temple—a *chenière*—small, sandy island—where the smuggled items were auctioned.

Brown pelicans perched on pylons as ever-watchful sentries. Fishermen in a small boat off to their left lowered their nets, unconcerned with their arrival. Grand houses perched on stilts amongst a background sea of blue, green, and gold. The delta created a labyrinth of waterlogged islands and marshes—a liquid land. Would it trap her in its midst or swallow her whole?

"It is perfect for our needs." Captain Dominique inhaled a hearty breath. "A deep harbor for our ships, a sheltered cove to anchor them during storms. The north and east lead into a labyrinth, where bayous, swamps, and rivers intersect. Only the seasoned navigator knows how to find his way."

"It sounds like an ingenious hideout for miscreants."

Captain Dominique threw back his head and laughed. *"Femme intelligente."* He nodded his head at her. "It doesn't keep out the riff-raff, but it does keep away government officials, and foreign invaders have a way of disappearing." He cackled at his own joke until his shoulders shook. His black eyes twinkled with mirth. He released a sigh and pointed. "See those young oak trees there?"

Lottie nodded.

"I planted those. Someday they will be giant and protect our island from storms."

She shifted to face Captain Dominique and tilted her head. "Why Captain, I never would have taken you for a horticulturalist."

"Now, *chérie*." He winked at her, "I have enough nicknames. I won't have you calling me the gardener. It would ruin my wicked reputation."

She folded her hands. "You have been nothing but kind to me. And besides, I believe it is good for you to have other pursuits besides raiding and smuggling."

"We are corsairs." His swarthy face grew serious. "One bit of advice. When you meet Jean Lafitte, do not call him a pirate, or things will not go well for you. We are privateers with letters of marque from Cartagena."

Lottie swallowed and inhaled a calming breath.

"I am unaware of the friendship between Lafitte and your husband," the captain said.

She only knew the one story of Lafitte being stung by a man-o-war, and it had happened a long time ago. Would Lafitte even remember? Therein lay the risk. *Lord, please let Captain Lafitte hold Nathan in fond regard.*

"But I shall champion you as best I can. Jean Laffite is a wise man, but also a sound adversary. He comes across as polite and charming, but do not be lulled into carelessness. He is hot-tempered and quick to raise his sword or pistol."

The oarsman jumped out and dragged the boat onto shore. Captain Dominique stepped out and offered Lottie a hand.

Crushed white shells littered the beach and outlined the path that led to Lafitte's lodgings.

The home stood out among the palmetto thatched roof huts, equal in size to some of the larger plantation houses on St. Kitts and by far the largest on Grand Terre. A wraparound porch stretched the length of the building where hammocks swung in the breeze. A grand wooden staircase led up to the porch and double-doored entry, which was wide enough to carry in bulky pieces of furniture. Bright shutters propped open with sticks accented the windows.

Captain Dominique pointed behind Lafitte's tropical luxury home to the slaves' barracks and a warehouse that held any goods not brought to the Temple for auction.

They ascended the stairs, and two slave men swung the doors to the entrance wide. "Jean is expecting you," Captain Dominique said. "I sent a messenger ahead."

He gestured for her to enter.

Splendor filled her eyes from every corner. Richly ornate Baroque furniture, Spanish glassware, silver candelabras, Axminister carpets, and heavy draperies filled the room with opulence. Captain Jean Lafitte possessed a taste for finer things.

Gruff male voices emanated from behind a closed door off the back of the house.

"He will not see you right away." Captain Dominique nodded to a slave woman dressed in a light cotton frock with a mobcap covering her hair. "Lena will see to your needs."

Lottie grasped his sleeve. "Will you be there when I—?"

"I cannot guarantee it." He shook his head and patted her hand. "But remember my heeding from earlier. Other than that, be yourself, and Lafitte shall be as taken with you as I am."

She nodded and followed Lena, but turned back to the captain. "Thank you." A nervous smile flittered on her lips.

He returned the smile before pivoting on his heel and striding off.

Lottie followed the servant down a hallway. On a half circle demilune table rested Chinese sculptures of onyx and jade. As they walked, she peeked through cracked or open doors and spied mahogany four-poster beds and matching chests of drawers.

Lena opened a door on the right and stepped aside for Lottie to enter. White cotton drapes billowed in the breeze from an open window under an ornate tasseled valance. A mountain of pillows was piled at one end of the large bed, which was dressed in silk linens, and a French gown splayed out on the coverlet with a matching pair of lace gloves. Another servant poured steaming water into a large porcelain basin.

This must be someone else's room.

Lottie spun on her heel, but Lena pointed to the tub and the gown. "You are to bathe and dress. The master will send for you to sup with him in an hour."

Lena excused herself before Lottie could ask questions. She scanned the room again. She may as well obey. The other servant aided Lottie's undressing for her bath. The water felt glorious, but the strange place and her unknown future kept her from relaxing.

What would Lafitte ask of her?

Lottie rose from the tub before her fingers pruned. The servant dried her off and buttoned her into the fine glazed fabric of the French gown. Rows of ruffled lace layered the hem, and a smaller ruff rimmed the square neckline. Odd, but it was a perfect fit. Maybe a tad too long, but the small heel on her kid boots would hide it. She slid the lace gloves over her fingers and sat as the maid wound her red hair into a lovely cascade of pinned curls.

Was she safe, or merely being dressed up for a human sacrifice as the Indians used to perform in the place now called the Temple?

Before the maid put away her old dress, Lottie pulled the

tiny Bible from its inside pocket. The pages were wavy and crinkled from her dousing, but still readable. She flipped to Psalm twenty three. *The Lord is my shepherd; I shall not want... Yea, though I walk through the valley of the shadow of death, I will fear no evil: for thou art with me; thy rod and thy staff they comfort me. Thou preparest a table before me in the presence of mine enemies: thou anointest my head with oil; my cup runneth over...*

A knock sounded on the door, and a footman appeared to lead her to the dining room. Lottie said a prayer with each step. *Be with me, Lord. You are my Shepherd. I'm trusting in You. Give me courage.*

He paused at the door to allow Lottie to gather herself. She swallowed her nervousness and nodded. He swung the door wide.

A swarthy group of men congregated around a long dining table. At the head sat a tall, dark-haired man, elegantly dressed, with unusually white teeth and dark eyes.

She peered into the face of the infamous pirate, Jean Lafitte.

CHAPTER 35

Keep a leery eye on Fielding. I daresay, he means to
crimp us and I shall not tolerate such trickery.
~ *From Captain Jean Lafitte to Captain Dominique You*

"Welcome, Madame Winthrop." Jean Lafitte rose
at the far end of the dining table.

He cleared his throat, and in unison, all of the men and the
few women present stood. Only one wiry man with burned
black skin, a horseshoe mustache, and a kerchief around his
head grumbled and pushed himself to a half stand. Lottie dared
to flick her gaze to each of the women's faces, hoping to find
camaraderie, but the grim line of their rouged lips appeared
ready to defend their territory.

Lafitte gestured to the seat on his right. "Please, be my
honored guest."

Lottie forced her watery knees to conduct her to the spot,
where a footman pulled out an ornately scrolled chair. She sat
and the men resumed theirs.

Lafitte raised one finger, and a footman rushed to fill her
long-stemmed crystal glass. The table was well set with fine

china plates, silver utensils, and gold candlesticks. The footman draped a satin napkin over her lap.

"*Capitaine* Dominique has given you high praise." Lafitte's dark hazel eyes studied her. "Praise is not readily offered by such a man."

Lafitte was impeccably dressed in a tailored jacket and neatly tied cravat. Thick dark curls, a bit unruly on top, graced his head and side whiskers and contrasted against his light skin. "I'm honored the wife of an old friend is able to join us." His slim pale fingers raised a glass in toast.

"I appreciate your hospitality." Lottie's heart wept with relief. *Praise God.* He remembered Nathan. She ignored the curious stares of fierce-looking men along either side of the table.

"I do hope your stay upon the *Le Tigre* was also enjoyable."

"Indeed. Much more so than my unfortunate time aboard the *Amory.*"

A muscle twitched in Lafitte's jaw. "*Oui.* And we shall do our best to remedy that, but such discussions shall wait until after we dine. One wouldn't want to sour the stomach."

Lottie folded her hands. Her nails were even and no longer stubs. What sort of fate did he have in mind if it would sour the stomachs of these daunting men? She glanced down the table, hoping to find Captain Dominique among the gathered guests. Instead, she caught sight of Captain Fielding and Captain Phelps. She shivered at the contempt in their eyes. How could she ever have believed Captain Fielding was a good man?

"May I introduce you?" Laffite asked.

She nodded. Lafitte certainly wasn't behaving as someone ready to seal her doom. Instead, his manners were impeccable, and he played the gracious host.

He gestured to the man across from her. "This is my older brother, Pierre Lafitte."

The man nodded. She could see the family resemblance, but

Pierre's features were more rugged, and one of his eyes was slightly crossed.

"Next to you is Louis Chighizola, or Nez Coupé, as we call him, and beside him his wife, Madame Coupé."

Long scars sliced Nez Coupé's face, but they were not as disturbing as the man's missing nose, hence the nickname, Cut Nose. His big-boned wife eyed Lottie with dubious curiosity.

"And you know Captain Jeremiah Fielding and Captain David Phelps."

She refused to meet their gazes, and instead nodded at Captain Lafitte.

When Lafitte completed the rest of the introductions, a small fleet of footman ladled out crab gumbo, drawing the men's attention away from her.

"So tell me, how fares Winthrop?" Jean Lafitte sipped from his spoon. "It has been an age. Does Gator still carry the weight of the world on his shoulders?"

Lottie smiled. "You did know him well then?"

Nez Coupe's eyes narrowed. "Is this a trick? Why would she ask if you know her husband if it was the reason she summoned this meeting? How do we know she's not a British spy?"

Lottie straightened, imposing the best impression of her mother. "I am newly married, sir. My husband has mentioned his schooling with the Lafitte brothers, specifically Jean Lafitte. I have yet to hear all of their stories, but I'm certain if your wife were in dire straits, you'd want her to call upon a past friend for aid." She placed her hands on either side of her place setting. "Besides, I am not courageous enough for espionage."

Nez Coupe snorted and focused on his gumbo.

"Well said, mademoiselle." Lafitte arched a brow. "Indeed, I did know your husband well. We sailed and sparred together at Maritime in St. Kitts. He was a valiant opponent, especially with a saber. I tried to convince him to join me in business, but he didn't hold the same passion for privateering as I, nor the same hatred toward Spain."

The other men growled at the mere mention of the country pitted against France.

"How did a Kittitian such as Winthrop, meet a beautiful woman in England? When his brother fell ill, it seemed he would manage the sugar plantation. Did his brother recover?"

"Sadly, no." Lottie put down her spoon and smoothed her napkin in her lap. "The fever not only took his brother, but also his sister and mother."

Lafitte's brow furrowed and his dark eyes softened. "My condolences."

"I did not have the privilege of knowing them, but I grieve for my husband."

"Rightly so. If Winthrop has taken over the plantation, how did you meet? He must still be sailing, or was it a family connection?"

"The land isn't producing the way it used to."

Several of the men nodded, including Lafitte's brother, Pierre. "The supply of sugar barrels at auction has decreased."

"My husband became an import and export merchant for the Leeward Islands to make up for the lack, and to keep those in his employ fed."

"It was wise to diversify." Jean Lafitte leaned back in his chair and swirled his drink. "But that doesn't explain how you met."

Lottie released a nervous laugh. "It's a comical story. Truth be told, Nathan rescued me from my overbearing mother."

"I'm intrigued," Lafitte said. "My men love a good tale."

"Aye." The men agreed.

"It's rubbish." Captain Fielding slammed his glass down on the table. "If you're looking for grand tales, I have better to tell."

Jean Lafitte's gaze slid in his direction. "I do not recall asking you, Captain."

Fielding shrank back.

"Please do tell." Lafitte lounged back in his chair.

Lottie started from their first dance at the Middleton ball.

"You asked Winthrop to dance?" Pierre Lafitte gaped at her.

"It wasn't that I asked him *per se*. We merely ended up dancing together."

"I enjoy a lady who is driven enough to seek what she desires." A half smile curled Lafitte's lips.

"I'm not... I don't desire..." Heat filled her cheeks.

"Go on. I want to know how Winthrop responded."

The footmen collected the soup plates and brought out roasted turkey and an array of sauces. She continued with her story until they stopped her after the candle incident.

"That's what you get trying to do the honorable thing—leg-shackled." Nez Coupe crossed his arms. "Like us providing goods for our country and not attacking American ships, yet Governor Claiborne won't rest until the whole lot of us rot in jail."

Jean Lafitte waved a hand for him to be quiet and focused on Lottie. "Please, continue."

She explained the wedding, being sick on the ship, and Nathan's care for her. They were disappointed when they heard Nathan had put her up at the inn upon reaching St. Kitts.

"A pretty thing to warm his bed, and he sleeps alone?" Pierre said. "Maybe Winthrop isn't the man you thought him to be."

Lottie frowned at him. "He was protecting me. He thought he was cursed."

The entire room of Baratarians recoiled.

Jean Lafitte eyed the table before meeting her eyes again. "We are a superstitious lot and can understand Winthrop's hesitation."

"But God is bigger than any curse." Lottie leaned forward. "It says in the book of Deuteronomy we can choose blessing or cursing. I choose blessing."

Several of the men made the sign of the cross.

"And my husband, in this instance, was wrong." She explained his witnessing the obeah slave's capture and the woman's words to Nathan. "And then his family died of fever, but God gives and takes away. We have to trust His plan in the good and the bad." She swallowed. "Captain Fielding, however, heard the tale of the obeah slave and justified the disappearance of the ship's cargo by blaming it on the curse."

Captain Fielding's laughter sounded with a hollow tone. "She does tell a good tale, but it's a fabrication. All of it."

Jean Lafitte's gaze lifted. He nodded to Dominique You, who stepped forward and escorted Captain Fielding from the room.

When had Captain Dominique entered the room?

"Pardon the interruption," Jean Lafitte said. "Fielding is needed at the Temple. Please go on."

"Nathan's fears grew when I too came down with the fever. He stayed by my side day and night until he thought death was upon me." She told of her miraculous recovery and her dream. She told of Adana and the hail storm. And then she told of overhearing Julia and Captain Fielding's plans, and her capture.

"If I don't return, Nathan will blame himself and the curse for my disappearance." She closed her eyes and saw Nathan's face, and the intense way his gaze had held hers the night they'd found the sea turtles.

She inhaled a breath and opened her eyes. Jean Lafitte was studying her.

"I'm sorry to cause you trouble," she said, "but I must return to him. If you could aid me in the passage, I will find a way to repay you for the efforts."

"What if he is on his way here?" Lafitte asked.

"His other ship is badly damaged. He has no means to sail, nor does he know of my whereabouts." Pain sliced her chest. "I have brought him nothing but worry and burden, but I won't rest until I'm certain he understands these unfortunate incidents were not his fault. He is not cursed."

"Are you trying to demean your value?" Lafitte arched a brow. "Do you not want Fielding to earn a single shilling?"

Lottie raised her chin. "You intend to purchase me? Even though I was never Fielding's to sell?"

Lafitte shrugged. "What if I say you are plunder taken from a British ship?"

"You will not honor your friendship and champion me?"

"It is still to be determined. I have yet to hear Captain Fielding's view."

Lottie swallowed hard against the fear rising in her stomach. "Captain Lafitte, I have been in bondage most of my life, a slave to my fears, a slave to my doubts, but I have found freedom through Christ. You may do what you want to me. You can throw me in chains, you can make me a servant, or sell me as a slave, but I will never be in bondage again. You may have me serve you, but I will be serving God. He is my protector and my refuge."

Jean Lafitte's black eyes held hers. He blinked several times, then a slow smile grew upon his lips.

~

a splash sounded to Nathan's right as another alligator dipped into the greenish duckweed. Hairs rose on his arms and neck. He hated alligators, but Laffite's smuggler's haven resided on Grand Terre in a maze of swampland where bayous, rivers, inlets, and marshes meshed together.

Laffite had once shown him the map of his grand plan and even asked Nathan's advice for fortifications. If Fielding sold Lottie to Laffite's men, she'd be brought to Barataria's Temple auctions.

Nathan and Baby paddled past the floating logs with hungry

yellow eyes. Middleton and Lady Etheridge balanced the boat in the center. Cypress trees dripping with Spanish moss lined the brackish water. Their root base fanned out like fingers dipping into a washbasin—some wider than he was tall.

The borrowed British frigate remained anchored in Dispute Bay, less than two miles from Grand Terre and out of sight. The *Katherine's* crew kept the British soldiers acquiesced by feeding them tales and rum. If that didn't work, Nathan had told Cobble to remind the men who had their captain and weapons. But he'd commanded them not to let harm come to anyone.

"No woman is worth risking a man's life like this." Anthony's chest rose and fell in rapid succession, winded from paddling.

A thud sounded behind Nathan.

"Ow." Anthony rubbed the back of his head.

Baby smiled a toothless grin and dipped his oar back in the water without missing a stroke.

"Cut that out." Anthony twisted in his seat.

"Harrumph." Lady Etheridge sat prim and proper behind Nathan. "You got off easy." She closed her parasol. "One more word and I'll poke your eye out." She held the blunt end up under his chin. "Maybe the pirates will mistake you as one of their own and keep you."

Middleton drew back. His panicked eyes pleaded to Nathan for help.

"Less complaining, more paddling." Nathan kept his tone commanding, but couldn't tamp down his smile.

A graceful white crane stood with its feet in the murky water and eyed their passing boat. It held beauty and grace, even though it stood in the muck with predators all around. Nathan's heart clenched. How was Lottie faring in this den of thieves? Was she scared? Had they hurt her? He jabbed his oar into the water too far out.

"Careful now." Baby leaned right to balance the boat. "We don't want ta go swimmin' in these waters."

Nathan forced his fingers to relax. He once again picked up the monotonous rhythm. The crane dipped its head and retrieved a crayfish with its beak. Somehow, the graceful bird survived. *God, protect Lottie. You're in control. I'm trusting in You.*

He mentally outlined their plan once again. Better to focus on strategy than on Lottie being hurt, or the alligators and other lethal creatures looming underneath the duckweed.

He had three hours to get to Grand Terre, locate Lottie, and get back.

CHAPTER 36

The pleasure of your company is requested to break our fast in the gold dining room promptly at nine in the morning.
~ *From Jean Lafitte to Lady Winthrop*

"*M*onsieur Lafitte has asked for you to join him to break yer fast, madame." Lena curtsied and left the room.

Lottie inhaled a deep breath. It was time to learn her fate.

So far, she'd been treated like an honored guest. This morning, another gown awaited her in her closet, this one a vibrant blue. She had no choice but to don it. The dress she'd arrived in had been disposed of, according to her maid. The girl claimed it was ruined and not fit to dine in amongst the company of the brothers Lafitte.

Lottie peeked into the looking glass. The color of her latest gown contrasted with her hair, accentuating the red so bright, her head appeared on fire. The last thing she needed was to draw attention. "Was there a bonnet or cap left with the gown?" she asked the maid.

"*Non*, madame."

So much for that.

Lottie slid on a pair of satin gloves and cracked open her door. The hallway was empty, and she strolled toward the dining area. It wouldn't be proper to keep the Baratarians waiting.

Fingers clamped on her upper arm, and she was yanked into an alcove. She winced as her shoulder bumped a shelf. A large Chinese urn wobbled but didn't topple.

Captain Fielding's face hovered inches from hers, his gray eyes as hard as the steel of a sword. A cynical smile twisted his lips.

"Enjoying yourself, *ma cherie?*"

She yanked her arm from his grasp. "Does Julia know you call other women her pet names?"

"The name for one lightskirt works as well as for another."

Her fingers curled into fists. "What do you want?"

"A great deal of coin, and you are going to help me get it. Lafitte shall pay plenty for you. There are men who prefer pale skin and red hair, and Lafitte knows it."

Her chest constricted. Was that why the vibrant blue dress had been left for her?

"You've dressed the part. Now I can name a higher price, but if you're thinking of getting comfortable with Jean Lafitte so you can live in this splendor, I hate to disappoint you. Lafitte doesn't care for fair skinned women. He prefers a blend of dark and light."

She had no intention of *getting comfortable* with anyone, but she had noticed several mulatto women in Jean Lafitte's company last evening.

"I shall warn you." His chin jutted forward. "If you keep opening your mouth and spilling your grievances, I shall return to St. Kitts with stories of how you ran off because Nathan wasn't fulfilling his duties as a husband. I will explain how you threw yourself into the arms of the handsome pirate, begging Lafitte to make you his own."

Lottie snorted. "Nathan would never believe you."

"Nathan believes whatever I tell him," the captain snarled. "And if you don't keep your mouth shut, I will make certain the curse itself falls upon Nathan. You wouldn't want anything to happen to your beloved husband, would you now?"

Lottie raised her chin, but said nothing.

Captain Fielding released a hollow laugh. "You still hold onto the hope that Lafitte will return you to him." He grunted. "As if Winthrop ever wanted you."

He pressed her back against the wall with the palm of his hand.

Lottie refused to cower in the face of such a man, despite the shooting pain in her collar bone. *I may be hard pressed on every side, but I am not crushed. I may be struck down but I am not destroyed.*

"Winthrop hated being shackled to a willowy, sickly, female he'd been forced to marry. He told me so himself." He strummed his fingers on her neck, a warning that he could squeeze the life out of her this very instant. "And even if Winthrop somehow had developed a *tendre* for you, he has no idea where you've disappeared to. And, even if he did, the *Katherine* is half sunk and almost beyond repair." His lips curled back in a snarl of a smile, and he punctuated his words. "You. Have. No. Hope."

"You're wrong. My hope is in Jesus. You may sell me to the highest bidder, or you may kill me, but you can't take that from me."

He snorted. "What good is an ancient dead man going to do you? Go ahead and pray. Not even God can save you now."

"*Bonjour*, Lady Winthrop."

Captain Fielding dropped his hand and stepped back at the sound of Captain Dominique's voice.

"Is this *le mec* bothering you?"

She stepped around Fielding and accepted Captain Dominique's arm. "Pardon me. I do not want to keep Captain Jean Lafitte waiting."

Captain Dominique escorted her the rest of the way to the dining room, ignoring Captain Fielding in his wake.

The men rose from the table as she entered. Captain Dominique seated her next to Jean Lafitte before assuming the chair on her right. Captain Fielding found an open chair down the table next to Captain Phelps. Everyone sat to a hearty fare of eggs, bacon, and tropical fruit.

"Did you sleep well, Madame Winthrop?" Jean Lafitte asked over a bite of eggs.

"Indeed, my accommodations are exceptional. I appreciate your hospitality."

"Do you flatter me in hopes to win my favor?"

"I do so because it is the truth, and it is proper to compliment the host."

"Spoken like a true member of the Quality."

More coffee and pastries of all kinds were served, and light-hearted banter switched to business topics, like Britain's demand letter to entice Lafitte to fight for them against the Americans, and Louisiana's Governor Claiborne's lack of response to the Lafittes' pardon request. Lottie's mind screamed to know her fate, but also dreaded to know the outcome.

Jean Lafitte's black eyes flashed. "We are Americans. We have never attacked an American ship. We are willing to fight for our country." He addressed Captain Dominique. "Have Grymes write up another compelling letter to Governor Claiborne and Blanque in the legislature. Dash it all. Pen one to General Andrew Jackson. He'll be coming to Louisiana to battle the British, and when he does, he will better understand the country's need of our help."

A young messenger ran into the room. His chest heaved with

the exertion. He whispered his message to Dominique You. Captain Dominique's expression hardened.

When the lad pulled away, Dominique leaned across Lottie's plate to speak to Captain Lafitte. "The British frigate we've been watching anchored in Dispute Bay. Three men and a woman in a dinghy are rowing through the marsh to Grand Terre."

A low snarl emanated from deep in Jean Lafitte's throat. "What is he thinking sailing into Barataria on a British vessel?" He crossed his arms. "I do not like all these British associations. Claiborne will think we are siding with England. I cannot invite more suspicion."

He pounded two fingertips on the table. "Have Grymes add the British papers with my letter to Claiborne. We shall be open about the British trying to woo our support. Tell Claiborne I am a stray sheep wishing to return to the fold and offer our services to fight for Louisiana." Lafitte scratched his sideburn. "Keep men on watch. If the frigate tries to leave the bay, seize it. Bring the others to me." Lafitte's dark brows drew together. "You say he brings a woman with him? What does he expect? A trade?"

Lafitte cast Lottie a sideways glance, and she held her breath. *A trade for who? Her?*

Captain Dominique chuckled. "It would not be a fair trade. The woman is well past her prime." He leaned back in his chair and relayed the orders to the messenger.

Laffite threw back the rest of his drink in a swallow and stared at his glass, but it seemed as if he was not truly seeing it. "A British frigate and a woman. Curious."

Lottie set down her fork, unable to touch another bite of food. What she'd already eaten swirled in her stomach. Everyone else continued on with their meals, laughing and telling tales. Their lives didn't depend on the decisions being made today.

An hour later, the footmen gathered the empty plates, and Captain Fielding raised a glass to draw everyone's attention. "It is Baratarian smuggled goods and the sale of black ivory that keeps Louisiana and the country happy and working."

"Aye!" echoed around the room.

Fielding leaned in. "Captain Lafitte." The sparkle in his eyes dulled. "I have brought you prime goods. It cannot be contested. Already my sugar and rum are being sold fer high prices in the Temple. I must request my compensation, so I may be on my way."

"Captain Dominique will settle with you for your cargo, minus the damage done to our ship."

Fielding's jaw tightened, but he didn't argue. "Fine, but I shall also take $2,500 for the fancy lady." He nudged his head toward Lottie.

Lafitte arced a brow. "And how does your friend, Winthrop, feel about you selling his wife?"

"Believe you me, he is happy to be done with the strumpet."

"I cannot in good conscience purchase a woman without her husband's consent."

"Since when does a pirate hold such scruples?"

Lafitte slammed his fist onto the table and half rose from his chair. "I am not a pirate."

Fielding stilled.

"My men are privateers, corsairs"—Lafitte's nostrils flared— "and above all, Americans."

"My apologies," Fielding spit out through tight lips.

"A man lives and dies by his honor." Lafitte's gaze dug into Fielding's pale face. "It is time to determine the truth." He raised a hand. "Let him enter."

A footman bowed and opened one of the doors. One of Lafitte's men shoved a dark-haired man in a billowing white shirt and buff breeches into the room. He stumbled to get his legs under him without the aid of his hands, which were tied behind his back.

Lottie twisted in her chair.

The man straightened, and a pair of piercing blue eyes sought hers.

"Nathan!" Lottie pushed her chair back, eager to lurch toward him, but Captain Dominique's fingers wrapped around her upper arm, holding her in place.

Nathan's face hardened, and he struggled against his bindings. "Unhand my wife, you scoundrel."

"Winthrop, old friend, good to see you." Jean Lafitte rose from his chair. "After meeting the beautiful Lady Winthrop, I had a feeling you'd turn up in these parts. I must commend you on your speed. I didn't expect you for another week or two, but then again, you were always a great sailor." He signaled to his brother to cut the bindings. "Please pardon our lack of hospitality. We needed to be certain it was you."

Pierre Lafitte pulled a cutlass out of his belt and sliced the leather bindings.

Nathan rubbed his wrists, but ignored his old schoolmates. His eyes remained locked on Lottie as if she were the only one in the room. "Are you hurt? They didn't…"

She shook her head. Her heart pounded as if attempting to break through her chest. *He came for me. He's here.* "How did you—?"

"Charlie found me." He stepped towards her. His eyes broke contact and shifted to Captain Dominique with an expression that could only be read as begging.

Nathan didn't beg.

Dominique glanced at Jean Lafitte, who nodded. Dominique's fingers released her arm.

Lottie stepped forward, but a sudden shyness washed over her. Nathan had never shown her affection in public. Would he desire it now?

Nathan closed the distance, clasping her to his chest against the thudding beat of his heart. The scents of salt and ocean air engulfed her, and she melted into his embrace, absorbing his heat and strength. A sob wrenched its way from her throat, and his shirtfront soaked up her tears.

He cupped her face in his hands and lifted her chin to meet her gaze. "I'm so sorry, darling. I promise to be a better husband. If you can forgive me, I will never allow you to leave my side again."

He claimed her mouth with his own. His lips, tender and ardent, slid over hers with a hungry, soul-reaching passion. His hands dipped into her hair, and he deepened the kiss. She could taste the tang of her tears on his lips as she clung to him, weeping like a babe yet filled to overflowing with joy.

Several whoops and whistles filled the room.

Lottie broke the kiss. The tips of her ears burned, and she chewed her bottom lip. She couldn't meet the eyes of the men who'd just witnessed their passionate display. Surely, they'd now believe her a wanton woman.

Nathan tucked a loose tendril behind her ear before stepping aside to face the jury of corsairs. He slid his hand down her arm and laced his fingers with hers.

"Where do you think yer going?" Nez Coupe's voice rang out in the silence of the room. He was facing away from them, and she craned to see to whom he spoke. "Lafitte isn't done with you yet." He blocked the servants' exit and pointed a cutlass at Fielding's belly.

"Indeed." Jean Lafitte planted his fists on his hips. "There is still much to be discussed. The number one thing being whether Captain Fielding is a cheat and a traitor?" He turned to Nathan. "I have heard Fielding's tale, along with your wife's. I'd like to hear what you have to say in the matter, Winthrop."

Nez Coupe grasped Fielding and dragged him closer so he stood on the far side of the table.

Nathan stiffened, and his grip on her hand tightened. With what seemed considerable effort, he turned away from Fielding and focused on Lafitte. "I have been deceived by a man I considered a loyal friend. It has been brought to my attention that Captain Fielding has been selling my wares on the black market and blaming their disappearance on raids made by your men."

Jean Lafitte lifted a brow. "Fielding has done business at the Temple and shared the profits, but he claimed the goods to have been taken from Spanish ships. Your name was never mentioned until your wife asked for a parley."

Nathan glanced at her, but returned his focus to Lafitte quickly. "Fielding kidnapped my wife because she overheard his plans. Someone informed me of Fielding's intention to sell her to bring in more coin."

"Julia." Captain Fielding bit out. "She will pay for her loose lips."

"Is she the woman outside?" Captain Dominique asked.

"Julia is Fielding's wife." Nathan lifted his chin. "By now, she has probably reached Florida and sold the house they built there with their smuggling profits. She plans to use the money from the sale to begin a new life." He turned his attention to Fielding. "She promised to repay me for the merchandise you stole."

Fielding's eyes blazed. He swiped at an empty chair, and it fell on its side with a crash. "That money is mine. Not yours. She has no right." He charged around the table toward Nathan.

Nathan pushed Lottie behind him, shielding her with his body.

"My grandfather plowed the sugar fields of St. Kitts long before you. The fortune your father made off sugar should have been mine."

"Your grandfather sold that land to pay down his gambling debts." Nathan sounded calm, but his muscles tensed under her fingers like coiled springs. "I hold the deed to prove it." He extracted a scrolled paper out of his jacket and held it up.

Lafitte sauntered over and plucked the deed from Nathan's fingers. He scanned it quickly, then looked at Fielding. "It is the deed to his lands, signed over by one Jacob Lewis Fielding on

August 8, 1773." He re-rolled the paper. "Tell me, Winthrop, do you always travel with the deeds to your land?"

"I believed it may be needed as a bargaining chip."

Lafitte paced back and forth, tapping the rolled deed into the palm of his hand. "For what did you plan to bargain?"

"My wife."

Lottie gasped and stepped out from behind Nathan. "No, not your father's lands." She gripped his arm. "Not the legacy you've worked so hard to protect."

"What if that is not enough?" Lafitte stopped pacing and faced Nathan.

"Then I shall offer my ships, the *Katherine* and the *Amory*."

Her heart dropped into her slippers. "Nathan, you can't sell your ships. What will you do?"

"The *Katherine* is damaged. What of the British ship?" Nez Coupe asked.

"I borrowed the British frigate, but I will find a way to pay my country back."

"No." Lottie tugged harder on Nathan's arm, but he ignored her. She pleaded with Captain Dominique. "You can't let him do this."

The man merely shrugged.

She strode to Jean Lafitte himself. "Please, you can't ask this of him. I'm not worth it."

A spark lit Jean Lafitte's eyes. "I believe Winthrop feels differently." He reached out and fingered a strand of her hair.

Lottie swallowed.

Lafitte raised a brow at Nathan. "A woman with titian hair and fair of face is a prize indeed. She can bring me some hefty coin."

Nathan's fingers coiled and uncoiled by his sides. "I would draw more coin as a laborer. Take me."

"No!" Lottie screamed.

Captain Fielding laughed an ugly, bitter sound.

She dropped to her knees at Jean Lafitte's feet. "You can't possibly mean to do this. Please, I beg you."

"Justice for my father has come full circle." Fielding's chest lifted.

Lafitte growled a low menacing sound. "Show this man the splendor of our backyard."

Nez Coupe stepped toward Captain Fielding.

"Winthrop reduced to an indentured servant." Fielding ignored Nez Coupe, refusing to budge. "If only Father were here to celebrate your fall from grace."

Nez Coupe shoved him toward the door, and Fielding sobered.

"Hold!" Captain Phelps rose. His wide eyes bounced between Lafitte's and Fielding's. His pale face indicated he understood the labyrinth of alligator-filled swamps and marshes that consisted of Grand Terre's *backyard*. Suddenly, he snatched his sidearm and pointed it at Jean Lafitte.

The double doors behind Lottie and Laffite flung open.

"I demand to see my daughter!"

Lottie stared at the sight in the doorway. It couldn't be.

But it was.

Mama strode into the room, Shorty in tow. She wacked Shorty on the arm with her umbrella. "Stay back. I'm tired of waiting. My patience has run out."

Nez Coupe used the distraction to dive across the table at Captain Phelps's midsection, tackling him. Dishes and glasses shattered on the floor. Phelps's pistol flew from his fingers, bounced off the table past Nathan and Captain Dominique, and skidded across the floor, stopping in the folds of Lottie's skirts.

Lottie fumbled for the pistol, raising it, along with a fold of her gown, into the air.

Fielding drew his sidearm, but instead of aiming at Lafitte, he pointed it at Nathan.

"Get down!" Nathan yanked the back of Captain Dominique's shirt and pulled him down to the floor.

Lottie closed her eyes.

The loud crack of a gun jerked her back. The floor shook as a body thumped against the ground.

Her eyes sprung open, and she lowered the gun.

She'd never fired.

~

*N*athan's heart slammed into his chest. For a split-second, Fielding's eyes had narrowed and shifted to Lottie. A bolt of terror slammed through his body, helpless to save his beloved who hadn't seen the new threat.

He scrambled on his knees to get to her, but a gun discharged. Lottie opened her eyes and lowered her weapon. A stream of black smoke poured from the end of Jean Lafitte's gun.

Blood pooled beneath Fielding's body.

Nathan snatched her against his chest. His whole being shook as he wrapped her in a tight embrace. "Don't look." He tried to block her view by pressing her face into his shoulder.

Nez Coupe grabbed Fielding's legs and dragged him around the table towards the servant's entrance.

Two of Lafitte's men held Captain Phelps's arms behind his back and roughly pushed him out the door.

"Are you all right?" Nathan asked.

She nodded, though he could feel her trembling in his arms.

"What in heaven's name is going on?" Lady Etheridge's voice boomed. "This is some welcome." Her eyes landed on her daughter, still kneeling on the floor, and her lips pursed. "Stand up, Charlotte. Etheridges don't lie about on the ground getting their gowns dirty like scullery maids."

Nathan rose and pulled Lottie up with him, careful to make certain her legs could support her before he released his hold.

"And stop slouching," she added.

Jean Lafitte pushed back his jacket and holstered his weapon. Shorty tried to take hold of Lady Etheridge's arm, but she jabbed at him with the pointy end of her umbrella.

Lottie's chin raised, and she stepped forward. "Mama. Put down your umbrella before you hurt someone. Our host will believe us to be ill-mannered guests."

Shorty's head drew back. "Mama?"

"What has come over you?" Mama said. "Etheridges don't—"

"I am not an Etheridge any longer." Lottie entwined her arm with Nathan's.

A smile twitched at the corners of Nathan's lips. He couldn't have been prouder. His wife had stood up to a roomful of pirates, a traitorous scoundrel, and now her own overbearing mother.

"I believe some late introductions are in order." Jean Lafitte stepped forward.

Nathan could no longer contain his smile as Lottie reverted to a well-mannered English socialite.

"Mama, may I introduce you to Captain Jean Lafitte of Grand Terre."

Her mother nodded.

"Captain, this is my mother, Lady Etheridge."

"A pleasure to meet you." Jean Lafitte bowed. "Your daughter is an amazing woman. I'm certain you are proud."

"Indeed." Lady Etheridge curtsied low. "She retained the best qualities of her father and me."

Lottie glowed with pleasure, and the sight stirred a great need in Nathan's belly.

"This is Monsieur Pierre Lafitte, Captain Lafitte's brother." Lottie stepped back. "And this is my dear friend, Captain Dominique You."

Lady Etheridge dipped her head to each man, and they bowed in return.

Jean, ever the elegantly mannered gentleman Nathan remembered from his youth, gestured toward the door. "I'm certain you must be tired after such a long journey. Why don't we retire to the shade of the porch, and I'll have refreshments served? We can finish our business where there's a better breeze and less of a mess." He turned to his men. "You may resume your duties. The threat is gone."

As the men filed out of the room, Jean stopped Nathan with a questioning look. "I'm grateful you sought to save my man back there"—Jean raised a brow—"but have you forgotten my dueling skills?"

He shook his head. "I have not."

"Do you believe my fingers have slowed or my aim become less true?"

"No."

"Why then did you seek cover? Fielding was dead before his fingers found the trigger."

"I wasn't worried Fielding would get off a shot. I was frightened my wife would."

An abrupt laugh escaped Lottie's lips, which she quickly covered with a cough.

"I do not understand." Jean's gaze pivoted between Nathan and Lottie.

Lottie swallowed her laughter. "I daresay my husband was frightened because, when I aim, everything in the room is in harm's way." She lost the battle against her smile. Mirth shimmered in her eyes.

Jean nodded to Nathan. "You have my gratitude for protecting my man, and you, madame"—he nodded at Lottie —"for not pulling the trigger."

Out in the hall, Anthony rose from a chair.

"Captain Middleton?" Lottie's slender brows drew together. "What are you doing here?"

"Quaking in his boots." Lady Etheridge wrinkled her nose. "He didn't have the courage to enter a room full of pirates."

"Privateers." Nathan covered her gaff

"Corsairs." Jean Lafitte corrected at the same time, but his temper didn't show itself.

"Aren't they one and the same?" Lady Etheridge frowned.

"No, Mama." Lottie slipped a hand through her mother's arm. "A privateer is commissioned by a country to raid foreign ships and protect the homeland from enemy combatants."

"I see. I beg your pardon, Captain Lafitte." She peered over her shoulder at Middleton. "Come along, Middleton, don't dawdle." She lowered her voice and leaned closer to her daughter. "I'm pleased you never married him. The man lacks a spine. He could never be half the man Winthrop turned out to be."

Had that been a compliment? Nathan gave himself a mental shake. No, he couldn't give Lady Etheridge that much credit.

They resettled into wicker chairs under an oscillating fan. Anthony pouted in the corner. A large empty hammock swung gently in the breeze. The sun shone off the water and the white sails of Lafitte's fleet. Nathan scooped Lottie's hand in his. He needed to touch her, keep her close, and memorize the feel of her. He needed to take in every detail in her face, her expressive blue eyes, the brightness of her smile, the creaminess of her skin. He'd need to cling to this moment, for it may be the last he saw of her.

Lady Etheridge crossed her ankles and locked her gaze on Captain Lafitte. "What is this nonsense I overheard regarding my daughter and son-in-law?"

"*Un moment, s'il vous plaît.*" Jean passed the scrolled deed to Nathan.

He accepted it but didn't put it away. "Why are you returning this?"

"You do not believe I would accept any payment from a man who saved my life?"

Nathan's brow furrowed. "That was a long time ago, my friend. I thought perhaps you'd forgotten."

"How could I forget a debt I owe to a friend who'd dive into jellyfish-infested waters to save a man?"

"Why the show, then?"

"I was merely curious to see what you'd be willing to sacrifice for her. She is a rare gem."

Nathan lowered his head nodding. "Indeed."

"Captain Lafitte." Lady Etheridge rose, and the men rose with her. "I would love a tour of your charming estate, and I do believe Middleton would like to return to his ship. They have far to sail before morning."

Jean didn't smile. He never had smiled much, but his eyes danced with mirth. Nathan rubbed the back of his neck. Maybe he'd underestimated Lady Etheridge.

She opened her parasol. "We shall also need passage for my son-in-law's crew to be taken to the *Amory* where they will await their new captain." She nodded at Nathan. "Captain Winthrop."

A servant escorted Middleton to a fisherman who'd row him out to the bay. Jean offered Lady Etheridge his arm, but before descending the steps to the lawn he eyed Nathan, "Lena will show you to your room when you're ready." He winked, or at least, Nathan believed he caught the wily look before Jean turned and pointed in the direction of the temple, explaining the large draw of the auctions. They strolled the grounds as Jean pointed out different islands nearby.

Lottie stared at Nathan's chest, and her hands slid into the folds of her gown. She was nervous. He'd grown fond of her endearing habits. God, he loved her. She was a woman of strength and firm faith. He slid onto his knees.

She bit her lower lip, and her eyes grew misty.

He enfolded her hands in his. "I'm sorry I've held back on telling you what has been in my heart for some time. Those things I said, the things I offered, I would give them up in a heartbeat for you. You are worth all of it and so much more." He pressed one of her palms against his cheek. "I love you, Lottie Winthrop. I've been blind and hardheaded. I don't deserve to be blessed with your love, and I will thank God for the rest of my days for putting you in my life."

Tears streamed down her cheeks.

"And if you let me, I'll spend the rest of my life ensuring you know the truth of it."

She slid to her knees in front of him and raised her palm to his cheek. "I love you, Nathaniel Winthrop, I promise to hold you to it."

A husky chuckle rumbled deep in his throat, and he gently brushed his lips against hers before capturing them in a kiss meant to sear their souls together. By the end, they were both breathless. Desire blazed in Lottie's eyes and matched the fire deep in his belly.

He issued Lena a slight nod and pulled Lottie to her feet. "Etheridges don't kneel."

"You're right." Her eyes danced, and a slow smile spread across her lips. "But I am a Winthrop."

Pride lifted his chest. "Then I yield to you, Lady Winthrop." He crushed her to him for another smoldering kiss.

Did you enjoy this book? We hope so!
Would you take a quick minute to leave a review where you purchased the book?
It doesn't have to be long. Just a sentence or two telling what you liked about the story!

~

Receive a FREE ebook and get updates when new Wild Heart books release: https://wildheartbooks.org/newsletter

Here's a sneak peek at the next book in The Leeward Islands Series!

The Sugar Baron's Ring

A ring is her only tie to a distant homeland, until a marooned Englishman anchors her heart.

CHAPTER ONE

Off the Coast of Nevis, Leeward Islands
April 1829

By day, the ocean blue sparkles with life, and sails fill with promise. Under the black curtain of night, the crewman fill tankards to cope with the monsters lurking beneath, the ones within and the ones below.
~ *Journaled the 4th of April, 1829*

If he lost his journal, he lost his future. Bradlee Miles Granville's hand grasped thin air as the leather-bound book slipped from his fingers. His writings were his only chance to prove he wasn't an irresponsible disgrace to his family name. The journal landed with a thud and skidded across the weathered floorboards, dangerously close to the spilt tankard of ale. His shoulder slammed against the ship's rail, and he winced. The hull emitted a groan followed by the crack of splintering wood. The eerie sounds raised the hair on the back of his neck and tingled his scalp, distracting him from the pain.

"Hound's teeth!" Colin Fitzroy pushed himself up from off the deck and frowned at the black stripe from the contents of Bradlee's inkwell, now staining his white muslin shirt. Whether his impeccably groomed grand tour companion swore due to the ship hitting bottom or over his ruined shirt was still to be determined.

The scraping of the ship's bottom as it ground against what must have been a coral reef held the same pitch as fingernails down slate and continued for almost a full minute. The stench of ale and rum wafted under his nose, blending with the briny air. Inebriated sailors cursed as the contents of their tankards puddled about their feet. The billowing white sails deflated, and the familiar whistling of the wind ceased, along with any forward progression.

The contents of one of the spilt tankards ran down a seam in the planks toward Bradlee's journal. He snatched it up and examined the pages to make certain the ink hadn't smeared, breathing a sigh of relief when his research notes from his travels appeared unaffected. He slid it into his knapsack for protection.

The ship could merely be stranded on a reef, or it could be capsizing.

Blood surged through Bradlee's veins, quickening his pulse. He hooked Colin under his arm, dragging him to a stand.

Colin's eyes widened. "The ship didn't just… Please tell me…" He raked a hand through his windblown hair and groaned.

"Sink me!" The captain cussed from the helm. He fumbled with his hat and plopped it back on his head. It fell over one eye. With his other hand, he wiped the ale off the front of his shirt. "We've run-agrounds." The captain slurred his commands, "Goeth below tah see if her keel hasth been breached." He grabbed the first mate's lapel and shook him, but in his foxed state, lost his balance and toppled the crewman in the process.

The panicked screams of the crew and passengers permeated the deck like a gale of wind. In the chaos, the crew bumped into one another. A couple of drunken sailors sprawled on the deck snorted and tipped back the last of their bottles while the halfway-sober men clambered to their posts on unsteady feet.

Colin's face paled whiter than the sails. "The ship is sinking, and the captain and crew are as drunk as wheelbarrows." His fingers dug into Bradlee's forearm. "We're going to die."

"No, we're not. Look." He pointed to the dark shape on the horizon and speckled lights. "We're in sight of land. We can always swim for it."

"It could be ten miles away."

"Try to be positive."

"Fine." Colin stared at the melee ensuing on deck. "I'm positive we're going to die."

Bradlee looped the strap of his satchel over his head and shoulder. "Stay here.

I'll be right back." He raced below deck to gather their belongings from the cabin. He couldn't afford to leave behind another one of his journals. They were his only hope of graduating, and he was not about to let them sink.

The ship groaned and tilted toward the port side. Bradlee grabbed the rail to keep from missing the stairwell. Men spilled out of the crew's quarters, pouring onto the deck. Bradlee pressed against the wall to squeeze by the outflow of people.

"We're taking on water, captain!" a sailor yelled.

Sure enough, below deck, an inch already filled the hold. The stamping of running feet splashed through the large puddle. Bradlee pushed through the narrow passage. Men brushed against him, knocking him back a few steps. He reached his cabin door and slid into the room as the ship tilted further.

Hurry!

He grabbed his journals from his bunk and a few spare clothes from the dresser and stuffed it all into his knapsack. He felt under his mattress for his meager change purse, but came up empty. As he flipped up the bedding, a piercing whine followed by a loud crack split the air. Bradlee slipped on the wet floor and whacked his head on the hanging oil lamp. He grunted and grasped the writing desk for support. His textbook on agricultural studies glared at him—a reminder of his father's expectations.

Confound it.

He disregarded the book and climbed uphill out of his cabin. Fewer men filled the passage now. The ocean trickled in through the cracks and seams like the Grecian fountains he'd seen in on the Continent. The water now sloshed halfway up his boots. He turned the corner and mounted the stairs leading above deck.

"Help!"

He froze.

"Someone, please," a brittle male voice said. "I don't want ta drown."

It sounded from the galley. Bradlee turned. The elderly cook clung to the pot rack on the far side of the splintered deck, unable to pull his weight up the steep incline.

Feet pounded above deck, and flashes of people passed by the opening of the hold, but no one stopped for the man's cries.

"Help!"

Bradlee picked his way over the cracked boards. The wood scraped against his boots and breeches. He grabbed hold of a beam and leaned over as far as he could. "Give me your hand."

The man stretched but couldn't reach.

Bradlee scanned the area for a rope or something to grab hold. Rations and utensils lay strewn about the floor, but nothing useful for aiding the trapped cook. Bradlee blew air past his lips. A loud groan echoed through the empty hold. The gap between them widened.

"Colin!" Bradlee yelled up the stairs.

No response.

His hand rested on the strap of his bag. He glanced down. It might work.

He unlooped his knapsack from around his head and shoulder and dangled the strap down to the man.

An inch short.

"Colin! Get down here this minute!"

After a long pause, Colin's face peered into the stairwell. "You told me to stay put."

"Since when do you heed me? Get down here. I need you."

He glanced back toward the upper deck. "We'll lose our place in the lifeboat."

"Dash it all. We'll be fine. Get over here."

Colin clamored down the stairs, grumbling under his breath.

Bradlee fashioned the strap of his bag around the beam. "Get a good grip and lean me out." Bradlee locked arms with Colin and swung over the splintered boards. Beneath the rift, crated cargo floated in the ship's hold. "Take my hand."

The cook clutched Bradlee's outstretched palm.

"Hold fast." Sweat broke out across Bradlee's forehead. He strained with all his might and heaved the man over the divide.

The cook didn't waste time thanking him, merely dashed up the steps. Colin handed Bradlee his satchel, and they followed in the man's wake.

"I'd heard being a hero was a thankless job," Colin hissed in Bradlee's direction.

His companion's aptitude for sarcasm didn't change even in a crisis.

They chased the cook up the stairs. Bedlam had erupted on the top deck as men pushed and shoved to claim a spot in the few remaining dinghies.

"Stay close." Bradlee pried away from the crowd and found a spot near the rail. A warm breeze flapped the loose sails. He sucked in a deep breath and blew it out past his lips. Stars twinkled brightly in the night sky and stood in stark contrast against the pandemonium that surrounded him on deck. The moon reflected off the water, shimmering in the rise and fall of the waves. Lights shone in the distance, a beacon of hope. "That must be one of the Leeward Islands. I knew we had to be close."

Bradlee searched the deck. "Here." He grabbed a small barrel full of rum and opened the stint. The golden liquid spilled over the wooden boards, wafting the scent of spiced vanilla through the air.

"What do you plan to do?" Colin snorted. "Toast to our demise?"

Bradlee ignored him. "Use this or anything else you can find to help you float."

The stream lessened, and Colin closed the stint. "Can't hurt to save some. After all this, I might need it."

"If we have to jump…" Bradlee gripped Colin's shirt near the collar and locked gazes. "Swim as fast and far as you can away from the ship. The suction might pull us under."

Colin nodded, and they both turned toward the rail. The sea seemed calm compared to the mayhem on board. One dinghy rowed toward land with slow, steady strokes.

"You realize this is your fault." Colin didn't look in his direction.

"My fault?" Bradlee's mouth dropped open. "You can't blame me for the captain dipping too deep and running the ship aground."

"It's your spirit of adventure that keeps getting us into these messes. Before this, I lived a peaceful life as a humble Servitor at Oxford."

"You hated serving the professors and students. You complained about dull discussions regarding the crop rotation of turnips. I saved you from boredom."

"Indeed, and you have excelled to an extreme. There is no time to be bored when you're caught in the middle of a Spanish bar fight, dodging Indian arrows, or clinging to a sinking ship."

Off the starboard side, a dinghy heavy with passengers tipped and plummeted its occupants into the black water below. The zip of the line hissed as it flew through the winch, and the rowboat toppled after them. Another loud groan reverberated the boards beneath their feet.

"Grab ahold—" Bradlee's boots slid as half of the ship upon which they stood pitched forward, dipping its bow into the ocean.

He gripped a metal cleat bolted into the decking. His satchel dangled in the air and bumped against his side. Colin clung to a rail post with one hand and the rum barrel with the other. Below them, men splashed in the water, stirring up white foam at the bow. Grown men screamed like children as the dark water swallowed them whole. Others grabbed barrels or masts as lifelines.

The sight made the confident words he'd uttered earlier seem foolish. This couldn't be the end. What about his family? Would they remember him only as their foolhardy son?

God, get me through this. I promise I'll go back and take my final exam—even if it kills me. I need to redeem myself in my father's eyes before I die.

Bradlee adjusted his grip to ease the ache in his fingers. His strength waned. He couldn't keep hold much longer.

Colin released the rum barrel to grasp the rail with both hands. It rolled down the steep slope of the deck, splashed into the water, and submerged. A second later, it bobbed in the waves.

A blood-curdling scream howled above the wails of the drowning men. A man frantically slapped the waves. His scream muffled into a gurgle. A moment later, he disappeared.

An eerie hush fell over the water.

And then someone else shouted, "Shark!"

Hannah Rose Barrington ducked out her bedroom window into the humid night air. Her Uncle Reuben's rantings pounded her ears. Miss Albina Kroft's screeching fury followed. Hannah cringed. The bickering between her uncle and his frequent guest had, as of late, exploded in full-out battles. Their tension permeated the house, easily spilling under Hannah's door and stirring her sleep.

She inhaled the salty air and the sweet smell of molasses drifting on the light breeze from the neighbor's boiling houses. Her feet knew the path down to the beach by heart. Small crabs raised their pinchers but posed no real threat. They darted into their holes before she passed by.

She crawled up onto her favorite spot, her uncle's overturned rowboat, careful not to obtain splinters from the weathered underside. Flakes of peeling paint poked at her skin as she tucked her skirt under her feet. The warm night hadn't allowed the sand to cool completely from the scorching heat of the day.

The ocean breeze played with her hair, and the rhythmic breaking of waves washed the day's tension away.

It's unsafe for a lone woman to be wandering the island at night. Lady Clark, the reverend's wife, warned after Hannah had mentioned slipping out in the evenings to escape her guardian's quarrels.

Hannah glanced over her shoulder at the house. The silhouette of Uncle Reuben tossing back the last of the rum in his glass showed in the lighted window.

She released a sigh and turned back to the tranquil ocean. Was it evil to find comfort in something that had taken everything from her? Twelve years next month. That's how long it had been since the sea stole her parents. She swallowed against the lump that still formed in her throat. Her hand moved to her chest and fumbled for the gold ring that lay hidden under her gown—her father's ring.

An unsettling sound drifted across the waves, raising the fine hair on the back of her neck.

A ship sailed into the harbor, its white sails illuminated by the moonlight. It was not an uncommon sight, but most ships came in on a different angle to avoid the coral reefs. Distant cheers split the air. The crew must be having a boisterous night, or perhaps they were celebrating reaching their destination.

Strange. It didn't appear to be moving.

She rose onto her knees and squinted at the black outline of the ship. It seemed to bend in half. She blinked to clear her vision, but the masts continued to tip in opposite directions.

Her heart stilled, and her veins turned to ice.

Merciful heavens.

The ship was breaking in half. Those weren't cheers. They were screams.

She scrambled down to the sand and pressed her hands against her ears to block the sound. Bile rose into her throat, strangling out her breath as she was drawn back to her six-year-old self, the night she'd run away from her nursemaid as the squall hit. The sailboat her parents had navigated toward the Isle of St. Kitts had been much smaller than the ship now fighting its battle. Her parents' skiff had sank fast, faster than any fishing boats could get there.

She had stood on the shore, screaming for her mama and papa, while they drowned.

Hannah pivoted back toward the house. Should she run into town and sound an alarm? By the time she got there it could be too late. What of her uncle? Would he be sober enough? Not likely. He'd probably pass out on the side of the road, or worse if he rowed out. He'd likely drown.

Hannah plunged her fingers into the sand, grasped the edge of the rowboat, and heaved it over. With a strength she didn't seem capable of on her own, she dragged the dingy to the ocean's edge.

This time, she wouldn't be helpless.

Get The Sugar Baron's Ring at your favorite retailer!

GET ALL THE BOOKS IN THE
LEEWARD ISLANDS SERIES

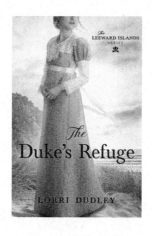

Book 1: The Duke's Refuge

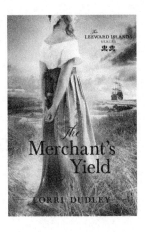

Book 2: The Merchant's Yield

Book 3: The Sugar Baron's Ring

Book 4: The Captain's Quest

ABOUT THE AUTHOR

Lorri Dudley has been a finalist in numerous writing contests and has a master's degree in Psychology. She lives in Ashland, Massachusetts with her husband and three teenage sons, where writing romance allows her an escape from her testosterone filled household.

Connect with Lorri at http://LorriDudley.com

ACKNOWLEDGMENTS

I thank God for the joy of writing and the opportunity to understand His love on a deeper level through story.

I'm so grateful for my loving husband and three boys who don't think I'm crazy when I laugh or cry in front of my computer. I'm especially fortunate to have such great parents who've been so supportive of my writing. My mom is the sweetest woman I know, and she doesn't worry when I write about an overbearing mother figure, and my dad proudly reads my romance novels.

Special thanks to Misty Beller, I'm going to call you the *Dreammaker*, thank you for making mine come true. I'm so blessed to get to work with such a wonderful and fun publisher. I don't know how you do all that you do. And to the Wild Heart Books team, thank you for designing a great cover and for your tremendous editing and marketing wisdom.

Erin Taylor-Young, thank you for drawing out the emotion within my characters and forcing me to dig deeper. You made the story shine in a way I could never have without your suggestions and encouragement. Robin Patchen, my amazing editor and friend, I'm so fortunate to have you to hone my writing and me in the process, and Robyn Hook, my critique partner, you are a tremendous blessing. Also, big hugs and kisses to my beta readers, Kristin, Shannon, and Michelle. Your excitement invigorates me.

I have been (and continue to be) blessed by all the people who have supported me in my writing, especially my blog readers and launch team. I'm humbled by the outpouring of love and appreciative of their encouragement and excitement. Many thanks to my church family, my small group friends who've kept me going, and Pastor and Stacy—you've had such an impact on my life. Keep fighting for God's Kingdom. I'm appreciative of my amazing family, my brother who has passed my books out to book clubs, my aunts who've approached librarians, and cousins who've been so supportive.

May God bless you all abundantly.

If you love historical romance, check out the other Wild Heart books!

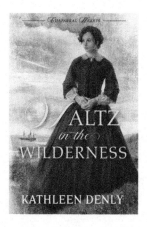

Waltz in the Wilderness by Kathleen Denly

She's desperate to find her missing father. His conscience demands he risk all to help.

Eliza Brooks is haunted by her role in her mother's death, so she'll do anything to find her missing pa—even if it means sneaking aboard a southbound ship. When those meant to protect her abandon and betray her instead, a family friend's unexpected assistance is a blessing she can't refuse.

Daniel Clarke came to California to make his fortune, and a stable job as a San Francisco carpenter has earned him more than most have scraped from the local goldfields. But it's been four years since he left Massachusetts and his fiancé is impatient for his return. Bound for home at last, Daniel Clarke finds his heart and plans challenged by a tenacious young woman with haunted eyes. Though every word he utters seems to offend her, he is determined to see her safely returned to her father. Even if that means risking his fragile engagement.

When disaster befalls them in the remote wilderness of the Southern California mountains, true feelings are revealed, and both must face heart-rending decisions. But how to decide when every choice before them leads to someone getting hurt?

~

Marisol ~ Spanish Rose by Elva Cobb Martin

Escaping to the New World is her only option...Rescuing her will wrap the chains of the Inquisition around his neck.

Marisol Valentin flees Spain after murdering the nobleman who molested her. She ends up for sale on the indentured servants' block at Charles Town harbor—dirty, angry, and with child. Her hopes are shattered, but she must find a refuge for herself and the child she carries. Can this new land offer her the grace, love, and security she craves? Or must she escape again to her only living relative in Cartagena?

Captain Ethan Becket, once a Charles Town minister, now sails the seas as a privateer, grieving his deceased wife. But when he takes captive a ship full of indentured servants, he's intrigued by the woman whose manners seem much more refined than the average Spanish serving girl. Perfect to become governess for his young son. But when he sets out on a quest to find his captured sister, said to be in Cartagena, little does he expect his new Spanish governess to stow away on his ship with her six-month-old son. Yet her offer of help to free his sister is too tempting to pass up. And her beauty, both inside and out, is too attractive for his heart to protect itself against—until he learns she is a wanted murderess.

As their paths intertwine on a journey filled with danger, intrigue, and romance, only love and the grace of God can overcome the past and ignite a new beginning for Marisol and Ethan.

~

Lone Star Ranger by Renae Brumbaugh Green

Elizabeth Covington will get her man.

And she has just a week to prove her brother isn't the murderer Texas Ranger Rett Smith accuses him of being. She'll show the good-looking lawman he's wrong, even if it means setting out on a risky race across Texas to catch the real killer.

Rett doesn't want to convict an innocent man. But he can't let the Boston beauty sway his senses to set a guilty man free. When Elizabeth follows him on a dangerous trek, the Ranger vows to keep her safe. But who will protect him from the woman whose conviction and courage leave him doubting everything—even his heart?

Printed in Great Britain
by Amazon

31546442R00225